THE TILSIT INHERITANCE

Ginny is summoned to England to take up the Tilsit inheritance. Unknowingly, she faces an implacable line of powerful and ruthless women who, even from the grave, exert their will to ensure that the inheritance shall pass unchanged.

With growing horror Ginny learns the truth about her forebears. She learns the price in love and hate that has been paid to keep the estate, the fearful cost of its continuance, the reason why her father disappeared.

She feels herself becoming possessed, and the climax comes when she learns the price she herself must pay, she and the man she loves . . .

CATHERINE GASKIN

The Tilsit Inheritance

F

Collins

FONTANA BOOKS

First published 1963
First issued in Fontana Books November 1965
Second Impression August 1968

© *Catherine Gaskin Cornberg, 1963*
Printed in Great Britain
Collins Clear-Type Press
London and Glasgow

BOOK ONE

CHAPTER ONE

The sun touched only the farthest corner of the garden now, the place at which Ginny stepped down from the cloister to cross to the bench where Mother Angela sat. For a moment her incredible blonde hair caught the sun, and then she was in shadow, walking slowly, a tall, slender girl, with a straight back and a way of moving that made you think, if you were of the generation that had known horses, of a high-stepping mare. She was not coltish, but graceful. Her manners, Mother Angela thought, until to-day had been impeccable.

" You sent for me, Reverend Mother?"

She gave the usual respectful half-bow with which the students approached their teachers, but in almost no other way did she seem to resemble the girl who had received her diploma yesterday. Mother Angela sat and looked at her for a few seconds, fighting the amused twitch that threatened at the corner of her mouth. She had seen this so often before. Most students came to it gradually; but with Ginny the revolt had come all at once.

" I see you're ready to leave us to-morrow, Ginny?"

" Yes, Mother." She had replaced the regulation blouse and skirt with a striped cotton dress, sleeveless, fitting her high firm breasts. The bright blonde hair, cut in bangs on her forehead, had been caught back in a rather amateurish but attractive knot. It would begin to fall down soon, Mother Angela thought, but for the moment Ginny had made her point. To-morrow, in the taxi on the way to the airport, she would put on lipstick. They all came to it—at one time or another—and they thought the nuns didn't know. Mother Angela could tell, after each vacation, which type of movie star was in vogue from the way the girls wore their hair. Once she had had to issue strict orders because of the popularity of the hair-style of someone called Brigitte Bardot. Girls were like that, and it was expected. Most of the Puerto Rican girls hoped to marry soon after they left school; their maturing went on before the nuns' eyes. But Ginny was of another temperament.

"Sit down, Ginny. I'd like to talk to you about Isobel Tilsit. I'm sorry I was away when she came. I had to visit the school at Barraquitas this afternoon. Now Mother Lucia tells me she is leaving San Juan for London in the morning . . ."

Ginny nodded. She was very nearly beautiful, Mother Angela thought. Along with the bright blonde hair that came from her mother, she had the Tilsits' winged brows and lashes, and their grey eyes. The bone structure of her face was defined and good—and it would endure; when she was old she would be a very handsome old lady. But now she was young, and in her first revolt. The grey eyes were defensive and wary.

"Tell me about your aunt."

Ginny shook her head. "I don't—I can't think of her as my aunt. I called her Miss Tilsit. I was very rude, I'm afraid."

"Tell me."

Ginny looked away from the nun. She seemed to be watching the tops of the trees that stirred in the constant breeze of San Juan. The nun waited patiently. The words would come, she felt. The ease and intimacy of this garden would work their usual charm. The garden almost never failed to help tear down the formal barriers between pupil and teacher, and she sensed that in Ginny, made angry and defiant by to-day's happenings, the barriers were nearly swept away. Mother Angela sat and prepared to listen.

II

It was the end of discipline, and, almost, the end of innocence. Ginny thought of the two things together, remembering that last day in the convent in San Juan. The discipline was finished—they told you that from now on you had to make your own discipline. The end of innocence was something you wished for, perhaps, though the nuns were more silent on this topic in the convent of Santa Maria. It was the age and the time when you knew you had outgrown the convent uniform, and the sounds of the world outside became urgent and compelling. Ginny also remembered this day as the one on which she had been made aware that there was significance in the fact that her name was Tilsit. This also was the beginning of the loss of innocence.

Everything was over by that last afternoon. Yesterday the diplomas had been handed out, and the junior classes dismissed. There had been a kind of special solemnity that morning in the last Mass for the seniors. Ginny wasn't a Catholic, but this morning she had knelt in the back of the chapel, unwilling not to be part of it, and wanting an expression and an outlet for the excitement that was like a knot in her stomach. The vestments that morning were green—the colour, they told her, of home. Father Garcia's sermon, in Spanish, was emotional and a little troubled. They never knew, the nuns and Father Garcia, whether the discipline would stick; the innocence, of course, must go. After the Mass there was a special breakfast, festive and lighthearted like a party; only the nuns were touched a little by sadness as they watched. It was their special treat of farewell to the seniors. To-morrow the parents would be there, and to-morrow night the school would be empty.

With her packing almost done, Ginny took a book to the garden, and then left it unopened on the bench beside her She wouldn't finish this book; she would return it to the library this evening and it wouldn't matter that it was unfinished. The discipline was breaking a little in her too. To-morrow morning her father would arrive; there would be the last interview with Reverend Mother—rather longer than most students had because John Tilsit had known Reverend Mother when they were both young in England. And then it would be over. Upstairs in a classroom there sounded the hollow bang of a lid on a desk finally emptied of its books, and a sudden explosion of excited, nervous laughter. Very young laughter. She could hear running footsteps along the second-floor balcony. That was something strictly forbidden at normal times. She leaned back against the sun-warmed wall behind her, closing her eyes lazily and at once becoming more conscious of the scents of the blossoms. The colours remained, too, imprinted against her eyelids as if they could never fade. In Puerto Rico there is very little that is not touched by the colour of the flowers, the brilliance of the greens. Here in the courtyard in the middle of Old San Juan there was the tall flamboyant tree, and

the white frangipani and the blaze of the scarlet bougainvillea against the wall. A few years ago, when she had
come here, the trunk of the vine of the bougainvillea had
been thicker than her hand-span; her hand was big enough
to span it now. The vine was older than Sister Aloysius,
who was the oldest nun in the convent; it was not, however,
as old as the wall to which it was clamped. No one
quite knew how old the Convent of Santa Maria was; some
parts of it had been standing even before the hurricane that
had destroyed the records almost two hundred years ago. So
you measured time against the growth of your hand-span,
but time didn't count much against the age of this city. Ginny
had measured time for herself in the small things that are
personal and only mattered in a small way, like becoming a
senior and having the privilege of using the roof garden
where the wind always blew from the harbour, and you
could see over La Fortaleza, the Governor's residence, to
the harbour entrance, to Isla de Cabras and Catano on the
opposite shore, and to the folds and folds of the blue-
misted mountains beyond that. But you could see other
things too. You could see down into the plaza, and often
there was a group of the slim, graceful Puerto Rican boys
who would wave and perhaps whistle. That was a measure
of time, too, when it first happened. Ginny, with her blonde,
straight hair, stood out sharply from the row of dark-haired,
olive-skinned girls who lined the wall with her and who
occasionally ventured to wave back. "El Yanqui" one of
the boys had once called out to her. She wasn't American,
but the boy would never know that. Nearly always one of
the nuns would hear the whistles and call them all back from
the wall; after that the privileges of the roof garden would
be withheld for a week. And to-morrow, Ginny thought,
it was all ending, and she would have to learn to deal
with the slim graceful boys and others like them. She would
have to learn how to deal with the world of men.

"Ginny!"

She opened her eyes. Luisa was walking towards her, a
beautiful girl, as full-blown as a Puerto Rican girl can be at
seventeen. Luisa knew by instinct how to deal with men; she
would be married a year from now.

"Wake up, Ginny," she said, half laughing. "You sit
there like a gecko in the sun. What are you dreaming of?"

"Men," Ginny answered promptly.

"Ooo . . ." Luisa giggled. "And to think Papa always says, ' Notice how Virginia is—so calm, so gentle-mannered—not with her head always filled with silly stuff.' And now you tell me—Men!" She giggled again, her whole body moving in a sensuous little wiggle that displayed her full breasts and hips. "Because you're not one of us. Papa doesn't understand anything about you, Ginny—he only hears your beautiful English." The rich full lips curved back mockingly. "Or so he says!"

Looking at her, Ginny was conscious of dissatisfaction—dissatisfaction with what she herself was. The excitement changed to a swift depression. There was so much time to make up, so much to learn wilfully when others like Luisa knew it already. Here she was, fully eighteen months older than Luisa, and like a child beside her in the ways of men. Partly it was because she had been kept too long on St. Nicolaas, where these things had a different aspect, and partly it was because she was an only child. But mostly it was, she thought, because she was slow. "Don't listen to your papa, Luisa. He doesn't mean it for you. He'll want you married with a couple of babies by the time you're twenty."

Luisa wiggled again, a quick glow of pleasure in her face. "We'll see . . ." she said, as if there were no doubt about it. "But perhaps now you had better go and find out what *your* papa says. I suppose it's your papa. Mother Lucia says there's a visitor for you."

Ginny straightened abruptly. "Already? He's come already? He wasn't to come until to-morrow." She got to her feet and began to tuck her blouse into the band of her skirt.

Luisa shrugged. "Mother Lucia didn't say—but hurry." She shook her head at what Ginny was doing. "Leave it —you can't do anything to make *that* look better." She surveyed the regulation skirt and blouse with distaste. "He won't mind . . . Here—what's this for?" she demanded as Ginny thrust the book into her hand.

"Take it back to the library for me, will you, Luisa? If he's going to try to make the last plane over to St. Charles this afternoon we're going to be rushed. I haven't finished all my packing . . ."

" All right . . . but one condition. While he's waiting for you, bring h.m back to talk with me . . . eh?" She gave a little breathless laugh, and again the wriggle. " I like your father. He looks like an English movie star." She called out the last sentence because Ginny was already half-way across the courtyard. Ginny waved her hand.

" I'll tell him you said so." She wouldn't, and they both knew it. John Tilsit would have gone scarlet with embarrassment if such a thing had been said to him. And he would have been angry too. As she ran along in the shade of the cloister and skidded to a halt on the polished tile floor before the great door at the end of it, Ginny reflected that Luisa might be right about her father. He would be wearing, of course, the washed-out seersucker suit he kept for visits to San Juan, and his shoes, though polished to fearful brilliance, would be cracking in the creases. All the same, he was a vaguely d.stinguished figure. Some people, Luisa among them, liked him, and some people left him alone, finding him too aloof for their taste. But he was never overlooked. Ginny added love to that, and groped for ways to express it. After a final adjustment to her blouse, she tugged at the chain which would ring the bell on the convent side of the door.

Like many of the buildings of Old San Juan, the convent and the school building were hollow rectangles. Each of them had a garden courtyard enclosed by three tiers of open balconies, presenting to the street smooth façades s.it by narrow shuttered windows and the three huge carved double doors facing into the plaza. The passage from the school to the convent was through the porch of the chapel, and the students went through to the convent only when they were summoned. A moment of appropriate solemnity fell on Ginny as she tugged at the chain. This might have had something to do with the fact that the deep shade of the cloister seemed slightly chill after the bright sun, and that the door stretched above her to more than three times her height. This place stood as a rel.c of Spain in the New World, the Spain of the Inquisit.on. And she was not Catholic. Crossing over from the school to the convent always reminded her of that.

Half of the door swung back and Mother Lucia's little brown face looked into hers. " Ah, Virginia! Hurry, child!"

"Yes, Mother."

The nun closed the door and preceded Ginny, her footsteps light on the tile, the invariable click of the long wooden beads strung from her belt accompanying her. The porch of the chapel was very large; it was a room of four doors—the two leading to school and convent, one to the street, and the entrance to the chapel itself. Behind the thickness of the three-foot walls the street noises were distant and remote; the light was dim, coming from windows high up. The doors to the chapel stood open, and Mother Lucia, in passing them and in sight of the altar and the small red lamp burning there, paused to genuflect. Ginny did not copy her action; it was part of the training that non-Catholics should merely bow their heads to acknowledge the religious beliefs of another person. The old religion had developed some tolerance in the New World. Ginny realised, as she passed, that she would miss the chapel. The stained glass altar window had been destroyed in the same hurricane in which the records had disappeared and had been replaced by clear glass. But the choir stalls had been carved in ebony in Spain three hundred years ago, and the tapestries hanging above them were Gobelin. An agent of William Randolph Hearst, the story went, had tried to buy the whole chapel to have it shipped in pieces to San Simeon. Since that time the chapel was on view to tourists by appointment only. Ginny looked back, thinking with some regret that she would see it in the future only when she took the trouble to call at the convent during visits to San Juan. The pupils of Santa Maria were expected to return to show off their engagement rings, and later, their children. That, too, was part of the training.

Mother Lucia's hissing little whisper reached her. "Hurry, child, hurry!" She held the convent door open. "I've put the lady in the First Sitting-Room."

Ginny pulled up short. "The lady?"

"Miss Tilsit. In the First Sitting-Room, Virginia."

Ginny did not move. "There's a mistake, Mother. There isn't any Miss Tilsit—it must be my mother who's come."

The old brown face wrinkled further. "Not your mother, child. I *know* your mother. It's your aunt—Miss Tilsit."

"I haven't got an aunt!"

Mother Lucia was old, which was why she had the duty of

sitting by the door all day to answer it, with plenty of time to read her office between rings. She did not like problems; now she looked troubled and perplexed. " But she *said* so, Virginia. And Reverend Mother is still at Barranquitas . . . so I put her in the First Sitting-Room and sent for you. She is an English lady—not an American. She talks like Reverend Mother . . ." Now she was pleading with Ginny to remember this English aunt and so relieve her of the responsibility of having let a stranger in. Then another, a worse thought, struck her. " *Madre Mia!*—suppose she's a thief!"

Now the little nun whipped past Ginny with a fluttering of her black veil, scuttling down the corridor to the room that was known as the First Sitting-Room. There were three such rooms for receiving parents and visitors; the First Sitting-Room was grander than the others, the place where the Bishop was put when he made his yearly visit. It had some valuable furniture in it, and Mother Lucia was in a panic. Ginny ran—on her toes in the convent manner—to catch up with her. The nun flung open the door without the discretion that was usually practised. What she saw caused her to let out a little screech of dismay.

" *Madre Mia!* I knew it! A thief!" The little black figure took a step backwards, trembling visibly. Ginny peered over her shoulder.

Inside the room a woman turned unhurriedly to look at them, a tall lean woman wearing the first woollen suit Ginny had ever seen, and a brimmed felt hat. What had caused Mother Lucia's cry was obvious. The doors of the cabinet which displayed the convent's prized collection of antique porcelain were open, and the woman actually held one plate in her hands.

" Child—quickly! Run to the kitchen and bring Sister Ursula and Delores. I—I will lock her in here! Quickly!" The nun's thin old voice cracked with excitement. She began to close the door.

" Wait!" The command came from the woman; it was peremptory, impossible to ignore. With the door almost shut, Mother Lucia hesitated. She thrust her head through the crack, and Ginny had to crane to see around her.

" Just a moment!" Very calmly the woman replaced the

plate in its rack, and brushed the invisible dust from her hands. Then she turned back to them, coldly.

"You are mistaken, of course. I was merely examining the pieces . . . I assure you I am not a thief." If English had been Mother Lucia's native language she would have felt the sarcasm. But it passed over her.

"Señorita . . ." She was at a loss for words, and wavering. "Understand, please . . . this collection is very valuable. Reverend Mother has brought it from England to the convent. It is strictly forbidden to touch it. Why—Reverend Mother herself dusts it . . ."

"And not very well, I notice." She gestured impatiently towards the nun. "Calm yourself! No harm has been done. And as for its being a valuable collection . . ." Her tone now assumed a kind of bitter amusement. "There are one or two good pieces—but there are also some quite inferior examples." The voice carried its own conviction. It was all they had to go on; the rest was a dark silhouette against the light from the big window, the face shadowed by the hat.

The nun remained unconvinced. She still did not budge from her position at the door. Her faint shrug seemed to ask if the evidence of her own eyes had not been plain. Had she not seen the stranger with a piece of the forbidden china in her hand, and were not the doors of the cabinet open?—the doors which were never locked simply because it was unthinkable that Reverend Mother's orders could be disobeyed. It was, she indicated, her duty to stand guard.

Then, behind her, Ginny spoke. Her lips were stiff with a kind of apprehension. "Mother—I am certain it is all right. This lady is . . ." The words died away. She had never seen this woman before, nor heard of her existence. But whether or not John Tilsit chose to ignore the fact, his speech, his gestures, the way he stood even, were all re-created in this woman.

"I know this lady," Ginny said finally.

The nun gave in grudgingly. Quite clearly she was still astounded by the audacity of the stranger who would dare to open doors that were closed, and to touch the precious porcelain. Only slowly she relinquished the door-knob, standing aside to let Ginny pass. "Then if you say so—it is all right."

The woman inclined her head, not in thanks but merely in acknowledgment of her due. " Thank you—now I would like some time alone with my niece."

" That is usual," Mother Lucia replied with icy politeness. She motioned Ginny into the room, and then turned back to the visitor. " May we offer you some refreshment, Miss Tilsit?" It was said with a great feeling of enjoyment, as if telling the Englishwoman that while she did not know her manners, here in Santa Maria they did. " Some tea perhaps?" Mother Lucia believed it was proper to offer tea at any time of night or day to the English. Was it not one of Reverend Mother's eccentricities to have tea every afternoon?—not iced tea, as anyone else would drink in this climate, but hot tea?

" Thank you."

The nun half-bowed, closing the door behind her with exaggerated gentleness. Ginny and the woman were left facing each other.

" Well," the woman said briskly. " I suppose I made a bad impression. One doesn't quite know the correct behaviour for these nunneries."

Ginny made no attempt to deny this. There was contempt implied in the use of the word " nunneries," and there had been scorn for the fears of little Mother Lucia. Suddenly Ginny felt grimly protective of both. " I imagine," she said, " that the rules for correct behaviour are the same in a convent as anywhere else."

Surprisingly the woman laughed, half turning at the same time, so that the light caught the side of her face. Ginny sucked her breath in swiftly at what she saw. Across the woman's right cheek, and extending on to the nose, was a livid scar, deep and almost purple, not a birthmark, but the scar of a wound. As she had laughed, the edges had drawn together. It was shocking on that delicate, transparent skin. It was a long-ago scar, healed but never repaired.

" You mean I was rude?" the woman said. " *Touché.*" She shrugged. " And that old nun was telling me I was rude? Well, she had a right to, I suppose." Apart from the scar, the face was good-looking, but hard. The touch of humour had been a saving grace but was quickly gone. Now that she could see her fully, Ginny thought the resemblance to John Tilsit was much diminished.

Ginny nodded. " It was a great shock for her. That cabinet "—she nodded towards it—" is never opened by anyone but Reverend Mother. I've never seen it open before. There aren't so many museums here in Puerto Rico . . . so what we have seems very precious. Mother Lucia —all of us—take it on faith from Reverend Mother that the collection is priceless." In spite of herself she smiled faintly as she spoke. After the first amazed reaction her feeling was almost one of admiration for someone who had the courage to actually handle the fabled porcelain because it interested her, someone who did not sit like a mouse, waiting. That was what it meant to be sure of oneself, a thing Ginny very much wanted to be. " All the same," she added, as if to explain her smile, " I was pleased to see it out of the case for once. It seemed to come to life . . ." She hesitated. " I mean—that one plate looked better in your hand. Outside the glass."

" Exactly!" The tone was still crisp, but warmer. " But they are right to keep it where it 's. Nothing that is beautiful should be within the reach of fools."

" I'm not sure." Ginny moved closer to the cabinet, wondering why she suddenly found it easier to talk to this woman, easier, for the moment, than it was with most people. It was as if this disagreement, this mild argument, had brought them more nearly level in age. She was not yet used to older people listening very closely when she spoke. " I think it's a shame to shut up beautiful things. They are meant to be seen. To be used, if that's possible."

" With discrimination. Only by those who know what they are."

" But how will anyone ever learn? Learning is . . . exposure." Ginny came to a halt, the thought unfinished and confused. It was puzzling, therefore, to see a look of approval on the other face, a nod of understanding.

" You are right." The words came out slowly, as if this woman was committing herself. " And you are young yet. You have time to learn to discriminate." Abruptly she turned away from the cabinet and walked to the window. " Shall we sit down? No, here in the light. Where I can see you."

Ginny did as she was directed. The woman had an automatic habit of command. They faced each other from two carved high-backed chairs set on each side of the long

windows that were open to the cloister, and to the enclosed convent garden beyond. The breeze from the garden
fanned them ; the scent and colour of the blossoms seemed
stronger here than in the school garden because of the deep
quiet. In the shade of the opposite cloister, a nun paced
back and forth rhythmically as she read her office. The
footfalls reached them faintly across the garden. Ginny
could feel the scrutiny of the woman upon her, lingering and
intent. The temptation was to shift under it, but she disciplined herself to remain motionless, and to return the gaze.
She didn't, either, voice the questions that waited on her
tongue. The woman sat with her hands resting on the
massive arms of the chair ; the royal heraldry of Spain rose
in the carving above her head. It was something to be said
for her, Ginny thought, that she looked not at all out of
place in such a chair, nor uneasy. The livid disfigurement
grew less shocking because the woman herself ignored it.

When at last she spoke her words were pronounced like
a judgment. " How like her you are—it's really quite
astonishing. I had wondered if you at all resembled her."

" Resembled whom?"

" Jane—Jane Tilsit."

" Jane?"

" You don't know?" The voice took an edge of anger.
" Is it possible he's never told you? I'm speaking of your
great-grandmother. A very remarkable woman." She leaned
forward in the chair. " Strange—none of us have so much
resembled her. Even the colour of the hair—though yours
is lighter. You're sure he's never told you about his grandmother Jane?"

" I'm sure. I've never heard of any of Father's family. Just
that he came from England. I thought there was no family
but himself."

The thin bluish lips twisted and the scar puckered. " Yes
. . . I might have guessed. When he left England he said
he would never come back. It was a surprise to find that
he meant it—he was never what you would call a strong
character. But to wipe us out . . ." Her lips made a clicking
sound. " Who would have imagined he would be so
stubborn as to keep every particle of knowledge of the family
from his only child."

" But I do know about my family. Grandfather Pieter van Meerten and Great-grandfather Heindrik left . . ."

" Your mother's side . . . the Dutch side," the woman interrupted. She shrugged, dismissing it. " I wasn't thinking about the Dutch side—though Dutch is better than Spanish if he had to marry a foreigner."

" We are all foreigners here," Ginny replied.

" Is that what he tells you? It sounds like John. He was always saying things like that—impractical, foolish th.ngs. He was always talking about what he didn't understand, and refusing to listen to those who did. Wrong-headed and stubborn—very stubborn. But who would have thought he could hold out so long? I have waited in England for more than thirty years to hear him admit his error. But he has chosen to remain silent. . . . Well, so be it. That is past and done. It no longer concerns me."

She moved her hand, and was silent. It was a brief, spare gesture, sweeping aside the span of thirty years. Her hands, Ginny noticed, were surprisingly beautiful, white and blue-veined, with long fingers. They were the only truly feminine aspect of this woman. Even unmarked by the scar, her features would have been too strong for beauty, and she made no attempt to soften them. Her clothes were uncomprom.singly ugly; the felt hat pulled down on her head to cover most of her short-cut grey hair, the laced brown shoes, the gauntlet gloves in the style of twenty years ago. She made no concession whatever to the warmth of this June day in San Juan, not even taking off the jacket of her thick tweed suit. Her linen blouse, immaculate and starched, was buttoned to the neck. It was impressive, as if such a thing as climate did not exist for this woman.

" I can see," she said at last, " that we shall have to teach you the fam.ly history. It's a considerable history . . . it goes back a long time."

" So do the van Meertens."

The woman ignored the statement. " It has been our misfortune that the Tilsits have not been prolific breeders. A family needs numbers for strength, you know—you can afford to disregard the weak members and there are still those to carry on. Jane Tilsit had only the one child who survived, and in our generation there was John and myself —I am Isobel. And now there is—only you."

"Only me." Ginny echoed the words, feeling the weight of them. For a moment she almost let herself be possessed by this stranger. It was a strong intoxication to learn that she belonged in a time and a place and a family she had not known existed before, to feel the sudden importance of carrying the history of that family in her own person. Isobel meant her to feel it; it was of vital importance to this woman or she would not be sitting where she was now, preparing to begin on a tale of things her father had chosen never to speak about. Ginny recognised that the gaze of the woman on her was fixed and rather fanatical; she felt herself draw back.

"Did Father know you were coming here?" The name was invoked as a kind of protection.

"No—I told you he no longer concerns me. His time is past."

"Yes—but you'll be seeing him, just the same. He'll be in San Juan to-morrow. It's usual for the parents to come and see Reverend Mother at the end of the last term. But then he comes and visits her every time he's in San Juan because he knew her when they were both in England . . ." A thought came to her and she looked questioningly at Isobel Tilsit. "Then you probably know Reverend Mother too . . ."

"Who?—oh, you mean Dorothy Hamilton? Yes, I knew her—slightly. I had heard she ended up here. That just makes another one who is finishing a life unsuitably very far from where she should be. She also evaded her responsibilities. She turned Catholic . . . and everyone knew she could have married the Cavendish son, too. I've no doubt she and your father hang together for mutual support in the bad decisions they both made. But no matter—that's beside the point. You're the only one who concerns me now."

"We will be flying back to St. Nicolaas to-morrow afternoon," Ginny said with what she hoped was a tone of finality. She was trying to draw herself together to resist Isobel Tilsit's compelling manner.

"That's time enough—time enough."

"Then you will be seeing Father?"

Isobel Tilsit shrugged. "Perhaps—perhaps not. After thirty years it hardly matters, does it? We can't have much to say to each other that's of great importance."

"Then why have you come?"

For the first time she looked away from Ginny to the garden. " It was a long journey," she said slowly. " It was a long journey to make when one is not quite certain of why it is made—no, don't interrupt me. It was a long journey made in a hurry, because one can never be sure if this time the doctors who usually are such fools have managed to hit on the truth. They tell me I have a heart condition and that I should not do too much. What rubbish! —as if I could stop with so much to carry on. I thought, though, that there was more time to contact you. I had inquiries made, but there was some stupid mistake. I didn't know until a week ago that this was your last term at Santa Maria."

" You could have seen me on St. Nicolaas," Ginny said coldly. " Father would never have refused . . ."

" Perhaps—but I have told you my concern is not with your father. I am not interested in having his permission to talk to you. I don't know that he would face me—even now."

" Why shouldn't he face you? Is there something for him to be afraid of—ashamed of?"

Again Isobel Tilsit shrugged. "That's for him to decide. I have no need to answer for him—or speak for him. What has become of John is not my doing. He knew his whole future lay there in England with me. But he chose to fight that, and to make his life away from England—on some god-forsaken little Dutch island. If he has regrets now it is hardly my fault."

" Father's all right." Ginny leaned forward now. " There aren't any regrets . . . he's been happy on St. Nicolaas." But she knew the words sounded desperate. Why had she used the word regret?—regret for what? And why shout at this bitter, lean woman that he had been happy. Did she know that? It was the first time in her life she had ever had to question happiness. She suddenly was aware of the extent of her father's silence about the past, a deep and complete silence which only in these minutes with Isobel Tilsit had come to seem unnatural. The questioning that Isobel had planted began to grow in her.

" Is John all right? Are you certain of that?"

" Of course I'm certain!" She said the words automatically because they had to be said. And then she closed her mouth against this stranger, this probing, troublesome stranger. But in her mind she could see her father's face, deeply sunburned and thin, like the rest of his body. It was a grave face, and often his expression, now that she attempted to analyse it, seemed worried and abstracted. What did he think of when he sat on the gallery at Oranje Huis, endlessly smoking his pipe and letting the ice in his drink turn to water—what indeed did he think? Did he think about the price of sugar and whether the seasonal labourers would want higher wages next year? Did he think about the books he pored over in the shops each time he went to San Juan and which he never bought because he could not afford them? Or about replacing the roof beams of Oranje Huis because the termites were in them? Or did he think about things that were far beyond her knowledge and, she guessed, her mother's knowledge also. What did he think about?—and was he really all right? That was what Isobel Tilsit had asked, and she didn't have the answer.

Isobel Tilsit began, in a fashion, to answer the question for herself. Her lips twisted upwards at the corners mockingly, and the edges of the scar drew in. " Don't you think I know about John?—the kind of life he has had all these years? I've taken the trouble to keep myself informed of him. It was a habit I'd grown into—being older than he I always had to make the decisions for him—to try to do what was best for him. Of course when he came to a certain age he decided he knew what was best—and that kind of folly led to worse folly. He never had the stuff in him to *do*— none of the men of the family ever had that. Can you understand what I mean?" Her tone was demanding, prodding. " So what became of him?—He drifted across the world and he became a sugar-cane planter. That's what became of him!"

Ginny edged forward in her chair; she could feel her face flaming and she knew a moment's fear that the tears which suddenly stung behind her eyes would show. It was imperative that Isobel should not see such a display of weakness. " What's wrong with being a sugar-cane planter?"

The woman's tongue clicked impatiently in the way that seemed habitual with her. " Don't they teach you anything in this place—no history?—no economics? The sugar-islands were gold-mines while there were slaves to work them. Without the slaves they were finished. What remains is worn-out soil and worn-out notions about clinging on to what has passed. And no capital to do anything real for the future. Your father has played a losing game ever since he was foolish enough to go into sugar. You must know that, surely? You must see that he works harder than anyone he employs, and what does he get for it? The price of labour and fertiliser and machinery keeps going up, and the price of sugar fluctuates. He's holding on to a shred of what was dead before he ever touched it. It's so like him . . . he has always been the same. He has always gone out for things because he wanted them, not because they were the right things. Impulsive, stubborn . . . always. A selfish, self-indulgent boy, and he grew to be a selfish, self-indulgent man. He has followed his own whims, and where have they led him? He's spent the last twenty years wavering on the edge of bankruptcy. I tell you this because I know it. I know everything about him. I even know how much he owes the bank."

" That isn't all there is to know about him!"

" It's all that matters in most people's lives in the end. The important thing is what one leaves behind one—no, I'm not talking about money now. Your father has evaded his responsibilities, he has failed to do what it was clearly laid upon him to do. So he leaves behind nothing of any value. He will . . ."

Ginny stood up, and the movement caused the woman to pause. " What is it? What are you doing?"

Ginny licked her lips. She hoped her voice wouldn't shake when she finally spoke the words she was desperately trying to frame in her mind. Never before had she wished so much for poise and dignity, and the gift of a few years, or many years, to lend weight to what she wanted to say.

" I'm going. I'm sorry you said the things you did. I can't pretend they haven't been said, but I'm going to try to forget them. Perhaps I could even forget about this whole thing. After all, it's only been a little while, and before that I never heard of Isobel Tilsit." Her voice wobbled. " I wish I never had." She drew in a large breath and slowly expelled it, hoping to gain control. " But before I go I'd like to tell you something about St. Nicolaas. It may be a god-forsaken little island that no one ever heard of, but we don't spy on our neighbours there. We don't make inquiries about them. If they need help we try to help them. We don't wait thirty years, either." It was all wrong. She hadn't said what she wanted to say. In any case, Isobel Tilsit would never understand.

" Sit down! You talk a lot of nonsense, but I'll put it down to your being young and ignorant. Sit down and we'll talk sensibly."

Ginny shook her head. " I suppose I'm as stubborn as you say my father is—as well as being foolish and ignorant. But I won't sit down. I finished school yesterday, and perhaps the only part of wisdom I got there was learning the right time not to do what I'm told."

A kind of exhilaration moved through Ginny as she went to the door. But it was such a very small triumph, really. Just to decide not to give in to this woman, just to decide that she felt more comfortable in the image of her father.

" Virginia, wait! You are not to go now! I've come too far for this—and it's too late in the day. There's no time for this foolishness . . . I have some very important things to say to you."

" You waited too long, Miss Tilsit. If there were things to be said they should have been said long ago."

" That wasn't the time. I had to wait until you were old enough. Until you could make your decisions . . . until you could understand."

Ginny shook her head. It was a very small triumph, hardly worth having now to see Isobel Tilsit's face so disturbed, the lips working strangely like a woman in pain. Nor to see the hand, that beautiful hand, that half groped towards her. It was a gesture of infinite loneliness and frustration. She didn't want to look at it, and she spoke quickly. " I'm sorry. I couldn't possibly stay. Surely you understand that? I don't know why you've come, but now I don't want to know, either. You haven't come to make up the quarrel with Father. You just want to carry it on. And what's the use of that? I can't stay here and listen to you talk about him this way—not understanding him in the least, despising him, not caring anything about him. You see, don't you?—it doesn't matter how important what you have to say is to you. It's of no importance to me—none whatever. If it didn't matter thirty years ago, it matters even less now."

Isobel Tilsit seemed to accept it. Her hand fell back. "You're making a mistake." With each word her face seemed to tighten back into its rigid lines; only the burning, puckered scar spoke for her. I tell you you're making a very great mistake."

"Then it's my mistake. No one else's. It's not my father's mistake this time. Mine, Miss Tilsit—*mine*! That's one of the things that happened yesterday, too. Good-bye, Miss Tilsit."

III

The dusk was coming to the garden as Ginny turned to the nun. "But why did she come? What would bring her all this way? I told her I didn't want to know, but of course I do."

"I don't know, Ginny. I don't know . . ." Mother Angela had an idea about what had brought Isobel on this journey. But because John Tilsit had never talked of the past to his daughter, she had felt bound always to respect his desire for privacy. So she said nothing now.

"I was rude to her," Ginny said again. "I let you down . . . but she was pretty sneering about the convent."

"I shouldn't worry. If politeness and the truth can't go together it's better to choose the truth. Though . . ." now the nun smiled faintly, "a little tact can be helpful too."

Ginny swept on. "But in an odd way I sort of liked her. In the beginning, that is. She didn't fling her arms around me. We had to start from scratch and she didn't assume that I was going to love her. But she did frighten poor little Mother Lucia, and I hated the way she talked about Father. But she was different . . . I don't know how to put it. I didn't really want to go—I wanted to stay and listen. I've never met anyone who did that to me before."

"Those who exercise power are often very attractive without meaning to be. They have their own kind of magnetism."

Ginny frowned. "What—what did you say, Reverend Mother?"

" Never mind. I was thinking aloud. Well—I couldn't imagine Isobel changing. And it seems she hasn't. I knew her, of course, when I knew your father in England."

" Poor Father! She made me feel sorry for him, and I've never felt that way before, either. Oh—and she was nasty about the china pieces."

Mother Angela laughed aloud. " Well, Isobel knows her china, if nothing else! It's a pity she didn't stay for tea. The tea-service is really a museum piece. And the two Sèvres vases in my office she would have envied. I always remind myself of those and the tapestry in the chapel when the builder comes around and tells me once again that the convent really needs a new roof. Together those things might pay for it for us. Go along now, Ginny. It's almost time for me to go in to Vespers."

The girl stood up. She seemed reluctant, looking at the nun as if she had hoped for a fuller explanation of Isobel Tilsit's visit, a scrap of information against which to exercise all the questions. Her brows were drawn almost into a straight line in the frantic, sudden worry of the young.

" Are we going to tell Father?" She said it as if Isobel Tilsit were a secret they shared.

Mother Angela had a moment of delighted thankfulness that Ginny was her friend. Occasionally a student left Santa Maria feeling that the nuns who had taught her were human beings, were women, not mere figures clothed in black and the mystery of their vocation. The woman in the black habit had not ceased to be a woman. Mother Angela was glad that Ginny should be one of the ones to know this.

" Yes, Ginny—we'll tell him. He won't like to hear it, but we must tell him."

When the girl had gone the nun sat on, watching the shadows under the trees deepen, and the soft Spanish arches of the cloisters begin to stand out against the depth of the shadow behind. It was a moment of tranquillity in which she permitted her tired body to sag from its upright position, in which she breathed in the warm evening scent of the blossoms and listened to the erratic tap of the branches of the flamboyant tree against the wall. The garden was her solace and her joy ; she sought it at every moment she was not required at her desk. It was an easier place in which to deal with problems and she loved it so much she some-

times wondered if she were not guilty of the sin of indulgence in coming here so often. It was the love of gardens
that was bred in many of the English, though the gardens of
old Spain she had found here were both more lush and more
contrived than the garden of her childhood. That long-ago
garden had been open and large, rather unkempt, windswept
too, when the storms came in off the sea. The same storms
that had cracked limbs off trees there had also lashed the
walls of the garden at Tilsit, five miles away. She pondered the memory and the name of the house. Tilsit . . .
for years she had not given Tilsit more than an instant's
recollection in her busy life. Tilsit was not a close nor a
particularly fond memory of the nun's early years. But
it was there. John had been a child of—how old?— perhaps
ten, at the time she had left to join the Order in Canada.
But she remembered Isobel—autocratic, arrogant even then,
very sure that she would, in the end, have things as she
demanded that they be. Mother Angela also remembered
Jane Tilsit—the fabled Jane Tilsit—still alive and still
dominant. Letters from her family to Canada told her about
the quarrel that was the talk of the country, and that John
had left England for the West Indies. In some way he had
learned that she had been transferred to the convent of the
Order in Puerto Rico. He had come to see her there, shy
and ill-at-ease at finding himself in such surroundings.
She had liked him for making the gesture of coming. In
time she had assumed the position of Reverend Mother at
Santa Maria, and she had known that her work would be
in Puerto Rico for the rest of her life. Then John Tilsit had
asked her to take Ginny at the convent even though she
was not a Catholic. " *You'll find her backward,*" he wrote,
" *though I don't believe she's stupid. She's had all the
schooling she can get on St. Nicolaas, which isn't much, and
for the last two years I've been pretending that I can fill
the gaps with what I remember from Winchester and these
old text-books I've got here which even I can tell are
wretchedly old-fashioned. I've been selfish keeping her here,
but I hate to see her go. I'm a rotten teacher, and she has
little inclination to learn. She needs girls of her own age,
and the incentive of competition.*"
Ginny had come and had been two years older than most of
the girls in the class she was entering; she had made up a

good deal of the lost time in school work. Of the rest of it Mother Angela had been rather doubtful until she had seen Ginny come towards her across the garden that afternoon. Whatever damage Isobel Tilsit's visit may have done, it had also worked some good. It had seemed to spark Ginny into a kind of revolt, had forced her to know that she was no longer a child. The knowledge had been late in coming, but it had come. She had been stirred to a defence of her father, and in that decision she had rejected Isobel. It was the first act of adulthood, and with it she had put aside her child's uniform and her child's way of doing her hair. Small things these, but to a woman who had watched many hundreds of girls come to the same stage, they were things of value and significance. Ginny had done them with purpose and knowledge, and that was what made them important.

So far it was well, then; the balance was in Ginny's favour. But the nun sensed that this was only the beginning. Isobel had not made the long journey from England without purpose; she was the kind who ignored things and people until she had need of them. The fact that Ginny had seemed to reject her would, Mother Angela believed, have made little difference to Isobel. If the need was there Isobel would continue her effort to have what she wanted. The nun felt she knew why Isobel had come. The reason still existed in spite of Ginny's reaction. Isobel had left it late —almost too late.

The nun began to see Ginny at the centre of a renewed struggle between John Tilsit and his sister. She might be called upon to choose between them. Whatever the decision, Ginny must not only make it, but also know why she was making it. That would need, not a knowledge of the quarrel itself, but a knowledge of the world. The nun looked about the gentle, serene garden, where the night was gathering rapidly in the shadows of the trees and the depth of the cloisters and she acknowledged that between this place and the backwater of St. Nicolaas Ginny knew too little. How did you bring a girl suddenly to know evil as well as good? How did you show her quickly the problems of power and of greed?—how make her less vulnerable without encasing her in an armour of suspicion? One could only hope that Isobel would delay and hesitate for a few more years. One could only pray that Ginny would be given time.

The nun rose stiffly from the bench and walked across the garden to the chapel. In the corridor she nodded to Mother Lucia, seated in her usual place waiting out the few minutes before she would ring the bell for Vespers. Mother Angela entered the chapel and went to her stall at the front near the altar. She genuflected, and although her very bones now were weary, she went on her knees. Her thoughts continued in the same line they had taken in the garden. For her long ago there had ceased to be a demarcation line in prayer. What existed for her now was a continuing dialogue. "*Dear Lord* . . ." Ginny would need help. She had to be helped quickly to an understanding of the world beyond the enclosed worlds of a convent and an island. They were a good beginning, but they were far from enough. If there had to be a defence against Isobel Tilsit, there had to be some time. "Find time for her, dear Lord . . . perhaps find a man for her."

The bell for Vespers rang, and almost immediately the chapel sounded with the soft footfalls of the nuns, the click of the wooden beads as they genuflected and took their assigned stalls. The novice whose duty it was lighted the candles. Mother Angela opened her book and said aloud:

"*Deus in adjutorium meum intende.*" Incline unto my aid, O God. Behind her, from the thirty-odd nuns assembled, came the response.

"*Domine ad adjubandum me festina.*" O Lord, make haste to help me.

"*Gloria Patri, et Filio* . . ."

While the accustomed words came to her lips, Mother Angela's interior prayer ran on. "To-morrow I must explain this to John Tilsit. Dear Lord, I think he'll be very angry."

IV

It was not only anger that troubled John Tilsit, but fear as well. During the thirty-minute Caribair flight to St. Charles, the American island where they would pick up the charter plane to take them on to St. Nicolaas, he tried to put the feeling away from him, but failed. He tried to ease his body back into the reclining seat, and to talk to Ginny about other things, but they both knew that he was faking, and so he gave it up.

The landing at St. Charles and unloading the baggage distracted him for a while. The day before he had made arrangements with Harry Parker, who ran the charter flights out of St. Charles, to take them across to St. Nicolaas. There was nothing to do but wait now until the pilot had finished his business at the Caribair counter. Albert de Kruythoff, the Lieutenant-Governor of St. Nicolaas, paused for a moment to tell John that he would be taking the charter flight with them: then he hurried off for a last-minute consultation with two Dutch officials from Curaçao, who sat in the coffee-shop. John watched him go, a lanky figure in an old white suit, carrying the inevitable battered brief-case; except for the brief-case, Albert never looked like officialdom. Ginny had left John's side, and he paced around the airport building alone, chewing without enjoyment on the third cigar of the day, an almost unthinkable extravagance. Above him were the huge posters advertising the hotels on St. Charles; their brilliant false gaiety seemed to mock his dismay. Why should he so much fear Isobel, he wondered, after more than thirty years? What could she do to him? Then he dismissed the thought. Of course it wasn't he that Isobel was interested in; he had long been wiped off. Ginny was what she now wanted, and there lay the root of his fear. The cigar in his mouth suddenly tasted filthy, and he threw it half-smoked to the ground. A moment later he had his pipe alight, but that tasted no better. He felt old and ineffectual and rather sick.

Harry Parker, walked away from the Caribair counter, signalled that he was ready to go. John, pacing by the coffee-shop, tapped on the window to warn de Kruythoff, and then he looked around for Ginny and caught sight of her through the plate-glass window of the gift shop, the striped dress and blonde hair were brilliant even beside the holiday clothes of the women tourists who lined the counters. There was always a crowd in the airport shop in these last minutes before a flight was called. St. Charles was a duty-free port, and the final temptations of perfume and silver, music-boxes and watches were laid out before their eyes. With his hand on the door, John paused. He was struck again, as he had been this morning, by how changed Ginny seemed, and he wondered for a moment if he were jealous because the little golden-haired girl had disappeared. Then he called himself a sentimental fool, and swung open the door.

" Ginny—Harry Parker's ready. He wants to take off right away."

She turned from the counter. " All right—I'm just waiting for something to be packed. I'll be with you in a minute."

He nodded. " I'll load the bags then. Don't be long." He strode towards the bags, feeling better now that they were almost on their way, already anticipating the moment of pleasure it would be to step out of the plane at St. Nicolaas. It was a sign of age, he supposed, that he was thinking of St. Nicolaas not only as a refuge, but as a hiding-place. Then he cursed under his breath because he knew also that Isobel had left him now no place to hide.

" Ginny will be along in a minute," he said to the pilot, as he began to stow the bags in the little four-seater Cessna. Albert de Kruythoff was coming towards the plane, his head thrust forward on his bony neck in the way that was characteristic of him. He slung his brief-case in under one of the seats, and started to crawl in, bending his legs almost double to fit into the bucket seat. He sighed as he leaned back.

" Well—they say there must be a new elementary school on St. Nicolaas next year, John." He nodded back towards the airport, indicating a weary patience with the two Curaçao officials. " So we have to start scratching around for some money. . . ."

The talk went on—about the difficulties of raising money, about the slight chance of getting more assistance from Curaçao, about all the other things that needed attention on St. Nicolaas besides the schools. Harry Parker chipped in occasionally with items about the St. Charles budget, but de Kruythoff and John listened with only half an ear. St. Charles was an American possession, one of three islands which were vital footholds for the United States in the Caribbean, comparatively rich from tourism. St. Nicolaas was an outpost of the Netherlands West Indies, an unimportant adjunct to Curaçao and Aruba, a sugar-island

that had become a backwater and slipped into decline. It
struggled to pull its population into the twentieth century,
to build roads as well as schools. There was no way to
compare St. Nicolaas with St. Charles. Sometimes St.
Charles, viewed from across the few miles of water that
separated them, seemed to be almost enveloped in a rosy
mist of prosperity. It was hard for John not to think that
Harry Parker sounded faintly patronising. Then he realised
that they had talked for five minutes, and still Ginny had
not come.

As he twisted about in his seat to look for her, she emerged
from the building. She was carrying a large cardboard carton
which bumped against her legs as she ran across the tarmac.

"I'm sorry, Mr. Parker . . . Mr. de Kruythoff. I didn't
think I'd keep you waiting so long. They were so slow
wrapping this."

John reached out to take the package. "I hope it isn't all
perfume, Ginny. You'll smell like the gift shop."

She laughed. "It's four ninety-five worth of china for
Mother." She slipped into the seat beside the pilot's, and
Harry Parker leaned across her to fasten the door. "They said
it would cost fifteen dollars in New York"

They tended always to think and talk in terms of American
dollars rather than Dutch guilders. The close proximity of
St. Nicolaas to the American islands and Puerto Rico, its
isolation from Curaçao, forced it to dwell in a half-way state
of mind. It was something of an anachronism that this little
island still remained officially Dutch.

"What can you have bought for Katrien for five dollars?"
John asked. The plane began to taxi towards the runway
that headed out to sea. Harry Parker tapped Ginny's arm.

"Fasten your seat-belt, Ginny."

"Sorry . . ." She did as he told her. Once the Cessna was
in position at the end of the runway, Parker began to go
through the drill of checking the instruments and revving
each engine separately. The noise was now deafening;
Ginny had to shout her answer above it.

"You don't have to tell her it only cost five dollars—I
just had enough money. It's one of those English early-
morning tea-sets. You know the ones—just one cup and
saucer and small plate, and the matching little teapot and
jug and sugar-bowl. It looked so . . ." She hesitated. "Sort

of *exclusive* to have just one cup in the set. Mother will feel like a queen sitting on the gallery having her morning tea."

Beside him, John saw Albert de Kruythoff nod in agreement, though he was too shy to comment openly on Katrien Tilsit. John thought for a moment that to this lonely, middle-aged bachelor perhaps his big-boned, blonde wife did seem a trifle queenly, with her graceful, unhurried movements. Ginny had made a good word for Katrien.

Harry Parker was talking to the flight-control tower. Then there was the swift run down the long stretch of tarmac that led straight to the sea. No one spoke until the craft had lifted clear of it, and the sea was green and suddenly a long way below them. They climbed to two thousand feet before the Cessna turned to take the run down the coast line of St. Charles and east towards St. Nicolaas. The busy humming life of St. Charles was briefly below them—the U.S. submarine base, the new salt-water distillation plant that was costing the U.S. Government, they said, a fortune to operate and test, then the town of Margretsted, the streets running up the hillsides and bisecting each other in an orderly fashion right down to the waterfront drive. The town and the Fort, with its cannons pointing out to the harbour entrance, were as the Danes had built them three hundred years ago. The Americans, when they had bought their islands from the Danes during the World War I, had supplied plumbing and electricity with a certain discretion. Only the square slabs of modern houses reaching up into the steep hills spoke of this century. John lifted his eyes from the scene below him, and St. Nicolaas was already plain on the horizon and growing bigger every moment. His eyes squinted against the glare from the brilliant sunlit sea. To the north were the British Islands. This cluster of the Antilles, he thought, was a tiny microcosm of the sugar-islands and of the wars that had been fought over them by the Spanish, the English and the Dutch. The Americans had paid cash for their three islands, which was more gentlemanly, if you had the money. John thought that it would be nice to have —in spite of Congress groaning—enough money to buy what you wanted. Then he told himself that he was grown into a sour, envious old man. He jerked his mind back to the conversation in the cabin.

" . . . since you're home for good," Harry Parker was saying. " You should get a job in St. Charles. Everyone needs help . . . you know, typing and all that kind of thing. Or in one of the shops . . ."

" Well . . . I don't know . . ."

Unexpectedly Albert de Kruythoff spoke—unexpectedly because he was painfully shy with women and John had never before heard him volunteer advice or opinion about one of them. " Surely Ginny will stay a little while now that she's come home?" This was nearly a plea in his quiet voice. Then he seemed to squirm in his seat, alarmed at the daring of what he had said.

In front of John, Harry Parker's powerful shoulders shrugged, seeming to dismiss de Kruythoff as exactly the kind of man who would think a backwater like St. Nicolaas was the place for a girl like Ginny. The motion suggested that de Kruythoff and St. Nicolaas deserved each other. " St. Nicolaas is dead," Parker pronounced. " And it will stay dead until you get some tourists going there. Until then there's nothing for a young girl on St. Nicolaas."

" Tourists!" John said the word almost in a whisper. It was a crime to talk against tourism in the Caribbean, but the thought of its coming to St. Nicolaas appalled him. It was coming, of course, and the cherished peace and obscurity of the island must vanish.

" Well—St. Nicolaas's turn is coming. There just aren't any more undiscovered islands in the Caribbean."

John edged forward in his seat to peer over the shoulders of the pilot, the better to get the full view over the nose of the Cessna, to reassure himself, if only momentarily, that the island still lay undisturbed, that nothing had really changed since he had left it yesterday, in spite of Parker's words. It was there, looking as it always did, and his emotion on returning to it was, as always, a deep relief that it was simply there. His eye followed the line of the coast on which lay the orange glow of the sunset. He marked the well-known bays and inlets, his mind saying over their names— Creel, Frenchmen's, St. Eustatius, and there, right at the end, and now out of sight as the plane descended, his own bay, Oranje Cove. From the darker blue the colour of the water gave to green inside the reefs, and the astonishing, glistening white beaches curved inwards from almost every rocky point. The ridge of the hills down the spine of the island were gentler slopes than those on St. Charles, making the growing of sugar-cane possible, if no longer very profitable. Like anyone who looked at St. Nicolaas from out at sea, his eye was drawn by the swell of Kronberg, the extinct volcano that rose at the north-eastern end of the island, and which was visible from every part of it. Its twenty-five hundred feet, rising out of comparatively low hills, was a landmark in the Lesser Antilles. St. Nicolaas lay as a kind of outpost along the crescent of the Antilles at the point where the Atlantic and the Caribbean meet, a shimmering, jewel-coloured thing which seemed to John almost as untouched as the first time he had seen it almost thirty years ago. In those days there had been very little air traffic in the Caribbean, and he had first glimpsed the peak of Kronberg from the deck of a trading schooner out of Miami. For him this had marked the end of a period of drifting from island to island about the Caribbean. He had stayed on St. Nicolaas. These were the years of the depression thirties, and sugar was bringing almost nothing in the world market. The land which he had bought cheaply from the widow of a sugar-planter had promised no more than a bare living. He had settled here, expecting very little from his life, and strangely, had gathered contentment to himself with every year. He had married the daughter of a man of Dutch descent who was his neighbour. He had asked nothing of this island except that it be not any part of England, nor asked of the woman, Katrien van Meerten, nothing except that she remind him in no way of the woman he had once wanted. Unexpectedly—undeservedly, he thought—there had been peace and a measure of happiness.

And there had been Ginny. He looked at her now, blonde, smiling, listening to Harry Parker's conversation, untroubled. He could not let her feel his fear, the sure and disturbing knowledge that the outside world was coming close, was even threatening in the form of his sister. He was made cowardly and old by the thought of Isobel; the memory of her worked on him like a cataclysm of pain. His heart seemed to contract in remembered bitterness. His only gift to Ginny could be an absence from fear, and greed, and he hoped he had given her that.

The landing-strip at St. Nicolaas was a bumpy field and

B

the Cessna bounced several times. At the end of the runway the craft turned and headed back towards the small white-washed building of corrugated iron which served as the terminal. Parker pointed towards the red steel skeleton that was rising beside it, and down towards the inland end of the runway where two orange bull-dozers were working.

" Well—there it is, Ginny. It's the beginning."

" What is it?"

" Caribair's starting a service from Puerto Rico in the New Year. They're extending the runway—and that's the start of a new airport building."

" I didn't know," she said, and the words were voiced with a kind of young excitement.

" That has to be the first step, of course," Parker said knowingly. " You can't get tourists here until there's some way to transport them." The plane had been taxi-ing gently over the rough ground and was now in front of the building. He cut the engines and his voice seemed to boom out in the sudden quiet. " You want to bet me there'll be two hotels by this time next year?"

De Kruythoff reached his long arm out past Ginny to unlatch the door. " Perhaps that," he said, " will be where I will get my money to pay for the schools."

They stood and waited while Parker got Ginny's bags out, and placed the cardboard carton down at her feet. " I wouldn't want to break your mother's china, Ginny, so perhaps you'd better carry that."

" Please—let me," de Kruythoff said.

They settled with Parker for the cost of the charter, de Kruythoff and John splitting it between them. De Kruythoff picked up his brief-case and Ginny's package. " I'll just carry this to the car, John." Then he turned back to Ginny. " The Governor is expected from Curaçao next week, Ginny. There will be the usual small reception. I hope you will come." He said it in his accustomed, unemphasised way, as if such an invitation were nothing, as if it did not mark the occasion, on St. Nicolaas at least, when a young girl was acknowledged to be grown up.

" I'd love to. Thank you."

" Very well. I shall include your name on the card to Katrien and John."

The Cessna had taken off again by the time John had loaded the baggage into the Volkswagen. The sound of the engine diminished and died; the island took back its accustomed quiet, and John felt the return of his longed-for security.

V

Oranje Huis stood on a high promontory above its cove. One end of the gallery that surrounded it looked south and gave a glimpse of the island's only town, Willemstad. But it was usually on the northern side, looking down into Oranje Cove, that the Tilsits sat. The great central hall was the living-room of the house, and its view was directly west over the chain of the Lesser Antilles, the British and American islands. From here at night you could see the light on Margretsted, over on St. Charles. There was a story on St. Nicolaas that the place had been named Oranje Huis when John Tilsit had married Pieter van Meerten's daughter, and gone to live there, the marriage awakening echoes of the one-time union of England and Holland under William of Orange. The story was not true, and was only told as a joke. The house of Katrien van Meerten's ancestors had been built more than two hundred years ago, and had always been called Oranje Huis. It was a stone and brick building with all its floors and galleries marble-tiled; it had been built by slave labour and had the large, high-ceilinged rooms of that time and easy economy. Each room opened by its own tall french doors to the outside gallery; there were heavy wooden shutters latched back from each window, waiting against the arrival of the hurricanes. The termites were in the shutters now, and John Tilsit doubted that the roof would withstand the next full hurricane. Whenever he spoke of it Katrien reminded him that the next hurricane might be twenty years away, and not to worry. But he did worry because he could not afford to replace the roof beams or the shutters, and before next harvest he had somehow to get a new truck and he could not afford that either. He wished he had the temperament of his wife.

John Tilsit mixed the punch rather ceremoniously on the evening of Ginny's return. Katrien now raised her glass towards her daughter. " Welcome back, Ginny." Katrien nodded, and her eyes approved the same changes that John had noted in his daughter. Katrien privately considered that Ginny had been far too long at school ; by temperament her daughter was a late-comer, and John's holding her back here on St. Nicolaas a year and more after she should have been at Santa Maria had been no help. Katrien was a realist who recognised the fact that she was married to a man of another stamp. She did not fight with the fact unnecessarily. Looking at him now, with his eyes fixed on Ginny, she smiled secretly.

Katrien was a large, handsome woman, fair-skinned, with a high colour, and very blonde still. A certain languor of her movements betrayed the fact that she had been born to this climate and knew how to live with it. She made occasional visits to Curaçao and San Juan for shopping ; she had been three times to Miami. Once John had taken her for a terrifying, bewildering week to New York. That was all she knew of the world beyond St. Nicolaas except for what she read in the newspapers and magazines to which she subscribed, and which were always weeks out of date. She had none of the sometimes nervous intensity of her husband and daughter ; her placid strength was rock-like behind them. The only sharp regret of Katrien's life was that she had borne only one child besides Ginny, a son who had died in infancy. She would have liked more children—more sons. Apart from this lack she was content, and reasonably happy, and she believed for the most part she had succeeded in making her husband so. She did not often pause to consider that it was no simple thing to have achieved this much. In her opinion, it was foolish and wasteful not to make the best of what one had.

" It's so quiet here after San Juan," Ginny said. " Every time I come back my ears almost tingle with the quiet. San Juan never seems to go to bed."

" There are worse places that San Juan," Katrien said, remembering New York. " The people are polite. . . . I always like the smell of the peeled oranges in the street. I've often thought I'd like to own one of those orange-peeling machines the vendors have . . . so cunning, they are. You know them, John?"

" I know them. Do you really want one?"

" I was joking."

The breeze moved in off the sea as they sat, stirring the trees in the garden on the hillside below the house. Like the house, the garden was a relic from another time, a time of unpaid labour and unlimited patience. It was laid out in terraces cut into the hillside and its soil had been brought from the more fertile parts of the island in baskets strapped to donkeys. The garden was a small miracle of mechanical engineering, planned to control erosion and conserve water and soil: in the years of its neglect it had become beautiful in a disorderly way that its careful Dutch planner had never intended. Its stone urns and balustrades, the marble-paved walks were cracked from the slight earth tremors which shook the islands; weeds grew in the cracks and vines clawed at the stonework, and Katrien's ceaseless labour never defeated them, merely held them back for a time. But things still bloomed there that never should have bloomed in the face of the salt winds from the sea. At the bottom of the garden a high wall protected the more delicate plants; it was crumbling—when a large section had fallen a year ago Katrien had not even discussed rebuilding it with John. There was no money for it, and they knew they must see the terraces and walls shift gradually, almost imperceptibly, year by year closer to the sea.

Katrien watched Ginny now as she sipped her drink, trying to gauge, as she did each time her daughter returned from San Juan, what the months of absence had changed or developed in her. Ginny had perched herself on the low balustrade of the gallery, and she was staring down into the cove. The German shepherd, Bo, who had been her dog for twelve years, sat at her feet, occasionally nuzzling his head into her lap to reassure himself that she had returned once more. The darkness was gathering; behind Ginny's head Katrien could make out the constant creaming of the gentle surf against the beach. The opposite headland of the cove was a darker outline on the night-blue sky. The stars had begun to show faintly. The girl's body was relaxed: she looked peaceful and happy, as if it were no exile to come back to this quiet. Her hand strayed over to fondle Bo's head; it was a gesture that seemed almost to embrace Katrien and John too.

Suddenly Ginny stiffened, leaning forward and staring down fixedly at one point in the growing darkness of the cove. "What on earth is that down there?—it looks like some kind of building . . ."

"*That* belongs to our neighbour, Jim MacAdam. And *that* is the start of a cottage hotel he's building on his end of the beach." John pronounced the words reluctantly, as if he hated to say them.

"He can't—not on our beach!"

"That end of it happens to be his beach, Ginny. I can't stop him."

"His beach?" she repeated. "What do you mean—*his* beach. *Who* is Jim MacAdam—I never heard of him!"

"You remember a man—an American—bought that northern headland from Katrien just before the war—no, of course you don't remember. It was before you were born. He was an American—he never came back here, and he didn't seem to have any plans for the land, except just perhaps a small house. We needed the money at the time, but every day I looked across at that land and pictured someone else living on it I regretted the sale. Every day that MacAdam didn't come back to the island has been a day of grace."

"You're very hard on him," Katrien demurred. "He had every right . . ."

"Of course he did. That's what made it harder to take. We sold him the right. The land was useless for sugar—far too dry and sandy out there. But I should have found some other way to raise the money. Now with the way land values have risen, I couldn't in a lifetime afford to buy it back."

Ginny turned again to stare into the darkness of the cove; her look was more concentrated now as she tried to discern the outline of the buildings. "A big hotel? How many cottages?" Her tone held shock and outrage. "I just can't believe we're going to be looking across at beach umbrellas and all that awful stuff."

"A small hotel, Ginny. Six cottages, I think—to begin with. But he has plans for more—and thirty acres on the hill behind that. With St. Charles's tourism booming as it is, and Cuba closed down by Castro, it's only natural that people are going to start exploring farther. I'm afraid it's the start of change here on St. Nicolaas, and there will be other Jim MacAdams. Money's the only thing that will hold him back. "

" Doesn't he have the money?"

" The money he's building with isn't his own—the value is in the land. He's put together a syndicate in New York to raise the capital to build this first part, and on the strength of it he'll probably get the money to do the rest. His problem will be to retain control, but I'd guess he'll do that too. He's one of these determined young men who have a remarkably single purpose in life."

" Young?" Ginny gave a short laugh. " What do you count as young, Father? You said he bought the land before I was born."

" His father, Ginny—it was his father who bought the land. He was a builder in Connecticut—he went broke, Jim told me, just before he died. Jim trained as an architect, but I suppose he's a builder like his father. He's building down there practically by himself. An odd man . . ."

" I *like* Jim MacAdam," Katrien said firmly. " He's a good man, and he's bringing money into the island. And we need that badly enough."

John sighed. " You're right, I suppose. The island needs it, and he's a decent enough fellow. The funny part of it is that he thinks we're bound to be as excited as he is about the hotel. He sits here and has a drink with us, talking about it, and I haven't the heart to tell him I hate the sight of his bloody buildings."

" And you'd better not tell him," Katrien said, " because I have him picked out as someone for Ginny to marry."

" Mother!"

" *Katrien!*"

Only John's exclamation had been a real protest. Ginny's tone had held amusement and curiosity. Katrien held up her hand to silence them both. " Well—and why not? It's not such a bad thing for Ginny to be married, is it?"

" Jim MacAdam," John said stiffly, " is in his thirties. He's too old for Ginny, and he's not at all suitable."

Katrien's large mouth stretched wider in a smile. " And how much older than I are you, John Tilsit? And are there so many other suitable young men around for Ginny to take her pick? This is a poor island, and the young men leave as soon as they can. Or is it because Jim's an American?—you always tell me you admire the American get-up-and-go! Or isn't he good enough for Ginny? Shall we import an Englishman?" Her tone was bantering, but she pressed her point.

"You know that has nothing to do with it." John always felt ridiculous when Katrien chose to tease him this way —especially when they both knew there was some grain of truth in what she was saying. "MacAdam's already been married, and there's no future for Ginny in a situation like that."

"Jim's wife died," Katrien said quickly. "I think he loved her very much—I *feel* he did. He won't be in a hurry to marry . . ."

"Well—I'm relieved to hear it." Ginny suddenly stood up, displacing Bo's head from her lap. They both turned to look at her in an instant's surprise. They were so accustomed to talking about her in her absence that for the first few days after her return it was hard to remember to stop. "I hope you didn't tell him you had a daughter all ready to make him change his mind." She walked over to the drink-tray. "I'll look him over, of course," she said sarcastically, "but I don't know . . . I don't think I could marry a man who put up cottages on our beach."

It was all a joke, of course, but Katrien noticed that Ginny's movements at the tray were suddenly awkward, self-conscious, a little defensive, warning Katrien to say nothing more about Jim MacAdam for the time being.

"I'll get more ice," Ginny said. "This is almost finished." It had been her task, since she was a small child, to keep the bowl filled during this hour Katrien and John spent on the veranda at dusk. Her resuming it had always been part of the home-coming. With the bowl in her hand she paused now in the arched doorway that led to the wide central room of the house. The kitchen was beyond that, separate from the main building. The bedrooms occupied the four corners. The house had great charm, and great inconvenience. This thought was in Ginny's mind as she turned back to her mother.

"We really ought to get one of those insulated ice buckets

the Americans make. It would save ice. I've seen an in-expensive plastic kind we could get . ."

Her father uttered a soft groan. "Plastic! The whole world seems to be turning into a plastic bag. I'd rather have the ice melting in front of my eyes."

Ginny shrugged and smiled. "Reactionary!" They listened to the spike heels of her new shoes tapping rapidly on the marble as she walked out through the house to the kitchen. Something of the same thought stirred in both their minds, but John spoke first.

"I'm surprised the nuns let her buy those cheap things she has on her feet. They're ridiculous—and she'll be crippled!"

"What would you have them do—keep her in baby shoes? They're not fools, those sisters, and not quite unworldly either. Girls have to follow the fashion, and they always wear heels that are too high until they learn better. John . . . we must let her make her own mistakes."

He shook his head, sighing. "I know—but I'm getting to be a foolish, doting old man, Katrien. I want to save her from—from everything."

Katrien turned partly towards him, but they could no longer see each other's features clearly. "You can't save her from living. She must know what it means to live."

He thought that it was a strange statement to come from a woman who had lived nowhere but on this island, and whose life, on the surface, would seem to have been one of immense tranquillity, even dullness. But Katrien was visited by these moments of sudden wisdom that owed little to experience and a great deal to instinct; these were the times when John felt vaguely uneasy with her, reluctant to think that he might have listened more to her through these years, might have learned from her, might even have talked to her of the things that troubled him, and have had the trouble lightened.

In the half darkness he looked towards his wife. "Mother Angela thinks Ginny should go on to university. Not in San Juan. She suggests the University of Miami."

He saw Katrien nodding her head slowly, and he hadn't known until that moment how much he had been counting on her disagreeing, and perhaps ending the matter there and then.

"Yes?" It was only partly a question.

"Some place like Vassar or Radcliffe would have been better," he continued miserably. "But of course it's out of the question as far as money's concerned. And it's too late to apply . . . It might be too late at Miami," he added with faint hope.

"So . . .?" Katrien took a sip from her drink and she seemed in no hurry to discuss the matter. It was almost as if the suggestion were no surprise to her. "Mother Angela thinks she should be away from St. Nicolaas? Away from us? She's probably right."

"You really think she should go? Will it serve any purpose?"

Katrien shrugged. "Who knows? Will it do any harm? She might learn a few useful things—but she's not very ambitious, our Ginny. What she needs is to learn about the world that is not on a small island—I suppose that is what's in Mother Angela's mind. The world has changed more quickly than we have. We can't help her with it much —she needs to discover it for herself. She needs to meet young men—enough young men to learn how to choose the right one."

He turned on her, bewildered, disappointed. "But a moment ago—why, you were pushing Jim MacAdam on her, Katrien."

"Not Jim MacAdam in particular." She gestured quickly. "Don't you understand—not *just* Jim MacAdam—though he's a good man and I would hope she'd do as well as him. No —not just him, but *a* man—some man. She has to get used to the idea of men. Have you looked at your daughter, John —this time? She's a woman, and in some ways she's a beautiful woman. She has a woman's body. She has to learn how to deal with herself—and with other people. She's better to do that with girls of her own age. The lessons are more painful, but they're better learned."

"But aren't they better learned here—where we can help her?"

"Parents can never help much," Katrien replied calmly. "We're always too far away, however much we love her. All we would do would be to wrap her in cotton-wool—or marry her off quickly to some good Jim MacAdam."

"Would that be wrong?"

" For Ginny—yes! She would wake up some day and say she has been cheated. Some tourist would come along and tell her she was wasted here, and she would believe him because she didn't know any different. If we send her away she has a chance to choose. At least she'll understand what there is to come back to—if she wants to come back. I don't want her to be discontented . . . unhappy. Do you understand me, John?"

" No!" he said wildly. " No, I don't. Why should she be discontented and unhappy? *You* were not."

" Ginny is your child as well as mine." She said the words gently, but he understood suddenly the extent of her knowledge of him, of his own discontent and the unhappiness that had come to this island with him and which had lessened so gradually over the years that he had hardly noticed its going. Now that he was forced to think of it he realised that only the slightly bitter after-taste was left. He had many reasons to be grateful to Katrien. It was a pity that it never seemed quite the right time to tell her so. Her voice went on, gentle, quiet in the dark. " Ginny is not all me —nor all you. She has two inheritances."

" Yes." He was glad she could not see his face nor see the panic that he fought to control. He did not wish part of himself in Ginny now, nor the kind of legacy that seemed to pass down in his family. He said quickly, " It would be better for her if she had only the influence of her good solid Dutch forebears . . ."

Katrien laughed, a deep laugh that came from her throat. " Solid? That's not a quality young girls wish for. Just wish for her to be happy, John—in whatever way she can. There's not much else you and I can do for her."

He acknowledged what a precious gift this was of Katrien's to be able to leave things alone. He supposed it might have been the reason he had asked her to marry him. He had admired her ability not to claw and probe and try to possess wholly. And now here he was—being all the things he could praise Katrien for not being—possessive and jealous, terrified that Ginny would slip away from him and so to Isobel, wanting to bind her close to him here on this island where Isobel could not touch her, and where the effects of the legacy the Tilsits seemed to bequeath to their descendants could be minimised. He was a panic-

stricken man, and he fought his panic only weakly. He
didn't want to listen to what Katrien had said. He didn't
want to send Ginny away. He wanted her married, safely
married. All his former hostility to the stranger who had
come to disturb Oranje Cove suddenly vanished. Jim Mac-
Adam or anyone like him, just so long as he was stronger than
Ginny, and knew how to hold her. He, her father could not
keep her safe from Isobel, but a husband might. In the
darkness John wiped the beads of perspiration on his top
lip with the back of his hand. Ginny's high heels were
clicking again on the marble.

One of the lights in the big main room was switched on.
The shadows of the gallery columns now fell darkly in the
garden below them.

"Mother—come here a moment, would you? I've something to show you."

"What is it?" Katrien rose from her chair slowly.

"A surprise."

Katrien walked towards the lighted doorway, a big-boned
woman, but not heavy in her movements. She paused in the
arched doorway, blinking; then John saw her start forward
again, more quickly. "Why—what's this?"

"For you," Ginny's voice answered. "I found it this
afternoon in St. Charles while we waited for Harry."

"It's beautiful, Ginny. It is just for me?"

John, too, got out of his chair and walked along the
gallery. He liked the pleasure in Katrien's voice, and he liked
Ginny for having thought of buying her mother the gift
with the last of the dollars saved from her school allowance.
There was strangely very little rivalry between these two—
a mother and her only daughter; they did not seem to seek
to dominate each other. Ginny was too generous, he thought,
to be a true Tilsit. His panic subsided a little. Ginny
would be all right. There was no need to fear too much,
because she would be all right.

He came to the doorway and then he saw it. Ginny
had set out the pieces of china on a tray while she was in
the kitchen. She had placed the tray on the low table
before one of the sofas and now Katrien was bending
over it. As John stood there she lifted the teapot, smiling
with pleasure at its perfect miniature shape. John clutched
the door-frame to try to stop the trembling of his hand. He

was mistaken, he told himself; he was mistaken because he had to be. But he was not. His hand slipped from the door-frame, and he strode towards the table. Ginny looked up, smiling.

"Father—what are these blue flowers in the border? Are they English flowers, do you know . . .?" The rest of her words died there.

Now he felt the rage and fear engulf him. The decorative pattern of tiny bluebells that banded the cup and saucer, the plate, the teapot he knew by heart. He had seen this pattern on the day it had been created—an action of his had been its inspiration. He had walked in the woods at Tilsit with Isobel and the woman he had loved; he had picked a dozen stalks and passed them to her; he knew they would quickly fade but he had wanted to see them lie in her hands. She had touched the tiny bells softly, delighted with their fragile beauty. "Wouldn't they look pretty on china?" she had said. Isobel had had the pattern created. "It's not distinguished, of course," Isobel had pronounced, "but it will do very well in the cottage ware." He felt he had stolen it, not for pleasure but for greed —and because everything at Tilsit belonged to her, even the bluebells. He stared at the china set out before him for a moment longer, and the remembered pain and rage grew beyond bearing.

Katrien saw his face. "John—what is it?"

"God damn it! Get that stuff out of here! Never let me see it again."

He could not stop himself. It was done in a second. He swept the tray and its contents off the table. They smashed violently against the marble tile, and pieces of the china slithered away to the corners of the room. As he left his shoe crunched on one in the doorway. He heard no protest behind him in the room, only blank astonished silence. He plunged down the steps from the gallery to the covering darkness of the garden.

For the moment Ginny and Katrien found nothing to say to each other. Ginny knew that questions would bring no answers; the shock and surprise was as clearly on her mother's face as she felt it on her own. Slowly she bent down and picked up one of the fragments at her feet. It was part of the saucer, the indented part where the cup would rest. She turned it in her fingers slowly. It was stamped with the maker's name:

TILSIT

BONE CHINA

ENGLAND

And the identifying mark, the large sloping T with the cross through it.

T

CHAPTER TWO

Bo ran on ahead of Ginny, down the steps and paths that led to the beach. There was a sudden return of youthfulness to him—in the way his head was held, in his eager dashes back to her side to assure himself that she was really following. Although she had been away from him so many times, Bo had always been Ginny's dog.

The tide was on the ebb, and the surf was barely more than the lapping of wavelets against the beach. The sun was not up yet. There was a grey cast on the water; it looked cold. But when Ginny kicked off her shoes and walked along the wet sand at the edge of the tide, it touched her feet and ankles with the familiar warmth. She searched among the debris of driftwood and seaweed to find a light stick to throw for Bo. He bounded out into the water after it as if he had been a young dog, rushing back to give it to her, shaking water over her and pleading to have it thrown again. While she played the game with him she kept her eyes deliberately away from the outlines of the new buildings at the other end of the beach. Then suddenly, a little more than half-way down the beach the line of debris from the tide changed. The seaweed and driftwood had all been removed; someone had begun to tidy the undergrowth of the sea-grapes At twenty yards distance a wooden bench had been placed in their shade. Ginny knew then that she was trespassing. She turned quickly and faced the other way. She threw the stick once more for Bo, but he was tired and he could no longer pretend to be a puppy. So she walked away from the water and seated herself on the high barrier of sand flung up by the tides. Bo lay beside her panting, one wet sandy paw laid possessively on her shorts.

The line of the horizon had been bright for some minutes now. Suddenly the sun touched the ridges of the hill behind her; in a few moments it would reach down here into the cove. Automatically she looked up at the house to see what signs of life were stirring, but she could see no one on the gallery. This morning, she thought, her mother would drink her tea standing in the kitchen talking with Wilhelmina, the cook. She would pretend that she had no time to sit on the gallery to drink it. This would go on for a week or two until the memory faded a little of the china lying in fragments on the floor. Then she would take to having her tea once again on the gallery in the ordinary breakfast coffee cup she had always used, and there would never be a mention of the Tilsit china.

Katrien had made that very clear to Ginny the night before. She had sent her to the kitchen for the dustpan and brush, and she swept up the pieces herself. " Never mention it to him, Ginny—do you understand that?"

" But why *not*? I want to know!! Are these Tilsits "— she held a piece of the china towards Katrien—" the same Tilsits as we are?"

" I don't know. I've never heard of them—and I won't ask him. And you're not to ask either."

" But why not! Why should he just be allowed to smash this—it was a present for *you*, Mother—and never explain why. It isn't fair. . . ."

Katrien leaned on the broom. " Ginny, you surely know by now that things aren't always fair—especially with people you love. If your father doesn't want to explain, he needn't. It's not your business to pry."

" You mean you're going to let him get away with it— just say nothing? *I* wouldn't—I would never do that!"

" You haven't loved a man yet, Ginny."

" I love Father! "

Katrien smiled faintly. " I didn't mean that." Then she resumed sweeping.

Soon after that they had heard the noisy putt-putt of his old outboard down in the cove. The moon was not fully up so they saw only the vague shadow that might have been the boat as it headed towards the point. Watching from the veranda, Katrien only said, " I hope he has enough gasoline."

It was very late and the moon was bright and full when Ginny woke at the sound of the outboard on his return. Later she heard the voices of her parents, at first soft and cautious, then more normal, and the smell of toast and the splutter of eggs frying in the kitchen. To Ginny's amazement there was even one moment of quiet laughter. It was all so removed from the drama of the smashed china, so ordinary. Ginny rolled over and fell asleep again, puzzled, and feeling ignorant and young.

There was the outboard now, called *Ginny,* drawn up on the sand at the bottom of the path to the house. It was old, and many times painted. It had the worn look of her father's seer-sucker suit, and the same kind of honesty. Now she turned and looked with great deliberation at the sleek lines of the cruiser which was moored a little out from the beach at the other end of the cove. It said speed and money, the kind of money her father would never have, the speed that had passed him by long ago. She resented it. It was cool and beautiful, the movement of the water reflected in the shining white hull. It represented the enemy and the intruder, and she had enough of Katrien in her to know that she must go and make the civilised gesture to the enemy, and have done with it.

So she got to her feet again, and this time she crossed that invisible barrier where the tide debris had been removed. There was no sign here, but in her mind she could see it as it was on some other beaches. PRIVATE PROPERTY—KEEP OUT. Perhaps, she thought, when the tourists came they would have to put up a sign of their own, facing Jim MacAdam's beach, or the strangers would come innocently wandering along to the point, perhaps even up the paths to Oranje Huis itself. They would be surprised that no one was anxious to have the house photographed. She passed the wooden bench. Now she was deep in the enemy's territory. Bo was ahead of her, recognising no barrier, as if the way to the straggle of half-finished buildings was a familiar one. Finally he broke into a run and left Ginny behind. It could have been the smell of the bacon which drew him, she told herself, or it could have been that the man who was cooking was Bo's friend.

She surveyed the building site critically, resentfully. One of the cottages appeared finished, the others in various stages of construction. They were of native stone and redwood—whole walls of redwood louvered to permit the breezes to pass through; all of them deeply shadowed by wide over-hangs of the roofs. Dominating them was the big curving cantilevered sweep of the roof of what would be, she supposed, the main building, the kitchen and restaurant. There was nothing like it on the island, bold and dramatic, but not obtrusive, its lines following the line of the ridge above it, hugging down to the earth and even seeming to fade back into the hillside. On this island, where all the archi-tecture was patterned in the colonial style, it was vaguely shocking, but none of it was ugly, as she had thought it would be. She was not yet prepared to admit that it was anything else. She began to pick her way through the piles of building materials towards the louver and screen door at which Bo was waiting.

The door opened before she reached it. The man seemed to accept Bo's presence as normal, as if he had been there often before. The dog brushed past him, into the cottage. Ginny knew a moment's jealousy at that act of familiarity. Then the man spoke.

" Well—who are you? The Golden Girl?"

Ginny halted. The tone was strange—cool, teasing, like the eyes of the man.

" I'm . . ."

He swung the door wider. " You're Miss Virginia Tilsit of Oranje Huis. Come in. And mind where you're walk-ing—you shouldn't be here in bare feet with all this stuff around." He was a tall man, wearing worn khaki shorts and a T-shirt and heavy workman's boots.

" I—I always walk on the beach in bare feet."

" Times change," he said. " You'll have to be careful until I can put it all back in order for bare feet again. Come in. I'm Jim MacAdam, your neighbour."

" Yes, Father told me."

" Ah, your father . . . He doesn't like what I'm doing
here. Although he tries to be polite about it in his civilised
English way. Your mother is looking forward, I think, to
watching life among the tourists. Whose side are you on?"

" I haven't made up my mind. If you'd just stop lecturing
me and asking questions I might have a chance to think
about it." She began to work her way around the piles of
lumber.

" I suppose I deserve that." He held the door wide. " I'll
admit I was pretty scared of you. I always talk too much
when I'm scared."

She moved past him into the room. It was large, with
the usual tiled floor, and the lights from the sea softened by
the louvers and the sea-grapes. As large as it was, it seemed
to Ginny that there was hardly space to move. The furniture
was scanty, and the floor was covered with books and
spread-out plans weighted down with odd pieces of wood.
The saucers Jim MacAdam used for ash-trays were overflowing. There was no table, only a tilted drawing-board
and a high stool; there were six empty beer cans with sharply
pointed pencils facing upwards like bristling cactus. Clean
laundry had been stacked in two piles on the floor against
the wall. Ginny carefully picked her way among the plans.

" Why were you scared?" she said at last.

He closed the door noisily. " I watched you down there
on the beach. I knew who you were, of course. Everyone
at Oranje Huis has been talking about you coming home for
the last week. I thought you were coming to pay a call. And
then I saw you turn back when you crossed on to my part
of the beach. I guess after that it was a toss-up between
your mother and your father. I couldn't make up my mind
when I saw you starting back down here again whether it
was your mother's friendliness or your father's sense of the
proper thing to do that had won."

" Well . . ."

Beyond the bravado that had swept her past him into this
room she had no resources. " The bacon is burning," she
said.

She watched him fish the bacon out of the pan and set it to
drain. The kitchen was a small rectangle balancing the
bathroom along the same wall. Her mother had said they

were called efficiency units. Jim MacAdam moved expertly in its space. Strangely the clutter of the big room didn't extend here.

"How do you like your eggs?" he called to her.

Ginny hesitated. No one had ever asked this question of her before. At Santa Maria you ate what was put in front of you; at Oranje Huis they knew the way you liked your eggs.

"Poached," she said at last.

"Sorry . . . you'll have to have them fried. I've only got one frying pan and it's already got bacon grease in it."

"Then fried will do . . ." It wouldn't have mattered whether or not she agreed. He was already breaking the eggs into the pan.

Then he put his head out of the kitchen. "Coffee's ready . . . see if you can clear some place over there to eat, will you?" He nodded in the direction of a low table in front of the bed, which she hadn't noticed because it was piled with books.

"I really shouldn't stay . . . they'll be expecting me at home."

"For Pete's sake, don't be so English! Will they send out the police? Are there so many places to go on St. Nicolaas for breakfast? Where else would you be except here?"

She moved obediently to clear the books off the table. Then abruptly she turned and looked back at him. "That's rather disappointing, isn't it?"

"What's disappointing?"

"I mean that they know where I'll be."

Ginny thought that it was the best and the worst hour of her life. She heard herself say most of the things she had rehearsed for the time when she had her first meal alone with a man; she said them, and they were mostly the wrong things. The best parts of it were what she had never imagined.

Jim MacAdam ate his breakfast hungrily, concentrating only on it for a time. He had not shaved this morning; the stubble of beard added to the look of a kind of raw strength in his lean-boned face. It was not exactly a handsome face —too long and squared-off too suddenly at the jaw. He had grey eyes under an untidily-hooked line of eyebrows. His eyes went to her face whenever she spoke and stayed there until she finished. It was a disconcerting habit; she wished the gaze wasn't quite so direct and without softness. Under this gaze she began to think about herself; her face was bare of make-up and her hair hung down long and straight like a child's. She was grateful he didn't treat her like a child. He didn't fuss over her. The acceptance of her presence there as a natural thing was what was most unexpected and unimaginable. It was the best part of it.

As soon as he had finished eating Jim's hand groped automatically for the pack of cigarettes as if he knew that they were there without his looking. She had noticed the number of opened packs that lay about the room. He extended it towards her.

" No—thank you."

His hands were large and looked strong. The nails were broken off and the skin was covered with small cuts and scratches. He had the swellings of sand-fly bites on his arms and legs. He took a long draw on the cigarette, half-closing his eyes as if to concentrate more closely on the smell and taste of the tobacco.

" Well, Golden Girl—what do you think of all this?"

She frowned. " I wish you wouldn't call me Golden Girl."

" Why not?"

" Because it sounds like someone who doesn't exist."

He nodded slowly, and for the first time since she had seen him he smiled. It was strange that in her nervousness she had not noticed the lack of a smile in greeting. " No one ever does exist for themselves in the same dimension that other people see them," he said. " God forbid! We'd all be stark raving mad if we did. But you've a right to object. It's stupid to put labels on people. I won't call you that again, Ginny."

" You make me feel bad because you said that."

" Why?"

" Because I've been calling you something. Not aloud —just in my mind."

" I know what you've been calling me."

" How do you know?"

" I knew when I saw you turn your back on this place.

Even from a distance, Ginny, you have a very expressive back."

" I didn't feel that way completely—or I wouldn't be here now, would I?"

"But it let me know pretty well what you think of all this. I needn't have asked that silly question. You don't like this, do you?"

" It isn't that I don't *like* it. It could have been worse. It could have been four storeys high and painted bright orange. It isn't what it looks like—I just wish it had never happened."

" Why do you wish that?"

" It was free here, and wild. No one ever came on this beach except ourselves. I remember when I was a kid I used to pretend that I was walking on and on, and that round that point was the rim of the world. The beach seemed longer in those days, and I half suspected I'd fall off the edge if I did get to the rim. Father said I couldn't fall off, but it seemed to be taking a wonderful chance."

" Poor Ginny—so in place of your lovely adventure at the rim of the world, the world has got to come down to size —precisely the size of overweight, middle-aged tourists lying on beach towels. I'm sorry."

" Why did you have to come *now*? You've left us alone all these years . . ."

He squashed out the cigarette in his saucer and stood up. " It's none of your goddamn business! You're too much like your father. You think no one's got a right here except yourselves—only he's a little more polite about it."

" I'm sorry—I didn't mean . . ."

He began to gather up the plates. " I hear the truck with the boys starting down the hill. You'd better go or the gossip will be all over the island to-morrow that you had dinner as well as breakfast here."

He was in the kitchen lighting another cigarette when she left. The only sound was the soft slam of the screen door. He broke the match between his fingers and started to go after her. At the door he stopped. " To hell with it!"

He stood still, though, watching her walk across the sand to the tide. Bo stayed by her side as if he knew that she would need him at this moment. Her long tanned legs in their brief shorts were very beautiful; her back and head were erect so that the straight blonde hair just brushed her shoulders. Her shorts and sleeveless blouse were faded and soft from washing, the colour was a pale yellow. As she walked down to the morning brightness of the water with that loose, free walk he thought that he had never seen anyone so integrated with their background.

" Golden Girl . . ." he said under his breath.

And then the truck started down the last rough section of the unmade road, and a minute later the crew of native workmen were swarming down from it. Jim stowed a fresh pack of cigarettes in his shirt pocket and the keys of the tool-shed. He didn't think about Ginny again in the following eight hours.

For the next week Ginny did not go down to Oranje Cove; she swam in the rocky inlet on the other side of the house. This was the start of the cane-fields, the land here was flatter and the soil richer, the slope of the hills was gradual and gentle, permitting the cultivation of the cane. The farther rise was crowned, as were many hills on the island, with the ruins of a stone sugar-mill, built in the days when each planter processed his own sugar. Now it was all handled at the one central mill. Her father passed her often in the jeep. While the cane grew the work of cultivating and fertilising was ceaseless ; he employed a small work force all the year round, and seasonal labour to cut the cane. He would wave to her each time from the jeep as he passed along the dirt road towards the fields.

" Dangerous swimming there, Ginny," he called.

" I'll be careful. I can take care of myself."

" Yes—I know."

Bo did not want to go down on that side. Each morning he obstinately took the path down to the beach, and she had to call him back. Once down there in the inlet, he refused to swim with her ; he stood on a flat rock, jumping backwards when the spray from a wave hit him. One morning, as she returned to the house for breakfast, he deserted her. She stood at the top of the terraces and watched his dash along the whole length of the beach to the door of Jim MacAdam's cottage. The door opened at once to admit him.

There seemed no way to be free of the awareness of Jim MacAdam. Every morning at seven-thirty Ted Gardiner's truck rolled down the road to unload the crew of workmen. About seven in the evening they heard Jim's jeep as he went into Willemstad to sit on the veranda of The Amsterdam with his whisky for an hour, and then to eat dinner afterwards either at The Amsterdam or at Sparkey's American Grill, which was a hamburger place; when he stayed at The Amsterdam he shared a table with Dr. van Buren, a cranky, ageing bachelor who was one of the island's best gossips. It was something of a shock to Ginny to learn that Jim MacAdam was already so much a part of St. Nicolaas that everyone knew if you wanted to talk to him he was on the veranda of The Amsterdam between seven and eight. People talked about him, too—because the new hotel was something to talk about, like the new air-strip. When Ginny went into Willemstad the next remark after the usual ones about being glad to see her back and was she home for good now, was always one about Jim MacAdam and the hotel. " Well, Ginny—how do you like your new neighbour?" and " The cottages must be making some progress now . . ."

The sounds of Jim MacAdam's activity were ceaseless. The cove rang all day with the noise of the hammers and the electric saws, with the grind of the cement-mixer, with the measured blow of the mason's chisel as he broke stone to the size he wanted.

" Jim's an architect, did you know that?" Katrien said to Ginny one day as she stood watching the *Oranje Lady,* which was what Jim had named the cruiser, speeding out of the cove and heading in the direction of St. Charles.

" If he's an architect, what's he becoming a hotelkeeper for?"

" Some men like to do as well as to plan. His father was a builder . . . I don't imagine Jim will stop being an architect because he runs a hotel."

" It's a bit of a come-down, isn't it—to be just a hotel-keeper?"

" Sometimes, Ginny, you're more than a bit of a snob." She said it without malice, but she meant it. " I think if Jim is doing what he wants to do then he has more dignity than many men I've met." Then she walked along the gallery towards the kitchen with more briskness than was usual with Katrien.

Ginny walked to the balustrade dejectedly, watching the

Oranje Lady growing smaller in the distance until finally it couldn't be distinguished against the blinding sunlit surface of the sea. It made the run to the West India Docks on St. Charles about once every day, and came back loaded with lumber and building supplies. Katrien had told her that Jim had removed all the plush leather seats from the cockpit to make this ferrying work easier. The glamorous lines of the craft looked ludicrous when she came back distorted out of shape by the lumber tied to the cabin room. The sight reminded Ginny a little of the homely clutter of Jim's cottage.

She wished she could walk down there now and talk to him. She wanted to be on hand when the *Oranje Lady* moored again. It would have been good to see the door of Jim's cottage open to admit her as it had for Bo, to take the magazines from Jim's one chair and sit down among the clutter. She was feeling a loneliness that she had never known at Oranje Huis before, a loneliness which sprang partly from the fact that the pursuits of childhood were finished and had not yet been completely replaced by more satisfying ones. But it was mostly the feeling of apartness that had come between herself and her father. John Tilsit was as he had always seemed—grave, mildly sardonic, and a little detached. He was her father, and he had always given to her whatever part of himself he was capable of giving. To give wholly would have been for him, she sensed, a violation of his great need of privacy. He gave what he could. Katrien had been content with that, but she, Ginny, was now asking for more. She no longer thought it enough to have only the part of him that he chose to reveal. That there was much which he was not revealing had suddenly been made clear to her with the visit of Isobel Tilsit to San Juan, and with John's violent and anguished destruction of the Tilsit china. She felt cheated and shut out. It seemed all very well that Katrien should demand to know nothing of her husband's background. That had been her choice long ago. But she, Ginny, was her father's flesh and blood. She believed she had the right to the deepest knowledge of him that was possible. He was her, and she had to know what that was. To have that knowledge withheld, to be shut out from it, was to be denied a part of herself. She resented it, and the resentment and frustration were growing like a wall between them. If she could, she would have torn it down, but the consent to that action had to be her father's. And he would not give it. Suddenly she knew that his kind and gentle façade was only that—a façade. They were apart because he held them apart by his silence. This had existed, of course, for many years; but she had not known of it, and therefore had not grieved. The knowledge was here now, and bitter.

One morning before dawn broke they had gone fishing together, she and her father and Bo, as they had been doing since she had been a child. Before this the silences had always been unstrained, the proof, to Ginny of their knowing and trusting each other so much that words would never be necessary. Now the silence was the evidence of betrayal. The sunlight broke across the grey water with its sudden tropical radiance as she had seen it do a thousand times; dawn and sunrise had always been a time of calm before this. Now the light of tension beat upon them. She had wanted to cry the questions to him, to scream them, to break the quiet with their fury. But his spare, straight figure in the bow of the boat was unmoving and, she thought, unmovable.

When finally she did speak, it was a whisper.

" Father . . . tell me about Isobel Tilsit. Tell me about the Tilsit china. Father, I want to know."

He hadn't even turned around.

" No, Ginny. It's no concern of yours."

And that was the end of it.

Soon after that he pulled in his line, went back to the stern and started up the outboard engine. It was an old, cranky engine, and it made a great deal of noise. But that didn't really drown out the silence between them, which was much larger. When they beached the boat Bo sprang out quickly and went off across the sand at a fast run, turning once and barking as if to entice Ginny after him. He was headed in the direction of Jim Mac-Adam's cottage.

John Tilsit whistled after him, summoning him to return. But Ginny cut him short abruptly.

" No, leave him be . . .!"

She thought that Bo was lucky because he knew the door would swing open.

CHAPTER THREE

The big high rooms of the house of the Gezaghebber of St. Nicolaas, Albert de Kruythoff, were filled with the buzz of talk that went with receptions. But it was a far less frantic sound than Jim was used to hearing at cocktail parties ; the pace was slower. People walked up the lovely double staircase that led straight out of the town square of Willemstad and they did not hurry. A bowl of punch stood on a white-clothed table near the head of the staircase ; you could help yourself right there, and perhaps never bother to leave the gallery with its view of the Fort, and the small craft riding at anchor in the harbour, and the late evening sun splashing against the soft pink and cream walls of the great airy villas the sugar-planters had built in the days when the islands had been rich. But if the atmosphere was relaxed, the occasion still had its ritual of formality, and Jim noticed that no one took a drink before going to greet de Kruythoff and the Governor, for whom the reception was being given. The Governor came once a year from Curaçao, unless there was an emergency. It was a tradition among the residents of St. Nicolaas to make the visit pass smoothly, regardless of the fact that you might have been fighting the day before with Albert de Kruythoff over whether dredging the harbour or widening Town Road had greater priority in the budget allocation. St. Nicolaas was governed from Curaçao. It only made sense, so the island reasoning went, to form a common front with de Kruythoff to get as much as possible in funds allocated and to fight about the exact way to use them afterwards. So everyone went deliberately, but still unhurriedly, to where the Governor and de Kruythoff stood.

It had surprised Jim, when his turn came, to find that the Governor recognised his name when de Kruythoff had spoken it, and there had been an immediate question about the hotel. It occurred to Jim that his might be the only new name, the only new face since last year's reception.

" It's moving along, sir. Slowly—getting materials is difficult. Even in St. Charles they're always running out of supplies—or just the size of nut and bolt you need. Then it's a matter of waiting until the stuff gets here from Miami."

The broad red face of the Dutchman broadened further in a smile. " In the old days the wait wasn't weeks but months, Mr. MacAdam. We make a little progress, you see. But then, things *are* slower down here—they always will be, I hope. That's what brings the tourists. Well—good luck with your hotel."

He turned to greet the next group of arrivals and Jim was free to wander away towards the long table where the official silver of the Lieutenant-Governor of St. Nicolaas was on display. To Jim's dazzled eyes it looked as if a small fortune lay here—the great punch-bowl, the tall candelabra, the serving dishes—all of these left over from the days when the sugar-islands had been worth fighting wars over. Now these symbols of wealth were the last remnant of empire, massive, intricately wrought things that had survived privateer raids, pillage, slave insurrections and stood here magnificent but tame, the finest handiwork of Dutch and English silver-smiths, and now the possession of bureaucracy in the form of Albert de Kruythoff. Jim accepted a glass of punch and the Negro behind the largest of the dishes smilingly served him curried shrimp on a Meissen plate, also from de Kruy-thoff's official pantry. There was a mad air of unreality to all this when Jim knew that the treasury of St. Nicolaas hadn't got two pennies to jingle in it. He took his curry and his punch and wandered out on to the gallery again, leaving by one of the side doors of the room.

Most old island houses were of this plan of big square rooms with long window-doors that stretched from the floor almost two-thirds the way to the fifteen-foot-high ceilings. Jim put his curry down on the balustrade, sipping his drink, his eyes professionally examining the craftsmanship of the builders of two hundred years ago. The walls were three feet thick ; the curving double staircase below Jim, crumbling and in need of paint, might have graced the house of a Renaissance prince. Unlike Oranje Huis, the shutters on these windows were iron, and their hinges were an iron-master's works of art. Although beautiful, they were more for protection than beauty, put there by the cautious sugar-king who had built this house, against the unwelcome arrival of a Spanish or English buccaneer in the harbour. The cannons of the battlemented fort across the town square faced out to sea, rusted, with grass growing through the cobblestones on the ramparts. The shops of Willemstad, those duty-free shops which Jim hoped would help lure the tourists, were the ground floors of the old merchants' warehouses, as old as this house, most of them. Their over-hanging upper storeys were supported on great pillars, so that every street of Willemstad was a colonnaded arcade. It was as lovely a town as Jim had ever laid eyes on. He took a larger gulp of his drink, wondering how his own effort at Oranje Cove to create something that spoke a little of the nature of the island could stand beside these monuments of other builders. In a chastened mood he picked up his curry and began to eat it.

Through the open doorway he could see the place where the Governor and de Kruythoff stood, the large fat man beside the thin, stork-like one, the movements of one slow and measured from all the years of such hand-shakings, and de Kruythoff's jerky and awkward, faintly embarrassed al-though he, too, had been doing this job for years. Jim thought that de Kruythoff would never do more than administer a backward, out-of-the-way island. For him there would probably never be the richer pickings of colonial service in Curaçao or Surinam. But looking at his house, and knowing de Kruythoff's tastes, Jim was inclined to think it wasn't such a bad fate. De Kruythoff's bad time would only be when the tourists became so numerous that they presented their own particular problems; the time, unfortunately, Jim thought, wasn't just yet.

He had come early, and there was still only a sprinkling of people in the large rooms, and only a trickle on the staircase. He had amazed himself by coming so early, to wander round these half-empty rooms like a man hungry for companionship. The level of noise rose a little in the group immediately around the Governor and de Kruythoff, but it was still unhurried and placid. Over near the main door someone laughed uproariously—there must have been a new joke imported from St. Charles or Curaçao. It would have made the rounds by the end of the party, and everyone would tell it again to-morrow at The Amsterdam. He said to himself, " I've been here long enough to know the jokes."

Then Jacob Geyl came up to him and told him the joke. It was a good one. Jim began to think about the possible variations he could add to it on the veranda of The Amsterdam.

Then Geyl said, " How's the building going?"

They asked him every day, anyone who met him. He really didn't mind. It was all part of the pleasant monotony of island life. And so he told him about his idea for the roof overhangs that were separate from the roof itself and so would give in a hurricane without taking the roof with them, about the outsize refrigerator and two freezers on order in New York, about the electrical generator for emergency power supply when the power failed, as it often did, about negotiations to get a chef from a hotel in Miami when the time came.

" He'll earn more the first five years than I will," Jim said philosophically.

Geyl listened to all this trivia eagerly. St. Nicolaas wanted to know every detail of the Oranje Cove cottages. Besides the old Amsterdam, built eighty years ago, there was no other hotel on the island. The islanders were tired of looking across the passage to St. Charles and wanting the things that they saw happening there to happen here. With tourists would come a real estate movement, and then perhaps the old worked-out land would start to sell as home-sites for those who wanted to escape the Northern winters. Although he was an outsider, some people looked on Jim MacAdam as a prophet. Just as some said that he would end up a millionaire, and others said he would lose his shirt. Geyl hoped he would be a millionaire, because in the process he would cause some other people to earn money.

And Jim, his plate of curry empty, suddenly knew why he had withdrawn himself from the main stream of the party to stand here on the gallery. The beaten-up Tilsit Volkswagen had just parked in the square and Katrien Tilsit was squeezing herself out of it with some difficulty. It was too small a car for Katrien. But Ginny, although she was tall, slipped out of it as if she were a cat, with a display of long legs that came enticingly and vanished as she stood upright. John Tilsit slammed the door and put on his jacket. Like most men, he had marked the appearance of the Governor on St. Nicolaas by wearing a tie.

Jim realised that he had stopped listening to Geyl as Ginny walked across the square.

She was wearing a blue cotton dress which Jim thought might have cost five dollars in a Puerto Rican store. The straps were very narrow on her bare shoulders; the cheap shoes had high spiked heels. She carried no handbag—nothing at all; Jim couldn't remember when he had last seen a woman who didn't need something to clutch, something to fumble with and wave at other people. She looked free and uncluttered. Her bright hair was caught at the back of her head in some kind of loose knot, an inexpert knot that looked as if it might come tumbling down. It was touching and young, the clumsiness of that hair.

After he had watched the Tilsits mount the stairs and pass into the main room, Jim addressed himself more earnestly to the party. The level of noise was higher now, the talk going on in the island's three languages—the official Dutch, the English which most people used, and some Spanish. He did his job of circulating as was expected of him, talking with all the people he had talked to yesterday or last week as if he hadn't seen them for a long time. The atmosphere at official parties was always rather strange because of the mixture of races. He noticed every white person there took a great deal of trouble to offer a greeting to every person with a coloured skin, to spend some time with them even though they might have had business together the day before. It amused him a little, that, because he thought that the coloured people could be rude or indifferent with impunity, and no one would accuse them of race prejudice. The coloured women, in their bright dresses, he thought were far handsomer than the white, though all of them aged too quickly and grew heavy. Nowhere could he see a single woman of the thin, talkative, New York type. There were women like that over on St. Charles, transplanted New Yorkers, who would never be anything else. He wondered if he missed those women, as smart as paint, eternally talking, afraid of not being noticed. And yet among those women he remembered from New York there was often a face, a voice, a manner of moving that was heart-stopping, that could not ever be forgotten. It was a face, a voice, a mannerism that could have belonged only to one city in the world. There were times when he thought that all

women should look as the women did at three o'clock in
the afternoon on Fifth Avenue between Forty-Second and
Fifty-Ninth. There were no women of that kind here.

His dead wife, Julie, had been that kind of woman.

When he got to that point in his thoughts he decided that
he had been polite long enough. He opened the door of de
Kruythoff's library and closed it firmly behind him. No
one else was in the room. It was not a party room, and
people knew that. It was the retreat of a bachelor, untidy,
rather dusty, the bookshelves long ago filled, and the
books now piled in stacks on the floor in whatever filing
system de Kruythoff had worked out for himself. There
were stacks of newspapers also—Dutch papers, and copies
of the London *Times* and the *Spectator*. Jim stretched out
to take one up, and then his hand fell back. He was looking
for distraction, and this one wasn't powerful enough. He
eased himself down into one of the deep worn chairs that
faced the long windows opening on to the back walled
garden. The springs protested, and he shifted uneasily
until they seemed to accept him in the shape that de Kruythoff had given them over the years. He stretched his legs
out before him, his hands and arms hung down limply,
accepting now the mood of detachment and aloneness that
had come over him. He didn't even want to fight it. Why
should he? The best part of him had been Julie.

The thought of Julie came unbidden in this way at the
most unlikely times, even the memory of the woman having
that quality of not being able to be overlooked which the
woman herself had had when she had been alive. At
moments when he was completely concentrated at the drawing-
board her face would suddenly be there—more powerful,
more compelling that the lines on the paper; her voice
would seem to break through the most important conversations and demand his attention. When Julie had been alive
her face and voice had been a small ghost beside him whenever they had been apart; now that she was dead she had
grown stronger, so that at times she seemed almost a second
part of himself, a twin grafted on him from whom he did
not want to be free. He remembered the bright, matchless
courage with which she had faced her death—a true courage,
not bravado. If he had not known her so well he might
have believed at times that she had not minded so much

the thought that she would die. But she had loved life, had demanded it in its fullest way, not accepting less than could be taken from it. He could not deny her the permanence she had in his thoughts, the way that she commanded, at the strangest times, that he withdraw and give himself over to her. Julie had earned that much ; it was her due.

Jim stared, with eyes that were deliberately seeking, at the flowering trees of de Kruythoff's garden, thinking that Julie would have enjoyed them. Even though she would have been a focal part of this party, as she had been wherever she went, she would also have managed to see this quiet walled garden, hidden here strangely in the middle of the town. She would have liked this house too, and been respectful of its shabbiness. She would have found the right thing to say to de Kruythoff about it, about his books and his two cats, about the orchards which he cultivated. That shy, retreating man would have warmed before her interest, and the party, the whole house would have been richer because she had come. Julie had been that kind of woman too.

And now he was half amused at himself to think that he had waited to watch Ginny Tilsit walk across the square. Her youth was touching, but it was gauche. Ignorance was a dangerous thing, and Ginny had much to learn yet. She would acquire by painful experience what Julie must surely have been born knowing. The two women, if you could call Ginny a woman, were in no way like each other. Julie would have been kind to Ginny's inexperience.

The library door opened upon him then, and he cursed silently, and turned with infinite reluctance to see who it was. It was something of a relief to see de Kruythoff's figure.

De Kruythoff was the kind of man who understood why it was sometimes necessary to go and sit in a room by oneself. But the Dutchman had not seen him, was not even looking his way. His whole attention was fixed on Ginny, who followed him. His neck was twisted in his own peculiarly awkward fashion. He stammered a little as he spoke.

" It's something I m—mm—meant to show your father. We—we should get him along to see it.".

Jim didn't think, somehow, that de Kruythoff really wanted John Tilsit to come and see whatever it was he intended to show to Ginny. He had the appearance of a man who had pulled off the unexpected, and can hardly believe his own good fortune. Jim felt a moment of compassion for this middle-aged man unhappily reduced to stumbling embarrassment before a young girl. He wished desperately that Ginny was better equipped to handle the yearning eagerness that he read in de Kruythoff's face. She would be no good at it, of course. She would fumble, and would wound de Kruythoff with the bluntness of her youth. Jim was reminded suddenly that Julie had always been able to manage these things so well.

He got to his feet. At the squeak of the ancient springs, de Kruythoff spun about, his face going briefly crimson, like a man caught in a gu.lty act. Jim wished he might have been able to vanish through the french doors and spared all three of them the explanations. Ginny had seen him now, and she stood in the doorway waiting, much more calm than de Kruythoff.

" I borrowed your room and your chair for a snooze, de Kruythoff," Jim said. " Do you mind? I must be getting old, or something. I always seem to doze off over a drink at night before I go into The Amsterdam. It's go.ng to be a habit . . ." It seemed more helpful to the Dutchman to place himself in that age bracket than in Ginny's. In fact he felt that he belonged with neither.

De Kruythoff waved his hand in vague protest. Now that his first surprise was gone he seemed almost pleased at Jim's presence, like a man rescued.

" No—no! Stay—please!" He motioned Ginny past him. " This is my own favourite place in the house. I'm always pleased when someone else discovers it. You know Miss Tilsit?"

" Yes," Ginny said.

De Kruythoff shrugged. " Of course—I forget. You're neighbours."

Ginny did not acknowledge the fact that they were neighbours. She swung rather abruptly away from Jim. " Where is the book, Albert?"

Jim gave her the credit of knowing enough not to have called him " Mr. de Kruythoff."

" The book? Oh, yes! The book! Over here—this pile, I think."

De Kruythoff rushed across the room and squatted before one of the untidy, dangerously stacked piles of books. His

movements were jerky and nervous. Jim watched him with
a return of the compassion he had felt when the two had
entered, and momentarily he disliked Ginny because she
remained so collected. She had no business to be that way
when de Kruythoff suffered in her presence. The thought
was confirmed by the sudden crash of books to the floor.
De Kruythoff, balanced precariously, went over with them,
sprawling ludicrously. He was a comic and pathetic figure.

Ginny reached him before Jim could. She did not attempt
to help him, but busied herself among the jumble of books,
giving the Dutchman time to recover himself. Seeing this,
Jim hung back.

"Oh, look—what a pity! This one got its spine broken!
And this one, though not as badly. Just as well Father isn't
here. He hates anything to happen to a book. You should
get some more shelves, Albert—or at least make Jansje stack
these better."

De Kruythoff was on his feet again, looking down at
Ginny as she knelt on the floor among the books. A shaft
of sunlight fell from the window across her young tanned
shoulders with their provocatively narrow straps. The knot
of golden hair had slipped a little farther and threatened
to tumble down. There was, Jim thought, a sweetness about
her then in her effort to help de Kruythoff through his
embarrassment. And she was utterly desirable. Jim recognised the kind of wasted sadness of de Kruythoff's gaze upon
her.

"It is my own fault, Ginny. I have told no one to touch
them until I had a chance to sort through them properly and
put them where they belong." He looked across at Jim now.
"They've been here more than six months—ever since my
last leave in Europe. There never seems time . . ."

"You're like Father. When he buys books he even delays
opening the package for a week. He won't admit it, but I
think he likes to save it up—like a child. The fun lasts
longer that way. Not that he's had much of that kind of
fun lately. There always seems to be more urgent ways to
spend the money."

"Oh, these didn't cost very much," de Kruythoff said
hastily, as if to apologise for his comparative affluence
beside the Tilsits' lack of it. "I got this lot in London—
second hand. One can stretch one's money very far in

Charing Cross Road." Jim had a sudden vision of de Kruythoff, rumpled seersucker suit and an umbrella dangling awkwardly, spending his whole leave among the second-hand book-shops of Charing Cross Road. The Dutchman bent now to take one of the broken books from Ginny. His hand on it was affectionate and regretful. He fitted the loose spine back into place. "A pity," he said. "I must see if I can mend it." Then he laid it back with the others. Jim saw that it was a work of philosophy, written in German. The Gezaghebber, he thought, took his pleasures seriously.

Now de Kruythoff was squatting before the books again, taking them down one at a time. "I thought it was on top," he said to Ginny. "I had it only the other day—in fact I had it out because your father was coming to see me and I thought he would enjoy it. But I got back late from a meeting and he had been and gone, Jansje said. So that was why I thought to-night . . . ah, here it is!" He had reached the last book of the pile. "Jansje must have been having one of her rare attacks of house-cleaning fever . . . yes, this is it. *English Country Houses*. I found it at Foyles—Mr. Mac-Adam, you're an architect. This should be your meat too."

Ginny was flicking the pages. "It's lovely," she said, but her tone was puzzled. She glanced up to de Kruythoff for guidance.

He smiled at her, the first relaxed movement he had made since he had entered the room. "But there's a special treat for you there towards the end. It may have no connection, of course—but Tilsit isn't a common name in England, and I wondered . . . I've been meaning to ask John for months, but I wanted to have the book with me." He suddenly took the book from Ginny's hands. "No—a little farther towards the back——"

"Excuse me, sir." De Kruythoff's Negro housekeeper stood in the doorway.

"Yes, what is it, Jansje?" He was abstracted, his eyes still on the pages he flicked.

"The Governor was asking for you, sir . . . and some guests are leaving." Jansje was devoted to de Kruythoff, as everyone on St. Nicolaas knew, and she was jealous in maintaining his official position above the two Landraden, the local councillors who assisted him. Her disapproving tone clearly implied that her master had no business here enjoying himself with Miss Tilsit and his books when the Landraden were busily improving themselves with the Governor. She held the door open, almost threatening.

De Kruythoff sighed. " Excuse me, Ginny. I'm afraid I'll never remember what the host's duties are." He handed the book to her. " You see how it is—I'm clearly not destined to be Governor of Curaçao."

" I hope not," Ginny said, and she smiled into his anxious face. " You'll be much too grand to know me then."

His protest came with a kind of a splutter. " Never mind, I promise——"

" Sir . . .!" Jansje's voice was clouded with exasperation. De Kruythoff gave in before it.

" At once," he said. " I'm coming at once." To Ginny he said, " I'll see you before you leave?"

She nodded. " Yes."

When the door had closed behind de Kruythoff, Ginny spoke directly to Jim for the first time. " Poor man—she rules his whole life. I never understand how he can stand it. The trouble is that she's not very good."

" In what way?"

" Well—I mean she pushes him on about the wrong things. She worries about the wrong things. You saw her now, worried that he might be neglecting the Governor, but she doesn't notice that he needs his socks darned, and a decent meal once in a while. She's the worst housekeeper on the island. Every time the Governor comes they have to borrow the van Aerssens' cook."

" But she has the main thing in mind—keeping de Kruythoff in the Governor's good graces."

Ginny gave a short laugh. " Oh, that doesn't matter. Everyone knows that Albert isn't going to be promoted to Curaçao or any place like that. He simply isn't! That's understood. Now why can't that woman let him enjoy the things that are important to him. It won't make any difference if he isn't under the Governor's nose every second."

" I'm surprised you know what things are important to a man like our good Albert. You're very young to know that."

With great deliberation she began flicking through the pages of the book. " I thought everyone of any sense knew such things. One doesn't have to be particularly *old* to understand them. Oh—and he's not *your* good Albert. You haven't been here long enough for that."

" I'm sorry," he said quite humbly.

She relented a little, glancing up at him quickly. " You see, we all like Albert the way he is."

" So do I. I said I was sorry."

" Well, all right. But he isn't a joke . . ."

" Has anyone said he was a joke? I told you I like Albert. Don't be so damn' touchy, Ginny—you're behaving just like a woman."

She giggled suddenly, a return to normalcy which relieved him. " I don't mind being a woman. I hear it's rather a good thing to be. Shall I tell you—— Ah! "

She had been idly turning the pages of Albert's book as she talked, glancing down and back to him with that instinctively feminine sense of timing which was her gift. Suddenly the fluid grace of her body vanished. Her limbs, without moving, seemed to stiffen. She bent over the book closely so that he could not see her face. He heard her breath drawn in hoarsely as if she needed air.

" What is it? What's the matter? " He was beside her, kneeling on the floor. She said nothing. There was just her fingers tracing the jagged edge of the paper where a page had been torn from the book. It seemed an act of senseless vandalism, but not shocking enough to cause this reaction.

" What is it? " he said again.

" Look! " The word came in a whisper. " Look here! " Her finger pointed to the page facing the jagged leaf. Jim leaned in close to read the words.

(Opposite) *Held by many to be the beau idea'l of medieval manor houses, Tilsit is exquisitely placed against its wooded hill. Built about two courtyards, its later buildings are Elizabethan and are but the culmination of centuries of building by its masters. That its origins lie in the days of the Conqueror is attested to by the remains of the Norman keep that command the skyline.*

He read the caption twice, struggling to rid himself of the sense of unreality which had hold of him. He tried to shrug, to remark to Ginny on the coincidence of the name. But the jagged edge of torn paper held him silent. He did not want to believe the thought that occurred to him, and he did not want to be the first to say what had happened.

So it was Ginny who spoke. "You see what he's done! I can't believe he would do such a thing, and yet he's done it!"

"Who?" It was better to pretend that the thought had not occurred to him, to lend it no strength other than what it already had.

"Faher, of course. Who else would want to do this?"

"Ginny!" he protested. "Here—hold on a minute! How do you know it was your father? It could have been anyone. After all, it's a second-hand book."

"But Albert saw this picture. That was why he wanted to show it to me. He meant Father to see it too. You heard him say he left it on the top of the pile the day he was expecting Father. You know what happened. Father waited here for Albert and he picked up the book—and did *this*!" In spite of himself Jim began to be affected by Ginny's sense of the horror and savagery of the act in a man like John Tilsit, the knowledge that to him the maiming of a book would be the beginning of barbarism.

"Why?" Jim said. "Why would he want to do this?"

She looked around at him wildly. "I don't know! I don't understand any of it. He was the same with the china. He smashed it as if he wanted every bit of it destroyed. As if he'd gone mad!"

"What china?"

"The Tilsit china. He smashed . . ." Her voice trailed away uncertainly. She closed the book, fumbling with it. Her head was bent and she seemed to be seeking a way to end the talk. Gently he took the book from her hands, placing it carefully on the pile. As he bent forward he saw that Ginny's mouth had sagged down in the corners. She seemed to be pulling her face into tight lines to prevent its collapse into tears. As he took her hand to help her to her feet he was shocked at its coldness.

"What china?" he repeated. He retained his hold on her hand, in the way he would have held the hand of someone wounded or in pain. Her tightened mouth suddenly trembled violently.

"I shouldn't talk about it. It's his business, I suppose,"

she said miserably. "I've no right to be discussing his affairs."

"I'm not completely a stranger, Ginny."

"No, you're not—but it still doesn't seem right to talk about him. If only *he* would talk . . . but he won't. I asked him, and he won't. I asked him about the china, and he just wouldn't say anything. He smashed the china on the night I came home. It was a present I bought for Mother, and he was pleased about it until he saw it. Then he went mad."

The story she told him, drifting into it as if she couldn't help herself, was a jumble of illogical sequences from which he managed to sort out the facts with difficulty. The irrelevant things seemed to hold her attention most; she clung to them as the ordinary parts of this extraordinary sequence. ". . . the pattern was so pretty—sweet little blue-purple flowers. I looked them up in one of Father's flower books later. Bluebells they were . . ." and ". . . it was such an odd mark on the back of the china. A big sloping T with a crooked top on it. That must have been why Isobel Tilsit was so interested in the china. Mother wouldn't talk about it either. She said I wasn't to ask. It didn't seem to matter to her . . ."

"Your mother's a very wise woman."

"But she should care! She should want to know—about the china and now about whatever was in this book that he tore out. It's stupid not to want to know."

"Perhaps it's the best of wisdom. Whatever your father wants to leave behind him is surely his affair. The wisest, most loving women I ever encountered always knew how to keep their mouths shut. It's not a bad thing to learn, Ginny."

"You mean I'm not to ask him?"

He shook his head. "I wouldn't—what good can it do, except to satisfy your curiosity? If you can, say nothing about it. Pretend you never saw this book. And try to forget it."

"But Albert—Albert will see it. He's sure to. And he'll ask—or make some kind of fuss about the torn page."

"Albert's manners are much too good to allow him to distress John Tilsit by making any reference to it. If your father did this, Ginny, he didn't do it just to vandalise a book. Albert will know this . . . I think you can be pretty sure he'll never mention it."

"And I'm to forget it, too? How can I?"

"Well, try, can't you!" he said impatiently. "Perhaps you could try being like your mother for a change. I never know why women always have to dramatise everything and pull everything out of shape. Just simmer down—take it easy. You may not want to believe me, but I hope you'll trust what I'm saying—and I'm saying to leave it alone. Forget it."

She broke her hand from his dispiritedly, but the gesture was one of unwilling submission. At the same time the strain had eased from her face; she no longer held it tightly together. She shrugged. "So what now? Do I have to go out there and pretend that nothing has happened? How shall I talk to Father? He'll ask me if I'm enjoying myself. He so wants me to have a good time. I suppose he's afraid if I'm bored or lonely I'll want to leave St. Nicolaas." She flung both hands wide, a strangely unnatural gesture in Ginny, he thought, as if she were a little frightened of what she wanted to say. "He tries to hold on to me. He doesn't want me to leave St. Nicolaas. I somehow think he feels I'll be safe as long as I stay here. He always talks about the rest of the world as if it's to be avoided. Perhaps he doesn't mean the rest of the world— perhaps he only means the Tilsits."

"You don't know what you're talking about," he said rudely. "I've never heard such a pack of fairy-tales in my life. Your father's all right, Ginny. You just leave him alone, don't pester him with questions—and trust your Uncle Jim."

The colour mounted rapidly in her face. "You're not my uncle. I wish you'd stop treating me like a kid, Jim."

"Was I? I didn't know. I'm out of practice in dealing with women these days. Don't be so damn' prickly, Ginny. I've had a rough day, and I can't take all this feminine nonsense. Shall we go?"

"Back there?" She seemed disappointed, and strove, in a woman's way, to hide it behind nonchalance. "I don't think I'm ready to face him just yet and pretend I'm having a good time."

"Well, I wasn't thinking of that—I was thinking of just leaving."

"You mean—just *leaving*?" A kind of astonishment broke on her face. "But how?"

He grinned, feeling good all of a sudden because Ginny was a pretty girl—he corrected himself—almost a beautiful girl, and she was unsophisticated and oddly comical. "It's done all the time, they tell me." He shook his head, and now that the strain was gone from her, he himself began to relax. He reached for the first cigarette in half an hour. "They sadly neglected your education in that place in San Juan. I mean, in things that really matter. Here—let me give you an example." He lighted the cigarette, and then pointed. "You see that door—it's open. The steps go down to the garden, and the gate to Albert's garden is never locked. Could anything be easier?"

He held out his hand to her again, in a different way this time. "Coming?"

"Yes."

The feeling of slight exhilaration and gaiety stayed with him all the way to the jeep. He waited while Ginny got her purse from the Tilsit Volkswagen. When he saw it, a cheap plastic thing, very worn, he understood why she had not wanted to carry it with her. He watched with pleasure again the swish of her full cotton skirt against her legs as she swung herself into the jeep. He remembered how long it was since he had observed this purely feminine reaction of coquetry to an unexpected invitation. He remembered how long it was since he had enjoyed the act of inviting a woman out—even if this woman now was really not much more than a rather naïve child. As the engine of the jeep came noisily to life, he glanced around the square. The usual crowd of loungers was there—a larger crowd had turned out this evening, though, to watch the arrivals at the Governor's reception. To-morrow the story would be all over the island that the new American and Miss Virginia Tilsit had left by the Gezaghebber's garden gate, and had gone off together. To hell with it, he thought; it would do them all good to have something new to talk about.

As the jeep turned out of the square he suddenly laughed aloud. The laugh hadn't been meant for Ginny to hear, but it had escaped him. "What's funny?" she said.

"Nothing much. I was just thinking . . ." He took the plunge. "I was thinking that this is possibly—just possibly —the first time that Miss Virginia Tilsit has left a cocktail party with a man without asking permission first. It seemed . . . not funny . . . good!"

"I'll go one better than that. It's not only the first time Miss Virginia Tilsit has left a cocktail party without asking permission, but the first time she ever left a cocktail party at all. Where are we going?" She asked the question without curiosity. There was only one place on the island to go, and that was The Amsterdam.

"St. Charles," he said.

She gave a short gasp. "St. Charles? No one goes to St. Charles just for dinner!"

He squashed the cigarette on the floor of the jeep. "Ginny, there are some things you have to learn about. Like the open door and the steps and the garden gate. People do it every day."

She lapsed into silence, and didn't speak again until he turned the jeep off Town Road, and headed down the dirt road to Oranje Cove.

At the slower pace of the jeep it made less noise. Her voice was quite soft as she said, "I forgot to see Albert before I left. I said I would."

Albert, Jim thought, had been born to be forgotten. He didn't deserve it, but it was true.

II

Ginny slipped off her shoes to help Jim launch the dinghy, and then waited impatiently, curling her toes down into the wet sand at the tide's edge, while he went to collect a pair of sneakers and a flashlight from his cottage. She felt vaguely uneasy standing here in the growing darkness. Involuntarily she kept glancing up towards Oranje Huis, its shape against the headland a slightly blacker mass than the land itself. There was no light there yet. She kept waiting for it to go on, as if it were a spotlight to reveal her here on the beach. Jim came at last, the bottoms of his pants rolled up, his jacket slung across his shoulder. He also was bare-footed, and carried his sneakers by their knotted laces.

"The moon will be almost full to-night," she said as he came close. "There'll be plenty of light when we come back." For some reason she spoke in a near-whisper.

"There'd better be!" he grunted as he pushed the dinghy down off the sand. "I have to gauge my drinking in St. Charles by the strength of the moon. Sometimes I need an awful lot of light on the way back."

They made the short trip to where the *Oranje Lady* was moored in silence. The oars made their monotonous thumping sound in the rowlocks and the noise seemed startlingly loud to Ginny. Jim tied up the dinghy to the buoy, and threw his jacket and her shoes and purse into the *Oranje Lady's* cockpit. Then he clambered over the side, and reached back to help her.

"Before the first tourist arrives I'll have to have a dock." His voice seemed to boom out across the water, and she wanted to caution him to be quiet.

"Why?"

"Haven't you ever seen tourists, Ginny? They come in all sizes and shapes, and very few of them agile enough to negotiate a ladder. Can't risk wetting the mink stoles."

"I *knew* there was some reason at the back of my head why I didn't like you," Ginny said. "A dock next? Where will it all end?"

"Ask me five years from now. I might know then."

The deck of *Oranje Lady* felt gritty under Ginny's feet. Its interior had been stripped of its fittings completely; not even a seat remained. The craft was low in the water from the pile of cement-filled bags which neatly balanced each other on port and starboard. Jim gestured towards them.

"Take a seat. Lucky they're still here—I didn't have a chance to off-load them before it was time to go and get ready for Albert's whing-ding."

But she didn't do that. Instead she went to stand beside him at the wheel, watching as the powerful engines sprang to life at the touch of the ignition switch. It was a small marvel to Ginny to feel the gentle throb of that power in the deck beneath her feet. Jim moved the craft away from the buoy quietly, a man long used to doing it and with no

need to show off. As they moved towards the headland
she looked, not out towards the open sea, but back to the
land, back to Oranje Huis. Someone, probably Wilhelmina,
had switched on a light on the gallery, and the single one
in the driveway against John and Katrien's return. Then
suddenly, as Ginny looked, she saw the flash of headlights
where the road to Oranje Huis turned off Town Road,
the swift brilliance appearing and disappearing among the
trees. Then the lights were extinguished, and she knew her
parents had come back. She felt a slight sense of panic
which she tried to bury by turning away from the sight
of the house. It was a relief to see that they were already
near the point of the headland, though the slight vibration
of the craft gave little indication of speed. She thought
of the many times in the last week she had listened to the low
sound of these engines from the gallery of the house, in
just the way John and Katrien must hear them now.

"This is a very expensive cruiser, Jim—are you rich?"

He laughed aloud, a genuine cry of amusement. "You're
about the only girl I've met who'd ask straight out."

"Well, why not? Is it such a bad thing to be rich?"

"No, not at all bad. I wish I had that trouble. I'm not
rich, Ginny. I don't think I ever will be. That beach back
there is my only asset, and I didn't even earn that—which
at my age doesn't make me a very smart fellow. I—the
syndicate, that is—is up to its ears in debt, and it might take
most of my lifetime to work it off."

"Father says only a poor man can't afford debts."

"By that standard I'm rich. I must remember to remind
myself of it every day. My credit is that beach, and if I pray
at all I suppose I pray that a hurricane doesn't swallow it
before I'm clear of this business. It would be too bad if it
had waited for me for over twenty years and then I missed
my chance. It was all my father had left when he died and
I'd hate to mess this one up on him. He always hoped
we'd do something with it together. We had to wait, though.
It took quite a long time for the tourists to get past Florida
after the war. They moved out, island by island, and
Dad watched the spread all the way. He used to say, ' Not
just yet, Jim. We'll go bust if we start yet. Give them
time to discover the place.' Then Pan Am put the jets
on the run to San Juan, and Dad said the time was nearly

right. Funny, he didn't come down here in all those years. He used to describe the place to me, and live on those old black-and-white photos he took back in the thirties. Those photos were so faded you almost couldn't see a thing, but he made it sound like paradise. I guess it was a kind of paradise to him. The place where he said he was going to die."

The black humps of the chain of British islands had come towards them rapidly, dark shapes in the sea that was lighted by stars. They rose steeply, these little islands, mostly uninhabited, with only tiny clusters of lights to mark a few houses at one of the harbours. The American island of St. Charles was unmistakable. The blue sodium lights along the waterfront drive of the harbour of Margretsted had always seemed unreal to Ginny, just the footlights to the whole brilliant spectacle of the hills behind the town dotted with lights, and even the lights that stood astride the saddle of the mountain reaching sharply above. She had grown up with these lights, seeing them increase year by year from the gallery of Oranje Huis. They had not been of her world; in childhood she had accepted them as a fairy-tale. They still held something of this same quality. Jim's father, she thought, had come here when the lights of Margretsted had been few and distant and faint. He had seen them once, and dreamed of this place ever since. He had never come back.

" Why didn't he come back?" she said. Shielded from the wind of their passage by the windscreen, and with the whole length of the *Oranje Lady*'s cockpit between them and the roaring propeller, there was comparative quiet here at the wheel. Their tones were almost low.

He shrugged. " Enough reasons, I suppose. The war . . . and then after the war he got involved with building big housing developments and he almost never left the job. I think he kept himself away from here deliberately, too— you know the way a man resists taking a drink because he knows if he does he's finished. I guess he needed this place as his . . . well, as his dream if you want to call it that. Most men have a dream. This was his, I suppose. I wish he'd lived long enough to see even the beginning here. But he always wanted to come down here with enough money to keep control of the whole thing in his hands. Maybe that's why he delayed so long and took such risks. He always worked in debt, but he never liked it. That's what killed him."

"How?" She knew he didn't mind the question because suddenly she had realised that he was hungry to talk to someone who wanted to hear of the things that had been familiar to him all his life but which meant nothing to anyone else on the island. He had come here, a stranger into the midst of strangers, and although he was accepted because of what he was and what he was doing, there probably had been no one in all these months who knew without asking what he meant by certain words. When he said "home," what did that mean? Or "wife"? No one here knew that either. She began now to sense the dreadful loneliness and isolation that must sit on this man at times. Perhaps he was only able to talk at moments like these—this swift passage across the channel to St. Charles, a small interlude between two worlds, and talking over the low sound of the propeller.

"A stroke," he said briefly. "But he'd had warnings for years, and he d'ed because he'd gone broke and he knew he couldn't start again. He did a pretty foolish thing in building, Ginny . . . he thought the public was ready to pay extra for quality, and he rode his hunch. It was a big mistake, and he lost every cent he had."

"But surely . . ."

He cut her short, anticipating her question. "Not just one house, Ginny. He could have survived that easily. A whole development of houses . . . you've seen those developments in Puerto Rico? Well, he built two hundred houses that had quality and design that were way above the heads of the k'nd of people who buy into big developments. Way above their pocket-books too. The forty he sold of the two hundred he had to let go at cost. And then his creditors closed on him. That was the end. You see, he'd got a reputation as a good builder who always brought the money home to his backers, and good profits as well. They trusted him on this without knowing fully what he was aiming at. He knew it would be his last development, and I suppose it was natural that he wanted something he could be proud of. The trouble was that it wasn't what people wanted—not those that could afford them."

"Did you . . . did you design the houses?" She didn't

know whether she dared to ask the question. And yet gaining knowledge of him had to carry its own risks.

He tossed his cigarette butt into the water. " No. No, they weren't mine, Ginny. We fought the most serious fight of our lives over that one. I told him he was making a mistake. I said I knew what kind of people bought expensive houses, and that they didn't buy them built in tracts, no matter what you did to the landscaping to make them look different. If people pay that kind of money they want custom houses, and Dad's gamble was that he could make a lot of money by building in quantity and still sell to the higher-priced market. I said it wouldn't work. He told me I was a status-symbol snob—a small-town Frank Lloyd Wright. We had a bust-up about it, and I didn't go to see him for more than six months. By that time he was well on with the project and sure he was going to make a small fortune. He meant to gather it all up and bring it down here. He said he wanted to build the finest small hotel in the Caribbean, and he was going to own fifty-one per cent of it. He used to say to me, ' Jim, I'm going to end my days walking on that beach. That's what I'm going to do.'"

" And so you came instead of him. That's why you came, isn't it?"

" Ginny, you ask an awful lot of questions." It was said, not unkindly, but with great finality. He was not angry, she thought. It was just that he had had enough. And the interlude was over.

They were almost at the entrance to the harbour of Margretsted, the shape of Pitt Island looming up on the left, Star Point on the right. Jim lined up automatically with the red and green navigation lights high in the hills above the town. He cut the speed of the cruiser now to avoid too big a wash to the craft in the yacht basin. The distance between their two worlds had been crossed, and the talk was over. The blue sodium lights seemed to rush up to meet them; the cars moving along the waterfront drive took shape and colour. Jim throttled back and edged in carefully to the dock, which was a cement wall fronting on the drive itself, and which gave anchorage to everything but the bigger vessels. These had to go over to the West India Dock. Most of the smaller trading vessels from

Puerto Rico tied up here, bringing the fresh produce and a good part of the building supplies which the island used. They unloaded their cargoes right here on the broad cement walk on the seaward side of the main drive. Boxes and piles of lumber were still here, where the end of the working day had left them. Along the sea-wall was a curious mixture of sailing and power-driven craft, craft for profit and for pleasure, and craft that joined the two functions, the charter boats, with advertised space and rates chalked on a board by their gang-planks, and occasionally a skipper soliciting the tourists who strolled by. There was very little suggestion of hurry in the scene though. In Margretsted, those who wanted business usually let it come to them, or looked as if they did. Beyond the blue sodium lights on their aluminium stanchions, the modernity seemed to halt abruptly. The drive was lined by the warehouses the Danes had built to house their sugar and the wares of their entrepôt trade, which had been the life of the island. The warehouses, with their glossily painted iron shutters, were now the sleek shops which lured the tourists with their free-port prices and the strange blend of sophistication and island informality. There were no neon lights there; if the brick façades had been painted, the colours were the soft sun-washed colours of the islands, pink, cream, faded blue. The signs were discreet, again in the fashion of an earlier time. Margretsted struggled to keep itself as the tourists hoped to find it. The I.B.M. electric typewriters were hidden in the back rooms of the shops; soft grass matting and a free daiquiri greeted the shoppers while they browsed. It was done with typical American efficiency, with only small and necessary concessions made to the climate and the slower pace of life. Ginny had always considered it, close to, almost as much the fairy-tale world it had seemed from the gallery of Oranje Huis.

She gathered up her shoes and bag. A line of grinning brown faces stared down at them from the sea-wall. Brown arms reached out to help her step ashore.

"Evening, Mister Jim."

"Evening, Sam. Jacky about?"

"Nosaar. Jacky ain't here. I'll look after the boat, Mr. Jim. Yessaar, I'll take real good care."

"O.K., Sam. You take good care. I'll see you when I get back."

"You goin' back to St. Nicolaas to-night, Mr. Jim?"

"Sure, Sam—sure."

And that was the first time Ginny knew for certain that there were nights when Jim didn't come back from St. Charles.

They ate dinner at Barney's on the waterfront. Ginny had guessed they would go there, had hoped they would. It was a restaurant-bar one level above the street, with a view over the masts of the craft anchored at the sea-wall, across the harbour to Pitt Island. Its roof of palm fronds disguising the corrugated iron was supported on great poles of bamboo, windowless and open on all sides except the north-east corner, which was the direction from which the trade-winds came and the brief showers of rain. It was the unofficial club of those who lived on the island, and those whose craft tied up regularly in the harbour. As Jim climbed up the iron staircase, perhaps six people among those ranged along the narrow horseshoe bar raised hands languidly in greeting.

"Hi, Jim—how're things?" A different kind of greeting than he would have received on St. Nicolaas; here it was the recognition by one man of another who was trying to make a living in paradise, and trying to make it seem as if it wasn't very hard. The Americans, the last-comers to the island, had more energy and more money, as a rule, to put into their ventures, but it was the fashion to pretend that one had come here to escape the rat-race of New York or Philadelphia or Chicago, or wherever they had come from that the winters were coldest. Down here, the competition was not less keen, but only on a smaller scale. So the lazily drawled "How're things?" only slightly disguised a precise and detailed interest in every aspect of the other man's affairs, and the desire to know whether he was "making it" in paradise.

"Hi!" Jim said several times, and did not accept any of the invitations implied in tones of the greetings. "Drink?" he said to Ginny.

She wanted to sit at the bar, so she said yes; it amused

her to do this because she sensed that Jim would have liked to rush her straight to a table and thereby announce that he was not available for conversation with anyone. The bar was crowded; he found a stool for her, and he stood beside her. While she sipped her rum collins several people did come and speak to Jim, and in the process were introduced to her.

" How long are you staying?" was the inevitable question. It was automatically assumed that anyone whose face was not familiar on the island was a tourist.

" I live on St. Nicolaas."

" Then you come over here often?"

" Fairly often."

" Funny—I don't remember seeing you before."

It had been that way with Harry Parker, she remembered. This same sudden discovery that she existed, the same surprise that she had not been noticed before. She grew tired of it in the end, and put her unfinished drink down on the bar.

" Could we have dinner now?" she said to Jim. " I'm hungry."

When they were seated at their table she looked around her—at the solid row of people still along the bar, at the group of sailors who had shore leave from the American light cruiser anchored in the harbour, at the trio of musicians who came to play here every night and who were now just picking up their instruments.

" It's a funny feeling, Jim."

" What is?"

" I've been coming to this place all my life. Father always has lunch here whenever he comes over—it used to be a day's treat when I was a child to come over to St. Charles —and now I feel as if I'm a stranger." She nodded towards the crowd about the bar. " I know some of those people over there—Father's been buying supplies from some of them for years. But they don't recognise me. They don't know me."

" People only relate to themselves, Ginny. They can't quite see the child in the woman, so they don't relate. They might remember the child, but they don't know the woman."

" And you—you only know the woman." It was good to her to hear him use that word.

"Oh . . ." He sipped his drink thoughtfully. "I guess I might know a little more than that."

"How?"

He smiled. "Well . . . I saw you starting along the beach that morning. You looked small from that distance. I saw you playing with Bo, and you looked like a child, and he was frisking about like a puppy. And then when you came to the beginning of my beach you turned back—which was a pretty childish thing to do. Then you thought about it, and you crossed over the line, and you got nearer and nearer, and you got bigger and more grown-up. It was like watching someone go through all the stages of childhood and adolescence in five minutes. When you finally arrived at my door, I'd got to think of you as a woman."

"Do you mean it?"

"I almost mean it."

It was late and quiet when they left Barney's. The moon was high now, outlining the nump of the cruiser and the bigger mass of Pitt Island. The tourists no longer strolled the sea-wall, and the loungers had gone home. Only Sam waited at the *Oranje Lady,* sitting on the foredeck, his arms resting on his bent knees, and he was asleep. He came to life when Jim paid him.

"Thank you, Mr. Jim. You gonna have a real sweet trip back now with that moon just like a silver road over to that island. You had a good time? That's right! Good night, now!"

"Good night, Sam."

Ginny didn't speak until they were past the headlands. "*I* had a good time, Jim."

"Did you? That's good. I hoped you would."

She wondered if he had even heard her, or if he really cared about what she had said. He seemed abstracted now, detached. He stared straight ahead of him, his hands resting easily on the wheel, not even glancing sideways at her when he answered. She looked backwards to St. Charles; it was receding quickly into the darkness like something seen dimly in a dream. The wake from the *Oranje Lady* foamed whitely in the moonlight. Ginny felt a sense of loneliness suddenly, a tightening of the throat, a chill about her body. She felt shut out, alone.

"What was she like, Jim?"

"What was who like?" he said abstractedly.

"Your wife. What was she like?"

Now he looked at her. Sharply. And she saw the sense of shock on his face, and an expression that was nearly outrage. His brows drew together.

"What the hell business is that of yours?"

"None . . . I have no right. Except that you've talked of everything else. But not her."

"Because it's no concern of yours or anyone else's."

"I'm sorry." Because of the tightness in her throat, the words seemed to break from her in a distorted garble. "I'm really sorry, Jim." She had had no business to ask, he was right about that. But the urge had been strong, and the answer would have been worth the risk. The urge had been stronger than her father's training of reticence, of a scrupulous avoidance of probing other people's lives. Or perhaps it was because of that training and the results it had had in producing strain and lack of understanding now between herself and her father that she had decided to take the risk. One had to dare something, to risk a great deal, if the need was great. She wasn't quite sure how great that need was, except that it was more than curiosity. It hurt her to think that Jim might suppose that it was just curiosity, the kind of stupid questioning that asks without having any real use for the answer that would come. And could she use it?—and why? She wasn't sure of that either, but she had sensed this evening that any true knowledge of Jim was tied up in knowing something of his dead wife. His avoidance of even the mention of her name was the key to this. A man who does not care greatly will talk easily; what is of importance will be held closely, as she had learned of her father. She felt again the familiar bafflement and frustration of his refusal—in just the way she had experienced it when her father had refused her the knowledge of the Tilsits which she demanded. And yet one could do no more than ask. If the refusal continued it had to be accepted.

Suddenly Jim spoke to her. She missed the first few words over the noise of the engine. She saw his lips moving, and she leaned in closer. He was speaking quietly, and she had to strain to hear.

" . . . a brilliant woman. Everyone admired Julie. But she was a kind woman too. Witty and generous."

" Was she . . . Well, was she pretty?" Why did her lips tremble? What was it to her what his wife had been? Or had she been hoping for some other kind of answer?

" Yes—she was even that, as well as all the other things. Some people thought she was beautiful—quite beautiful."

" Why did she die, Jim?"

" Leukaemia. She was braver than I imagined anyone could be. All that she grieved for was the baby she wasn't able to carry."

" So you lost that too?"

" I lost everything."

There were no more words to say, and no more questions that could be asked. She had asked her questions and the answers were cold and brutal and pitiful. The price of knowledge had always to be paid, and her feeling of inadequacy and unimportance was the price. She felt diminished, cut down to size, like the child that has tried the adult gambit and seen it fail. Perhaps her father had been right in his refusals. You had to be able to take the answers to the questions you asked. The rest of the journey passed in silence.

He brought the *Oranje Lady* into the buoy smoothly and tied up. Ginny picked up her shoes and bag and scrambled into the dinghy without waiting for his help. Up at Oranje Huis a single light burned on the gallery. She wondered if her father was still awake, waiting for her to return, listening to hear the cruiser come back to its berth. She almost hoped he was awake ; she had asked her questions of him, too, and had been forgiven, because she was loved. After these cold and frank answers from Jim, she needed the familiarity of that love. The dinghy scraped the sand, and she stepped out ankle deep in the water. Immediately there, nuzzling under her hand, she felt the rough shape of Bo's head.

" Been waiting, have you?" she said softly. Then she turned back to Jim. " Thanks, Jim." There was no point in saying it had been a lovely evening.

" I'll walk you up to the house."

" No!—don't trouble. Bo's here with me. I'll be all right."

" It's no trouble."

She made no further protest, although she didn't want him with her now. She thought he came unwillingly—no, worse than that, he didn't care whether he came or not. It was literally no trouble, but it wasn't anything else, either. They walked the length of the beach without speaking, Bo moving quietly between them. When they started to ascend the path to the house they went in single file, Bo ahead of Ginny, Jim behind her. The moonlight made the tree shadows deeper; the air was heavy here with the perfume of the chinaberry tree. The bluish-lilac blossoms lay on the path to be crushed under their feet, the white radiance of the moon drained their colour. Then they reached the foot of the steps that led up to the gallery and the yellow light from the lamp burning there was softer and gentler than the moonlight.

"Good night, Jim."

"Good night, Ginny." Without haste he bent and kissed her on the lips. His hands did not touch her. The kiss was a gesture only, no more than a pat on the shoulder. She turned and hurried up the steps, and at the top she stood and listened until the sounds of his footsteps on the path had been lost.

"Hallo, dear. Had a good time?"

Her father stood in the doorway of the living-room. The space behind him was in darkness. He wore his pyjamas, rumpled, with the bottoms too short, and his lean wrists poking from the sleeves. Strands of his hair stood on end, giving him a softened, tired, old look.

"Yes, thanks. A good time—we went to St. Charles for dinner. To Barney's."

He nodded. "Yes. I was just going out to the kitchen to make a cup of tea. Want some?"

"Yes."

"All right. Don't switch on the light—go quietly now, and don't wake your mother."

She followed him, glad to be back with him, grateful for the gentleness that was his, or at least the belief in that gentleness.

CHAPTER FOUR

The languid, humid summer months came down fully on them now. On St. Nicolaas, as everywhere else in the area, they listened daily to the weather forecasts for hurricane warnings. Tropical storms were born in the South Atlantic and moved across the Caribbean, sometimes gathering to the intensity and giant strength of a full-scale hurricane, sometimes turning east and dying feebly out in the middle Atlantic. Two hurricanes, with their graceful, ironic, feminine names, threatened the American mainland that season, and twice turned aside without striking. One storm brushed Puerto Rico, and passed on northwards. St. Nicolaas had some days of heavy yellow skies and rain, but no more than that. Then the hurricane season was over, and the islands began to prepare for the winter season of the tourists and the cruise ships.

For Ginny these days and weeks had the crust of idleness and frustration upon them. She had enough to do, and none of it mattered. She helped Katrien in the garden and the house, and was aware that most of the tasks were manufactured to keep her busy. She did some typing for Albert de Kruythoff and some filing of his untidy stock of reports, but she knew it would have made hardly any difference if none of it had been done.

The only movement on the island, even through the heavy still days of the hurricane season, seemed to be down at Jim MacAdam's beach cottages. Steadily they took shape —six cottages built of the wood and stone that Jim loved, and the restaurant building. Curious cargoes came from Puerto Rico now. One day Katrien called her excitedly to the gallery, and below them in Oranje Cove was a sailing vessel with six royal palms lashed to the deck. Jim and the botanical expert who had come with them to supervise their transplanting, and who stayed for two weeks, hovered over them anxiously.

"They cost a young fortune," Jim muttered to Ginny. "I probably was a fool to get them, but somehow palms

87

seem to belong to Caribbean islands, and the tourists seem
to expect them in the travel folders. Any rate, I *like* them."

They were planted, and the sun-bathing deck started to be
shaped about them. It was almost possible for Ginny now
to look along the beach and forget that that end of it had
ever been empty.

"He's doing a good job," Katrien said. "I knew he
would not make something ugly, that man."

John Tilsit said nothing, and that itself was an admission.

Jim went himself to Puerto Rico on buying trips, and
twice over to Miami. The days that he was gone seemed endless to Ginny. She sat on the gallery with a book in her
lap waiting for the sound of his jeep on the dirt road. The
worst of it was not knowing which day he would return, and
hanging about the house in case she would miss that moment.
It might be two hours or half a day after he got back
before she would see him start to walk along the beach
towards the path. But he always came after an absence, and
sat with them on the gallery with a drink, and always
accepted Katrien's invitation to stay to dinner. Ginny
began to think he regarded it as a kind of duty call, made
not unwillingly, but as a part of the routine. He brought
small gifts for them—*flacons* of perfume, a woven handbag
of the kind that was popular in Miami, some Japanese
slippers, a new shower curtain because Katrien had com-
plained that hers was stained with mildew. They were
impersonal gifts, chosen either for Katrien or Ginny, and
handed out without distinction. When Katrien protested
he merely said:

"I have to take care of my family, don't I?" and Ginny
knew that there was no more to these small presents than
that. Jim was grateful for the routine of walking up to
Oranje Huis at the end of an absence because it gave
him the semblance of a homecoming. He did not come
back to her in particular, but to them all. There even came
the day when he felt relaxed enough with John to bring him
a box of cigars, and have them accepted. They were taken
with a brusque shyness that was almost rude, but they
were taken. After dinner the two men sat in the darkness
of the gallery smoking in companionable silence, and Ginny
didn't even bother to say good night when she went to bed.
Jim didn't seem to notice her going.

The summer, though, brought some good with it. As the days passed and Ginny never again saw a return of the look of pain and anger which her father's face had worn on the night when she returned from San Juan, the thought of Isobel Tilsit, the Tilsit china and Albert's mutilated book slipped to the back of her mind. It was still there; at times she still brought it out to worry and nag the questions that the name of Tilsit raised, but she did not again ask the questions aloud. Albert, as Jim had predicted, never mentioned the book, which told Ginny plainly enough that he had seen the missing page and had decided that it was no business of his; neither did Jim ever speak of it. Ginny had not told Katrien of it either. There seemed a conspiracy of silence between them all to protect John Tilsit.

There was some discussion of the University of Miami, but it was only discussion. "Perhaps after Christmas," Ginny said vaguely, and her father was content to leave it at that. "Ginny is not very ambitious," Katrien said again, and Ginny acknowledged that it was the truth. Reluctance or laziness held her there—perhaps the desire to please her father, or the desire to stay close to Jim. She let the days slip by her, uncounted, waiting for something. She fished with her father often in the mornings and it was almost as it had always been with them. If there was any restlessness in her now at the times when they beached the outboard, it was only because that day that faced her had too little in it. She found herself too often at Jim's door, and she tried to keep from her mind the image of a beggar. But whatever shame there was in begging, she still did it.

The door always swung wide to admit her, and if Jim didn't show great pleasure in her arrival, he didn't show annoyance either. She kept watching for it, ready to draw back, but he was always the same, laconic, off-hand, not given to fussing over her.

"Hi—had breakfast? No? Well, get the bacon on then." She only dared come for these early-morning visits because the rest of the day he worked harder than any two men he employed, and she had the sense to keep out from under his feet. To have come in the evening would have been to beg too plainly. So she found herself often cooking bacon and eggs, and pouring the thick black coffee Jim liked, while he puttered about the cluttered room, eternally smoking, flipping through plans, scanning the advertisements for hotel furniture that came in every mail.

" I can get more for my money buying the Danish imported stuff duty-free on St. Charles than anything they have in Miami. It's better-looking too."

" Yes." She didn't want to be drawn into comment, because whenever she did, he would look up, challenging her mockingly.

" How do you know? You haven't seen any of the other. In fact you haven't seen anything in the whole wide world, have you, Ginny?"

" Oh, shut up! Is it my fault I was born here?"

" No—but it'll be your fault if you never leave here."

" Well, you *came* to this island, didn't you? It can't be such a bad place."

" It isn't a bad place at all. It's a wonderful place, but not for anyone who's never known anything different. And don't give me that bit about the convent in San Juan, either. The only thing you learned there was how to write your name."

" I suppose you think that's all I know."

He grinned. " That's about it, Ginny."

She couldn't leave it there. " What about my mother? She was born here and she's never lived away from the place —but I notice you don't treat her as if she were a fool."

" Because she's not. She's right in her own time and generation. But *you*—with planes at your doorstep and the whole world stretching in front of you, you have to be a kind of backward little girl to be content to sit in one place."

" I'm not content."

" Then don't moan—do something about it!"

She went away in a savage bad humour and didn't go down to the cottages again until Jim himself walked up the path to Oranje Huis one evening several days later. Ginny and Katrien were sitting on the gallery; John Tilsit had gone into town to see Jan de Hoot, the manager of the sugar mill. They were waiting for him to come back.

Jim addressed himself to Katrien. " I gave your daughter a telling off the other day, Mrs. Tilsit, and she's not speaking to me. That being the case I can't ask her if she'd like to come into St. Charles for dinner. So I thought if I could persuade you to come with us, at least I'd have someone to talk to."

" You seem very sure I'll come," Ginny said.

" I'm counting on it."

" Run and dress, Ginny," Katrien said briskly. She was laughing as she spoke, but she meant what she said. " There aren't enough young men to take you out that you can afford to be proud."

" Aren't you coming?" Jim said to Katrien.

She shook her head gently. " I have never been away from this house any time that John has returned, in all the years we've been married, and it's far too late to start now."

" We'll wait for him—take him along with us."

" Now you're pressing your luck, Jim. Just be thankful that John has stopped turning his eyes away every time he looks down to your end of the beach. It's too much to expect that he would submit just yet to getting in your lovely cruiser as if he approved of it." She nodded towards the doorway through which Ginny had gone on her way to change. " Stiff-necked, both of them."

" She'll learn," Jim said.

Ginny heard both remarks, and she thought over them furiously while she dressed. It didn't help her frame of mind to find Jim, when she returned to the gallery, slumped in a seat beside her mother, looking content and pleased, and not in the least impatient to take her to St. Charles. She thought he would have preferred to stay where he was.

" You didn't have to ask me, you know," she said to him when the *Oranje Lady* was out of the bay and heading across the channel to St. Charles.

" I thought I'd better." He looked sideways at her, jesting. " I somet.mes think that perhaps you might be a fairy—perched up there in your castle on the hill. And Bo is your familiar—that's what they call a witch's companion, isn't it?—a familiar? If I offend you, I'm afraid you might turn my poor little hotel back into sand. Though I must say that's being a bit rough on Bo. He wouldn't hurt a fly."

" But I might?"

" You might."

" You like to make a fool of me, don't you, Jim?"

He shrugged. " No one *makes* a fool out of anyone. Relax, Ginny, relax!"

It was the pattern of all their times together—these trips to St. Charles, the hurried breakfasts in Jim's cottage, the hours Jim spent at Oranje Huis under Katrien's discerning eyes, and John's anxious ones. Jim was good-humoured, teasing, and seemed to Ginny completely detached. His teasing at least was a positive thing to which she could react with laughter or irritation. Much harder to bear was his absent-mindedness—to sit in front of him and feel herself fade from his sight and mind. She wondered at these times if she was replaced by the image of another woman.

By degrees that summer she learned more of Jim's wife. It was always in small pieces, and she slowly put together her picture of Julie with no confidence that it was a true picture. Jim still spoke of her with reluctance through which pride and love sometimes broke.

Jim was making a small effort to put in order some of the piles of books and magazines in his cottage the day that she got her fullest and most frightening portrait of Julie. It was late on Saturday afternoon ; she had been swimming, and Jim's shout from his cottage had drawn her.

" Hi—want a drink?"

She didn't want a drink, but she would never have said no to an invitation from him. She found him standing in the middle of the stacks of periodicals, trade journals, books, and the inevitable rolls of blueprints. " Just tidying up," he said as he handed her the Scotch and water.

What he was doing was browsing, not tidying. He would pick up a paper or book to file it, flick through it and become engrossed. And that would be the end of the tidying for that day. Ginny had seen him play this game often. It exasperated her, and still she liked this human failing in Jim.

" Here—let me help. Now—let's see. What about starting a stack of back numbers of *Architectural Forum* over there, and then you can stack some of the smaller magazines on top? Jim—are you listening?"

" Um . . .?" he said, not looking up.

" When are you going to get some bookshelves?"

' When . . .? Oh—well I'm not going to put bookshelves in here. They'll be built when I have my own apartment.

That's going on the side of the restaurant block—look, let me show you. Throw me over that roll of prints, would you."

"Never mind—not now. Just tell me if I can start to stack these magazines. I think you should get rid of most of them. What use can they be when they're out of date?"

"Very useful. And you just leave them alone. How do you know that I'm not planning to steal precisely a roof-line that some clever guy used on a Texas house six years ago? There's nothing new under the sun, and we've all been borrowing and copying from each other since the Greeks. The application is what matters. And I'll be needing every one of those numbers when I start to build houses again."

"Are you going to build houses?"

"Of course I am."

'Oh!" She said nothing more for a time, just went ahead with her self-imposed task of stacking the magazines according to date, and thereby satisfying partly her own sense of order. Jim went on reading. She sipped her drink slowly as she worked, and she was happy. She didn't mind his forgetting her presence now; it was a comfortable forgetfulness, as if she were an expected part of the background. "Jim?" she said presently.

"Yes? What?"

"What about these copies of *Business*—they're way out of date and I can't see anything in them to do with architecture . . ."

"Leave them alone!" he said curtly. "There's some of Julie's best work in there."

"Julie's work?" A sense of shock and bewilderment ran through her. The magazine she was holding almost slipped from her nerveless fingers. In grabbing to save it from falling, she tore a corner of the cover.

"Careful!" Jim sprang to catch the magazine; he took it from her as if she were a clumsy child who could not be trusted with anything of value. He fitted the two torn pieces back together with anxious, careful fingers. "It's almost impossible to get back issues of some of these. I know because I've tried to get extra copies. Some of these issues Julie handled almost alone."

"I'm sorry, Jim. I didn't mean to damage it. Here—let

me fix it." She went quickly to get the roll of Scotch tape from the rack above his drawing-board.

"No—I'll do it." She stood by watching as he mended both sides of the tear, measuring and placing the tape in position with infinite care. She hardly seemed to breathe while the operation went on. "I'm sorry," she said again.

"It's all right. No harm done." But she felt there had been, as if profane, insensitive hands had touched something that was precious to him.

"Jim—what did you mean by saying that some of those issues were almost all Julie's work? I don't understand . . ."

"Julie was assistant art director for *Business* for two years. Her boss collapsed with an ulcer for a couple of months and Julie ran the show. Do you understand what that means?" And now Ginny knew that his pride in his wife struggled with the reluctance to talk at all. "That means she was responsible for the total look of one of the prestige magazines of the world. It had to be good and solid and always just a little bit slick—but never so slick as to look as if it was in a hurry. Do you understand any of this, Ginny?"

"Not much—but I want to know."

He looked down at the magazine in his hand. "Julie was one of the best there was. And she wasn't one of those bitching career-women either. She didn't have to be that, because real talent is rare enough, even in New York. When you combine it with courage it's an unbeatable combination. Julie came out of a poor family, so she knew how to fight, and she expected to work for everything she got. She had her M.A. in the History of Art when she was twenty-four. And she was a pretty good artist in her own right along with that. But what she mostly had was an incredible ability to put the right pieces together, for getting the best, the most inspired stuff out of the people she hired to do the art-work—and a memory like an elephant for the work of every artist she'd ever seen. All of this before she was thirty, too."

The words came very quickly, and with them the effort to appear casual and to disguise the pain. Ginny was frightened by the knowledge of desolation which the words uncovered, the quick speech that sought to find the essence of a woman who was lost.

"Given time," he said, "there wasn't anything that Julie wanted to do that she couldn't have done or been. But the greatest thing was that she was happy. Can you imagine that—to be happy in the possession of a talent! She had the gift—the way some people can sing or stand on their heads. This was the greatest gift and she had it. She was the most fortunate of women, the most blessed, and I had the good luck to be married to her. And she went and died on me. That's what Julie's grandmother said to me at the funeral . . . Julie's family is Irish. . . . She said to me, 'Well, boy, so she went and died on you!' And that's exactly what she did!"

Then he laid the magazine down with the others, the movement tender like a lover who touches his beloved. The gesture held a sense of agony and loss, of utter aloneness in the face of a life that has to be lived, has to be continued in some fashion. The physical hardness of the man seemed to vanish, though the gaunt lines of his face were accentuated. In that single gesture of gentleness and love towards his dead wife, Ginny had an intimation of what it might be like to be loved by him.

She made an excuse and left quickly, defeated. She knew as she shut the door behind her that it would be some time before Jim knew that she had gone.

Katrien came on her later, huddled on the steps that led from the garden at Oranje Huis, huddled as if, sitting in the hot sun of the late afternoon, she were cold. She lowered herself down on the step beside her daughter.

"What is it?"

Ginny turned her face towards Katrien; her eyes seemed over-large, staring almost stupidly, wildly. "Mother, did Jim ever show you a photograph of his wife? Did you ever see one?"

"Yes. Why?"

"I thought he might have. Because he trusts you—I thought he might have wanted to show it to you."

Katrien nodded. "It was just after he came. The cottages hadn't been started, and he had a lot of time on his hands, poor man. I asked him about her, and he seemed quite glad to talk. It was only once, though."

"What did she look like?"

" Does it matter, Ginny?"

" Of course it does!" The tone was high pitched, not quite in control. " Was she pretty?"

Katrien didn't lie; she knew what it meant but she didn't lie. " She was more than pretty, Ginny. She had a wonderful face—I've never seen any quite like it. Beautiful, and yet strong at the same time. In the photo she was half smiling, but you sensed that she was laughing a little, too. Dark hair and light eyes. Blue or grey—I don't know. I've never forgotten her face."

" No—I don't suppose it's an easy face to forget. He hasn't."

" Did you expect him to? Do you want him to?"

" Oh, God! I don't know! I don't know what I want." She got to her feet abruptly and left Katrien sitting there in the last of the sun.

On the following Monday morning she caught the ferry from Willemstad to St. Charles. She was in Barney's at noon when Harry Parker arrived and ordered his Rum Collins. She slid into the stool beside him at the bar.

" Harry—do you remember you said I could get a job any time over here? Where should I start asking first?"

She worked for a month checking stock and selling china, watches and Swiss music-boxes at The Treasure Trove; this was the month when she learned how to write out a sales cheque, make out an order for china from whatever pottery in England manufactured it, learned by heart the Customs regulations and the art of packing delicate things so that they did not break. She learned how to help the tourists order more china than they had intended to. The Treasure Trove did not carry Tilsit china, so there were no slips made out in her own name, and no questions to be answered.

With the start of the tourist season in December she had an offer of slightly more money from the St. Dennis Boutique, a branch of a fashionable, expensive resort-wear store in San Juan, so she went there. It was both more difficult and more interesting to sell clothes, and she was finding that jobs on St. Charles in the tourist stores were more or less interchangeable. Every shop was short of help, and training didn't much matter. The same number of women rotated in the same jobs, augmented only when a new permanent resident decided that there had to be more to do than to sit on the beach each afternoon. Ginny was accepted as one of these, and she learned, by imitation, to make admiring sounds at whatever dress or swimsuit a woman would choose to try on. The real work of selling was done by the Negro alteration hands who quickly and skilfully made the garments actually fit. At first Ginny wanted either to laugh or cry when she saw the spectacle of the too-fat or too-thin woman standing in front of the dressing-room mirror, hopefully, trustfully waiting for those deft, silent seamstresses to work a magic that could be worked on the clothes but not on the customer. She saw expensive clothes pawed roughly by greedy women, and she suffered the familiar protest of the young woman who covets a dress and sees it bought by an old woman. But these feelings didn't last long. After two weeks she had learned to shrug and mentally count her commission.

"Well—that was what you went to learn, wasn't it?" Katrien said when Ginny told her.

She was accepted by the lunch-time crowd at Barney's, and by the small crowd who took the once-a-day eight o'clock ferry to St. Charles from St. Nicolaas every morning. Now when she walked through the streets of St. Charles she was greeted by a dozen people with that off-hand, casual American "Hi." In so short a time she had the stamp of belonging, because in an island that was growing so fast, where new faces appeared every day, to have been born to this life was a mark almost of antiquity. The tourists she met always looked slightly astonished when she said she lived on St. Nicolaas. Nearly always these introductions took place at Barney's, and she would watch their quick glance towards the harbour, and the channel to St. Nicolaas. "You mean you live over there? It's a French island, isn't it?—oh, Dutch? And you come to work by water every morning? Well, it sure beats riding the subway."

She learned to say the flip, casual things that went with the conversation at lunch-time, even to participate a little in the island gossip. This was a much livelier activity than on St. Nicolaas because the American island, in the middle of its boom and profiting from the menace of Castro in the Caribbean, had been discovered in the last few seasons by the crowd that had once gone to Miami and Cuba. Mil-

lionaires were building homes in the hills above the town,
a few celebrities were to be seen on Main Street, a film star or
two. In the absence of any more startling news, or the hint
of a scandal, there were always the TV programmes to
discuss. St. Charles had two TV channels.

The few weeks she had been at The Treasure Trove
Ginny had remarked on the difference between the two
islands to Lillian Marshall, the manager of the shop; and
Lillian's flat, sarcastic voice had drawled back, " Oh, yes,
darling—we've got everything here. We've got beaches, and
nice houses and shops and public health. Everything's
so nice and pleasant I sometimes think I could drop dead
of boredom. I walked through the square yesterday and
someone was nailing up a notice announcing that next
week was Mental Health Week on St. Charles. Just think
of it, darling—Mental Health Week in Paradise!"

And a blonde, lean-faced girl in tight-fitting black pants
leaned in close to the group who ate their lunch-time hamburgers at Barney's and said flatly, " You're all kidding yourselves down here. My family sent me to St. Charles for the
winter to rest and get over an operation because they'd
heard it was nice and quiet. Funniest thing I ever heard!
This is practically New York crowded on to a pocket
handkerchief. Man—you can have the wildest times on this
quiet little island . . ."

Then the girl left them to saunter back to her part-time job
behind the counter of Jackson's, the largest store for selling
duty-free liquor in town, and Susie Marshall, Lillian's
daughter, shook her head and half laughed. " That wasn't
any operation. That was a nice juicy divorce they sent her
down to rest up from." Susan had finished that year at her
Connecticut boarding school, and she was not yet reconciled
to island living. There was an infectious restlessness about
her.

' How do you know?" Ginny said.

Susan opened up her wide green eyes. " Well, everyone
knows, don't they? That's Tracy West. She's Arnold J.
West's daughter."

" Who's he?"

Now Susan laughed outright. " You've never heard of
Arnold J. West? Well, he's . . . Arnold J. West. I mean, he's

. . . well, just rich, you know. Gee, Ginny—you mean you don't *know*."

She usually went back to St. Nicolaas on the evening ferry with a day-old copy of the *New York Times* which Mrs. Marshall saved for her. The *Times* was flown in every day. It was a continual small wonder to her the way overtones of New York clung to the people who came to St. Charles to settle. For some reason her father disliked seeing the folded paper tucked under her arm when he met her at the ferry. He always refused it when she offered it to him. Because she felt vaguely uncomfortable reading it under his eyes, she saved it until she was in bed at night, and then she only skimmed the news stories and gave most of her attention to the advertising. She conceived a strange picture of a city where everyone was marvellously well dressed and slim, where they ate foods she'd never heard of, and went to the theatre every night. She studied the photos and sketches of the models eagerly, hungrily. Was this a Julie MacAdam? Or this? Was this the kind of woman Jim admired?—or this one? Did they all know how to dress and talk, and no one was dumb or poor or shabby? Reason told her that this was not so, but still the pictured models took on the fascination of paper dolls.

Sometimes, when she walked towards the ferry, the *Oranje Lady* would be tied up at the sea-wall.

"Hop in," Jim would say briefly. "I had to come over late, so I thought I'd wait." There was a difference, though, the night he appeared freshly shaven, with jacket and tie to put on, and announced that he was taking her to dinner at Estate Louise, which was the Great House of one of the old sugar estates. It was the best place on the island to eat, extremely expensive, and the most formal. Jim had always spoken of it disparagingly as a tourist trap, but to-night he said nothing. Over the meal he questioned her about her job.

"Well, it's all right—I'm enjoying it, up to a point. There's not much to do, and once you've learned how to do it, that's that. But there's no other kind of job, either. I suppose I've learned a few things, but mostly I must seem pretty stupid to these people over here."

"Stupid? You're not stupid! Why should you feel that?"

" Oh, there are so many things I don't know anything about. Things like who is Arnold J. West."

Jim exploded into laughter. " Well, I admit in certain sections of society it's pretty important to know who Arnold J. West is, but you won't die if you don't know. What are you looking for over here, Ginny? A quick course in sophistication? The real thing isn't here, you know." He gestured, indicating the lovely candle-lit formality of the room, the view of the harbour lights below them. " This is all imported. If you haven't got it, you have to go to the outside to acquire it. Now Katrien—she's got a certain kind of realism that's the better kind of sophistication. She'll never need to know who Arnold J. West is."

" But I do."

" No—but you need to know that it's really not important."

She dug her fork into the curried rice savagely. " Jim, you talk to me as if you were my grandfather. Why are you always *telling* me things?"

" Because I thought you wanted to know. How else do you get an education?"

" I don't know," she said gloomily. " Well, you can go on telling me things, but try not to sound as if you're doing it, will you?"

He laid down his own fork. " Perhaps I should tell you something else, Ginny?"

She looked up. His tone had altered abruptly; it no longer had the bantering, half-jesting inflection which he seemed to reserve for her. She stared at him in unbelief because she thought that, for once, he was nervous. A wild, unthinking hope suddenly found birth.

" What is it?"

" Did you know your father is sick?"

She closed her eyes. She was ashamed to realise that her first reaction was disappointment that he had not begun to say what she wanted him to say. For a while she couldn't focus on what the meaning of his words were. For these few seconds all she thought of was herself; then that passed, and she thought of her father.

" Sick? How sick? What's wrong with him?" Even now she asked the question mechanically. Her ears seemed to ring with the very absence of what Jim had not said.

" I don't know how sick. It's his heart."

Now the words were real, and they hit her. "Heart? How do you know?"

"He had a bad spell to-day. I happen to know because Katrien asked me to go for the doctor—he was out on a house call where they had no phone. Apparently it happened like this before when you were away. Ginny—don't look like that! It wasn't very serious, the doctor said. A warning, he called it. He'll have to go gently for a while. Fortunately it's not cane-cutting for a few months yet—he'll have time."

"And you came over to tell me? It was good of you, Jim."

"I didn't want you to be frightened by someone else telling you the wrong thing. It really isn't serious . . . Hey, what's the rush? He knows I've come to tell you—they don't expect you early. They didn't want you to come early."

"I know." She was on her feet. "But you'll take me home now, won't you, Jim? He won't want me to come early, but he'll want to see me."

Jim signalled the waiter, and nodded. "Yes. I'll take you."

As the *Oranje Lady* cut through the water swiftly in the passage of the channel, Jim saw that her hands, pressed against the dashboard, were rigid with tension, looking almost claw-like. Her face was down-drawn and little hollows had seemed to appear at her temples. Instinctively his arm went about her shoulders. Even they felt young and vulnerable.

"Try to relax, Ginny. It isn't bad. He was all right when I left. He was joking in that strait-laced English way of his. He said to be sure you got a good dinner, and that he'd be meeting you at the ferry as usual in a few days."

She nodded and moved in close under his arm; the gesture was one of acceptance and weariness as if she had somehow been made older by this hour.

"It was the same with her. She was afraid of her heart . . The doctors didn't want her to come."

"Who was afraid?"

"Isobel—his sister."

"It doesn't mean anything. Forget it. I tell you he's all right. He just has to take care."

They were approaching Oranje Cove and he held his arm

about her only a second longer. He felt her shoulders lift
a little and he guessed that her eyes, like his, had automatically sought the lights of Oranje Huis. There was only
one on the gallery, and the sitting-room was lighted. Nothing
more; nothing unusual. " You see—it's all right," he said.

When she heard their footsteps on the path below the house,
Katrien got up from her chair in the living-room and went
out to wait for them. Bo, who had gone down to the
beach at the sound of the boat, was the first to appear at
the top of the steps, and then, a second later and, half
running, was Ginny; Jim was behind her.

" Mother—how is he?"

" Hush!" Katrien gestured towards the corner bedroom.
" He's asleep—quite normally. He had a mild sedative, that's
all that was necessary. The attack wasn't bad. There's
nothing to be concerned too much about."

" You're sure?"

" Yes."

Ginny dropped into the nearest chair in a graceless, heavy
motion; she rested her head in her outspread hands. The
slump of her shoulders and back were eloquent, as if the
sudden release of tension had left nothing to support them.
Katrien started towards her, but she checked herself when
she saw Jim make the same movement. He put his hand
on Ginny's disordered hair; then he squatted down beside
her and pulled her head against his shoulder.

" Easy, Ginny! Easy!"

She stayed that way for a minute or more, under the
firm stroking of his hand; then she lifted her head and looked
at Katrien.

" I panicked. I'm sorry. I didn't believe what Jim told
me. I should have believed him, but I didn't. But when
I saw you I knew it was all right."

Katrien looked hard at her daughter, and now she saw
that the resemblance to John Tilsit was stamped in every
line of Ginny's face. It had never been so before. There
had been traces of him, expressions that belonged to him,
quickly coming and going, obscured by a childish roundness
and feminine moulding. Now Ginny's gaunt, anguished face
was the face of her father. Her cheeks seemed hollow,

sucked in, in John's familiar look when he was disturbed; her lips were a thin bloodless line, and held with great firmness against trembling. Her jaw line was sharp, almost angular. Abruptly she had gone over to her father's side. To Katrien she seemed completely identified with him, face, body, temperament, and now, finally, this new experience of fear and pain kept tightly under control.

Inside herself Katrien sighed because she knew now that Ginny would make life hard for herself.

But when she spoke, her voice was calm and steadying. "Yes, it's all right, Ginny. It's going to be all right now."

And so it was, until Christmas Day.

11

Katrien did not linger after the service ended at the Dutch Reformed Church in Willemstad on Christmas morning. This was a departure from her usual custom; she had always enjoyed the ritual of the seasonal handshake and greeting with her neighbours; but this morning she hurried Ginny into the car. John Tilsit was not with them; the church, packed to the doors for the occasion, would be too stuffy he decided, and added his weak joke that in any case he had already heard Herder Verheul's Christmas sermon twenty-two times. Ginny, as she slowly manœuvred the Volkswagen between the crowd of people on the road outside the church, knew that Katrien's hurry was part of the routine that had come into being since John Tilsit's attack, three weeks ago. Thinking over the three weeks, Ginny realised that Katrien had hardly let him out of her sight in that time. It was she who drove her husband in the jeep through the cane-fields when he was well enough again to make the journey, and she who met Ginny at the ferry in the evenings. Katrien was a bad driver, who drove without zest, and hated it. It was the only visible indication of concern for her husband that she insisted on doing it.

"It's only for a time," she kept saying. "You must have no strain for a time, John. None at all."

"I don't know, Katrien, that it isn't safer to let me drive," he said, in an attempt to make the occasion a jest.

" Most men with perfectly good hearts would be in a bad way to see you at the wheel."

She laughed, but took no notice of him. And the contrast between them seemed savage and cruel to Ginny—Katrien's ample, healthy body and her strong arms and hands that managed the heavy gears of the jeep without strain, and her father, whose leanness had suddenly seemed to become thinness, looking fragile and worn. It seemed at times that Katrien tried to will her own strength to her husband, and was always tragically defeated.

It would be the usual Christmas celebration at Oranje Huis; the gallery and living-room were decorated with the flaming red poinsettia, the Christmas flower of the hot climates. The table, set with the fine damask cloth and silver that Katrien had inherited from her mother, had a row of the scarlet blossoms laid down the centre, and the pride of place was given to the white orchids Albert de Kruythoff sent each year. There was no evergreen Christmas tree, and John refused to have the imitation ones that were sold on St. Charles. So the presents were piled on a table on the gallery, and Katrien's silver punch-bowl would be filled and waiting for their return from church. Albert would join them as soon as he was finished with his duty of standing on the church steps and shaking hands all round, as he did every Christmas morning. He had been coming to Oranje Huis every Christmas dinner since he arrived on the island nine years ago. This year he would be joined at the table by Jim MacAdam. It was this fact that made it a different Christmas for Ginny, and she put her foot on the accelerator joyfully and the Volkswagen bounced in the ruts on Town Road.

Jim was already there when they drove up; he followed John Tilsit through the living-room to the gallery on the land side of the house. Ginny swung quickly and parked in the shade of the banyan trees, suddenly enjoying the sensation of showing off a small skill. She was conscious of two things—that her father, walking down the steps to meet them, did indeed look better, as Katrien had been insisting during the drive; and the second one was that Jim, leaning against the stone pillar, glass in hand, was smiling and nodding, and the nod seemed to be of approval. Ginny walked

towards her father, consciously swishing the full skirt of the
new dress she had bought at discount from the St. Dennis
Boutique and which had cost almost all of next month's
wages. She wore a hat with a sensationally wide brim,
and her hair was drawn back expertly, because Susie
Marshall had taught her how it was done. The new perfume
was by Givenchy, and very expensive. The pulse in her
throat seemed to flutter with excitement as she walked forward into her father's outstretched arms. Everything was
all right. It was going to be a good day.

She knew her father had caught the excitement and pleasure
of the moment too. His arms went about her in an uncharacteristic gesture of emotion.

"Did I forget to say it before you left? A happy Christmas, my Ginny. Many more of them!"

"Happy Christmas, Father." And over his shoulder she
smiled at Jim.

Jim sipped at his punch and pondered the scene. She was
changed—God, how she was changed in all the external
things. He remembered the time he had watched her in
just this way on the evening of Albert de Kruythoff's party
for the Governor nearly six months ago. He remembered her
as she had been when she walked across the square, with the
golden hair threatening to tumble down, and the touching,
slightly pathetic quality of her youthfulness. And sadly she
had known how young she was, and how late had been the
moment of her arrival at adulthood. She had run very hard
these last six months, and had covered ground, but he sensed
that she didn't fully know why she ran. The job on St.
Charles was a desperate attempt to make up for lost time,
to claim a piece of the world that was not her father's,
to discover something for herself. She tried very hard
and some of the results were plain and obvious. The dark
printed cotton and the brilliant orange straw hat were a far
cry from the pale blue childish dress of the Governor's party.
But she had learned the externals only. She still didn't understand the full power of the provocation of her walk, or the
heightened beauty of the face under the hat. She knew what
she did with her body, but not why. You can, he thought,
give beauty and the quality of sensuality to children and

watch them wreak havoc on men. And mostly they never understood what it was they had. The young, he decided, were savage innocents.

And Ginny had left her father's brief embrace and was walking towards him. Why did he not marry this girl, he wondered? She was there for the taking, if he wanted her. She would come for the asking, and she would make him a good, loyal wife, because there was enough of Katrien in her for that. She was beautiful, or nearly so. Such a marriage would be approved; although some people would say he was too old for her. Katrien, he suspected, would like it to happen, and John would be glad that Ginny, in getting a husband, had had to go no farther than the other side of the beach. That was what was wrong. Ginny had been no farther in life than the other side of the beach. He could take a risk and marry her, because he was a man and needed a woman about him—and the trips to St. Charles and Miami were not the permanent answer to that need. But the risk was there. She had seen nothing, but that was no guarantee that one day she would not have her eyes opened by someone else. His little untutored Ginny might have a violent awakening to life, and then the other side of the beach would seem too short a distance to her. And for him the risk was boredom. She was young and beautiful—and she knew nothing. Beyond her body, which was eminently desirable, she had nothing to give.

Thus, coldly, he looked at her as she came up the steps towards him, at the smiling, excited face raised hopefully to his. Without love, the risk was too great. And he did not love her. He had once loved a woman called Julie, who had had passion and wit and beauty. Beside her, this girl was a pale thing. A thing of beauty, but a pale thing, and too great a risk.

So he bent and kissed her warm, smooth cheek, delicious in its smoothness. He experienced the familiar, pleasurable glow through his body at the feel of the firm, silken texture of her bare arm under his hand. She was indeed desirable, but desire, now, was not enough.

So after that brief, seasonal salute, he drew back. " Happy Christmas, Ginny."

She sensed the withdrawal, and quickly she looked up and her eyes sought his. She didn't want to believe what she had felt so swiftly, but she was beginning to. She hadn't thought that the end could come like this, in the midst of people, on an occasion like this. She said fumblingly, " Happy . . . happy Christmas, Jim."

Albert de Kruythoff came hurrying through the living-room with his loping stride, his head thrust forward, his unbuttoned jacket flapping. " I'm sorry," he said to Katrien. " Even on Christmas Day the problems don't go away—or is it because it's Christmas people think I have more money in the budget. . . .? Happy Christmas!" He took Katrien's hand briefly. " Happy Christmas, Ginny—John!" He waved the punch glass which John had put into his hand towards Jim. " You're first on St. Nicolaas, Jim. I hope it's the first of many happy ones."

They drank, and Jim nodded and said, " If they're going to be happy ones then this is the first and last quiet one. I hope by this time next year I'll have to put up cot beds to accommodate all the people who want to have Christmas in the sun at Oranje Cove."

" If they come," Katrien said slyly, " send me the over-flow. A little whitewash in the outbuildings back there—better than sleeping on the beach. And I won't charge as much as Jim, either." After the laughter that followed, she added, " And the cooking will be better too. I've been thinking that I'll just add a lot of spices to the ordinary things we eat, and give them Dutch names and tell the guests they're recipes from the Netherlands East Indies."

" And they'll believe it, I'm sure." John looked across at Jim. " And if it's a success will you—will you build more?"

" I *have* to build more. Six cottages isn't an economic proposition. It's only a beginning. But I'll have to have more money, and somehow it's got to be raised. That is going to be tough to do until I can prove that people are willing to come to St. Nicolaas. Ben White, one of the people who's in this syndicate, is coming down soon to look it over. There's money to be had up there in Wall Street if only you can convince them that there's more of it to be made down here."

" You'll have some competition, Jim," Albert said. " A Mr. Philip Hayes from Miami was here the other day. He and his partner are planning to start building a sixty-room hotel on their land over at Seagrape. And Martin van Ness has sold forty-three acres to a real estate developer."

"The more the better. What we need is people coming to this island. The rest . . ." He broke off, because through the living-room came the sound of a car in the driveway, and the rapid slam of a door.

Katrien got to her feet. "Excuse me. I'll just see . . . Why, it's Jan Withoff. What can he . . .?" More loudly she said, "Come in, Jan . . . a happy Christmas to you!"

Jan Withoff, the head of St. Nicolaas's somnolent postal service, advanced through the living-room towards the group on the gallery. He was dressed for church, with jacket and tie on. The perspiration lay wetly in the fat rings around his neck. His broad, good-humoured face was further extended in a wide smile.

"A happy Christmas to you all. To you, Mr. de Kruythoff. Thank you, John, yes—I'll have a drink. But it will have to be quick. Martha won't like it if I delay dinner on her after all the preparations . . . I missed you at church, Katrien. I waited around, and then someone told me you'd left early. So I came after you."

Katrien raised puzzled eyebrows. "You wanted to see me especially, Jan?"

"Oh, it didn't matter—not you especially. Any of you would have done. The package is addressed to Ginny, but anyone can sign for it. It came late yesterday evening, you see—long after the last delivery had gone out. Someone had chartered a plane and the post office put a few things on it. So I thought I would bring this to church this morning. Against postal regulations, of course. . . ." He set his punch down on the table and dug into one of his bulging coat pockets. "You see, it was air-mail, express delivery . . . and I thought you would want to have it for Christmas."

Wonderingly, Ginny got to her feet. "It's for *me*, Mr. Withoff?" She held out her hand to take a slim, flat package from him.

Suddenly John Tilsit's voice broke in. "Where did it come from?" It was not an ordinary question, but a demand.

Withoff beamed. "From England. That's why I thought Ginny would want to have it to-day. It's from your family,

John. I never remember you getting letters from England all the years you've been here, so I thought this was important. You see the addressee's name—I. J. Tilsit. Yes—just sign there, Ginny." He looked around all of them happily. "Good, isn't it, that it came in time? Families should think of each other at Christmas . . ." Now he heaved himself out of the wicket-chair. "Well, thank you for the drink, Katrien —and that's my Christmas good deed done. Now I must get back to my Martha. Such a fuss if I'm late, with the grandchildren come from Curaçao for the holidays, and a visitor from St. Maarten." He bowed deferentially to Albert as he took his hand in farewell. "And a good New Year to you, sir. Is it this next year you go on leave? No? A pity! Well, I shouldn't mind a trip home myself. There is to be a great convention of postmasters this next year in Geneva. Such wonders they have . . . automatic sorting, they say. Did you hear of that new post office they have in America where no one ever touches the mail? Just think of it!" Katrien walked with him through the living-room to his car on the other side of the house. His voice drifted back to the group on the gallery. "They say it doesn't work, of course—but can you expect everything?"

They waited in silence for Katrien's return; Ginny stood unhappily with the package in her hand and the thick, straight handwriting seemed to her almost to shout in the silence. She looked at the name in the top left-hand corner —*I. J. Tilsit*. Isobel would write like that, authoritatively. She did not write "Miss I. Tilsit" or "Isobel Tilsit." She turned the package over and saw that her hands, suddenly damp with perspiration, had left marks on the brown paper. Katrien was coming back through the living-room. Ginny looked towards her mother expectantly; she had not yet dared to let her eyes go to her father's face.

"Well?" Katrien said with a forced brightness. "That was kind of Jan to bring it, wasn't it? Now—I think dinner is ready. Shall we go in and sit down?"

At her words there was a quick movement from Jim and Albert to obey her, glad to have the strain of the silence eased. John Tilsit's voice arrested them. "Wait! Aren't we going to open the presents? Isn't that what we always do before we eat dinner?"

Katrien shrugged. "Oh—let's not trouble. Dinner is

ready and we can just as easily wait until later." She tried
to smile. " After all—you *know* that I've given you the new
lens for the telescope you wanted, John. There's no surprise."

" But Ginny," he persisted. " Ginny must open her presents.
Look, Albert has brought something for her—and Jim.
Ginny has *always* opened her presents before dinner." He
stood rooted by his chair, his two hands clasped about his
glass and his fingers opened and closed compulsively. There
were two hectic spots of colour now in his thin cheeks, and
the sinews of his neck stood out in hard cords.

" Please, John—come now."

" And then," he went on, ignoring her, " there's that
parcel Ginny got from England. What could that be? Who
could have sent that, I wonder?"

" Please, John—our guests . . ."

" Damn the guests! I want it open! Now!"

Ginny looked at her mother desperately; Katrien sighed,
and then nodded barely perceptibly. Ginny began to fumble
with the string and sealing-wax. It resisted her fingers.
In the waiting, tense quiet, Jim took the package from her
and cut the string with his penknife, then handed it back to
her. She had to put it down on the table as the unwrapped
it because her hands trembled. She gave a last, despairing
glance at her mother as the final wrapping came off. Instinctively everyone moved a little closer, even Albert, who
had been gazing out to sea and trying to pretend that
nothing was happening.

In Ginny's hands lay a thin oblong box, covered with blue
imitation leather and stamped in gold with the single
word

TILSIT

Inside, in a groove in the blue velvet lining, lay a cheese
knife. The heavy white ceramic handle was decorated with
a design of gold and deep blue whose brilliance and strength
was startling in the sunlight. Ginny lifted it slowly out
of its groove. The curved and forked blade caught the
sun in a sudden dazzle. She had to shield it to read the
words engraved there.

Tilsit   England

It was John who spoke first. " Well, Isobel's caught on to the export drive, I see. Take home a gift from Britain—all wrapped in a handy little gift box." His tone was strident and mocking, derisive. He touched the box. " Look at that! A piece of cheap showmanship. Tilsit!—she uses the name as if it were Crown Derby or Sèvres. *Tilsit!*" But the last time he spoke the word his voice wavered, and there was hurt and longing in it now. He held out his hand to take the knife from Ginny. " Here, let me see that!"

As they watched, his fingers ran over the small handle with a gesture that was loving and knowledgeable. He stared at it for some moments, and when he spoke again the others knew that his words were for Ginny alone.

" See that? Beautiful, isn't it? Not overdone—not too rich or too sentimental. She has a good designer. This is a new pattern—I've never seen this one. See this blue —how rich and deep it is. It could have taken four—maybe five firings in the kiln to get that colour. It's hand-painted each time, of course. There's no machine yet that can do that. And the gold—that's hand-applied too. And hand-burnished with fine sand after the kiln. There's pride and craftsmanship in every line of this, Ginny. It means something in a mass-produced world, doesn't it?"

Then he turned back to them all. " You've probably gath-ered that I don't feel much love for my sister, Isobel. My instinct is to toss this down the hill there and let it lie somewhere among the rocks and be forgotten. In time the salt air would rust and corrode the blade, and it would disintegrate. But the ceramic, I think, would endure. It's already been through the fire, and its beauty and strength is because of that. When you washed the muck off, the colours would be there, as rich and true as ever. If I were to pound at this I would destroy it, but not, I think, any other way."

Quietly he laid the knife down beside the box on the table. His bony shoulders came together in a shrug that indicated a kind of helplessness. " And who am I to try to destroy it? There are too many other people beside Isobel involved in the creation of this one simple, complicated little thing of beauty."

While he spoke his hands had automatically begun to sort and smooth the wrapping paper, because by nature he

was an orderly man. And now, caught in the tissue in which
the box had been wrapped, and discarded by Ginny in those
first nervous moments, his fingers closed on a white envelope
marked again with Isobel's heavy upright script. For a
moment he fingered the stiff expensive paper, then he handed
it to Ginny.

" For you."

She ran her tongue over her lips, eyeing it mistrustfully.
" I'll read it later."

" No, now. It will be brief. Isobel always comes to the
point." This was not an order, as it had been when he had
told her to open the package. Now his words had a kind
of resigned acceptance of the situation. She hesitated only
momentarily before she slit the envelope with her fore-
finger. The letter was brief, as John had predicted. There
was writing on only one side of a single sheet of paper. They
watched Ginny's eyes flick over it.

" Read it," John said.

She didn't protest this time ; it would have been useless.

*Dear Virginia—Superstition has it that a coin should accom-
pany the gift of a knife so that the recipient may be able
to pay the giver for the gift, and so the ties between them
shall not be cut. I do not enclose the required coin. Not
only do I not hold with superstition, but I am well aware
that no ties have been permitted to form in this case.*

*The enclosed is a part of what Tilsit is. I invite you to
come here to discover what the rest of it is.*

Isobel Tilsit

" Well!" A painful smile twisted John's lips. His arms
hung limply from his hunched shoulders. " Well—so you're
bidden come, Ginny. She wants you at Tilsit. She invites
you—no, she commands you. An invitation is always a
command from Isobel. She wants you there, so you will
be there. Her mind is made up."

" No one's mind is made up." Quietly Katrien touched his
arm. " I remind you, John, that Albert and Jim are waiting.
Dinner is waiting for us. Now let us go in and forget
all this. Come, Ginny. Leave all that now. There's time
for that later."

She almost succeeded. The calm voice was a sound of sanity that held at bay the near-frenzy of her husband. Albert turned quickly to go with her, relieved to be rescued from this nightmare of embarrassment which thrust him into the Tilsits' affairs. Jim also responded, motioning Ginny to go ahead of him. In the general movement towards the dining-room door John was almost caught up and drawn along. Katrien led the way, but at the door she paused to look back to her husband. "Come now—leave it, please."

He shrugged. "You'll have to excuse me, Katrien. Albert and Jim—my apologies I really don't think I can eat. It's the heat, I suppose. I've always thought it was a bad idea to eat a heavy dinner in the tropics just because it happens to be Christmas. I think I'll just sit this one out, if you don't mind. Excuse me, Katrien."

"I'll stay with you." Although her mother frowned and shook her head, Ginny ignored her. "Look, Father, I'll bring my dinner out here. I'll have it with you out here. Just wait a minute . . ."

His expression warmed briefly, and in that instant lost its desolate acceptance. Then he shook his head. "That's kind of you, my dear. But I won't take you away from Albert and Jim. You go in and enjoy it. I think I'll just take a stroll down to the beach. I'll be with you later."

"Father . . .!"

"Go along now, Ginny—that's a good girl."

His bearing seemed altered strangely as he walked towards the steps; it had become not the careful walk of a man who has been ill, but the shuffle of an ageing man. Ginny let out a little exclamation of dismay, but Katrien waved her to silence.

"It is better to let him go." She marshalled them all again with a gesture. "Now—we will have dinner."

For ten minutes they made a show of normalcy at the table decked with the flaming red blossoms. The food was served, and Jim opened and poured the champagne he had brought, making more of a ceremony of it than he needed to cover John's absence. Katrien had quickly removed the extra place-setting, and had waved Albert directly to the head of the table; he had gone without protest. Now he shyly offered a toast to the coming New Year in Dutch, and Katrien responded. Ginny translated it roughly for Jim. "He wishes us peace and prosperity and our heart's desires."

Ginny saw the red blossoms waver through the straw-coloured bubbling wine as she raised her glass to her lips. "Yes, and happiness," she murmured. It was a wish for the end of waiting.

And then, as the glasses were lowered, they caught the sound of the outboard kicking over down in the cove.

"My God!" Ginny said. "He's taken the boat out! He's mad! It's too much strain—he'll kill himself!"

Jim pushed back his chair. "Shall I go and get him, Mrs. Tilsit? The *Oranje Lady* can catch up with him in a few minutes. Ginny's right, I guess . . ."

Albert clicked his tongue in distress. "He should not go alone." He half rose as if he would go with Jim.

"Everyone—sit down!" Katrien's voice snapped out like a command. "No one will do anything. You must leave him alone."

"It's cruel . . . it's wrong," Ginny objected. "I don't see how you can let him . . ."

The lines of Katrien's face tightened with severity. She looked her age as she rapped on the table for silence. "Let us all understand something. My husband is a man. He is not a child to be ordered to do this—do that—do something else. I will not have anyone sent after him to fetch him home as if he had behaved badly. Yes—I know—he is wrong-headed and stubborn. But he has been that way for a long time. He injures himself—he injures more than just his heart when he does this. But would you have me drag him back here with no respect for what he suffers from this letter to-day?" She waved her hand, dismissing the idea. "No—it lacks dignity. If you take that from my husband he has nothing. So leave him be. We must take the chance that he will be all right. Now—please eat your food. It grows cold."

They obeyed her silently. It was she who said the last words about her husband that day. "I hope he has enough gas."

III

It was almost fully dawn when Ginny woke on the morning after Christmas Day. She stirred sluggishly, wondering, half asleep still, why she had stayed awake so long the night before. There was a residue of tiredness in her brain and body, but as she struggled up out of sleep the worry and concern exploded fully once more. All through the afternoon and night she had waited for her father to return, and he had not come. And still Katrien had refused to allow Jim to go out looking for him. Ginny's concern had boiled up into a quarrel in which she had accused her mother of indifference, and had been coldly put in her place by Katrien.

" I've lived with him far longer than you, Ginny. You've only begun to notice your father because you've only just become a woman. He's been doing this for years—since we were first married and before that. I've never interfered. I never will. Now go to bed. I will wait for him."

" I want to wait too."

" That is not your privilege. Good night, Ginny."

So she had gone, unwillingly and sullenly, conscious of a jealousy towards her mother that had never been acknowledged before. She was aware now of the power in Katrien which made Jim respect and admire her, and which always brought John Tilsit gratefully back to her. Her father, she knew, would recognise Katrien's right to wait up for him alone. Sleep had been a long time in coming as she pondered this and strained for the sound of the outboard down in the cove. She calculated that it was well after midnight before the first, fitful, uneasy doze had taken her.

Now she flung aside the sheet and groped for her cotton robe in one blurred motion; the tile was cool against her bare feet as she hurried out to the veranda.

Her father was slumped there in a chair. On the table beside him was a tray with empty teacups and a pot. He sat with his legs extended, and his arms lying along the arms of the chair; his head was thrown back and his eyes closed. For a moment, as she looked at the dark, set lines in his face under the tan, the bluish tinge of his thin lips, she felt a terrible fear seize her. She gasped, as if the fear had squeezed the breath from her lungs. She tiptoed nearer, and then she saw the soft movement of his chest, and heard his own breath. Suddenly, sensing her there, he opened his eyes.

"Well, Ginny . . ."

"You're home! I've been so worried . . ."

He smiled faintly, with some amusement. "No need to worry. I always come home."

"Yes, but you shouldn't have gone like that—alone."

He shook his head. "No good if it's not alone. Got to think things out a little. Get them straight. I always feel better for it, and your mother's sensible enough to know that. So she lets me go."

She peered at him closely. "You look tired. You should be in bed."

He nodded. "I am tired. I'll go to bed in a little bit. I sent your mother off. I said I'd come in a while, just as soon as I got the kink out of my bones."

"You haven't eaten anything since yesterday morning. Let me get you something to eat."

"No—no . . . I'm not hungry. Katrien made some tea. I'll eat after I've had some sleep." He pointed suddenly at the chair opposite. "Sit down. I want to talk to you."

She did as he said. The light was growing; soon, on the other side of the island, the sun would touch the horizon, and from here they would see its flush on the high point of Kronberg. Ginny's sense of intimacy with her father was linked in a long chain of continuity with this time of day. It was a world of passing—these fleeting minutes when the night was gone and the day not fully arrived. She could feel herself a little girl again with him at this time, trusting him, trusting that there was no trouble he would not solve and take away from her. At this time of day all things were possible, were hopeful, even when she knew there was no hope.

"Well," he said, "what do you think?"

"What?" Lost in the delusion of having re-established herself back in that time when all things were possible, she did not understand what he had said.

"Will you go? Will you go to Tilsit, Ginny?"

"Tilsit?" Her brow wrinkled. "Why should I go there?" In the hours since she had read the letter there had been little room for it in her thoughts. Concern for her father had blocked out almost everything else, and even when she had first read the note it had had a feeling of unreality about it. She hadn't believed it, not deeply. The lovely little knife was tangible, and so had been John Tilsit's lonely yearning over its beauty. But the sender, Isobel, she had no substance for Ginny. She was the image who had appeared for one single occasion in the sitting-room at Santa Maria, and then had gone. What remained of Isobel was only a shadow like the tail-end of some nightmarish dream. The only strength she had in Ginny's mind had been imparted to her by her father's fear, and his refusal to talk about her.

" You were invited—remember? That's what she said. ' I invite you to come.' Will you go?"

She shook her head. " No. The thought of going never entered my head. Why should I go? I didn't like her. And she didn't like *you*—so why should I go?"

He moved his hand wearily, gesturing to dismiss the notion. " You don't know what you may be losing. What happened between me and Isobel all those years ago has nothing to do with you. It doesn't make any difference. We quarrelled seriously—no, it was far worse than a quarrel. But you were no part of it, so it doesn't affect you. You're free to go if you want to."

Glancing sidewards she saw that the sun had already touched the peak of Kronberg. Soon it would rise higher, the light would start reaching down the hillslopes into the flats. The day had truly come, and with it the time of reality. The illusion was gone that she was a child again, and that her father held all the wisdom of the world in his hand to dispense. She turned back to him and read what was in his face. His words had been false, a pitiful, brave attempt to convince her that the agony of his fear and revulsion from his sister could not affect her. He would tell her that she was free—free of any commitment to his emotions or to what had driven him away from England. But it was naïve to suppose that she could be free. She had loved him, and still did ; and she knew that he loved her— unfairly, possessively, with all the inequalities of love that demanded loyalty without reason. He had her loyalty without her understanding the cause in which it was given. Now he tried to resolve her from its ties and he didn't realise that it couldn't be done. She had made that decision in the first minutes that she had talked with Isobel Tilsit. She had not changed since then, and she would not. Her father was foolish to suppose that the essentials of their bonds could be dissolved by speaking a few words which were not the truth. For the first time she felt superior to him.

" It makes no difference. I don't want to go—to *her*."

He bent his head—a gesture of strange humility in John Tilsit. " If that's what you've decided. . . ."

She folded her arms across her body, gathering her robe in to her. " That's what I decided *not* to do. There's something else I must do."

His head shot up. " What?"

" I must go away from here."

" Go away?" He was bewildered. " Why? Go where?"

" Can you understand?" She held out one hand in a kind of appeal. " I was born here—I've lived here all my life, and if I'm not careful I'll die here without ever knowing what any other kind of life is! No!—let me finish. It isn't like Mother. It was all right for her to stay. But times are different, and I have to be different too. I have to *learn* something. Do you understand that? I have to learn far more than what I'm getting over on St. Charles."

" Learn? What do you mean? Go to college?"

She shrugged. " Perhaps—but that isn't the kind of learning I mean. I just have to know more than I can find out here."

He said slowly, " Yes, I see. I suppose I'm old-fashioned. If you were a boy I'd understand why you would want to go away for a while. I'd know, of course, that you needed an education. But somehow one doesn't think with a girl . . . it used not to be considered essential. I'm behind the times, I suppose. Where would you go—to Miami? I think that might be managed. I'd like one of the good Northern ones. Vassar or Smith." He sighed. " But places like that can't be afforded, Ginny. They simply can't be afforded. And I suppose there are all kinds of entrance difficulties now. Things used to be easier—if you could pay, you could get in."

" I wasn't thinking of one of those places, Father. That wouldn't be much different from Santa Maria."

"Yes, but the Florida colleges aren't at all like Santa Maria. They tell me things are very . . . progressive . . . there now. From what I hear of Fort Lauderdale at Easter, it's very—wild." His brow knit in sudden consternation. "You wouldn't want to go *there*, would you?"

She twined her fingers together hesitantly. "I wasn't thinking of Florida, either. I want to go to New York."

"New York! Good God, why! Why *New York*?"

"Because . . . because it's the most of everything there is. If you want something, it's there ten times in New York. I need so much so quickly, Father. I don't know where else to go to get it. Look at me! I'm ignorant—I'm not stupid but I'm ignorant. I've never seen a great painting, or been to a concert. I've never seen a play. Susie Marshall has a name for my kind of person. She calls them hicks—she doesn't think I know that she includes me in with them. But I *do* know that I'm one of them. And Jim says . . ."

He caught at the name. "Ah, Jim . . . isn't that what the great urge to learn about the rest of the world is all about? It isn't because Susie Marshall thinks you are a . . . hick. It's because you're afraid that Jim does. Isn't that right?"

"Perhaps."

Now he leaned forward in his chair, and put his hand on her knee. "Ginny . . . Ginny, why don't you marry Jim?"

She seemed to shrink back from his touch. She stared at him, and words formed on her lips which she couldn't speak at once. She ran her tongue over them. "Jim?" The sound was a croak. "Marry Jim?" Suddenly she let out a wild, mirthless laugh that caused him to pull away from her as if he had been struck.

"Marry Jim? God, if only I could! If only that wonderful thing would happen. But it won't!"

"Why not?" he demanded. "Why shouldn't it happen? You're a beautiful girl, Ginny."

"Not enough! It's not nearly enough. I've had that thought in my mind all these months, but I was suddenly sure about it yesterday. Jim's *been* married . . . He's a man—he's not a boy who'll marry the first girl that's put under his nose. If you'd ever taken time to find out anything about his wife you'd understand. Beside her I'm an ignorant little nobody. And that's why I have to go away." Her tone was rising, coming near to hysteria.

"And you think going to New York will teach you to be what she was? That isn't right. You can only be yourself."

"Oh!" She waved her hand in an angry dismissal. "I know that much. I said I wasn't stupid. But I can't hang around here waiting for him to marry me or take me to bed —yes, *bed*, Father—in a moment of boredom, or because I'd manœuvred him into it. You have your pride—and I have mine. That makes two stiff-necked people in this family. Well, my pride says I've got to get out. I love Jim, but he doesn't even see me. I don't know how to make him see me—but perhaps this is a way . . . a beginning. Perhaps there are even other Jims in the world, but how will I find out if I don't go and look? I don't really want to—but I have to."

"You might not come back." His hand made a tentative, grasping motion towards her, as if he would hold her there and keep her.

"That's a chance we'll have to take, isn't it, Father? It's like the times when you go off in the boat. All we can do is wait and hope that you will come back again."

IV

Once the words were spoken Ginny found herself caught in the current of the action she herself had set in motion. The acknowledgment that she loved Jim was the truth spoken aloud for the first time ; it was the moment after which there was no withdrawal. It demanded its own action, and she did what she did instinctively, not really because she wanted it, but because the intolerable thing would have been no action at all. And so a month after she had first put this idea to her father she was comm.tted to going. It was Sunday, and her last day on St. Nicolaas, and she found herself in the last act of desperation knocking once again on Jim's door.

A Sunday quiet lay over the cottages, the afternoon stillness had a quality as solid as the heat of the sun burning down on the sand. The sea-grapes and the six palms moved softly in the breeze from the sea, but did not really break the stillness. And no one came to answer her knock. The place felt deserted, and she had a moment's fear that she had left it too late. But Bo still pressed expectantly against the door; the redwood louvers were almost closed, and she couldn't see into the room, so she turned the handle and opened the door slowly.

She saw that Jim had wakened just at the moment the shaft of sunlight fell across the floor and the bed where he lay. He blinked for a moment, struggling to focus; Bo darted forward and thrust his nose against the pillow.

"Well—come in." He smiled, and then yawned. "I was snoozing," he added unnecessarily.

"Yes—I'm sorry I woke you. It's a shame when you have only Sunday . . ."

He raised himself up on one elbow. "No harm done. It's time I was stirring. What time *is* it?"

"Just after three. I wondered . . . well, would you like to take *Oranje Lady* and go over to Lindemann Island to swim? I've packed a picnic tea . . . you've never been to Lindemann, have you? It's supposed to be the best beach in the whole Antilles."

He sat up. "I've heard that fable. I've always promised myself I'd go over there some day and do some exploring. Perhaps *that's* the place for the next hotel." He scratched his head and grinned at her. "Can't you just see it? Millionaire's hide-away on an uninhabited island! Wouldn't that be a tourist trap?" He got to his feet, stretching and yawning again. He looked soft and rumpled from his sleep, and Ginny's instinct was to go closer to him, to put up her hand and smooth the lines on his cheek from the wrinkles of the pillow. She forced herself to stand where she was.

"If you have those kind of thoughts in mind I won't take you to Lindemann. It's the loveliest place in the world, and I won't have you spoiling it."

He pulled a mock grimace. "How's a man ever to make a buck when there are people like you in the world?" He made a move towards the bathroom. "I'll be right with you. Out of the way, Bo!"

She waited while he puttered around—getting his swimming trunks from the rail where he had hung them that morning, discarding an empty pack of cigarettes and finding a fresh one, searching for the keys of *Oranje Lady*, forgetting his sunglasses and going back for them. He even stopped on the edge of the surf to take up a piece of driftwood to throw for Bo, teasing him a little with it when he retrieved it. It was Jim in his Sunday mood—careless, indifferent to time, almost deliberately inefficient and forgetful. Ginny clenched her fists to control her impatience. Jim did not know that this was her last day here; he didn't know how precious the very seconds were.

They were moving at last, Bo in the cockpit with them, the dinghy trailing behind because there was no jetty at Lindemann. They headed north-east, and began threading their way through the chain of the British and American islands, lining up in this strait like a string of beads in the perfect, calm sunlit sea. Jim held *Oranje Lady* back from full throttle, not smashing the water but letting her ride at an easy speed that lay well in the mood of the afternoon. Under the shade of his peaked cap, Ginny saw that his eyes half closed and crinkled with pleasure. He held *Oranje Lady* on course with a touch of one finger. They rode down the middle of the strait as if they were in a long, fantastic gallery, the hump-backed islands pillars on both sides.

" It's the next one—there on the left. That's Lindemann. The best beach is directly ahead. You see that deep inlet that's opening up? It's easy going—there are no rocks."

" Whose island is it? British or American."

" No one's sure. The boundary line on some maps curves one side of Lindemann, and on other maps it goes on the other side. It's never been important enough to finally settle. It won't matter until someone wants to settle there."

" Why hasn't there been any settlement—with beaches like these?"

She smiled, glad to be able to tell him something at last. " The Spaniards and Dutch and French didn't come for the beaches. There's never been any springs on Lindemann. It was never any good for sugar."

He nodded, and *Oranje Lady* rounded the point of one of the headlands which guarded the long, almost rectangular inlet at whose end the beach gleamed like a strip of softly-coloured metal burnished and hot in the sun. It was palm-fringed, the shadows were languorous and beckoning. Jim gave a low whistle.

" Why haven't I seen this before?"

" Almost no one does," Ginny answered. "Every time Father and I have come here it's been the same—no—just once there was a cruiser anchored. It's not a favourite place for yachts for overnight anchorage. Although it's so sheltered and there's no surf, they say you get a long swell in here. You see how the headlands go straight out—they don't circle in at all, and you can't get behind them to shelter. I'm glad it's this way. It's so untouched—so perfect. It looks as if it never existed until the moment you saw it for yourself."

He cut the engine of *Oranje Lady,* and let the craft drift for just a moment. The silence was complete. Looking down he could see through the transparent green water to the sandy bottom twenty feet below. The fish that swam beneath the boat shot silver light off their darting bodies. When he tossed the anchor out the sound of the splash seemed to echo back off the hills that sloped away from the beach and headlands like a glad whisper. Then the silence came back to this lonely and perfect place.

They swam in the clear, calm water that was sun-warmed like a pool; they swam lazily, or floated, turning faces to the blinding brightness of the sky. To Jim it was an unearthly feeling to hover there, suspended in this calm; there was nothing hard to touch or feel, no dimension to measure against, only the line of the horizon, the bar of white that was the beach, and the aching blue above. In sudden restlessness he turned and dived down through the water, scattering a school of tiny fish. Down here it was cooler, the depths were greener, and the fish cast their own shadows on the sand beneath them. His chest tightened in the need for air, and he started to ascend to the surface. Then he saw Ginny's body above him, beautiful and swift in the long dive. The dive ended close to him. She trod water momentarily, her bright hair waving above her like a nimbus. Suddenly his hands sought her and he pulled her close to him. The hard thrust of her young breasts was against his chest as they rose to the surface together. They broke water and his lips fastened on hers and found the dimension and the firmness that had been lacking in this indolent soft afternoon. Her lips moved beneath his eagerly, searchingly.

" Jim . . ."

They went under again, and the words were lost as they both sucked for air that was not there. Their bodies, arms and legs entwined, unclasped now. They rose to the surface again, spluttering, apart.

He reached for her again, pulling her to him by the shoulders, and this time his kiss was longer and more tender.

" Did I hurt you? I didn't mean to hurt you."

Her reaction was violent. " Do you think I *want* you to be gentle?"

She broke away from him savagely, and swam with her quick strong stroke towards the beach. More slowly, he followed her. As he walked up the beach towards her she was towelling her hair with an angry briskness.

He dropped on his knees on his own towel spread on the sand. She was above him now, legs spread in the characteristic attitude of swimmers, her body outlined against the horizon. Her face, her expression, half hidden by the towel, he could not read.

" Well—what do I do? Is it so wrong to kiss you? Pretty girls are often kissed, Ginny."

Her voice came muffled from the towel. " But why *now*? If it had been sooner . . ."

Abruptly she withdrew the towel and the face he saw was young and troubled.

" Why sooner? What difference does it make?"

" It makes a difference. To-morrow I'm leaving to go to New York."

" You're *what*?"

" I've already said it. You heard. I'm leaving to-morrow to go to New York."

" But *why*? No—don't dive back into that towel." He reached up and pulled her roughly down beside him. " Now just you come down here and tell me why—and why all the secrecy? Why couldn't you tell me?"

" I didn't want to. I didn't want to tell anyone. I was going to tell you this afternoon—but not this way."

" Why not tell anyone? Why not?"

" Because I'm afraid." She turned on him angrily. " Can't you see that I'm scared stiff. I just couldn't take all the advice and the words of wisdom. I'd only have to listen to enough reasons why I would be miserable in New York, why it was not the place to go to, and I'd back out. I'm frightened enough to be talked out of it pretty easily."

"Then why go at all?"

"Because I must—you've said yourself . . ."

He nodded. "So you decided to tackle the hardest and the toughest place of all—the brightest, the most glittering, the hardest of all."

"Don't! Don't! It makes it harder."

"The rewards are great too—if you come prepared. If you know what to expect. How long are you going to be there?"

She shook her head. "I don't know. As long as I can stand it. I'm enrolling for some courses at N.Y.U. I suppose I'll get some part-time work. There isn't much money. . . . I know Father's been scraping to get it together. I feel badly about it, especially now with the harvest time almost here and he'll need every penny. But I've got to go, and he knows it. He didn't even try very hard to talk me out of it. He's said just about the things you've said, but sadly —as if he never expects to see me again. And yet he knows I have to go somewhere . . ."

"Because of the letter from your aunt? He's afraid that if you don't have one thing, you'll take the other?"

She looked down, and dug her fingers into the sand, not replying quickly, letting the grains run out in a slow stream. "Yes, that's why. He's taking the lesser of two evils. I wouldn't go to her, but he can't quite believe it. So he gives me something else. He can't quite see the sense of what I'm doing, but it's better than the other thing."

"Do you know the sense of what you're doing? Do you know why you're going?"

"That's part of why I'm afraid," she said haltingly. "I don't really know what to expect from all this. I know no one is going to open out the city for me to understand, as if it were a book. I'll get some sort of job—they told me I could get a job on my visa if I worked for some kind of foreign agency. I've told Albert—he couldn't understand it, of course—and he's fixed me up with a letter to the Netherlands consulate. I can probably do some typing for them, he thinks. And I can type in Spanish, or speak it if I have to. Susie Marshall has written to a friend, and I'm going to share an apartment—in the beginning, at any rate. So you see I've got all the tangible things lined up, but that isn't really why I'm going, I suppose. Mother pretends to understand it . . . and I suppose she does, better than Father." She looked up quickly. " He seems so *hurt* about it, Jim. As if I'd betrayed him, or something like that. He doesn't say anything, but he looks it. All he can think of is that Isobel offered me one thing, and he thinks this is the counter-offer. It isn't that way at all. I'd want to go whether or not Isobel had written. If I could only explain to him a bit better . . . If I only knew why myself, Jim."

" The getting of an education . . . the making of a woman," he said, his voice so low that it was almost a murmur.

" What?"

" That's it, isn't it? That's just about the only reason anyone picks up and goes somewhere when they're your age, Ginny. Of course, most don't go anywhere. It takes guts to pick yourself up and go."

She said quickly, " Do you think I've got guts?"

" Yes—you've got guts. And now let me kiss you properly, and don't pull away like a silly kid. You're going to be kissed a lot of times where you're going, and who better to teach you than old Jim?"

She came into his arms willingly. " I wish it were only you," she said. " I don't want to go . . ." Then her words were stifled by his mouth on hers.

" Shut up," he said. " You talk too much." He pulled her with him as he lay back on the towel; her mouth was sweet and tender. Her breasts, through the thin swimsuit, were pressed against him again in a way that increased to an almost unbearable pitch the desire that had been stirred by the sight of her in the water. He slipped down one strap of her suit, and caressed them wonderingly. " You're very beautiful, Ginny. A great many men will want to make love to you."

" Do you, Jim? Do you want to really make love to me."

" Of course I do." His hand tightened on her breast, and his lips left hers, and he kissed her throat and moved downwards. He felt her sharp intake of breath and her hand on his back gripped, and she moved herself in tightly against him.

"I won't go, Jim. If you would just say it . . . I wouldn't go to-morrow. I'd stay here with you. If you would make love to me . . . I want it, Jim . . . from you."

He heard the words in a kind of daze of desire, and it was a slow agony to force himself to relax his hold on her, to relinquish the softness and beauty of her body. As he sat up he heard her give a little sharp cry of protest. With a blind, scrambling motion he fumbled among his clothes on the sand beside him to find his cigarettes. It wasn't until he had lighted one and taken two long deep draws and felt the steadying effect of the tobacco that he could speak to her. He stared out to sea, not wanting to witness the hurt and humiliation that he knew would be here.

"That was a pretty silly thing you just said, Ginny. But I apologise to you for it, because if I hadn't been such a damn' fool it wouldn't have been said. You must never say anything like that again until you're sure—terribly sure—of what you're doing."

He felt her movement behind him. When she spoke her voice was muffled. "I meant it! I *am* sure." Glancing back he saw that she had turned on her stomach and her face was turned away from him, half buried in the towel. There was something utterly defenceless about the wild tangle of her wet hair and the clutching motion her outstretched fingers made in the sand.

"If you'd only say you'd like me to stay—then I would stay. Can't you love me, Jim? I think you could love me if you would let yourself."

For a moment he put his hand on her head, lightly, affectionately, almost without passion. "Poor Ginny. Things are pretty rotten for you, aren't they? It's hell to think you love someone and they don't—or won't—love you."

"I don't think—I know I love you." The words were a wild, desperate cry, muffled in the towel.

"If I said I loved you—if I made love to you, Ginny— you'd want me to marry you. And you'd be right. That's what people always hope for when they love, if it's a decent love."

"But you'll marry again! You'll marry *someone*—in time you'll stop thinking about her, and then you'll marry. Why can't it be me? Why can't it?"

He considered for a long time before he tried to answer her. She moved restlessly on the towel, like a child who writhes in a rage of non-understanding. He pitied her, and he wished the sentence he was trying to frame in his mind didn't sound so unsympathetic, so lacking in compassion. Suddenly she lifted her head and half shouted at him.

"Well—isn't that true? You *will* marry again, won't you?"

He drew on the cigarette heavily. "Yes—probably I will. Once you've been married—happily married—the chances are you'll marry again. Even if it's been unhappy you'll probably try again because you figure you got a bad break the first time. That's why those rich guys go on and give it a whirl the third and fourth time—and settle up a million dollars each time. They're optimistic, I suppose, but maybe it's because they've caught a glimpse, at some stage, of what the whole thing is like when it really works out. Maybe a lot of people get sour because what they thought they had falls apart on them, or maybe they never had it at all. And then there are people like me—lucky Joes who really had the lot. And it doesn't fall apart or fade away slowly. It gets taken from them."

He stubbed out the cigarette in the sand. "I had it, Ginny. I had everything there was to have in a marriage. Maybe it wouldn't have always been that way. Maybe the bright edges would have rubbed off in time. But I don't know that, do I? All I know is that I had it, and I'm still living with it. It's there in my mind every morning that I wake. I still live in that other place, Ginny."

She turned and sat up.

"I could wait," she said softly. "I could stay here and wait until you were ready."

"No—you're too young to be made to wait. You have to go on and find what you can for yourself. The timing is wrong for you and me, Ginny. We're out of step. You're ready now, and I'm not. Maybe at some time when you're gone—I mean gone for good—I'll realise that I wanted you to wait. But I don't know it now. All I know is that I'm still living back there in that other place. So that's why I can't let you wait—and I can't let myself make love to you."

He reached out and took her hand in his.

" It's tough luck, Ginny. And that's one of the things you're going to learn quickest when you are up there—that most of the time life's pretty unfair."

v

John and Katrien came with Ginny the next day. But it was Albert de Kruythoff who saved them all from too much awareness of the moment of leavetaking. He came hurrying into the airport building less than five minutes before the plane was to leave for San Juan holding a brown-paper bag stiffly before him.

" They tell me that all the American women wear these when they're leaving New York. I thought you might do it in reverse, Ginny. I think in Customs in New York they'll take them away, but you'll have them until then."

The paper bag contained a long spray of tiny green-spotted white orchids from Albert's garden. He hovered anxiously while Ginny pinned them on. " Too long," he pronounced. " They don't look right. I shouldn't have brought them."

" No—don't cut them. They're beautiful just as they are."

And then the p.a. system announced her flight, and she kissed Katrien and John quickly. Albert took her small luggage. " I'll walk with you to the plane." It was one of the few times Ginny had known Albert to use his position as Lieutenant-Governor; he walked without question past the official at the gate. At the bottom of the steps to the open door of the plane, Ginny took her bags, and then swiftly reached on tiptoe to kiss Albert's cheek. He turned a dull red, and took a stumbling step backwards. He opened his mouth, mouthed a word that had no sound, and then closed it again.

" Father will be all right, won't he, Albert? You think he's well again now, don't you?"

" I think he's well, Ginny. But if ever he isn't, I'll let you know. I promise you."

And then he turned and went loping across the tarmac, the too-long, ill-fitting shorts flapping about his thin reddened knees.

At San Juan airport she was alone. There had not been time for the expected courtesy call to the convent; John had wanted her to go and stay overnight, but Katrien had objected. " Let her go all in one piece and get it over with. It's hard enough as it is." She telephoned Santa Maria and was told that Mother Angela was at Barranquitas ; the novice who took her message was new since last June and wrote down Ginny's name without any recognition.

She had a Coke at the stand-up bar, checked her ticket again, and her money, and there was nothing else to do but walk among the interior gardens and flowers of the airport and feel slightly homesick already for the garden at Oranje Huis. She tried not to think of Jim and did not succeed. He was there in her mind, and he was going to be for a long time ; she understood, better than he knew, what he had said about living back in that other place of his marriage. She was glad that he had not come that morning to say good-bye to her under the eyes of Katrien and John ; she was glad that he knew better than to make that gesture.

She took her place in the long line of Puerto Ricans who were always present for the departure of every jet for New York. It was easy to pick those who were travelling and those who were staying by the heavy coats carried on the arms of the travellers. There seemed to be about six relatives for every traveller, and they all stood in line. At first she stood aside politely and let them in, and then she learned that you stuck fast to your place in the queue, and wriggled forward when you got the chance. It was very different from the leisurely, friendly procedure of flying to St. Charles, where you probably knew half of the people who were flying, and no one would have dreamed of fighting for a favoured seat for the thirty-minute journey. She thrust herself forward, packed solidly into the middle of the queue, and told herself grimly that if it was different, the difference was what she was going for, wasn't it? She occupied herself in the last ten minutes by practising her Spanish as she listened to all the tearful farewells ; it wasn't eavesdropping ; they were demonstrative and thoroughly public.

The flight number was called, and the metal gates drew back. Now the surge forward in the queue was real and earnest. She was prodded in the back, and pushed from the sides, and then as she edged nearer the official who checked the tickets, over the din she heard her name.

"Ginny! Ginny! Hold on a minute."

She stood still at the sound of Jim's voice and the thrust of the crowd nearly pushed her off balance. Then, without being able to see him, she turned aside and began the task of fighting her way out of the queue. Once she was on her way, the forward movement of the crowd expelled her. It was like being squeezed from a tube.

"Ginny—here. Over here." Then he was there, standing before her.

"What are you doing here?" she managed to say.

"I had to come over suddenly—business. Good thing I managed to catch you."

The quick hope that had risen in her died just as quickly. "Why?"

"I dug out this for you. It's the sheepskin coat I used to wear during the very bad weather up north. It used to reach above my knees so it shouldn't be much too long. Or cut a hunk off, if you want. The sleeves will turn back— it's fashionable that way, I think. Any case, do what you like with it."

"You came just to bring me this?"

He shrugged. "It suddenly occurred to me that you mightn't have anything warm . . ."

She indicated the coat lying across her arm. "Susie lent me her cashmere. I have a cardigan to put on under it."

"Cashmere—that'll do nicely for spring. Ginny, where you're going it's *cold*. Do you have any money to buy some warm clothes?"

She stiffened. "Father's given me enough."

"Well don't get all English on me. I was only asking . . . If you need anything, let me know. You hear, now? Well, you'd better get back in the scrum."

He bent down and kissed her lightly. "Good luck. And don't get lost up there."

And then he seemed to disappear among the crowd of relatives, and she was straggling at the end of the queue, clutching the great bulky sheepskin coat.

CHAPTER FIVE

Ginny found in the city some of what she thought she had
come to find, but she never was able to put a name to
it. She wrote to Jim: " *It is worse than I thought, and I am
more frightened than ever. And I am cold—cold right down
to my bones and right inside my brain so that I keep stepping
off the sidewalks in front of cars. If I don't die of cold there's
a good possibility I'll be killed in a street accident. At the
same time I'm more alive than I've ever been in my whole
life. I've been shocked and shaken out of my senses, and when
I come home at night I'm so tingling with what I've seen
that I can't go to sleep. I think my eyes and my ears have
grown to twice their size.*"

Home was a third-floor walk-up apartment in a brownstone in Greenwich Village shared with a girl called Barby
Hutchinson who was an older sister of one of Susie Marshall's
school friends. It was also shared with whomever Barby
could persuade to move in and help pay the rent. It was
dirty and over-hot at times, with sudden piercing draughts
that came from the ill-fitting window-frames; cockroaches
scuttled away whenever anyone switched on the light in the
kitchen, and the bathroom was perpetually damp from the
strings of underwear and blouses that always hung there.

" I get so sick and tired of listening to that damn drip,"
Barby said. " Next thing Du Pont wants to do is take the drip
out of the drip-dry."

Ginny grew accustomed to seeing total strangers unpacking
in the tiny back bedroom that she shared with whomever
else was Barby's other tenant at the time. Three came and
went in quick succession—Anne, Lee and Judith; there were
two others, but by that time Ginny just called them by any
name that came to mind. Barby herself lived in solitary
state in the larger bedroom in the front of the house, and she
both bossed and patronised the occupants of the back bedroom. " Look—you've got any problems?—come and see
me. I've worked in this man's town since I finished college,
and I know all the angles. Men?—bosses?—wolves—those

bitches you work with? Believe me, Barby knows all about them. Only don't come about money, because you won't get it. And don't bring boy-friends here to sleep overnight, because I'll throw you and him both out. Oh—and whose turn is it to clean up the kitchen? It's a mess!"

It was never Barby's turn. Ginny, and whoever shared the second bedroom at the time, were both resentful and tolerant of Barby's tyranny, putting up with it because she provided a haven and a rock of cynical common sense to which they all clung. And she did seem to know all the angles. She was a tall thin girl of about thirty, whose plainness was unnoticed because of an imaginative and daring flair with clothes. She was a secretary in a modelling agency, and was saving to start her own. When it didn't cost her money, she was generous in giving thought and energy to the problems of anyone who asked her help, seeming to enjoy arranging the lives of those about her. She was formidable on the telephone, bullying and cajoling, lying when it suited her, and she was nearly always successful.

"You want to do typing for the Netherlands consulate?" she said to Ginny. "You'll be doing them a favour! Who in this town can type in Dutch? Why, I'll bet you even have a hard time getting a Dutch dictionary!"

"I'm not very good," Ginny said—"I mean I couldn't do a complete translation. We always spoke English at home."

"I hope you're not going to tell them that!"

It was Barby who made the appointment for Ginny's interview, and sent her with a note to a dress manufacturer on Seventh Avenue to buy some clothes. "See that he gives you at least forty per cent off. Sam owes me favours." It was Ginny's first introduction to the system of discounting with which New Yorkers seemed to be obsessed. "Doesn't anyone pay the right price?" she asked Barby.

"What right price? *You* decide the right price."

She got the job at the consulate, which was routine and dull, but would provide some money and take the strain a little off John Tilsit.

"I should charge you commission, you know," Barby said, "for arranging the job. But I'll let it go this time."

"I assume Lieutenant-Governor de Kruythoff's letter had something to do with it."

Barby went back to filing her nails, shrugging. "Don't start pulling titles on me. I'm not impressed."

And Ginny, remembering the unimpressive qualities of Albert unless one knew him well, did not say any more. She was suddenly homesick for the gentle backwardness of St. Nicolaas, for the very fact that there was no one to be impressed with. It was a place where there seemed very little in the way of commission or discounts for anyone, and the prices were the same for everyone. That wouldn't interest Barby very much.

She worked very hard—the typing job, which was mostly trade reports, in the morning, and courses at N.Y.U. in the afternoon—English Litt. and French. She didn't know why particularly these, but they were a beginning. And then, without mentioning it in her letters to St. Nicolaas, she also enrolled in a course in the History of Art. This led her scuttling uptown to the galleries and museums, aware that most of the time she didn't even begin to understand half of what the instructor was talking about. When her papers went in they invariably failed to get a passing mark. One night the instructor, a fat, good-tempered man, asked her to remain after class.

"Miss Tilsit—may I ask why you're taking this course? I hope you don't imagine that this is one of those snap things you can take without trying."

"I don't think that at all. I've tried harder at this than I've ever tried at anything before," Ginny answered miserably. "It's just that I've hardly seen six paintings in my life and it's pretty confusing trying to sort out all this new stuff. I'm trying, though. I . . . I have a particular reason for wanting to learn about art. And design."

He adjusted his glasses and looked more closely at this girl with the wonderful blonde hair and the sun-tan that was only now beginning to fade. She had stood out in the usually anonymous class by the very intensity of her interest. The papers she sent in had been a shocking disappointment.

"Why, may I ask? Do you intend to make a career in design?"

"Oh, no!" she said quickly. "Nothing like that! It's just that a friend of mine . . . well, I'd just like to learn about it. This seemed a good place to start."

He nodded, but didn't comment. He had encountered many students in his classes, mostly women, who were trying to cram a subject they weren't interested in because they were in love with someone who was interested. " You understand, of course," he said, " that I'll have to fail you at the end of this semester."

She looked at the floor. " Yes, I understand. It's . . . it's to be expected, I suppose. There never was much of a chance I could make it."

He shrugged. " Try it again if you like. Take a summer course. If you look at enough of this ' stuff ' as you call it, something will take hold."

A weak smile filtered through her grimness. If she hadn't looked so tired she might have been quite beautiful, he thought. She was dressed as many of the young women students were—bulky skirts, black sweater and black cotton stockings. He wished they wouldn't dress that way; it was so damn' depressing. And this girl came to class wearing a sheepskin coat that was abnormally large for her, and made her look like a waif, or something equally old-fashioned. He supposed she was poor but it irritated him that anyone should misuse their looks the way she did.

" Yes," she said. " I'll try that. Thank you." She was about to turn away when he spoke again.

" By the way—do you happen to be connected in some way with the Tilsit china people? I understand it is a family name."

The faint smile vanished. " No—no, I'm not connected."

He shrugged. " I just thought I'd ask. My other subject is ceramics—there's a notable Tilsit china collection in England which is often represented in text-books. I thought I'd mention it . . . seeing that you're English, and it's not a common name."

" I'm not English. I was born in the Netherlands West Indies."

" I apologise, Miss Tilsit." He was amused, and he suspected that she wasn't telling the truth, not about the Tilsits anyway. " I hardly knew there was a Netherlands West Indies."

She nodded, as if to accept his apology, and in that instant all trace of the humble student seemed to be erased. There was more than a touch of the grande dame in her walk,

in her stiffly held back, in the angle of her head with its
windblown hair. It was wildly incongruous in this setting, in
those clothes. He felt like laughing, but even with her back
turned, he didn't even permit himself a smile, in case that
head should turn again, and he should find those wide grey
eyes fastened on him. When the door closed behind her
he began to collect his lecture notes, wondering, a little, why
she had bothered to lie to him.

That it had been a senseless lie was brought home to
Ginny the day that the card arrived from England. It bore
no message beyond the power expressed in its very brevity
—the heavy oblong of pasteboard alone in the envelope, the
name engraved in thick black characters: Miss Isobel Tilsit,
Tilsit, Dorset. On the other side was the handwriting she
remembered. *The Tilsit Showroom, 75 East 52nd Street,
New York City.*

Ginny placed it, guiltily, among the pages of a notebook,
and she did nothing about it for two weeks.

A light sleet was falling the afternoon late in March that
she finally went looking for the number on East 52nd Street.
Having no classes that afternoon, she had been at the Metropolitan Museum since she had left her job at noon,
wandering among the galleries indiscriminately, pausing sometimes, sometimes going through whole rooms at a rush,
taking in what her eyes could catch—furniture, jewels,
pictures, sculpture. It was a brilliant kaleidoscope of colour
and form and shape, pounding upon her senses in too swift
a time, so that she grew depressed by the very immensity
of the task she had imposed upon herself. It could never
be learned, she thought, starting from scratch. It could
not be learned in ten years, nor perhaps a lifetime if you
did not develop the eye and the turn of mind. The excitement she could catch, but the substance depended on the
kind of knowledge she did not possess. It did not seem
enough to just enjoy. She told herself that she was a fool
because she was chasing after some shadow of what Julie
MacAdam had been and had known. She was worse
than a fool to be trying so hard in so many directions,
and succeeding—where? In hardly any place, she thought.

She had spent half an hour slowly moving before the
showcases that displayed the Altman collection of Chinese

ceramics, gripped and entranced by the splendour of the colours, the simple beauty of some of the undecorated shapes . . . peach-bloom, ox-blood, imperial yellow, cobalt, turquoise . . . the brilliance of *famille rose* . . . Ch'ien Lung period, K'ang Hsi . . . how was she to remember? . . . the Four Seasons vases, peony for spring, lotus for summer, chrysanthemum for autumn, prunus for winter . . . beautiful and closed behind glass, all of them. She went downstairs to the section of European ceramics, the first time she had been there, this again out of some vague feeling of loyalty to her father. The French galleries . . . soft paste from Vincennes and Sèvres, astonishing jewel-colours, the Italian galleries, florid, quickly rushed through, the Dutch delft, the German galleries and the experimentation to discover the Chinese secret of hard-paste porcelain, and the final triumph of Meissen; the French galleries and the Wedgwood vases and pitchers in jaspers ware, the Chelsea figures and birds, the brilliant enamel blue of Royal Worcester. No Tilsit. Abruptly she turned and left the galleries and made her way back to the front entrance of the museum.

Out on Fifth Avenue she huddled into Jim's coat, and thrust her hands deep into the pockets. The March twilight was gathering in the distances of Central Park, dark blue going off to black. The trees along the Avenue shone wetly in the ghostly radiance of the street lighting. She shivered; her feet grew numb with cold but still she did not take any of the warm, crowded buses that would have carried her downtown to the Village. She walked on; two men spoke to her, and she took no notice; that was something she had learned quickly after coming to New York. And here was the end of the park and the discreet expensive elegance of the Plaza Hotel and the Bergdorf Goodman's windows. She stood for some moments studying the clothes on the models, trying to teach herself the line and the colour. In a month's time copies would be selling in the cheap stores downtown, and she had to remember. Then she crossed to Tiffany's. The subtle humour of the displays here had fascinated her from the first moment that she had taken this walk along Fifth Avenue. She had never thought of treating jewels as anything but pieces to be laid on black velvet. She smiled now to remember how it had been the first time that she had come here, and how she had gone back and forth between

these windows and the costume jewellery counter in Bonwit
Teller next door, trying to fix in her mind the difference
between the real and the fake. Now, with the approach of
Easter, there was a single emerald suspended on a near-
invisible wire above a golden eggcup. She stood there for
some minutes watching the emerald revolve in some slight
current of air; smiling at the sheer beauty of it. Then two
other people crowded against her at the tiny window, and
she was aware of the cold, and her aching feet.

She told herself she would walk as far as St. Patrick's,
look at Sak's windows, and then cross over and take the bus.
Four more blocks and she was at the corner of Fifty-Second
Street, and she was turning east, and her lips were repeating
the number written on Isobel's card.

She came opposite the number and stood on the sidewalk staring up at it. It was a narrow building, and on the
second floor the whole width was framed in one single
window which bore the words TILSIT CHINA in heavy gold.
Inside the coat pockets her hands clenched as she was caught
in the sudden surge of curiosity and excitement. She started
across the street without looking, and instantly there was
a sickening screech of tyres on the wet slick surface and
behind her a practised string of abuse from a cab-dr.ver.
Instinctively she ducked towards the lighted glass entrance
of number 75 and the refuge and escape it offered her. The
small self-service elevator was there, open, ready, and a man
standing in it with his hand poised to push a button.
" Going up?" he said.

" Er . . . yes. Two, please."

He pushed the button and took off his hat. The elevator
jerked upwards, and then stopped. The outer door slid open,
and the man pulled back the inner cage door. She had no
choice now but to step out; the two doors closed again
with great finality.

The showroom was long and narrow, carpeted in green,
and lighted warmly and brilliantly by great crystal chan-
deliers. She blinked in the light, and the reflection of the
lights bounc.ng off the surface of the china laid out on the
display tables and in racks on the walls. She turned her head
in bewilderment, and a new sense of panic as a man in
a thin dark suit and very white stiff shirt started to walk
towards her from the back of the showroom. She stared

at him like a rabbit hypnotised, wanting to turn and go, and unable to. Before he reached her with the silent quick salesman's walk, she knew that he had noted every detail of her appearance, and he knew that she had no real business here. She was acutely aware now of her wet shoes and coat, of the straggling ends of hair, and of her dirty woollen gloves.

"Can I help you, miss?" His accent was English.

"I just wanted to look. That is—may I?"

He gave the slightest bow, and frowned. "This is a wholesale showroom. If you wish to purchase anything we have to give you the name of the retailer who stocks it."

"Yes—that's what I want." She grasped the idea eagerly. "I want to choose something for a friend—a gift."

His expression told her plainly that he knew there was no friend, and no money for a gift. He nodded. "I'll be happy to supply you with any information you need." Then he looked at the clock at the end of the showroom. "We close in ten minutes. At five." Then he stepped backwards and came to rest with his back against the wall near the elevator, his hands clasped behind him. She knew he meant to watch her every second she would be there.

In a daze of confusion she turned and began a slow promenade down the length of the showroom between the display tables. It was all laid out before her, row upon row of place settings, dozens of different patterns, great richness and variety of colour—ruby, gold, jade green, a bold sepia figure on a white plate. Her eyes saw these things quickly, but without much comprehension. She felt a mist of tears before them so that the designs and colours wavered and dimmed. She could sense the gaze of the man in the black suit upon her, and she felt an interloper here. Suddenly there was the familiar tiny bluebell pattern of the china that her father had destroyed. And here was the cheese knife. She laid her fingers upon it tentatively, and at once the figure near the elevator stiffened more rigidly into attention. Ginny moved on.

This was Isobel's room, she thought. She, Ginny, had no business here, touching Isobel's things, moving in Isobel's world. She had said no to that long ago in the convent sitting-room; it was not safe to linger and to touch. She could grow to think that she belonged here, and that these

were her things too. She came to the end of the showroom, to
the partition which separated it from the offices behind.
She sighed, and half shrugged, and had started to turn
back when the portrait caught her eye. It was the portrait
of a man, a middle-aged man in a high, tight Victorian
collar—a colour copy of an original oil, framed in an oval
of black velvet and gold. She stepped in closer to read the
words inscribed on the tiny brass plaque beneath the picture:

*George Martin Tilsit—Potter—*1880

She drew in a swift breath of excitement and her eyes went
once again to the face of the man. It was a round, gentle
face, with gentle eyes that peered through steel-framed spectacles. He had a fuzz of greyish sideburns down his cheeks,
though his chin was clean-shaven. Above the respectable,
almost stern black of his coat, the stiff, choking cravat,
he had the eyes, the soft, curving lips of a dreamer. Inaudibly
she mouthed the name—George Martin Tilsit. Who was
he?—was he her grandfather? She counted back swiftly—
no, her great-grandfather he would be. Her father's grandfather?—or great-uncle? It could be that George Martin
Tilsit had founded Tilsit china. There was nothing else
to discover about him. Just the single word of description,
potter. It had a humble, earthy sound that went well with
the face of the man. She studied the portrait again. Even
behind the spectacles the eyes were warm, inquiring. There
was none of Isobel in this face, and nothing of her father's
lean, ageing handsomeness, either. She wondered if he
had left nothing of himself to his descendants other than
the products of his industry and skill. She would have liked
to have known that she was some small remainder of this
man, but the link was missing. She had no knowledge,
and there was no one to ask. Rather sadly she turned
away.

The man was still standing by the elevator as she walked
back down the green carpet between the tables. He pushed
the button to summon it.

" I'm sorry—I'm afraid it's closing time. A minute past."

" Yes. I'm just leaving." She could hear the elevator
start on its way up. In a last moment of desperation she

turned to the man again, trying to ignore his obvious impatience.

" That portrait back there—George Martin Tilsit. Is he the founder of the pottery?"

"Who? Oh—that one." He shrugged. "I don't know. I suppose so. Mr. Green would be the man to tell you—but he's in England now. I've only worked for Tilsit two months. I used to be with Wedgwood." His tone clearly implied that the job and the product of Wedgwood had both been infinitely superior. "Will that be all now?" The elevator had come.

"Yes. That's all."

She never went back to the Tilsit showroom to ask Mr. Green about George Martin Tilsit. There would have been in that act too much of an admission of her interest, and it would have been something she would have had to hide from her father. There was also that strange feeling that had grown upon her in that room that she belonged there, a feeling to be resisted lest it should become too familiar and necessary. So she did not go back. What she did was to look up an encyclopædia of English pottery and porcelain in the Public Library. *Tilsit, George Martin; Master-potter and chemist. 1830-1883. Apprenticed to Wedgwood, but returned to his birthplace of Torrington, Dorset, where he perfected the techniques of making a translucent, very hard porcelain using china clay from Cornwall in combination with local clays from his own quarries. Assuming the name of Tilsit in 1865, he founded the china works in that same year. The Tilsit pottery now one of the most modern in England, having begun the conversion to electric kilns in 1939.* Then followed the mark with which Ginny's was now familiar:

She copied the entry into the back of a notebook where her eyes fell on it almost every day. Almost every day then, for a few minutes she pondered the question of why a potter called George Martin had assumed the name of Tilsit in 1865, and she lived with the remembrance of that gentle, homely face in the portrait.

I I

Spring came to New York with an abruptness that was usual to those who knew the city, but which to Ginny had all the violent swiftness of jerking back a curtain. The days had grown longer but the cold weather had lingered, grudgingly the temperature went above freezing for two weeks in a row, but nothing seemed to happen to the city, no leaf appeared, no urgency stirred. Then one afternoon, suddenly, Jim's sheepskin coat was far too heavy, and so was the sweater she wore under it. She walked across Washington Square in the direction of West 10th Street, where Barby's apartment was, and the people were sitting in their shirt-sleeves in the sun, and even the old men playing chess and checkers at the game tables had peeled off their heavy coats, and some of them had bare heads. For the first time since she had come here Ginny felt a lightening of her loneliness; she experienced a sense of oneness with these people sunning themselves on the benches. It was as if, with the harshness of the winter, they had lived through a time of testing together, and had achieved the bond of something shared. She felt friendly, and among friends.

When Barby got back to the apartment Ginny was ironing blouses and humming lightly.

" Well—what's got into you? Got yourself a boy-friend?"

" No—but maybe that's what I need. It's spring fever, I think. I've only read about it before—I never expected it to really *do* anything to you. There isn't any spring that you'd notice in the tropics."

" Some place!" Barby commented. She dumped her over-size handbag on the floor. " Well, now's the time to do something about it. Go get yourself some clothes, and a decent hair-cut, and stop looking like something left over from beatnik week."

" Is that what I look like?" Ginny moved over to the mirror above her dressing-table. She smoothed back the loose strands of hair, peering at her own image. Her fading tan made her look washed-out, her eyes were darkened with fatigue. Her hair was just hair—nothing more.

" Most of the time you look as if you haven't caught up with yourself."

" Well, I haven't! I'm here, but I'm not quite here. Do you understand? It's been like a kind of exile."

" You take yourself too seriously, Ginny. Just think of all the millions of kids who'd like to be in your shoes. Relax—live a little. Enjoy the spring, and go buy yourself some clothes."

" The money . . .?"

" Forget the money—just for once. I'll tell you something, Ginny. At your age there's always a little money coming from somewhere—somehow. This is the time of your life you invest in yourself—not stocks or a savings account. Now, if I looked like you . . ." Barby shrugged. " Well, I don't, so what am I kidding myself about? Listen, why don't we skip cooking to-night and go eat some clams and spaghetti at Mario's? Like I said—live a little."

Even when Ginny remembered afterwards that she had paid for the dinner for both of them, it seemed worth it.

" The days are warmer, and the little green swellings on the trees have broken into buds," Ginny wrote to her father. *" I can't believe how different I feel. As if I had shed a skin or broken out of a cocoon."*

And John Tilsit wrote in reply: *" Down here it is as changeless as ever. Most of the cane is cut. The days are warmer, but not much longer, the same trees and shrubs bloom as continually—poor things that never knew a change of season. When I remember the English springs I know that you were right to go. No one should ever live a life in which there has never been a spring. But don't stay for ever, Ginny. I miss you."*

As the tension of the winter slipped from Ginny, when there was no longer the need to half-run in the streets to escape the numbing cold, the city began to change for her.

Until now it had been a thing of brilliance and glitter, the dazzling radiance of the tall glass buildings under the cold, sunlit sky. It had worn the improbable icy beauty of the diamonds casually displayed in Tiffany's windows. The winter city was a city of the rich, with fur coats commonplace on the streets, and all the opulence and display closed in behind drawn curtains and double glass doors. In the streets there was only the cold.

Now the streets were touched with the softening magic of trees in leaf, and people strolled with no more aim than to look and smell the air. Sidewalk tables sprouted about some restaurants in the Village, and the bright sun-awnings went up on the windows. The ice-skaters were gone from Central Park and the picnickers were taking over. There seemed more to do for less money. The city stopped looking in upon itself, seeing only its own glitter and beauty; it suddenly seemed to explode into the surrounding countryside, leaving the centre quiet on week-ends, as if everything interesting was happening elsewhere. The suburban dwellers came into their own, and the apartment dwellers, high in their cliffs, replanted their terrace gardens, killed by the winter frost and soot, and checked their air-conditioners.

"You think this is quiet?" Barby said to Ginny. "Just wait until July and August. It's dead!"

The restlessness of the city came upon Ginny now. She felt as if she were drifting a little, uncertain of direction now that the first months were over, and the first strangeness worn away by familiarity. She discovered that she was tired, and perhaps, too, that she was bored by the routine of work she had set for herself. The warmer, softer days encouraged her to idle. She got to her job, and she attended the classes she was supposed to attend, but now she strolled in the streets when she left the consulate at lunch-time, and forsook the galleries of Madison Avenue to gaze into the windows of the fashion speciality stores on Fifth. The library books she had set herself as extra-curricular reading often went back unread. She looked about her, seeking to break the isolation of the long winter, and in the very act of seeking she found that the break was already made. She stayed to have coffee with small groups after classes, and the invitations followed on that. She accepted them all.

Barby watched her dressing for a party that an aspiring

textile designer was giving in a loft on 23rd Street. She was lounging in the doorway with a cigarette in a long holder between her teeth; she nodded slowly. "Well—so you're breaking out at last. I was beginning to think that shell of yours was permanent." She nodded again. "That's a pretty good-looking dress Sammy picked up for you. You can tell him I said so." Barby insisted that Ginny could look in Fifth Avenue shops all she wanted, but that she was not to buy there. Sammy would get it for her wholesale.

"As a matter of fact I picked it out for myself. Sammy thought it didn't do anything for me."

"It does things all right. Here—I'll lend you my coral necklace." She went and rummaged in her room for a while and came back and dropped it about Ginny's neck, with a knot tied low in the front. Ginny looked at herself in the mirror and giggled.

"I look like those old photos Mother has of herself taken back in the twenties."

"You look damn' good."

Other people thought so too. She began to have a lot of dates—foreign movies and coffee with some of the boys from her classes at N.Y.U., each always paying for themselves because no one seemed to have any money. And meals at Chinese restaurants because they were cheap. Sometimes she dined more expensively uptown with young men she met at parties in the Village. These were more ritualistic performances, and perhaps the young men expected some return on the expensive steaks and martinis, because a few kisses in the taxi going home seemed not enough. Ginny was sometimes grateful for the rules Barby had laid down. "I share the apartment—I'm sorry you can't come in."

"Well, look—let's go to my apartment for a night-cap. I've got a wonderful old brandy that's not quite finished yet."

She found that if she managed to evade the invitation the first time, she was often given a second chance. A second refusal would mean the end of that particular young man. There wasn't much time to waste in New York on girls who didn't co-operate.

"Don't worry," Barby said. "At your age there are always more men."

There were more men, and after a time to Ginny they

began to seem frighteningly the same. The ones who were not students seemed all to wear the same careful, correct clothes, and she began to recognise the image that she had seen in the advertisements in the New York Times. They worked in brokers' offices, or advertising agencies, or insurance companies ; they were going to marry at the right time, and when it was the right time to have children they would move to the suburbs. Sometimes, in the middle of dinner, Ginny found herself calling one of them by the name of the last one.

"Look—I'm not Joe. My name's Frank—do you mind?"

The world of the students was less controlled, but it had its own kind of conventions. Even in a few weeks she learned that. She went to beer parties in loft buildings, and in houses like the one Barby lived in ; they were all much alike—the folk songs and the jazz, and the late into the night discussions of art and books and music that went wildly beyond her experience and understanding. She began to suspect that a lot of the talk was faked, was jargon that was learned and came easily. In this discovery she found that there were many of the young men and women who were just like herself—who knew no more of the essence of the city than she did, and who struggled as painfully to find it and grasp it. The heart of this city was ambition—sometimes accompanied by talent, but often not. To be immune from this fever seemed to mark one as something of a fool. Ginny found that she couldn't lie about herself easily. When she was asked why she had come to New York, it seemed inadequate to say, "To study a little —just look around," but it was not possible to deceive herself or anyone else that a few courses in English Litt. and French constituted any real purpose. She couldn't point to any goal. It wasn't possible to say, "There's a man down on a little Dutch island in the Caribbean that I'm in love with and I'd like to marry. So that's why I'm in New York." She couldn't even fake ambition. She learned to recognise the posturings and the attitudes of ambition, but she never learned to fake it.

Her lack of involvement seemed particularly irritating to Phil Hart, one of the students from her art history class who was preparing to become a scenic designer. He took her a few times to off-Broadway theatre, and to some parties given mostly by people on the fringe of show business. She was having a hamburger with him one night after the theatre, only half listening to his dissection of the play and the scene design and thinking that it was six weeks since the last rather brief letter from Jim, when he suddenly slapped down his mug of coffee.

"For God's sake, Ginny—what's with you? Aren't you interested? Every girl I've ever known has wanted to be something—or do something. Don't you want to act—or paint? You go to that art history class and you really don't care a damn about art, do you? And the play to-night? Did you even try to understand it?"

"I tried. But I think anyone who says they understand for a certainty what Becket or Ionesco is trying to put across is a liar. Perhaps I just want to know that such things exist. It's possible to want to know without becoming too involved." She smiled at him. "I'm not very ambitious, Phil. I can't help it—it's just the way I am."

He softened under her smile. "Well—maybe you're lucky, at that."

It was Phil who took her to the party where she met Eliot Russell. It was a Saturday night late in June; the temperature that afternoon had been close to ninety, and the heat still lay like a thick cloth over all the city, so that each movement seemed difficult, and it was too much trouble to talk. There was a somnolence about the gathering, a deadness that whisky and gin did little to liven. The party was in an apartment on Riverside Drive—an apartment that seemed to Ginny as big as a house, with rooms that opened like whole wings off the central foyer. "It kills you, doesn't it?" Phil said. "Genuine Victorian too—or almost. The whole of Riverside Drive has got places like this. You could get lost in them. Someone lent it to Marty's girl-friend for the summer. I hope they get it back intact." He forced a path through the groups in the hall, and surveyed the huge crowded living-room professionally. "There's no one here," he pronounced.

"I would have thought there was, if you hadn't told me," Ginny answered.

"I mean no one who counts," he said without a smile. "It's too late in the year—everyone's already doing summer stock. Marty said that Saltzman was going to be here, but there never was a chance of that. You wouldn't catch Saltzman in New York on a Saturday night in the summer." Even to Ginny the name of Saltzman was familiar as one of Broadway's most prolific producers. She had grown accustomed by now to hearing the rumour going round these kind of parties that so-and-so was coming, and then the girls would all go into the bedroom and re-do their hair, and re-apply their pale lipstick, and the men who wanted to be actors would seek to draw a group around them as an audience. More often than not the rumours were wrong— the producer, director or famous critic did not appear.

It was a very long night for Ginny. For some reason she was bored almost from the moment she entered, bored and tired. It seemed too much effort to talk, or to play the gullible listener which was a role she found more successful than any other in this place where everyone wanted to talk about themselves and eternally sought the reassurance that whatever they were doing was right. Phil had left her side long ago—he usually did at parties, restlessly seeking the very heart of whatever was to be found in the room. He would bring her and leave with her, but that was about the only contact they had in the hours they stayed. Phil was in the habit of staying late. She wandered from group to group, the ice melting in her glass to warm water, hardly bothering to try to enter any of the conversations on which she eavesdropped. The party was not going well— not for her or for most other people. She heard arguments that grew into near-quarrels. Everyone seemed to be drinking too much, and the food had been eaten long ago. Many people began to leave. The heat sat in upon the room in a damp fog. Looking around she saw that only the younger ones remained ; the voices were loud and slurred. There was ash spread like a film over the silken green Chinese carpet, and wadded balls of paper napkins. On one of the many sofas, a couple were in passionate and oblivious embrace. Ginny bent down and picked up a cigarette butt at her feet that someone had ground into the carpet. Close to her a man's voice said, " What are you doing, Beautiful— cleaning up? There are better things I can think of to do."

He was drunk. He put his moist hand over her bare

arm, and his fingers pressed into her breast. "Why don't you and I go off for a little quiet talk somewhere, sweetheart? Outa all this noise."

She stepped back quickly and slammed into the wall. The shock of it numbed her for a moment, and the man, smiling, moved in close again. He was quite young, handsome, the clean white collar of his shirt only a little wilted from perspiration, his suit looking freshly pressed even in the heat. He was the young man of the advertisements, and he disgusted her.

She turned and hurried along the hall towards the bedroom where she had left the little clutch purse she had brought. He stood in the living-room and watched her, not moving, just waiting. She turned the handle of the door and it was locked. Behind her the man laughed. As she looked back he wagged his finger. "Ah—ah! Not there, sweetheart. Marty and Sylvie have engaged that one for the next half-hour. But there are plenty of others . . . loads of room here. How about it?" Almost beside her another door opened, and a girl and a man came out, the girl tucking in long strands of her red hair that escaped the high knot. "There!—whadid I telya! Loads of room." Ginny felt sick as she stared past the couple to the rumpled bedspread and the spilled glass of liquor on the floor. "Whasamatter, sweetheart? You're not frightened of Johnny, are you? Ol' Johnny can take care of you." He had walked up close to her again.

She didn't speak. She just pushed against his chest and he responded like a wobbly toy, staggering backwards a few paces. She moved past him, down the hall.

"Sweetheart? Aw, com'on!"

Where was Phil? She looked quickly into the living-room and couldn't see him. There was a lot of noise coming from the kitchen. There were about half a dozen people there and Phil wasn't among them either. Beyond the huge kitchen was a maid's suite, with the door closed. She was suddenly aware of all the closed doors she had passed. Abruptly she turned on her heel, walked back along the hall to the front door, opened it and snapped it shut behind her. The man called Johnny had stood watching her, and he gave a bleat of protest as she closed the door. She rode down in the self-service elevator.

She had to wait for the doorman to come and unlock the outer door of the lobby.

"What time is it?"

"Some time after two, miss. Will I call a taxi?"

She hesitated. "No. Thanks."

She stood on the top of the white marble steps. The Drive was quiet. No traffic moved for the moment; the dense bulk of the leafy trees almost obscured the grey-black glimmer of the river. The air was very close and heavy. Behind her she could feel the doorman watching through the glass doors. She supposed she should have had him call a taxi—she could have had the driver wait at the other end while she got the money. She regretted the little clutch purse left behind in the locked bedroom with Marty and Sylvia. Phil was always telling her not to leave her purse around at parties. She never carried more than a single dollar in it—just enough for a taxi if it was necessary. The heat oppressed her. It would have been good to walk for a while, but no one but a fool walked alone at this time in New York. She stood poised at the top of the stairs, as if she were held there between two worlds— the dimly-lighted rococo lobby behind her, the heavy smell of dust in the velvet sofas that stood about, and out here the dried earthy dust of the strip of the park between the Drive and the Henry Hudson Parkway. Cars moved on the parkway like beetles under the blue glare of the sodium lights. She was reminded swiftly of the blue lights along the waterfront at St. Charles and how they had always sym-bolised fairyland from the gallery of Oranje Huis. Her eyes misted suddenly with a wave of homesickness; she wanted away from this damp, oppressive heat and the trees that smelled of dust and tar, and the river that stank at low tide. She turned back to call the doorman, wondering how she would say that she had no money to tip him.

The voice seemed to come from a distance, but the tone was low. "Want a lift?"

She spun around. "What?" She looked down at where the voice had come from, and wondered how she had not noticed him before—a man sitting in a small open car parked at the kerb. His face upturned to hers in the light was young and extraordinarily handsome. He was un-smiling. His words weren't an invitation, just a question.

"Want a lift?" he repeated patiently. "You don't seem quite to have made up your mind to leave the party or go back."

She came down three steps towards him. "Were you there? I didn't see you."

"We were introduced. I don't think you saw very much up there, did you? Well—are you leaving or going back?"

She liked the sound of his voice. It was grave and low-pitched, and coldly sober. "I wasn't planning to go back. I left my pocket-book up there, but there wasn't anything in it except a dollar and a lipstick." Then she smiled because it seemed such a foolish thing to say. "But it's the dollar I need."

He shook his head. "Whenever a girl leaves without her lipstick, she's in a hell of a hurry. Where do you want to be taken?"

"I live in the Village. But aren't you waiting for some-one?" She advanced across the sidewalk towards him. He hadn't once smiled and even now he made no gesture of invitation. He simply switched on the ignition and the car instantly responded with a roar of a powerful engine. "No. I'm not waiting for anyone. Just sitting. Better get in. It's no time for a girl to be wandering around alone." He reached across and opened the door. She had to walk out on the traffic side to get in.

"Thanks." She slid into the low bucket seat beside him. "I'd better get it over with," she said, "because everyone must ask what kind of car this is the first time they get in it."

"Alfa Romeo." He didn't elaborate. He was heading north on the Drive, going quite slowly, not in the way she would have expected anyone to drive who owned a fast sports car. He didn't look at her at all, but stared straight ahead, his face composed and rather cold-seeming in the light from the street lamps. She glanced at him several times, sideways. He was more than handsome; he had one of those rare faces that in a man can be called beautiful. She guessed that he was in his late twenties, though it was his manner that spoke of his age, rather than his face. There was no eagerness in him. Only a kind of weary patience. They reached an intersection and he stopped for a red light.

"Are you in a terrible hurry to get home? I mean—would

you mind if we went across the bridge for a few minutes of air?"

"Is that why you were sitting there—deciding where to go?"

"Perhaps. I really don't know why I was sitting there. Sometimes you just s't. What does it matter where it is? Well, will you go?" He asked the question but she thought that he was almost indifferent to her reply. If she said no, that she wanted to go home, she guessed that he would turn without protest and head downtown. She also guessed that when he had dropped her he would do what he had originally intended to do, and she would regret that she had not gone with him.

"Why not?" she said. "I was standing there on the steps a moment ago thinking about home and wish'ng I could for a moment get away from this smell of dust and gasoline."

"Where is home?" He turned the car swiftly on to the parkway.

"A little island called St. Nicolaas—in the Netherlands West Indies."

He merely nodded, and said nothing. She was pleased that he had asked none of the usual questions. He just left her to herself, and she sat while the hoardings and the warehouses of this upper end of the parkway moved by her, and the bends revealed the string of lights, like a delicately hung necklace, of the George Washington Bridge. The wind whipped by her face; it was a little cooler here by the water. Her hands lay limply by her sides; for minutes at a time she closed her eyes and let the air fan by her unseeingly. She had a curious feeling that it didn't matter to the man beside her what she did; it was a conviction, there from the moment that he had first spoken, that he wanted nothing of her. She opened her eyes, and they were already up on the bridge, and Manhattan was behind. The tall towers of lighted apartment buildings diminished as they sped away; looking over her shoulder and down-river, she thought that hazy hot air made them look less formidable, less brittle than they had seemed on the only other occasion she had been on this bridge—a cold brilliant dusk in February when she had walked its long length just to be able to write to Jim that she had crossed the Hudson at last and had been in New Jersey. And he had written back laconically and asked, "*Why New Jersey—what's there?*"

They slowed at the toll booths, and then flashed up the ramp, and Ginny read the sign Palisades Parkway. Manhattan seemed far away across the river, huddled, toy-like. She stared in fascination, and found an answer to Jim's question—from New Jersey you can see New York. She was taken unawares when the car suddenly pulled off the parkway into a lookout promontory. The young man cut the engine and the lights. The breeze coming at them from the darkness now had its own sound back again, the rush of wind up from the water and the lifting of the leafy trees behind them.

"And what are you doing so far from home?" he said, as if the conversation had never been broken off.

"Pottering about—dabbling." For some reason she knew she didn't have to make claim to any ambition with this man; she felt suddenly free to say what she liked. "I don't have any real reason for being here. I'm not doing anything seriously. Just passing some time because one has to pass time somewhere. And I suppose most people, once in a lifetime, want to come and see that." She pointed across the river to the apartment towers, and the whole mass of the island down-river, the bridge, the moored yachts.

"Well, that's home for me. At least that's where I was born."

"Aren't you at home there?"

He shrugged. "Who is? You're only at home in that place when you're trying to win something from it. My father and his father won it all for me before I was born. In a kind of a way that takes the zest out of it. There are no rewards when you don't have to try." For almost the first time he turned to look at her. "Ginny?—that's your name, isn't it—Ginny?"

"Yes."

"Ginny—why are you here if you don't want anything from it?"

"I'm here because—I suppose I'm waiting here. I'm hoping for something to happen and if it doesn't perhaps I'll get used to the idea—or perhaps I won't get used to the idea, and then I won't be able to go home."

"So you're away from home rather than in New York?"

"I suppose you could put it that way—yes, that could be what it is. But if I was going to be away from home, then the place had to be New York. There's a reason for that."

And now she found herself telling him about Jim. She talked with no sense of restraint, and no embarrassment. The man beside her meant nothing to her, and she meant nothing to him. She knew that to talk to him about a stranger, another man, did not offend him. He had asked her into the car only because he had felt like company. She probably would never see him again. For a short time he could bear the burden of her months of silence and loneliness; he would take it because they both knew he did not have to carry it for longer than this hour. He sat very still as she talked, only his cigarette moving in the darkness, and she took his stillness for acquiescence.

"So you see how it is," she said finally. "Every time something comes up here that means my getting more closely involved I run away from it because I keep telling myself that I'm not here for ever. I *have* to keep telling myself that Jim will change. And so I don't want any ties that will hold me here. I go to awful parties like the one to-night, and it doesn't really matter to me what those people do because I know I'll never see them again. I just don't care."

"And if Jim doesn't change?"

"Then I'll have to change, won't I? At the moment I can't believe that I won't get what I want, but I suppose I might have to come to believing it one day."

"Most of us do, Ginny. But hang on as long as you can—the day you give up is a pretty bleak one."

He snapped on a lighter to light a fresh cigarette and for a moment his face was clearly revealed. It wore, for the moment, a look of strain and it was older than she had at first thought. She said suddenly: "Thank you for listening to me. I haven't ever talked about this to anyone. I've never wanted to."

The lighter snapped off. "That's all right. I'm a pretty good listener."

"You're a patient one. It's very late."

"Yes. I'll take you back." He reached over and flicked on the ignition switch. Now the noise and the vibration was between them again and the time of quiet was past. She felt that he had counted himself among those of whom she had said she didn't care that she would never see them again; he had probably never intended it to be different. Now she thought that she would like to know him better, but the chance was gone. Then it struck her that she didn't even know his name. She thought then suddenly that this might perhaps be the essence of what was meant by living in a city as big as this one—the realisation that you could give your whole life in intimacy to a stranger for an hour, and still not touch his hand or know his name.

As they turned out of the parking area the headlights flashed briefly on a sign: NO PARKING AFTER MIDNIGHT. They had to go a long way north on the parkway, to a place called Alpine, before it was possible to turn south again. When they did the skies over Manhattan were lightening with the dawn.

He spoke only once during the drive, to ask the street and the number she wanted. He had stopped in front of it before he spoke again. "Call me some time, Ginny —when you feel you want to talk again."

"I've talked enough," she said stiffly. "I'll wait for you to call. What's your name?"

"Eliot Russell—I have a Third after my name. So don't call my father's house by mistake. He's Eliot Russell Jr. Though he'd probably be delighted to have a girl calling about me."

Before she could reply he slid out of his seat and came to open the door on her side. "I'll call that apartment later to-day and go get your pocket-book for you. No reason why you should lose it because other people act like pigs." Again she felt the coldness that had seemed to characterise him as he sat in the car by the kerb. "I'll leave it here for you, at this address."

"If you like to take the trouble, I'd be grateful."

"It's no trouble." He said it without enthusiasm, walking beside her to the bottom of the flight of steps leading to the doorway of the brownstone. Ginny was puzzled by this strange combination of courtesy and lack of friendliness. It was as if he performed these gestures mechanically. And yet she had been in New York long enough now to know that such things were never done without reason. What cost time and trouble was valuable in this city. This man had listened to her with patience, given his time, and was now saying that he would go out of his way to retrieve a cheap pocket-book for her. And yet there was a coldness and indifference here. She felt as if she had been rebuffed, and it was humiliating not to understand why. With her hand on the stone balustrade of the steps, she turned to face him fully.

He spoke first. " Don't ask your questions, Ginny—I'll tell you." For just one second he put his hand lightly on hers where it rested on the balustrade. " I'm not going to kiss you good night. I don't like to kiss girls. Do you understand, Ginny?"

He left her staring after him as he strode across the sidewalk and slipped back into his seat. The roar of the engine shattered the dawn stillness of the block.

Ginny slept through most of Sunday, and when she woke Barby was drinking coffee and writing letters. The day was stiflingly hot. The heat had lain in the apartment for weeks now ; even when a cooler wind sprang up there seemed no way to flush the dead air from the small rooms. Ginny felt that her skin had dried out, as if she had been lying in the sun. In her nightgown and bare feet she went to drink a cup of coffee with Barby.

" Well—Handsome brought back your pocket-book about an hour ago." She lifted her glasses and looked hard at Ginny. " I thought Phil Hart took you to that party?"

Ginny wrinkled her nose. " Oh, it turned out to be one of those messy affairs—you know, people going off into bedrooms. I didn't wait for Phil—I just left."

" And found Handsome? Who is he?"

" His name is Eliot Russell—the Third, he said."

" Eliot Russell?" Barby dropped her glasses back on her nose. " Well, kid, you got yourself something. I suppose you know that?"

Ginny shook her head ; the movement hurt because her head was aching. " Should I know?"

" Eliot Russell the Third." Barby's eyes narrowed. " Well —let's see—that would be the old boy's grandson, I suppose. Oil—and lumber, I think. One of the last of the big-money boys. Almost a robber-baron, I suppose. Not a Rockefeller, you know—but not doing too badly, either."

Ginny digested the information, then shrugged. " So

what? He gave me a lift and brought back a pocket-book. I suppose he has ordinary manners like everyone else . . ."

"Don't you know yet—money is never ordinary. It's——" She leaned closer. "Ginny, what's the matter?"

"Nothing!" Ginny snapped. "What should be wrong?" because you don't look like that for nothing. Come on now. Tell Granny."

Ginny hunched over her coffee, sipping it slowly, for once not minding its bitterness.

"Shut up, Barby! If you must know, Eliot Russell isn't for me or for any other woman. He doesn't like women. He told me so himself. He came right out and said it!"

"Is that so . . ." Barby's finger-nails rapped lightly on the table. "Well, Ginny, it looks as if you just found yourself a brother."

III

In Eliot Russell Ginny made contact, her first and only contact, with money as it was understood by the rich— money big enough to assume almost an identity of its own, having a power that performed actions nearly of its own volition, that could force decisions and bring influence and pressure without having to move itself. It was the kind of money that made money just by standing still.

In the person of Eliot Russell the image of money was not clear, but it lay all around him in the inevitable trappings of wealth. Through him Ginny began to see wealth in one of its aspects, which turned out to be an attitude of mind. It was a way of looking at things and at life in a manner in which the problem of money never arose, and after a while she began to realise that if this had been an attitude since birth, then each day had a curious flatness to it because one whole aspect of struggle for material needs was missing. For the Russells, money had gone beyond the point where there was any need either to display it or to think much about it. Its preservation demanded their attention, but that was all. For the rest it was a fact of existence.

"That's the difference," Barby said, "between being very rich, and just being rich."

When she first knew him, because she had been expecting otherwise, Ginny said to Barby, "He doesn't seem to enjoy what he has. He doesn't seem to enjoy himself at all."

"My heart bleeds for him! Just try him without all that money as padding and see how much less he enjoys himself."

After the aloofness had been probed there was a quality of humility in Eliot Russell which touched Ginny strongly. She was struck by it on the day, a week after the party, that she came out of the consulate at noon and found him waiting on the sidewalk. He was better-looking than she remembered him—the classic face under the brown-blond hair, the cheekbones and firmly modelled lips. He was dressed with masculine severity and plainness that seemed to attempt to distract from the beauty of the face above it ; his body was ramrod straight. He did not permit himself to look at any of the people who passed by. Ginny had a swift intuition of an extraordinary self-discipline that came sometimes near to breaking, that wore itself out and in its shredding allowed Eliot to express himself in a contempt towards women, to let them know, initially and finally, that they were rejected. He had chosen to do that with her, in defiance and shame, at four o'clock in the morning on a street in Greenwich Village. Now his eyes became fixed on her in a wary scrutiny, and it occurred to her that he was waiting nervously for her reaction, as if he might expect a rebuff to cancel the one he had offered her. As early as this, then, she began to pity Eliot.

She held out her hand. Something like relief broke on his face, an expression which he quickly cut off. " Hallo, Eliot."

" Hallo, Ginny. Are you busy for lunch? Would you like to have a bite with me?"

She nodded. " Yes—please! " He automatically reached to take her large leather bag, a cheaper copy of Barby's. " I'll carry it," she said quickly. " It isn't heavy."

" No—let me. When I first saw you you hadn't anything at all in your hands, and you looked so darn free. . . ." He had her elbow and was guiding her across the street. It was a strange feeling of being taken in tow, as if he had to exert some degree of masculinity in any way he could.

At the same time she sensed that the very gentleness of his actions was a plea to her not to go against him, not challenge his precarious authority.

They had lunch at the Museum of Modern Art. Eliot ate sparingly, hardly at all, she thought; she looked up from her plate with some embarrassment to find him staring at her. She flushed. " I'm sorry—I'm terribly hungry."

" Good!" And he went off to the counter and got another salad and a cream cake. " I'm indulging you for once," he said, smiling slightly. " But watch the cream—you'll ruin your complexion and your figure." Ginny felt it was exactly as if a woman had spoken. Eliot sat in silence, drinking coffee, while she finished.

" Do you have classes this afternoon?"

" No—I'm being lazy for the rest of the summer."

" Good—then we'll go downstairs and take a walk through the galleries." He drew out her chair for her. " I don't like your Jim MacAdam very much, Ginny. I think he's an arrogant, self-opinionated bastard to pass by a girl like you. I'd like to tell you to forget him, but I know that wouldn't do any good. So—since you've come to New York looking for a liberal education, we might as well start here."

He led her through the galleries, pointing, explaining a little, applying where he thought it was necessary. He was clever, Ginny thought. There was no trace of patronage, and he never explained the obvious. He left her to ask the questions, and when the answers came they were more lucid and revealing than anything she had yet heard at N.Y.U. My God, she thought, he's brilliant and he's rich, and he isn't cocky about it.

Suddenly she said, " Eliot—how old are you?"

" Does it matter? I'm twenty-nine. Why?"

" Nothing—you seem to know an awful lot, that's all."

" I've had a lot of time to learn." The words were thrown backwards at her, over his shoulder, angrily. " Come on —let's go somewhere else."

They rode uptown in a taxi to the Frick Collection. Eliot again took her arm up the short flight of steps; Ginny felt that he clung to her. The guard came to attention a little and nodded.

" Good afternoon, Mr. Russell."

" How are you, Morgan?"

" Fine—just fine, sir."

" Do they all know you?" Ginny whispered when several more guards had acknowledged Eliot.

" Most of them. I'm here pretty often—they know the family."

It was to Ginny an astonishing fact to discover that anyone could be as well known in Manhattan as she was in St. Nicolaas. It was the first time that the city ever got a human proportion for her. Then later the impression was corrected when she began to understand that the Russell money had more than human proportions, that Eliot made no move without the knowledge of the money somehow foreshadowing him.

He dropped her arm now, and moved slowly through the rooms of Henry Frick's house, turning to the Van Dycks and Rembrandts as if they were friends, well-beloved friends. Here he made no attempt to give Ginny anything but what her own senses gave her of the richness and colour. He moved more by himself, pacing the huge rooms with a certain authority. Ginny thought that he belonged more to this scene than back in the stark purity of the Museum of Modern Art. He seemed less defensive here, as if he walked on home ground.

He said abruptly, " Henry Clay Frick and my grandfather did business together once. They were both of them—in one degree or another—crooks." Then he took her arm again. " Do you want to see my collection now?"

" Yours?"

" My own." He smiled. " It's only a few blocks. Let's walk."

They went north on Fifth Avenue. As they waited for a traffic light at one of the corners Eliot jerked his head towards the tall grey stone house beside them. " My parents live there."

It was briefly shocking to Ginny that he could walk by it in this fashion. He turned and caught her expression and laughed. " Oh, I visit them sometimes—nearly always by arrangement. We're not what you'd call a close-knit family."

" Is there anyone else in the family?"

" I have a sister. She's been in Europe for the last three years. You see—being a girl she doesn't have to pretend to be a solid citizen. She attends film festivals, and spends the other half of the year on the beach at Cannes. Which is about what I'd like to do."

"And what *do* you do?" Ginny asked the question very carefully, knowing that he had invited it, knowing that what she was hearing was said to few people whom Eliot Russell knew.

He sighed. Even over the rush of the traffic she heard the sound and it was empty, a declaration of nothing. "I help to take care of money—my father's and my own. And I help to give it away. There's not much I do that pleases them——" He jerked his head back towards the tall house. "Neither myself or Lucy—that's my sister. The least I can do is help take care of the money. The sacred money! You know something, Ginny? You know something interesting? Money invested at four per cent doubles itself in seventeen years? It's very safe that way, and dull. We have a staff that sits and watches it doubling itself, and then they decide how to give it away. It's a great system."

"It sounds wonderful—and sad."

He gave a bleak and wintry smile, shrugging. "I wouldn't know how to do without it. I haven't the courage to be a Lucy."

His hand tightened possessively on her arm as he guided her towards the entrance of a large modern apartment block. She felt as if she wanted to draw back, but she could not; the grip was tight and seemed to defy her to escape it. She knew suddenly that he was asking payment for that hour over on the Palisades. She had talked to him then, compulsively, to a stranger who would help her bear the burden of love and loneliness. And now he had asked her to hear him, demanded that she listen. His face was taut with strain as he approached the elevator and nodded to the porter.

He pushed the button for the penthouse, and looking upward at the indicator as the floor numbers flashed by him he said, "I don't know why I should have trusted you the other night, Ginny—or why I trust you now. But I do."

Ginny had expected Eliot's apartment would in a lesser way resemble the richness of the Frick setting; when he

F

swung open the door then it was a shock to see the blank
white walls and the bare floor of highly polished wood
block. A single piece of twisted metal sculpture broke the
line of the foyer walls. A sense of chill struck at Ginny as
she followed Eliot into the huge white room that opened from
the foyer ; she looked around her, puzzled, a little frightened,
and then she realised that this was a small private museum.
There was almost no furniture—two large chairs and a sofa
made of black leather and steel, all of them facing the
view from the glass-walled terrace. Around the room was
hung a collection of abstract paintings, their colours the
only thing of warmth to be seen. Down the length of the room
there were three more metal sculptures on pedestals, their
shadows thrown eerily on the polished floor. The sun
shone through the west-facing windows, with the view over
Central Park. Eliot went at once to draw a transparent
curtain across them, cutting the direct rays. The big room
was bathed in softer light.

Ginny began to walk slowly before the paintings. They
were extreme abstracts, some a whole song of colour and
rhythm, one no more than a single yellow square placed
near the bottom left-hand corner of a white canvas. She
turned to Eliot, who stood watching her.

" Don't expect me to have anything discerning to say
about these. You know that I *don't* know." She flung her
hands out suddenly, gesturing at the room, the black furniture,
the white walls, the bold marks of colour that were the
paintings. " I didn't expect this. I somehow got the impression that you wouldn't care much for abstractions—you
seemed to be so much at home in the Frick that I thought
you would . . ." The sentence trailed off. It seemed rude to
walk in and immediately criticise. She had begun to realise
he was vulnerable.

He shrugged. " These are not the ultimate choice. I don't
give a damn for them except as investments." He put his
hands in his pockets and started to pace the long bare room.
" Buying contemporary art is like playing the stock market,
Ginny." He nodded towards the wall. " These are growth
stocks—even though some of them were pretty high-priced.
You have to second guess the market, and like the market
there's no such thing as the sure thing. In ten years I'll
know if I've made the right choice. I hope I'll have got rid

of the duds by then. And when the time comes to sell, I'll part with them with as little sentiment as if they were shares of stock in a company."

He stood still for a minute, looking at each of three canvases which hung in a kind of bay; the look was critical and quite cold. "These are not," he said, "what I want to live with all my life. I want to own Rembrandts and Goyas—even an El Greco if I thought I had the courage to live with it. It's going to take a lot of money and a lot of patience before I can have what I want. It could be worth it . . . even the game of tracking them down could be worth it."

He wheeled suddenly. "You've had enough enlightenment for one afternoon, haven't you? Then let's go and cook dinner."

"You cook?"

He was already slipping off his jacket. She followed him quickly down a passage to what she later discovered was the second apartment on this level which he rented and had had joined with the other that was the gallery. He called after her. "I'm the best cook in the world. And if you tell me your mother is, I have to ask you to leave."

The meal was what he promised—broiled lobsters, zabaglione and champagne, a brie at the right temperature and age, firm dark grapes. It had been cooked with a minimum of fuss by Eliot in the kind of kitchen that Ginny had never believed existed—with a row of fifty cook-books on a shelf and enough shining copper saucepans to furnish a small restaurant. He was used to an audience; there was a table and two small chairs, and Ginny sat and sipped her drink while she watched.

"You're right," Ginny said when they had finished eating. "My mother isn't the best cook in the world—but then I never thought she was, and she didn't either."

"Then she's a rare woman—and so are you, Ginny."

They were dining in a small room across the passage from the kitchen. In here the warmth in furnishings and wood panelling wiped away the memory of the exhibition room for the paintings. A Sisley and a Corot hung on the wall. Eliot met her eyes across the candlelit table. He poured the last of the wine, and proffered a cigarette.

"You see what I shall become, Ginny," he said, as he

lighted it. "I shall become a fussy gourmet, a collector, a dabbler. In time, no doubt, I'll give up drinking hard liquor because it ruins a palate, and I'll bore my friends talking about vintages. God, what a future!" He rose suddenly, the movement so sharp and quick that he almost upset his chair. "We'll have coffee in the living-room, will we?"

She started to stack the dishes to carry them into the kitchen. "No—leave them there. Harry comes in in the morning to clear up." The coffee was already perking in the automatic coffee-maker. He had plugged it in while he made the zabaglione. The coffee-tray was set and ready in the living-room. Ginny had found throughout the apartment the evidence of a staff to back up this appearance of seeming effortlessness. There were no servants to be seen or heard, but you knew that a squad of them appeared every day, and withdrew, leaving Eliot to appear to complete the work. It was a harmless form of showing-off, executed with great skill and nonchalance.

"A dilettante, you see, Ginny," Eliot continued. His gesture indicated the room lined with books, the tables furnished with magazines that ranged from *Diogenes* to *Fortune,* the piano with the open score on its rack. "I'm in everything. I stick a finger in every pie that offers itself. I invest in Broadway shows—and in young musicians. I got my father to endow a scolarship to the Juilliard and to bring over three students each year from Nigeria. Nigeria! Think of it." He gave a half laugh. "Like most other Americans I'd hardly heard of Nigeria four years ago, and now I have these kids here and introduce them around and pretend I'm doing something for peace and understanding."

He had walked over to the glass wall giving on to the terrace—in this room the windows faced south over the view of the skyscrapers, lighted now, and close enough so that Ginny had, for one moment, the wild and unreal feeling that these too were Eliot Russell's private toys, piled on his terrace, waiting their turn for him to come and play with them. He slid back the glass door and stepped outside. Ginny put down her coffee cup and followed him. She seemed always to be following Eliot. She stood beside him at the terrace wall, which was also glass enclosed in fine mesh wire so that no inch of the view was lost. Every minute of gathering darkness made the lights of the office blocks stronger and more brilliant; at this height a breeze stirred, carrying with it, though, the smell and taste of dust.

"Eliot, I'm dazzled," Ginny said quite simply. "I never knew there were so many worlds to all come together in the one place—or in one person. I . . ."

He broke in, "Well, I meant you to be dazzled!" His voice rose shrilly. "Cheap—cheap histrionics—that's what you've been seeing, Ginny. I do it every now and again. I show off my possessions and talk big names in the theatre and art and music, and I think I can trick people into believing for a while that I share the talent just because I recognise it. That's never been true, and it never will be." He flung down his cigarette and stamped on it.

"I'm sorry, Ginny. I apologise to you. I should know better. When my family were struggling up in the social world my father got it drummed into him that it wasn't the right thing to talk about money or to hint at what it can do for you. But I'm expected to know that by instinct." He turned to look at her. "My grandfather started in a coal-mine. There's some truth in that old chestnut about shirt-sleeves to shirt-sleeves in three generations. Mentally I'm in shirt-sleeves. I try for a bit of cheap notice because I'm neither a coal-miner nor a latter-day robber-baron—nor am I anything like the financial wizard my father turned out to be. I have to be something. So I am what I am."

"Eliot, why do you apologise for what you are?" Her voice was very low. If she had dared she would have put her hand upon his. But Eliot would never have permitted that —not of her, and only, she believed, of a very few other people.

"I have to. The world is not a very friendly place to my kind. I've been holding it at arm's length most of my life. There have been very few to trust—I said that to you before. In these last years there's been nothing to hope for, either. Money breeds mistrust, Ginny. The right kind of people shy away because they think *you* think they want something of you. The wrong kind comes too easily. Even inside a family money seems to breed its own kind of mistrust. We all have the means to lead completely separate existences —to tell each other to go to hell."

He rested his hands on the railing and stared out over the night city.

" But sometimes this separate existence grows separate beyond bearing. Then I have to break out of my box and try to make contact with the human race again. I do things I would rather forget. Or I behave as I did to-night —foolish, but not evil. I still have to apologise. I'm ashamed." He looked back at her. " That's all. Do you want to go home now? "

" I'd rather stay."

" Thanks." He wheeled and walked back into the living-room. " I'll get you some more coffee."

IV

Ginny found that the hold Eliot had taken upon her that afternoon grew stronger and more possessive. At first she did not try to shake loose because there was a kind of satisfaction in being needed, and a lessening of the sense of loneliness and perpetual struggle which seemed to be part of the city's back-handed gift to everyone who came freshly to it. She was aware of pity, and the surprising knowledge came that Eliot was as lonely as she. There was need on both sides and they fell together.

Barby did not approve, and she said so loudly and often. " You're doing yourself no good, Ginny. What's in this for you? It's dead-end—the whole thing's completely dead-end."

" He needs me—I think."

" Needs you? He will *always* need you—or someone like you. And it can never come to anyone. He'll use you. You'll be his mother and his sister—you'll be everything he needs a woman for except a lover and a wife. That you won't get—or if you do it'll be such a sorry thing you'll wish you'd never tried it. You're camouflage!—don't you see that, kid? You're a pretty girl to take about and be seen with. And it looks better that way for Mr. Eliot Russell. After all, he's got a position to keep up, and he's got to be damn' discreet. A thousand people may know about him but as long as he puts on a front of normalcy no one minds him. Because of his family he's got to try to look like every other guy, and you're part of that front. Try to get that into your head, Ginny. That's all you are! That's *all*."

"That's part of it. Yes, I'd admit that's part of it. But it isn't all. He needs me . . . perhaps I need him." Her lips hesitated over the word "compassion." In her heart Ginny was afraid to use it in case it, too, would be demolished.

"You need nothing from Eliot Russell. Don't kid yourself. The giving is all on your side."

"It . . . it isn't for ever. I can stop seeing him whenever I want to."

"Can you? Can you, indeed? I wonder. It can get to be a habit—you know. Money can get to be a habit, and good eating places, and always knowing you've got somewhere to go on a Saturday night, and someone to take you. It's tougher the other way, Ginny. It's always tougher alone. Soon you'll stop dating the other guys because they'll suddenly start to look awfully crummy beside Handsome, and a subway and a cup of coffee is going to seem pretty small time after Pavillion and a chauffeur-driven limousine. Just watch it, Ginny. It can get hold of you before you know it. You see, kid, I get the scent of lilies about you these days, and it doesn't suit you."

"Oh, shut up!—and mind your own business."

But the words stayed. They lingered in Ginny's mind through the summer when Eliot opened a different world to her, they persisted as a continuous interior dialogue to sour the taste of each new experience. There was a kind of confession of guilt and uneasiness in the fact that she did not write of Eliot Russell in letters to St. Nicolaas. This was the first sin of omission it had ever been necessary to commit.

She went with Eliot twice to the Southampton house of his parents, and glimpsed the world of the Bathing Corporation and the Meadow Club. This was not her world and she knew it, as did everyone else, but for two week-ends she saw it, and knew, instinctively, that if she had wanted to thrust her way in through Eliot, it might have been hers. "You're really quite beautiful, my dear," Eliot's mother once said to her. "And fresh. Where did Eliot find you?"

"In the Museum of Modern Art, Mother. She was on exhibit."

Eliot's mother was a coldly handsome woman who treated her son like an occasional, distant guest. But the formal manner of almost icy politeness towards Eliot broke sometimes to reveal a rage of disappointment and contempt that Ginny knew must have struck him like a blow. Ginny was herself included in the polite manner, but she knew the other woman did not like her.

"Well, did you expect her to?" Barby asked scathingly. "But she's glad enough to have you make an appearance with Eliot, I'll bet. It looks better!"

There were visits to other houses as well. Eliot would take her driving and suddenly say, "I think we'll call on the Matsons. They have a couple of good pictures I'd like you to see," or, "Let's go and see who's playing tennis at the Whitakers'." The houses began to look much alike, and she met some of the same people a number of times. The conversation was quick and light. To be amusing was the only thing that mattered. "I never say anything amusing," Ginny once said to Eliot.

"Don't worry—at your age you're not supposed to. It's enough to look the way you do." Suddenly he gave an uncharacteristic roar of laughter. "It's the English accent that has a few people bothered. They don't know whether you're a shy little English heiress or just a girl working over here for a year as a housemaid."

"Eliot, I very much suspect they think I'm the housemaid —except that you *should* be going out with heiresses. Money marries money, doesn't it?"

His face darkened momentarily, and then he decided to treat it lightly. "They've all given up expecting me to marry. I've been through the debutante cycle. I don't seriously count as eligible any more. They've even stopped asking me to the coming-out parties because I never accept. And I've put in my time around the International Set, too—Lucy's had me to Klosters and Venice and Nice at the appropriate times. But I kept coming back because it's pretty hard to get away from the conviction that you're meant to do something with your life. I got tired of packing my bags, and parties began to bore me. You need a hell of a lot of stamina and a head as hard as a nut to keep up. Poor Lucy doesn't have a very good head for drink, and she's thin as a rake now."

" What were you doing at that party on Riverside Drive?"
Ginny said. " Somehow—it didn't seem your kind of thing
—too messy." As soon as the words were out, she regretted
them. It did not do to ask what Eliot's business was anywhere ; the answer might not be palatable. The thing that
was wrong with their relationship was that she could not
ask these questions. There was a whole area of Eliot's
life that was blocked off from her, never referred to except
in bitter, self-accusing asides.

" What was I doing? Well—he didn't show up! Is that
what you were expecting me to say? God, Ginny, mind your
own business!"

That was what she had said to Barby, and the words came
home.

The fall came to New York and she knew why people
talked of its days that were made of golden wine. The
air seemed to tingle with life, the skies were a deeper blue,
the grey haze of summer heat was gone. There was a sense
of exhilaration, and excitement, of new beginnings. The
people came back to the city.

" I feel as I did in the spring—only better. I belong a little
bit now," Ginny said.

And now Eliot took her driving north into New England
for the colours of the autumn woods that she had never
seen before, the golds and browns and deep slashes of crimson
reflected in still blue lakes, the little steeples of the white
wooden churches that cut the folds of the valleys. There
was the scent of mould and wood-smoke. " I expected
autumn to be sad," she said. " But it's the most brilliantly
wonderful thing I've ever dreamed of. Father never told me
that it was like this."

" It isn't like this in England. It's colder here—the colours
are better."

" Have you seen an autumn in England?"

" Yes. There's a lot of sadness in the autumn rain in
England."

" Eliot?"

" Yes?"

" Why do you take all this trouble to show me these
things?"

" Because I see them again for the first time with you,
Ginny."

" That makes you sound so old. Why do you make yourself so old?"

" I am old. I thought you knew that." One of the difficulties was that she never knew when Eliot was joking. They were walking on the wet sand of an autumn beach on the Cape when he said it. The sun shone, but it had no warmth in it. Eliot's beautifully modelled head and features were sharp in profile against a cold-looking blue sea. He was at that moment both young and old, a beautiful young man with the touch of destruction on him. These were the times that Barby didn't know about, she thought; the times when compassion was uppermost, and the need was evident.

New York came to life in the fall with the round of new art shows, Broadway openings, the Philharmonic season, the Metropolitan Opera season. Eliot went to most of them, and Ginny was usually with him. The first cocktail parties were interesting because the people were new to her—they were not the Southampton people, or the students, or the ones who had stayed through the summer in the city. These were the ones who moved the art and show-business world along, quick-eyed people on the make and on the go, to whom the city was a fever in the blood. But by November Ginny began to think she had seen them all many times before—or people with faces and voices just like them. And why, she wondered, did all the women wear black? At two formal dinner parties given by Eliot's mother, she saw some of the Southhampton faces again, though by now the names were beginning to blur into the dozens of people she had met since then.

" It defeats itself," she said to Eliot. " I've met so many people that I don't know one of them."

Clothes now became a problem because the little fifteen-dollar linen sheaths of the summer could not be suitably matched. She thought of writing to her father for extra money, but was ashamed to do it. By cutting out one of the courses at N.Y.U. she was able to take a Thursday night and Saturday selling job at Macy's. Eliot found out immediately and he was furious.

" Surely you know I'd be glad to help! After all you come to these things because I ask you to."

" My father wouldn't like it, Eliot. I wouldn't like it either."

" Does your father have to know?"

She didn't reply and her silence was acceptance; and she was ashamed of this too. It wasn't until later that she remembered that Eliot had made no comment on her own objections. It was possible he didn't think them important. She made vague self-justifications for her decision, or rather for letting Eliot make the decision, and as a conscience-salver she went back to the course in the history of art, and enrolled for advanced Spanish. And then she let Eliot take her shopping. She let him choose the clothes and critically supervise the fittings, acknowledging that his instinct here was better than her own. Most of them came from de Pinna. She couldn't bring herself to ask the prices, and Eliot never did. Barby pounced on them when they were delivered to the apartment.

" What do you mean—you don't *know* what they cost? Can't you see? A couple of hundred bucks each!—all of them!" She rustled the tissue-paper angrily. " All right —you can call me a jealous bitch if you want to, but I'm telling you again this is all wrong. What's more, you know it's wrong. Oh, hell, Ginny—it's not the clothes! Eliot Russell can afford anything he fancies. For you it's wrong. Most kids I'd say—go ahead, get what you can. But you don't seem to know it's fairyland you're living in up there. It won't go on for ever, you know, and it's a hell of a long tumble down to earth."

" If it is fairy-land, then that's what the clothes are for— *only* what they're for. You don't think I'm fool enough to suppose they're to be worn here—or to work, or to classes? Don't you see?—they're Eliot's clothes. They don't belong to me. They never will. Except for the times I'm with Eliot, they'll stay hanging in the closet."

And they did; they hung there, the Cinderella clothes of Eliot's world. She regarded them as something apart. She wished she could have written to her father about them, but he would never have understood the pact she had made with herself that they were to be worn only as the passport to enter Eliot's world, nor would he even have understood the hunger to experience, however tentatively, what that world was like. She knew that this experience was not hers to possess for ever, as the clothes were not, but she counted it as much a part of what she had come to New York to discover as the packed subway rides to work and the stand-up lunches at Nedicks.

The evening of the first dinner party his mother gave at the Fifth Avenue house Eliot called for Ginny, and on the seat of the cab with him was a dark mink wrap. " Put it on, Ginny. No—don't look like that. It belongs to Lucy— she has a lot of things in storage here, and I take care of them for her. I think she'd like you to wear it a few times. Go on—*it's all right, Ginny*. I didn't steal it, and I didn't buy it. It honestly is Lucy's."

" Then won't your mother be surprised to see me wearing it?"

" She won't recognise it. Mother never knew what Lucy had and what she didn't have. Do you think it's any accident that I have charge of the storage claim checks?"

She found that he told the truth because when Ginny gave the fur to Mrs. Russell's maid she saw the initials L. R. on the lining. She wondered afterwards if the maid had also noticed them and reported the fact to Mrs. Russell. When she got back to the apartment she laid the wrap in a cardboard box on the high shelf of her closet, away from Barby's eyes.

It was the white silk coat that made Ginny truly uneasy, the single thing that most bore out what Barby had been saying about Eliot. Eliot brought it with him when he called for her on the night of the formal opening of the Metropolitan Opera season. The Russells were in San Francisco and he was using the family box that night. From the newspapers Ginny had gathered that this was a night of special importance in New York, and she was, without understanding quite why, a little nervous as she dressed. She was glad Barby was out. The girl who shared her room, Judith, just lay on the bed and stared.

" God—I've never seen anyone actually wearing a thing like that!"

The dress was white silk, stiff falling in a straight line from bust to toes, with wide straight shoulder straps. There were gloves reaching above the elbow to go with it. When Eliot came he nodded approvingly, and then handed her the white coat he had carried over his arm. " It's getting too cold for Lucy's little fur," he said.

Ginny stretched out her arms to take it, but for a moment they froze there. The edges had fallen open, revealing the lining of white Russian broadtail. She gave a little gasp.

" This isn't Lucy's," she said. It was made in the collarless horizontal fashion of the moment. It was certainly not what had been worn three years ago when Lucy had gone to Europe.

" Does it matter so much? You have to have something to wear."

She began to make a protest, and then it died. She was already condemned by the dress she had on, and the gloves, even the foundation garment without which the dress would have been ruined. They were all Eliot's. There was nothing of Ginny here; she had reserved no area of independence for herself. It all belonged to him, and she was the dummy wearing his clothes. She felt humiliated and it was too late for protest. The time for that had been before the first dress. Silently she took the coat from him.

" Just before you put it on—since it's *the* night at the Met I thought you'd enjoy wearing these." He slipped his hand into his suit pocket and when it came out he held a necklace of emeralds, set in diamonds, and carelessly bunched as if it were a plaything. " This is Lucy's—and it will go back into the safe deposit vault to-morrow morning, so you can stop looking as if I'm asking you to accept ill-gotten gains."

She stared in fascination. Seen here, in Eliot's hand, the colour of the emeralds was infinitely more warm and living than the tantalising but remote gems she had gazed at in Tiffany's window. They held her spellbound, and at the same time they were somehow ludicrous in Barby's cluttered, crowded living-room. " Lucy," she said slowly, without lifting her eyes from the stones, " could never agree to letting a complete stranger wear her jewels. She couldn't!"

" She did. I cabled her. Lucy's not possessive—she's not much like me. Which is perhaps why we manage to get on so well with each other."

" I don't believe it. Why would she have jewels locked up here? Why doesn't she wear them herself?"

" In Lucy's crowd at the moment it's the chic thing to wear ceramic jewellery that looks like nothing and costs a small fortune. A kind of throw-away, you know. She sent these back here because she's a pretty careless girl, and she knows it. In time she'll want it all back, and Cartier in Paris will make a new setting, and she'll be in style again." He smiled faintly. " So you see, Ginny, it will do no harm for you to wear them for just this one time. Jewels need to be worn—they get cold and faded in a vault." He moved behind her, and she could feel the weight of the necklace suddenly against her throat, and his fingers on the clasp.

" It's nothing new," he said. " Every second woman will have borrowed or rented jewels on to-night, and the models will be hired by the jewellers to appear in some new design and make a big splash in the hope of attracting some other woman to buy them."

Ginny said nothing. This was not a separate happening which she could dismiss ; it was all a part of the whole which had begun with the first dress. She submitted to Eliot's holding the coat for her to slip into. He led her down the four flights of the shabby stairs, the sheen of the silk seeming to light the dimness. The necklace grew warm against her throat. She knew that at this moment she was utterly and wholly the chattel of Eliot Russell's money.

It was the Saturday before Christmas when Ginny knew that the end was coming with Eliot—either the end or a change. Strictly, it was Sunday morning—about three o'clock, Ginny thought—but she was so tired that the beginning of the evening with Eliot seemed days away in time. They had been to a Broadway musical, and then to supper, and after that Eliot had wanted to go to the night-club he favoured, where the humour was low-keyed and off-beat, and there were no show girls. He sat on and on, smoking, but not drinking much, and Ginny felt the weariness gathering in her brain like a fog. She was conscious that she did this too often now—stayed out so late that she hardly seemed to sleep at all before it was time to go to the consulate. Two weeks ago she had fallen asleep during a lecture. Her neighbour had nudged her awake, but she had felt the gaze of the professor on her. This, too, was part of a pattern. She had not had a passing mark in any of the courses she had taken this semester except Spanish, and she knew that some kind of reckoning was close. They would not keep her at N.Y.U., nor could she ask to stay. She looked now at the comic who was finishing up his routine on the tiny dance floor, and she suddenly realised that she hadn't heard a word he had said. She had laughed mechanically when Eliot did, and now with the comic taking his final bows, Eliot had risen and was holding out the white silk coat for her. As she buttoned it, it seemed to her like some garment of punishment, a stifling, choking thing for which, although it had cost her no money, she had already paid far too high a price. She waited while Eliot got his coat, and they stepped out on the sidewalk together. This was the first they knew of the snow.

The flakes were small and icy, and were sticking. Driven before the wind, they had already piled in small drifts in the gutters and against the sides of the buildings. All the canopies up and down the street were white with it, and it lay stiffly on the little evergreen bushes at the entrance to the club.

" I had them move your car down here, Mr. Russell." The Alfa Romeo was parked right beside them. The few times when Eliot chose to use it in the city, Ginny noticed that he had never parked it himself, but miraculously it always was at hand when he emerged from wherever he was. There was never a parking ticket on it, and such services cost far more than the price of a taxi.

" When did it start snowing?" Eliot asked, while the doorman was handing Ginny into the car.

" About an hour ago, Mr. Russell. Heard on the radio that Boston's already had seven inches, and we're due about twelve inches here by noon."

Eliot slammed the door on his own side. " A good day to stay in bed. You need some sleep, Ginny."

" Yes."

He said no more all the way downtown to the Village. They rode on Park Avenue, and the tiny flakes of snow swirled about the car closely, blotting off the tall buildings, screening the other side of the wide avenue, sticking on the windscreen until it seemed they rode in a tunnel. The lighted Christmas trees were frosted with snow. The city was dead quiet. Ginny could hear only the noise of the windscreen wipers and the sharp little hiss of the icicles against the glass.

She leaned back, feeling the warm softness of the fur lining against her bare shoulders, letting herself drift in this white and quiet world.

Then beside her Eliot spoke. "I'm very fond of you, Ginny."

She made a mechanical, off-hand response because fatigue seemed to be numbing her senses. "I'm fond of you."

"Ginny—I think I'd ask you to marry me, only it wouldn't work out. I've known men like myself who've made marriages and had children, and it seemed to be all right. But it doesn't work—not if you feel the way I do. I'd be unhappy, and I'd make you unhappy. It wouldn't work, would it?"

"Are you asking me a question, Eliot? Do you expect an answer?"

"No!" Unnecessarily and dangerously on the ice-covered road he gunned the engine, and the quiet was destroyed by its noise. "No—I'm not asking. I'm telling you it wouldn't work."

V

Ginny had never experienced anything like the blanketed quiet to which she woke. She lay still for some time to focus on the clock. It was past noon. The strange quiet persisted, and she moved her gaze to the gap in the curtains; the streak of daylight had a bright, unnaturally sharp quality. The window was open a crack, and the air of the room seemed frozen. For a moment she stared in some puzzlement at Judith's neatly made-up bed across from hers; and then she remembered that it was only two days before Christmas and Judith had gone home yesterday to Chicago. The thought of Christmas and of going home depressed her, and with it was associated the feeling of vague guilt that now seemed built into her days. She turned over and drew the blankets closer about her ears. Forget about Christmas for a while, she told herself, and about home and about Eliot. In the living-room the phone rang, and very indistinctly she heard Barby's voice. She closed her eyes again.

The next time she woke there was the sound of voices—

Barby's strident and rather excited, and another, a low, masculine tone. She lay listening for some minutes while she struggled out of sleep, and then she realised suddenly that she had been anticipating the rhythm and the cadence of the man's voice because it was familiar and loved.

She jerked upright; the shock of the cold brought her to full wakefulness. She strained now for the sound, and she was certain. In an instant she was at the door and had it open.

" Jim—is it you, Jim?"

He was on his feet by the time she got to the living-room door. Jim, looking strange to her in a tweed jacket and tie, but still Jim with the bronzed face and the toughened look of a man who has worked out-of-doors for the last two years. The room was flooded with a stark white light, the reflection from the snow piled on the rooftops, piled in the street below and thick on every window-ledge. It was an unearthly light, harsh, unreal; seen in it, Barby's face looked ghastly, with the vivid red mouth drawn across its pallor. The light was the city, brilliant and cold.

He put down his coffee cup. " Jim?" She was still unbelieving. " You're here?" He met her as she moved across the room to him, and he seemed to cradle her in his arms, as if she had been a child running to him, warm from bed, freshly awakened from a long nightmare. His hand smoothed the sleep-roughened hair in the remembered way, and her weak tears were the tears of a child weeping from relief and exhaustion. She felt him rock her gently.

" I'm glad you've come, Jim."

Later she went back and got a dressing-gown and slippers, and put a comb through her hair. Her face in the bathroom mirror looked tired and faintly tinged with green. She put on a little lipstick, and then wiped it off because it made her look worse. When she got back to the living-room, Barby had brewed more coffee, and Ginny took the cup gratefully. She held it defensively in both hands, partly shielding her face from Jim's appraising stare.

She was controlled enough now to ask the questions. " When did you get here? Why . . .?"

" I've been in Boston for the last three days talking money to the two brothers who came into the syndicate as partners six months ago. I think there's a chance of doing some really big things on St. Nicolaas, but it took some selling to make them see it. I think the money will be put up, but you can never be sure until the cheque is signed. These money-men aren't the romantic kind, and you can't sell them the palm-fringed beach idea unless it's got solid profits behind it. Damned inconsiderate of them, I think." He grinned happily as he flicked his ash towards the ash-tray, and Ginny recognised anew that forcefulness in Jim that had always compelled her, that stirred action of its own accord. She knew suddenly that he relished the prospect of the battle ahead to prove that he had been right about St. Nicolaas. There was a complete absence of wavering in Jim.

"The talk in Boston went on longer than I thought, and I only got out of there yesterday afternoon—just beat the snow. I called you from Boston, but no one ever seems to be at home in this apartment. And last night I missed you again. Between telephone calls I interviewed two Cubans who got out from under Castro and who used to work as assistant chefs, they say, in the Hilton Havana. I have to believe them, because the French guy from Martinique who's running the kitchen at Oranje Cove is screaming for some experienced help. These two guys jumped at the chance of some work, and the thought of getting back to the sun. They were recommended and I just have to take their performance on trust because I need them. On St. Nicolaas the local help still has the idea that it's pretty foolish to hurry because the guests might get indigestion if they had to eat a meal in under two hours. So I told the Cubans to pack their bags, and if they work out all right we'll talk about bringing their families down. They're travelling back with me."

"When?"

"The first plane to San Juan after they get the snow cleared off the runways at Idlewild."

"No—you can't! That could be to-night, and I haven't had time to see you . . ."

"Listen, Ginny," Barby cut in, "this guy has problems too. He tells me he has a hotel full of people down there all expecting a bang-up Christmas, and no one to run the place except a few well-intentioned friends, including your mother. He had just better be there, *and* his two assistant chefs! Boy, some Christmas!" Something in Barby's voice made Ginny glance at her quickly. She was more animated than usual, more girlish, and her eyes were fixed on Jim as if she meant never to take them away. She had made no gesture to leave them alone, and Ginny didn't think she would either. Suddenly Barby's voice cackled in an unaccustomed, frivolous giggle. "You don't happen to need any barmaids for a while, do you? I can mix a real mean martini." This from Barby, Ginny thought, who thought St. Nicolaas was the end of the earth.

Jim smiled. "When I can afford to hire you I'll give the word. Even if it's only to watch the bar bills and the change. It isn't that they're dishonest . . . they just think it's too much trouble to count."

"Then I'm your girl," Barby said. "Just say the word and I'll be there. No one ever made two cents of wrong change from me in my life."

"Useful . . . very useful. I'll keep you in mind . . ."
Ginny got to her feet. "Excuse me. I'll go and have a shower. I look a sight."

"You certainly do that," Jim agreed. "I don't think even Bo would recognise you in that night-club pallor."

"Oh, shut up!" Ginny said rudely. She closed the door, not gently, when she left. It didn't help her mood, either, as she showered and dressed, to hear Barby's hoots of laughter coming regularly.

"I've never known Jim to be *that* funny," she observed to her reflection in the glass.

They beat their way down through the snow-filled streets to Mario's to eat. No traffic moved except a solitary bus on Fifth Avenue through the two lanes that the ploughs and bulldozers had managed to open. The traffic noise was gone—it was the noise Ginny had missed when she woke—and in its place was the sound of the steel snow-shovels scraping against the side walks, and the shouts of the scraping against the sidewalks, and the shouts of the middle of the streets. The cars were buried up to their windows and some of the small foreign makes had disappeared altogether under the drifts. There was an air of novelty and good humour in the scene; people talked to each other as they shovelled off their steps and made paths through the snow.

"It's because it's Sunday," Jim said. "Any day they had to go to work as well as shovel out from under fourteen inches of snow you wouldn't find them so merry about it." He gripped Ginny's arm tightly through the sheepskin coat. "Well, you'll have your white Christmas. They won't dig out from under this for a week."

"And you . . . you'll be gone." They had come to Washington Square and Jim paused for a moment to let Ginny watch the bulldozer piling up the snow in small mountains for the trucks to take it away. "I almost wish they didn't clear it so quickly. . . . I wish it would snow again and then you wouldn't be able to get away. I'd like you here for Christmas, Jim."

"And my customers down at Oranje Cove would like me there." He tugged at her. "Come on, before you freeze to death. Now—where's Mario's?"

"Two blocks over." She followed reluctantly, not liking the cheerful way he had talked of being in St. Nicolaas for Christmas. "He's open Sundays . . . but perhaps with the snow . . ."

Jim half pulling her along. "You'll be surprised how many New Yorkers will carry on as if nothing has happened. It's the suburbanites who get overwhelmed. Look there —that's it, isn't it? The lights are on, and . . ." With a flourish he opened the door. "The OPEN sign is on the door! What did I tell you?"

The lights were on, overhead and at the bar, but the place was empty. The tables were covered with their usual red-checked cloths, but no places were set. It was deadly quiet, as if they had come to a feast on the wrong night. Jim went over to the bar and rapped on it. The baize door from the kitchen swung open and Mario himself appeared.

"You open for business?" Jim said.

Mario shrugged and spread his hands.

"You see how it is. We are open, but there is no chef and no waiters. Weaklings, they are. A little snow and they stay in bed. One just called me. 'Listen,' he says, 'the subways aren't running out here. What do you expect me to do—walk!' In the old days, they would have walked! However, I can offer you a drink, since I see that you and the young lady are walkers, and walkers need sustenance."

Jim signalled Ginny. "A drink we'll have. What do you say, Ginny—a very dry, large martini? And maybe there's some olives and celery in the refrigerator? And perhaps even a slice of salami?"

Mario rushed around from behind the bar, a beam suddenly splitting the melancholy on his face. While Jim took Ginny's coat, Mario held out a chair for her. "Over here, young lady. It's warmer near the radiator. And those boots—better take them off since they're wet." He waved aside her protest. "Who will see? Take them off and I'll fix you, sir, the finest martini in New York, with a salami that's poetic, and the brown bread that will make you weep —even if it is yesterday's. Anyone who walks through the snow deserves food."

As he turned to go, Jim caught his sleeve. "Mario—how long since you cooked?"

The Italian's eyes narrowed; a look of speculation came into them, a mistiness that was pure pleasure. "You want me to cook?" He rubbed his hands together. "You will take whatever I prepare?—now, listen." His eyes went from one to the other. "A full anti-pasto . . . baked clams oragonato . . . maybe veal parmigiano." He shrugged. "We'll see what comes."

Ginny smiled weakly at the thought of the food. "I'm very hungry," she said.

Mario bent his gaze on her for a moment steadily. "For you, lady, I will cook."

Three minutes later he placed the big stemmed martini glasses before them, clouded with the chill of the liquid. He pointed to Jim. "You, sir, can you tend the bar?"

Jim sipped before he answered. "I'll never beat this martini, Mario—but yes, I can tend the bar."

At the kitchen door, Mario hesitated, and then walked with great deliberation to the front door. They watched him as he peered up and down the street, and then he shook his head. "Who will come on such a day?" He removed the OPEN sign from the glass, and switched out all but the lights over the bar and two near the table where Ginny and Jim sat. The dimness of the room was filled with warmth and the scent of garlic. Ginny stared at Jim and pressed her cold feet against the radiator. She sipped her drink and let out a great sigh of contentment. All the disparate pieces of New York, all the fragments that the city had tossed her way in this last year, seemed suddenly to have come together.

It was a meal of wine and good humour and a blessed sense of rightness that seemed to Ginny too rare ever to come more than once or twice in a lifetime. They gossiped and talked like lovers who have had time and space in which to become friends. The year of exile was over and she was older, and Jim was free, she believed, of the obsession with Julie. She felt that she could afford to waste time because there was much time ahead for them.

As she stuffed on the food that Mario kept bringing he teased her gently. " You begin to look like a woman now. I thought you were some half-starved dummy Barby kept about when you appeared this morning."

She just laughed. " I had to have my touch of dissipation, didn't I? Why else would I come to New York?"

She thought he would say then that the time in New York must end now, that she should come home, but he didn't. Instead, he thumbed in his wallet for a moment, the ghost of a smile flickering on his lips. It was pretty high-class dissipation, as far as I can see." Out of his wallet he drew a news clipping and passed it to her. " It was Susie Marshall who spotted it, of course, and she made sure I got it. You know you've really moved into big time when you can impress Susie."

She looked down at the paper in her hand. The column and the picture seemed to blur before her in the sickness of guilt. It was a clipping from *Time* magazine and the picture was of Eliot Russell. Behind him she saw her own face. She was wearing Lucy Russell's emeralds and the white gown. The caption read: *Russell at Met opening.* Underneath was the news item: " *To mark his thirtieth birthday last week, Eliot Russell III, playboy grandson of oil-and-lumber tycoon, Eliot Russell, was presented with his second trust fund of ten million dollars. Quipped Russell, ' It will come in useful to buy a few paintings.' "*

Ginny laid it down on the table. Her own face stared back at her, impersonal, cool, wearing the look of someone who is slightly bored. " I didn't see this," she said. " I didn't know it was Eliot's birthday last week—or about the money."

"I suppose if you're already loaded a few extra million wouldn't be worth mentioning. But Susie's right—that *is* pretty big time."

She tapped the clipping with her finger. "It isn't true. Eliot isn't a playboy. If he ever was that he isn't any more. He's . . ."

Jim's eyebrows were raised sceptically. "And you're not doing too badly, either, I see. All this must make St. Nicholaas seem pretty dull and pretty poverty-stricken." There was a trace of bitterness and hurt in his voice. "That's an awful lot of ice you're wearing, lady—an awful lot! Or are they fake? Somehow I don't associate Russell money with fake diamonds . . ."

She could do nothing about the wave of crimson that flooded her face. "They're borrowed—*borrowed*," she almost shouted. "They were loaned for that one night only. Jim —don't look at me like that, Jim! Don't! Did you imagine Eliot actually gave me something like that? You've lost your mind if you think I could ever accept such a thing."

He shrugged defensively. "Who am I to say what are the habits of the rich? First of all you've got to know someone to borrow these kind of things from, don't you?"

"Jim . . ." She let out her breath in a long sigh. "You don't believe me?"

He looked suddenly at his watch and rose. Standing over her he bent down close. "You're John and Katrien's daughter," he said. "You're too stiff-necked and proud to sell independence or anything else for a necklace or a night at the opera." Before she could reply he rushed on, checking the words she might have used.

"Excuse me a minute. I've been forgetting the time. I should have called Pan Am an hour ago."

While he was gone she tried to fight the sense of desolation which came upon her. The golden mood was gone, vanished, as soon as Jim had taken out the clipping. Jim didn't believe her, or didn't care what she did. The implication in the picture, the implication of the money and the necklace and the gown were of something that did not exist, and never would. She looked for Jim to come back again to tell him, to begin the long and complete explanation that would be a compound of loneliness and the astonishment at having revealed to her through Eliot the small and closed world of the very rich, the world that had the fascination of being a place utterly out of reach, and at which, in quieter moments, she had shrugged her shoulders. He had to listen, because there was much to tell.

But Mario came first, with the coffee, black and bitter Italian coffee, and the bottle of Remy Martin. And Jim was right behind h.m, urging him to sit down and share with them. She raised her eyes questioningly to Jim.

" What did Pan Am say?"

" More news in an hour. Call back, they said—and they have the hotel number, th.s number, and Barby's apartment." He said it lightly, as if the prospect of going w..s of little importance. She sa.d nothing as Jim filled her glass and Mario's. He looked at Mario as he raised his own glass.

" Mario, it was a supreme dinner. As one restaurateur to another, I salute you." His voice was thickened a little, and the glass seemed to waver.

Mario paused. " You have a restaurant?" His hand slapped down on the table. " I knew it! I knew there was something. Not for anybody do I close my restaurant and go back to the kitchen! No, sir! But when it is one of the profession . . ."

Jim held up his hand. " Hold it, Mario! I really don't belong in your class at all. I'm a hotelkeeper, and I'm trying to learn how to feed my guests. I've just hired two assistant chefs . . ."

Mario's expression lit as if he had heard a battle-cry. " Then, sir, let me say . . ."

For an hour, while Ginny listened, they sipped Remy Martin and talked food and wine, chefs, table linen, flatware, pilfering, bulk ordering, the pressure of the unions in New York, the trouble of the untrained help in St. Nicolaas. And all the time Jim seemed to sl.p farther from her. Her eyes sought his and he always seemed to look .away, and the discussion with Mario would grow fiercer. " But this is a little hotel," Mario protested. " Only six cottages?— that many people I could feed with one hand tied behind my back! And a Frenchman in the kitchen!—with two Cuban assistants! My friend, you will have trouble. Tell me one thing—what language will the kitchen speak?"

" It's only six cottages now, Mario, but eight more are

building. And more to come when they're finished. This is an expensive hotel . . . I've got to give them good food . . ." Then the telephone on the bar rang, and Mario hauled himself out of his chair and went to answer it.

" Jim . . .?" Ginny said.

" For you, Jim," Mario called.

Jim was at the telephone in a second. Mario sat down again with Ginny. " He's crazy, your friend. I like him, but he's crazy. Why is an architect running a hotel? To build houses—that's good. People sleep in them, eat in them, have babies in them . . . that's good. But to run a hotel, you've got to be crazy . . ."

Jim was standing over them. " That was it, Ginny. Pan Am say they expect to have a runway clear in about three hours, and everybody is on stand-by for departure any time after that. So I have to collect my two boys and get moving . . ."

She nodded, and bent down to search under the table for her boots. This was it, then, as he had said. He had come and was going, and a whole year was going with him. The mood of this dinner was an illusion only, born of nostalgia and wine, and it had had different meanings for them both. What was in her mind was not in Jim's, and it probably never would be. She was near to accepting this as she stood up and offered Mario her hand.

" Thank you. It was one of the best meals of my life."

There was a matter of pride, too, she thought, and Jim would not see her weep for the second time on this one day. And so she left behind her the child's part of her love, the part that could cling to him for protection and reassurance, whose hair he would stroke in an absence of anything better. She was no longer the little girl on the beach with her dog, and he should know it.

Outside a bitter little wind had risen, lifting the powdery snow off the window-ledges and the rooftops, swirling it madly and then dumping it again. The gritty particles of ice stung Ginny's eyelids as they faced into the wind. There was barely room for her and Jim to walk together in the narrow paths cleared along the sidewalks, but he stuck beside her, and when the wind pushed against them, she felt his arm about her shoulders, drawing her close. They walked along with heads turned sideways to escape the flying snow. The early dusk had come; the children were gone from the streets and so were the snow-shovellers. There was no further sound of good-humoured talk, only the whistle of the wind through the narrow streets.

They stood for a moment uncertainly in the hallway of Barby's brownstone. Ginny felt Jim's kiss on her lips but she was the first to draw away.

"Good-bye, Jim. Have a safe journey. Give them all my love down there."

"Don't stay away too long, Ginny," he said quietly. "Try to plan to come down soon."

There was more in his tone than the conventional leave-taking. She looked up at him sharply, searchingly. "What's the matter? Is there something wrong? Jim—is it Father?"

He nodded. "I honestly don't know how bad. Katrien wouldn't say. And she wouldn't let me write you about it—nor Albert, either. She said not to spoil things for you . . ."

"Has there been another attack?"

"Two since October . . . not severe, I think . . . but then I'm not sure," he finished unhappily.

She put her hand on the stair rail and held on tightly. She felt his hand close over it. "Poor Ginny—I have spoiled things, haven't I? I thought about it a lot, and I can't agree with Katrien. I thought you ought to be told about it."

She ran her tongue over dry lips. "I'm glad you told me. I will come. Soon."

His hand patted hers. "That's my Ginny. It will do him good to see you. I know it will. Make it soon."

"Yes—soon." She withdrew her hand sharply. There would be no further dependence on him in every crisis; she had resolved that, and it must begin here. "You'd better go now. There's your plane . . ." That was as much as she could say. She turned and ran up the stairs.

"Ginny . . .?"

By the time she reached the third floor she heard the street door bang.

"Barby, can you lend me seventy dollars to get back to St. Nicolaas?" As she saw the outrage in the other girl's face she said quickly, "If you can't do it, I'll borrow it from

Eliot, but I don't want to borrow money from him. But money I've got to have—wherever it comes from."

Barby agreed only after she repeated what Jim had told her about her father. "O.K.—but I want it back, you hear? I don't like lending money. Now go and get packed and I'll see if I can squeeze a seat for you out of Pan Am or anybody else who flies down there."

She came into the bedroom ten minutes later. "Not so good. . . . All they can say is that if you come out to Idlewild first thing to-morrow morning they'll put you on stand-by for a cancellation. It seems to me they've got half New York City out there waiting to get off the ground."

"I'll chance it," Ginny answered. "There isn't anything else to do."

Barby lighted another cigarette, lounging back against the door-frame and watching Ginny closely as she folded clothes. "It wouldn't be Jim who's taking you down there in such a hurry? Because if it is then I'm not lending the money. That's a guy and a half, and you don't deserve him, and I'm not going to help you get him."

Ginny raised her head. "I wish to God it were Jim. I wish I thought it was any use going on his account. He isn't any nearer to me than he was a year ago. Farther away, I think. He used to feel a little sorry for me then, and try to teach me things. But now, after a year in the big city, he thinks I can take care of myself."

Barby gave a shrill little laugh that ended in her usual cigarette cough. "Well—this seems to be one time when it would have been better to stay down on the farm. Of course, knowing guys like Eliot Russell hasn't helped, has it? Some of it rubs off—has to! And a guy like Jim could tell it in a minute. No fool he."

"You liked him, didn't you?" It was hardly even a question.

Barby made no bones about it. "I could go for him—real big. It's a guy like that who makes most of the local talent look so poor. I mean, he's going to be what he is, and he doesn't give a damn what anyone else thinks about it. He's selfish, you know—wouldn't make concessions, but God it's good to meet a man once in a while who's sure about himself and what he's doing. Yes—I could go for Jim."

Ginny said nothing in reply. Instead she pointed at the dresses that Eliot had paid for hanging in the closet. "Can I leave them?"

"Will you be back?"

"I don't know. I'll write you when I know about Father."

Barby shrugged. "Well, I'll have to pack them away in boxes. Got to leave some closet space for the next tenant. . . ." She nodded in the direction of the clothes. "What are you going to do about *him*?"

"Eliot? What is there to do? There never was anything for me there—or for him either. He'll get along without me, as he did before I came. Eliot will manage—I'll call him —no, I won't call him! He'll start fussing about getting me reservations and all the rest of it. He'd probably call the chairman of the board of Pan Am. And somehow . . ." She turned away from Barby and half buried her face in the clothes that still hung in the closet. "This time I think I've got to do without Russell influence. I think I've got to go home as plain Ginny Tilsit with no strings pulled for me, and no Russell red carpets laid out. It has to be just as it was before. That's the only way I can go home."

Barby drew deeply on her cigarette. "When you go home it's never just as it was before."

The next day she waited at Idlewild for sixteen hours, amid the crowds of passengers that the storm had held there, those that waited like herself, in the hope of cancellations, the crying children, the ever-present queue at the snack bar and the toilets. Pan Am terminal, the umbrella of glass and concrete, seemed to grow soiled and tarnished by the very passage of people through it. There was no thaw, so the snow stayed, and every road and walkway through the whole airport had to be cleared. It was one of the few diversions of the sixteen hours to watch the people who had left their cars in the parking lot before the storm, trying to find them among the indistinguishable humps in the snow. In sixteen hours she had four hamburgers and eight cups of coffee, and counted her change very carefully. The time of waiting was a slow nightmare. When she could find no seat, which was every time she came back from the snack bar, she paced the terminal, with the reflected light from the snow harsh through the unscreened glass walls. The distances of the runways seemed immense and endless; the jets rose constantly, with black smudges of burned fuel against the grey sky. When the darkness fell she could see no more than the other lighted terminals of the airport; the planes moved unseen except for the brief flash of the navigation lights. Then her own reflection looked back at her from the windows, because of the darkness without. Sometimes, with a sense of grieving and loss she seemed to see her father's face there also, and Jim's, disembodied, floating like the reflections of all the other people in the vast lighted room behind her. Once she turned swiftly, with a half cry, because she was certain it had indeed been Jim she saw. But there was no familiar face among the crowd. She resumed her pacing.

Once she telephoned Barby and asked her to tell the Netherlands Consulate that she had been called home and didn't expect to be back. A second time she called just for the sake of having someone to talk to. When she was finally given a seat on a jet due to leave in forty-five minutes, she sent a telegram to Eliot.

It was an hour before midnight on Christmas Eve when she left New York. The plane landed at San Juan at two-thirty in the morning of Christmas Day. The Caribair counter was closed, but from the Pan Am desk she learned that the once-a-day direct flight to St. Nicolaas left at noon. One of the Pan Am agents, who had worked for Caribair, remembered her from the days of flying into school in San Juan. From him she borrowed two dollars for some breakfast and some aspirin, and then she went to sleep on one of the benches in the garden courtyard of the airport. She kept waking every few minutes, disturbed by the bites of the sandflies and the nagging worry that she would sleep deeply and somehow miss the plane.

The plane landed at St. Nicolaas airport, the new airport that was strangely like all the others, at twelve-forty on Christmas Day. While the baggage was being unloaded she went to the telephone.

" Father? It's Ginny. Am I in time for Christmas dinner? I'm at the airport. Could you come and get me?"

CHAPTER SIX

It was in Katrien that the change was most apparent. It was vaguely shocking to Ginny, that change, because it was unexpected. As Katrien came running down the steps at Oranje Huis when the car stopped, Ginny saw that the bloom had gone. Katrien, who had been a beautiful woman holding her youth into middle-age, was now quite definitely middle-aged. Still beautiful, a little heavier, the lines of her face were more marked, the folds of the skin beginning to dry and toughen. Ginny realised then that it was Katrien who had borne the changes of her husband's illness.

Her father, when he had come for her at the airport, had seemed no different. She had looked for change, but she could find none that was significant. The deep permanent tan of thirty years effectively hid any signs of a colour change in his face. The sinews of his neck and forearms stood out as they had done for years, in the way that thin men aged in the tropics. The bony, patrician cast of John Tilsit's face was unalterable.

In the beginning he blessedly asked no questions. She felt only the strong emotion of his greeting in the tightness of his embrace. " Welcome home, Ginny. We're glad to have you back."

At Oranje Huis Bo had flung himself down the steps before the car stopped, running with the stiffness of an old dog. Ginny felt a momentary prick of tears as she bent to support his weight when he stood on hind legs to put his paws on her shoulders. Waiting until the first greetings were over, Albert de Kruythoff came forward, his shy, mournful face lightened in a rare smile. He kissed her quickly on the cheek, and grasped her hand. " You see, you still have your friends Bo and Albert. And I must have guessed you would be back because I brought an extra spray of orchids."

Jim was missing, of course. She had looked around for him expectantly, and then remembered that there were no more private days for him, no more days when he did not work. Bo's head nudged her hand possessively as she strode along the gallery to the side that overlooked the cove. There were the brightly striped umbrellas that she had dreaded and joked about, there was the jetty with *Oranje Lady* moored to it, there was the finished restaurant block, with tables under its sweeping cantilevered roof. The first six cottages were finished, and so quick was the growth of Jim's new planting that they already were almost hidden. On the hill behind were the raw scars of the new construction, with careful barriers around the trees to protect them from damage. It was all there—Jim's world of expensive man-made beauty that wholly absorbed him. Her father came up beside her, with a glass of the special Christmas punch in each hand. He handed her one.

" Well, he's done it," he said, nodding down towards the cove. " He's worked like six men and he's done it."

She turned away from the sight and looked back to where Katrien and Albert were standing, Albert trying to keep the smile on his face, though he, like the others, had not missed Ginny's directness in going immediately to see what this year had been in Jim's life.

John raised his glass. " Happy Christmas, everyone."

" Happy Christmas! "

She sat on the veranda with them, sipping the punch, and staring across to the remembered view of St. Charles. There had been no real sleep for two days, and her weariness was monumental, like a load she could carry only for the hour or so until dinner would be served and eaten. Recognising this, they left her in peace, and the talk flowed on past her, almost as if she had not come back, as if she were not there. The talk was of small and familiar things—the crop, how much the island expected to harvest, the budget Albert was preparing for Curaçao, the new school. The throb and roar of New York faded and almost died. She felt herself lean back against all of it, the solidity of the family and the house, the boring, repetitious routine that was their life and Albert's life, in which small changes seemed violent ones in this minute pattern of existence, but in which the big changes had a tradition of hundreds of years to wash against, and in which finally to imbed themselves.

She closed her eyes against the glare of the sunlight that now seemed painful to them, and she fell asleep with the glass of Christmas punch clutched in her hand.

II

Albert had said, the first day, " You have that pale Northern look, Ginny—and you are too thin." For two weeks she slept almost until noon each day, and in the afternoon, when the sun was past its zenith, she lay on the beach. She ate her mother's food in long, leisurely meals during which she talked to John and Katrien about New York. They did not ask many questions, but let her tell them what she had selected to tell them. After a while she realised that it was deliberate. The idea amused her. " They are more sophisticated than I thought." It was a time of recuperation, as if she had been ill.

There was nothing she could do for her father, and she never told him that she knew about the attacks. Let him believe, if he wanted to, if he could, that she had come home because she was tired. To Katrien she talked.

" How bad is it?"

Katrien, turning to her, for a moment seemed unable to speak. " It's not good. They sent him to San Juan for a week for tests—to make sure, too, that he stayed in bed. No one can say about these things—how long—when. He has to be very careful . . . to rest . . . not to get excited or worried. It is that part of it that is impossible. How do you tell a man to slow down who boils inside? How do you coddle a man so independent—so much alone?" The gesture of Katrien's hand was one of exasperation and despair. " It is like trying to rope down a cat."

" Can I help?" Ginny said it humbly. Before this she would have been sure she could help.

" Just stay with him—for a while. It helps him to have you here. If you have to go away again, then that must be, I suppose. But try not to let him know that you're staying because of him."

The letters came from Eliot, a small bombardment of them, angry at first at what he considered was desertion by Ginny, and then appeared the streak of feminine pique, shrill and a little spiteful. " *Well—has Jim come through at last? Or is he still vacillating, and what are you going to do to help him make up his mind? A woman's oldest trick, I suppose . . . the lazy, obvious way to get a man who*

*probably isn't worth having . . . Will I come down there?
Is there anywhere decent to stay on that island of yours
besides Jim's egotistical hotel?"*

The thought of Eliot on St. Nicolaas filled Ginny with
a kind of panic. There was nothing for Eliot here. He
was not a tourist and he had too much energy to want
to lie on the beach for more than a few days. She could
not see him away from the controlled environment which
was his New York life, the world that money fashioned.
She knew she was probably being unfair to him in this,
but the feeling persisted. There remained, however, the
softer, vulnerable side of Eliot, the aspect of him to which
she had always responded.

"You could have had anything you wanted, Ginny," he
wrote. *" I think I would have done whatever you asked if you
had stayed."* It was impossible to reply that there had been
nothing to ask of him that she really wanted. *" You gave me
a great deal . . . I felt the touch of silk, and I'm grateful."* He
was scornful of that. *" If gratitude's what you feel, I don't
need it. Will you come back to New York?"* And she had
to reply, *" Perhaps—I don't know."*

Barby wrote brusque little notes: *" I called your boy-friend
Eliot to come and pick up the fur pieces you rich people don't
seem to care about, but so far he hasn't bothered to do that.
I wonder at what stage possession becomes the law?"* She
added finally: *" Stay where you are, kid. You're better there."*
Better, Ginny thought, for what?

The island was beginning to stir with the preparations for
the harvest. The mill which served the farmers of the whole
island, after being closed for months, had begun the process
of overhauling its equipment. John spent most of each day
in the shed which housed his trucks. With his foreman
he worked to get them into the best condition which their
ancient engines could achieve. It was always a matter for
worry during harvest that they should remain in working
order so that he could get his cane hauled quickly to the
mill. Once cut, the sugar content of the cane deteriorated
rapidly, and if it was not processed within forty-eight hours
it could be useless. With everyone else on the island harvest-
ing, it was often impossible to borrow or rent a truck, so
over the years he had become, in a rudimentary fashion

G

because he had never cared for things mechanical, his own mechanic. There were also the barrack-like sheds at the other end of the plantation to get in order. These were for the itinerant cane-cutters who came from the British islands and from Puerto Rico for the months that the harvest required. Every year there were the damages and deterioration of the previous year to repair—the broken windows and plumbing, a leaking roof, the posts that, touched with a hammer, suddenly revealed their insides eaten away by termites.

"This is the worst time," Katrien said. "There is so much to be done, and I don't know how to spare him. I could do most of it myself—after all I was born with sugarcane—but it would hurt his pride." She nodded confidentially to Ginny. "I think that John's hurt pride is worse for him to bear than his damaged heart."

"You spoil him," Ginny said. "You take too much on yourself. You don't let anyone else share the burden. Why," she demanded, "didn't you let me know when he was sick— and in hospital? I would have come at once. You know that."

Katrien nodded. "Yes, I know you would have come. But for what purpose? To set up a death watch on him that might go on for ten years?" She dismissed the thought with a single gesture. "You came in your own time, and that was right. It has never been right that the young should be sacrificed to the old and sick. That you love him doesn't make it any more right either. You have your own life to live . . ."

"Sometimes you astonish me," Ginny said mildly. "Just the way you used to astonish Jim when he first knew you. He was always singing your praises at a time when I used to think you were a nice but perfectly ordinary kind of woman." She smiled at her mother. "I'm glad I found out in time."

Katrien paused in her task and looked down at Ginny. She didn't smile in response. She was standing on a stool stacking up bars of soap on a high shelf of the pantry. To store large quantities of soap to allow them to harden was one of her economies. Ginny passed the bars up to her two at a time.

" Do you still listen to what Jim says? Or has New York taken all that away?"

Ginny shrugged. " I listen—if he cares to say anything. But I can't stand waiting for the word for ever. It may never come."

" Give him time." Katrien put out her hand to take the next two bars.

Ginny, squatting to pick up an armful from the floor, stayed there, rooted.

" Time!" she said. " Time! How much more time does he need. I tried hanging around him, and I tried staying away. What difference did it make? Jim can talk to me whenever he wants, and I'll listen. But I'm beginning to think that he'll never have anything to say."

" Time," Katrien said, " is short for him and long for you. He's a man with a load of debt on his back and a hotel to get built and start paying its way. He doesn't want entanglements. Who would? A young wife and probably children. These things could seem only like burdens to him now. Give him time."

Ginny straightened, and began again the rhythmic passing of the soap to Katrien. " And what am I to do while I'm waiting?"

Katrien shrugged, concentrating on getting the stacks in alignment. " That's what I thought you went to New York to learn. Do what you can."

They finished up the job of the soap in silence.

When her mother put the stool back in its place, Ginny reached down the pair of garden secateurs which always hung inside the kitchen door. " I'll cut the flowers for the dining-room. What do you want?"

" Oh—oleanders for the tall vase. Whatever you like for the table-bowl."

" Hibiscus," Ginny said promptly. " Do you know, it was one of the things that shocked me most about New York —the price of the flowers. And all shut up in glass refrigerators. They died as soon as you took them out. I used to think about our garden and just being able to run out and pick something whenever we wanted it. It didn't seem real somehow. It's one of the things only the rich have in places like New York—as many flowers as they

want. I decided it was easier to be poor in a hot climate
than a cold one."

"Poor!" Katrien gave a hoot. "If I thought you meant it
I'd be seriously concerned."

Ginny made a face at her, and the screen door slapped
closed behind her. Katrien heard her footsteps on the paved
walk. Then a minute later the screen door swung open
again.

"There *are* ways I could help him without him really
noticing. I mean, if I did it gradually it would be a habit
before he knew what had happened."

"Jim?"

"No," Ginny said impatiently. "I mean Father. I could
stay through the harvest, and just go out in the fields with
him every day—drive the jeep, and do all the running to and
fro for him. I'd say it was just to get experience in the
beginning—after all, I haven't been here at harvest since
I started going to school in San Juan. I don't have to *say*
I'm doing it to help him."

"He'll know. But I don't think he'll tell you not to do
it." She nodded, thinking about the proposal and agreeing.
"Yes—why not? It would be a help, and he'll take it better
from you than from me. And it will keep you busy—
less time to fret about Jim."

"Jim? Who says I'm fretting about Jim?" The screen
door slammed again. Ginny's voice drifted back to Katrien
defiant and full of longing. "I couldn't care less."

With the months of the harvest Ginny found the island again,
made her peace with it, and the slow rhythm of its life,
sensed her oneness again with the people and the ways of
its living. On the canefields the sun was burning and relent-
less, and the dust of the roads dried and choked the throat
and the nostrils. But the steady movement of the cane-
cutters across the broad gentle slopes of the island was a dance
movement whose beauty and drama had been bred into her,
and to which she responded as if to the touch of a hand. She
stood in the sun watching the Negro workers, the muscled,
graceful black arms shining with sweat, the single precision
of the stroke of the machete learned through generations
of cane-cutting since the time their ancestors had been brought
as slaves from Africa. The brief soaking showers came and

passed, and often she did not bother to run to the jeep
but stayed and got wet through and let her clothes dry on
her, as the workers did. There was no shelter on the canefields. She was alternately soaked and burned by the sun.
Her skin burned and peeled, and then took back the tan
she had known since childhood. Her legs and arms were
covered with scratches from the cane. Her hair seemed stuck
to her scalp with sweat and dust. But it was a time of
triumph and of a strange contentment. In a kind of exaltation
born of the days of fierce sun and nights of exhausted sleep,
she seemed to find some of Katrien's physical strength and
stamina. After the first week she began to relieve her father
in the job of driving the trucks piled high with the cut
lengths of cane. Bumping over the roads to the mill,
her body shaking with the reverberation of the ancient engine,
she felt a fierce and wonderful joy.

"Has it always been like this?" she said to her father.

And he, understanding, didn't ask of what she spoke.
"Sugar is a feminine crop," he said, speaking slowly and in
a low tone as if he said it for himself. "It's a child of sun
and rain and humidity—a voracious feeder, exhausting the
soil. And yet what other crop will give you eight cuttings
from the one planting, and what other crop will give you
this yield and this tonnage, like a fertile woman who gets
pregnant every year? Sugar is the world's sweetener, Ginny,
and there's fire in its rum. A feminine crop—and the sugar
islands are feminine too, beautiful and voracious."

There was no time, no time at all it seemed, to think about
Jim. The image of him would come before her at moments
during the day, but something else always demanded her
attention, and so he claimed no large part of her hours, nor
of the few minutes before she slept at night. The kind of
satisfaction she had found in working with her father in
the canefields was in itself a source of strength which allowed
her to lean towards her mother's view of patience. It made
it easier also, on the two occasions she went to St. Charles
on errands for her father, not to brood too much over
the information Susie Marshall gave her that Jim had been
seeing a good deal of a young American divorcee, Pauline
Thomas, who had recently discovered St. Charles and was
in the process of opening up a bookshop and art gallery.

There was talk, though Susie couldn't confirm it, that Jim was designing the house she intended to build, and that she had been to Puerto Rico and Miami with him to choose furnishings for the Oranje Cove Hotel. Ginny attempted to shrug the information aside.

" He's an architect, isn't he?"

On Sundays she shared Jim's work. He had asked her to take over the cash register and bar during the lunch and dinner rush. Oranje Cove was beginning to attract customers from all over the island, and on the week-ends the cove now held a few yachts from which parties came ashore. The *Oranje Lady* plied back and forth between the two islands, taking guests to planes when they couldn't wait for the once-a-day direct connection to Puerto Rico, or picking up tourists who were tranferring from hotels on St. Charles. There was a sense of bustle in the cove that had nothing to do with the slower tempo of the island until this time, but it was a tempo that was being picked up and repeated where the second hotel and the housing development were being built. " The tourist bustle," Katrien called it, and on Sundays Ginny lived in its midst. It was like moving forward a century in time from the canefields. Late at night, when the bar was closed, Jim always called her for a brandy and coffee in his cottage, which adjoined the restaurant and office.

" Not the choice location," he remarked when he showed it to her, " but I have to have everything under my eye. The thing I didn't realise," he said, handing her the glass, " was that there were so many things to keep under my eye. I guess I should have gone to Harvard to learn hotel administration—they're bound to have a course in that at Harvard. I suppose I was pretty simple thinking that merely building the hotel would be enough."

" You're doing all right," Ginny answered, leaning back in her chair and surveying the strangely unnatural neatness of Jim's new establishment. One wall of the room was entirely given to storage, and all Jim's scattered possessions seemed to have found their place. It made her nostalgic for the days of the old muddle and intimacy. " You're doing very well, I'd say."

" We'll do all right when we get the next twelve units built. At the moment we're carrying too many in staff for the number of guests. But we knew it would be that way. As long as the boys in Boston don't cut off the money, we'll be all right."

"It's a beautiful hotel," Ginny said, rather unwillingly. Somehow she didn't want to praise him. He had so much already. "When I first saw it I didn't think it could work out like this. It's grown into the background so well. Except for the new construction up on the hill—oh, and the beach umbrellas—you almost wouldn't notice it from Oranje Huis."

Jim nodded in agreement, but there was a kind of humility about him, as if he were thinking quite detachedly about the work of someone else. "I spent a month climbing all over this site before I put the first line on paper. I knew every tree that was to be left standing, and where the new ones were to be planted. I've got the site for every cottage located as far back as my land goes. It had to look like this or it would have been no good." He roused himself suddenly, and looked at her directly. "God damn it, Ginny! This wasn't a hotel I'd build and walk away from. I knew I was going to *live* here. I couldn't spoil it for myself. Fortunately the Boston boys saw it my way. As soon as they don't, I suppose we'll part company." Then he added, as if there was really no thought of such a thing, "They're thinking of putting a marina in—the hotel is an attraction for the yachtsmen and the yachts are a distraction for the hotel guests—a nice backdrop to dinner."

"The cove will be busy—from Oranje Huis we used to see nothing but one or two dingy lights in Willemstad, and the lights on St. Charles. It's all so changed . . . and still changing."

"But Oranje Huis stays, doesn't it, Ginny. It doesn't change. It's the permanent and enduring landmark." He held up his glass only half jestingly in toast. "I try to do nothing down here in the cove that will be an affront to the building up there. They built, those old Dutch ancestors of yours—they really built. The guests ask about the house all the time—what it is, who lives there? And do you know what I tell them?"

"What do you tell them?"

"I tell them it's the castle of the princess with the beautiful golden hair, and that a wicked fairy has placed a spell on her so that every Sunday for all eternity she is compelled to work behind the bar at the Oranje Cove Hotel. I'm cunning, you see. It always makes them want to stay until Sunday."

" For eternity? I thought the spell was broken by the kiss of the prince?"

He put down his glass and reached his hand towards her, gently drawing her to her feet. " My story never went as far as the prince," he said before he bent to kiss her. Her lips met his with all the violence of the time and the differences that had separated them, trying with this one single act to force the changes in him, to break the aloofness and the caution. She felt his response, the tightening and urgency of his body pressed into hers, and his mouth was no longer gentle.

" Jim . . . can't it be this time? Can't it?"

He drew back. It was a complete withdrawal, physical and emotional, and she knew that she had again damned herself with haste.

" Whoever breaks that spell had better know what he's doing." His hands released her. " I'm a man, Ginny, not a prince." He reached down and took his glass again, finished the brandy with one gulp. " Don't look like that! You're not scorned—you never could be. But don't let anyone trick you into settling for less than you should have. When it happens for you it should be because it must be—not because you think it's the way to make a man love you. For you, Ginny, sex isn't an item for barter— it's something much better and much richer. You'll know what I mean when it happens. It may be with me—but more likely with someone else. What matters is that it be right—and good."

She was quietly weeping. But not reaching towards him for comfort as she had done before. She felt alone, not dependent on him, but just alone. She didn't turn her face away, or brush the tears from her cheeks. There was a kind of pride in standing there before him and letting him see the tears, as if she had been naked.

" Come on," he said softly. " Wipe the tears, and I'll walk you home. There's too much ahead of you for tears at this stage, Princess. And you do have beautiful golden hair."

III

The cutting of John Tilsit's canefields was finished. Ginny drove the truck back to its leaky shed for the last time; the migrant labourers were paid off, and the plantation went back to patient routine of fertilising and weeding the crop. John Tilsit came back to Oranje Huis with the slackened look of a man suddenly relaxed who has borne tension almost beyond his endurance.

He said, " I don't know yet whether we made or lost money, but the cane is cut." And then he sat down in his chair on the gallery, and except for meals and the reluctant change to bed at night, it seemed to Ginny that he hardly moved in the next week. He spoke very little at this time; he just sat and stared across the strait.

Then at the end of the week he began to stir. He inquired what there was new to read, and even went down to borrow some books from Jim. He announced that finally he was going to teach Ginny to play a decent game of chess. And he went fishing with her at dawn.

Katrien didn't want him to go. " He hasn't been out alone in the boat since the last attack. Don't let him start the outboard. You'll have to do it—or don't start it at all."

Ginny did it, and they had their hours fishing together. It was a strange pleasure to be back with him here. The last time they had fished together she had been tangled in her resentment against him for refusing to tell her about Isobel. Now, in a way she could respect his reticence. After the turmoil of New York, after a year of hearing people talk when talking was disaster, she knew that a man had a right to silence, if he chose it. In the mood of having absolved him from blame, she grew nearer to him in age.

As they drew in their lines one morning, when the sun had touched the far side of Kronberg, he said to her, " Do you miss New York? I hope you don't—but I'd like to know."

" Only in small ways. And it grows less. It is one of the things that you're glad to have done, and glad you don't have to do it again." She looked back towards the island, the slopes of the hillsides brown in places where the cane had been cut and changing to vivid green where the canefield ran off into brush in the higher areas. The ruins of the old stone sugarmills stood out against the sky. The colours were beginning to come with the sun, the green to glisten as the first light hit the foliage, the beach to wash with pink for the first ten minutes after the sunrise, a cool pink when she knew that it would glow white and hot as the sun grew stronger. Kronberg dominated the scene as always, but it did not brood or menace. At this hour it was a fair and peaceful landscape.

" It's good to be here," she said.

Her father nodded, knowing what she meant. " I hope it's all good. What of Jim?"

" Jim? What of Jim? Either I have him or I don't. It can't alter any of this. I have something, don't I . . . I have a lot."

" I'm glad you know it now. The knowledge came a little late for me." Then she saw that he was going back to start the outboard and she scrambled to be there ahead of him. There was no more talk between them, and she remembered afterwards that it was the last time they talked together before the cable came.

IV

Ginny spent the late hours of the afternoon that the cable arrived working with Katrien in the garden—the continuing work of clipping, pruning, weeding—Ginny matching herself to the kind of leisurely rhythm which was Katrien's special gift. Ginny watched her mother's skilled careful hands on the trees and shrubs and vines, and she was conscious of a sense of pleasure in what she saw and in the knowledge that she had come to recognise it. Although Katrien still directed her, as she had always done, they worked together as two women, and equals.

They were far down the slope of the terraces and did not hear the van from the post office pull up at Oranje Huis. Shaded by the trees, they did not notice the passage of the sun until Katrien, looking down into the cove, saw how the shadows had moved across the beach.

" It's late," she said. " John will have the punch mixed before we have time to clean up. Better gather up the tools

and go in." Ginny nodded, and took the tools to the shed.
Katrien still lingered, moving some pot plants about, and
when she had finished, standing with her hands on her hips
staring out across the strait. Ginny left her, and began
the climb up the terraces to the gallery to where her father
had been sitting all afternoon.

As her eyes came level with the floor of the gallery she
saw the yellow slip of paper lying on the tile where the breeze
had lifted and placed it. Even at that moment it stirred again,
and slithered across the marble towards her father's chair.
He was asleep. She moved softly, so as not to disturb him.
As she came near she saw that his head was not bent forward
in his usual posture when he fell asleep in that chair.
Instead his whole body was slumped sideways his head thrown
back and his face turned upwards so that she looked fully
into it. The face was rigid. His lips were stretched in a
grimace of pain.

It was long after her first cry to Katrien, and long after
they knew that John Tilsit was dead that she thought to read
what was typed on the yellow paper.

V

A tropical downpour marked the burial of John Tilsit. The
mourners had gone to the graveside in bright sunshine, then
the squall had moved in with its usual swiftness from the
sea, and they heard the last of the service read in the stinging,
drenching rain. Most of the crowd around the grave moved
back into what shelter they could find under the trees ;
it was a big crowd, and it was studded, Jim thought, with
faces that John Tilsit, aloof and touchy as he had been,
might have been surprised to see there.

With the crowd withdrawn the figures of Katrien and
Ginny commanded attention. Someone had produced an
umbrella and passed it to Albert de Kruythoff ; he opened
it and held it above them. Ginny shifted to give her mother
the benefit of its shelter, and soon she herself was soaking,
the white dress clinging to her and her hair pasted to her
head. She stood there, perfectly still, upright. It seemed
to Jim that she had very swiftly grown to Katrien's level

in these brief hours since her father's death. Each woman's face bore the marks of stoic acceptance; their calmness acknowledged the uselessness of tears. As the service ended so did the rain; immediately the sun was out again and the earth was steaming. Katrien accepted Albert's proffered arm, but did not lean on it. Her walk was almost stately as they moved towards the gate of the cemetery. The crowd parted before them. Jim, like the others, hung back, strangely awed by the immense and uncontrived dignity of the two women.

Finally even Albert and Jim had to leave Oranje Huis. Those who had come back after the funeral had gone long ago but they had lingered, hung on doggedly, waiting for the appeals for help, at least for guidance and advice, that their sense of what two women would need told them would come. But it did not come. Katrien's calm remained; her grief was private and, while she acknowledged that they had a right to offer sympathy, they both felt, Albert and Jim, that she would be glad to be left alone with it. In answer to a few diffident questions from Albert she offered the information that John had left a small insurance policy; she further volunteered that she would probably lease the canefields to Pieter Cats to work. And that was all. There was nothing more offered, and there was nothing further that could be asked. It finally came home on the two men that the women were actually waiting for them to go. So they left, concerned, baffled, rebuffed by the wall of silence and self-sufficiency that suddenly had rung down between them and the women at Oranje Huis.

For Jim the night became a kind of vigil. He lay on his bed and smoked and watched the light on the gallery at Oranje Huis. He went periodically to stand by the window, his hands gripping the louvers, and the light up there both beckoned and held him back. The chair in which Katrien usually sat was out of sight below the level of the balustrade, but several times he saw Ginny as she paced, and twice she came to the beach side of the gallery and stood and seemed to stare down at him. He felt the weight of the darkness between them, and his exclusion from whatever was happening there. He counted the number of times Ginny went to the kitchen and made fresh pots of tea and carried it back to the

gallery. He watched her pacing back and forth, and sometimes she disappeared and he guessed she was sitting opposite
Katrien drinking the tea; and all the time he knew the
talk continued, and he didn't know of what they talked, or
why.

He was possessed and gripped by the thought of Ginny,
and by the suddenly realised fear that she might somehow have
slipped beyond him. The swiftness of death and burial in
this tropical climate had given no pause; he had had no
moments alone with her, there had been neither time nor
opportunity to say anything more to her than any other
friend would have said. All that he had been able to observe
of Ginny in these days had been what everyone had seen,
and it had been the picture of a woman emerging. She had
come through this time clothed in a maturity that was new,
but which already sat well upon her. If he could have
shared this new aspect of her it would have pleased and
warmed him, but he was shut out and all he could do was
wait.

A little before dawn the light on the gallery went out. He
stubbed out a cigarette and permitted himself to close his
eyes. He didn't know what wakened him a little later; he
was abruptly awake and full of a sense of expectancy and
hope. He went to the window and stared out into the
half light, and the beach was empty. He turned and searched
for a cigarette, and when it was lighted he came back to
the window. It was then he saw Bo emerge at a run
from behind the lowest of the crumbling Oranje Huis walls,
and Ginny herself, walking slowly. He nodded to himself in
satisfaction. She was coming here. They would cook breakfast and drink coffee, and they would talk. The pattern
would be re-established. He wanted them all back, all the
things that had been before.

But she did not come. He saw her stop at her father's
outboard, *Ginny*. In an instant he had crushed out the
cigarette and grabbed his shorts and T-shirt. He flung them
on, the screen door slapped behind him, and he was running.
There never was any warning, he thought. You held off a
woman, and backed away from her, and then suddenly there
you were, running.

She did not even return his wave; Bo came racing towards
him, but she remained still. She was faced in his direction,

but she seemed to be looking more towards the sea than to him. For the first time he felt a hesitation as he approached her. He corrected himself—no, not the first time ; yesterday in the cemetery he had hesitated also. He was no longer quite sure of this Ginny, no longer sure that she would accept him—what he did, what he was—without question. He knew that he wanted back all the things that had been, the old pattern re-established, but he also recognised that it was going to demand more from him than merely swinging open the screen door to admit her. She turned her face gravely to him as he came. The trace of a smile she gave him was not the eager one of his recollection. He missed it ; quite savagely he wanted it back. He felt, unreasonably, that she had no right to withhold it now, just when he had discovered that he valued it.

" Good morning," she said. She was most like her father when she slipped back into all his habits of English reserve and convention. He knew that all her superficial Americanisms were just that—forms that she adopted the way she spoke another language.

" Good morning, Ginny." She looked woefully tired, her face greyish and pinched. She was not at all beautiful now, without make-up, her hair lank and her pale lips held in a tight, straight line. And yet he thought that he had never found her more appealing, though the childish quality was gone and in its place was the rather aloof dignity that she seemed to have taken directly from her dead father. A sense of strength seemed to rest with her now, a kind of steeliness that had been lacking before . She had met the fact of her father's death and was living with it, not protesting it vainly. In this single happening, Jim thought, she appeared to have crossed the line into his own country. They lived in the same place now. He no longer wanted to offer his protection as he had so often in the past. She didn't ask it ; she didn't seem to need it. Now he wanted to possess and subdue and keep her. He didn't desire her at this moment ; he wanted just to be sure that she belonged to him.

" Are you going fishing? Will I come with you?"

It came as a shock when she shook her head. " No. I'm going out alone."

She made no sort of apology or excuse, and he was filled

with panic. It was worse because the rebuff had been given unthinkingly.

" Ginny . . ."

" Yes?"

" I'm sorry. If you want to talk . . . if there's anything I can do."

She made a gesture that was nearly a shrug " There's nothing to be done. It's empty up there now. There seems no way to fill it."

" Ginny, I want to help you. I want you to let me help you. You won't go away again, now that he's dead? I know you'll want some kind of work. I was going to suggest . . . I wanted to talk to you about it, but yesterday didn't seem the time for that. I wanted to say—well, why don't you come and work at Oranje Cove full time. I could use your help. There's plenty . . ."

He hadn't meant to say that at all. He knew that he had meant to ask her to marry him. But she was strangely unattentive to him, absorbed in something she would not share with him, or could not. The words, waiting to be said, having been asked of him by her for so long, faltered now, and changed as he hung back these last few minutes before the final commitment.

" But I have to go away," she said.

" Do you? Are you sure about that? Are you sure about where to go? Is New York really what you want?"

She looked at him in some puzzlement, as if she somehow expected him to know what was in her mind. " I wasn't thinking about New York. You see—you don't know, do you? No—there hasn't ever been time to discuss it until last night. Mother decided—no, I decided. Finally I decided for myself."

" Decided what?" In a gesture of impatience he took her arm and shook it a little. She was wasting time, holding up the things he meant to say to her. " What the hell are you talking about?"

" I decided what to do about the cable."

" Cable?" Looking at her he was visited with a wild and inexplicable certainty that it was already too late.

" A cable came from Isobel Tilsit's solicitors—the afternoon Father died. He got it, and I suppose that was what brought on the attack."

"Isobel? What of her?"

"She's dead. She died . . . well, they're not sure how she died. There's to be an inquest."

"You mean you're going to England for the inquest? But that's nothing to do with you. It isn't your concern."

"I'm not going for the inquest. They would like me there for the reading of the will. The cable said it is important for me to come if it's at all possible."

His hand dropped away from her. He was not impatient any more; she was not going to hear the words he had meant to say.

"Then it's not a little thing. Lawyers don't ask you to come across the world for a small legacy."

"I don't somehow imagine it's a little thing. It was very important to Father, whatever it was. It was important to her too."

"There are other ways to find out what was behind that cable." He was saying this uselessly, and he knew it. "Call these lawyers. Tell them you're not rushing across the Atlantic at the drop of a hat. They'll have to tell you what they want you for."

She was shaking her head, as he had expected.

"That's not enough. I can't be satisfied with a solicitor's talk on an overseas telephone connection. There's too much piled up now. There's even his life. If he hadn't died I might have been able to treat it the way I treated the letter she sent. But he was afraid of what was in that cable. The fact that he's dead is what makes it very important now. I have to understand *why*. I have to. I want more than just the name of Tilsit stamped on the back of a plate—oh, yes, and I want more than the name we saw in that book of Albert's."

He didn't argue. He said helplessly, "What—when will you go?"

"To-morrow. At least as far as New York to-morrow. If I can get a reservation, I'll go straight on to London."

"So quickly? Why . . .?"

"The cable said as soon as possible. It will be sooner or later—and so the sooner the better. I need the answers. We both do—Mother and I. We both lost a part of him to whatever happened there in England. We both have a right to try to understand the reasons."

"I suppose so," he answered dully, not caring for the reasons. She didn't seem to hear him—as she had not appeared to have heard any of his words, nor seen his face, nor been aware of him fully since the moment he had come running along the beach to her.

"So there's no reason not to go," she added. "And no reason to stay."

He thought for a second that her eyes had misted with tears, but he was not sure because she turned away at once and put her hand to the bow of the boat. "Help me run this out, will you? I haven't much time—but I wanted to go out just once before I left."

He pushed off for her, and started the outboard and watched her go. The words he had wanted to say had long ago died on his lips. He had refused to say them before when the girl was there to receive them gladly. And now the woman had taken over from the girl, and this woman no longer expected to hear those words. She had ceased to listen for them. She was gone, lost. A curtain had rung down, and she could not see that he wanted to be let through. He had waited too long, and once again he and Ginny were out of step. She was moving on, into her own time and her own experience, and he was left behind.

He walked back to the cottages, Bo trailing him. He took no pleasure now in the sight of them—not the finished ones which were filled with people who were paying to be there, not the mass of unfinished construction that rose on the hill above them. Not that, nor the dream of the final thing that had lived with him for so long. All it represented to him at the moment was a colossal gamble in which he might or might not succeed. It was a huge debt that stretched ahead of him for, seemingly, the rest of his lifetime. He could not call her back to come and share it with him because she had other things offered now, and she might misunderstand the words. The timing was wrong, and she might misunderstand.

"God damn it, Bo! I held back too long—and I went and lost her."

VI

An impulse of loneliness urged Ginny to send the cable to
Eliot Russell when her plane was delayed in San Juan.
She thought afterwards that it had been a foolish thing
to do, that she could expect only Eliot's fine and pointed
indifference to what was no longer his concern, and that she
had only revealed to him the trace of the dependence
on him that still lingered. It would please him to know
that she could not even pass through New York without
letting him know, and he would pay her back for her flight
at Christmas by ignoring the cable.

But he was there at the arrival gate when she struggled
along the ramp from the jet burdened by the three small bags
she carried and the old-fashioned camera that Albert had
made her accept. Eliot's face seemed to swim towards her
through the crowd of Puerto Ricans who were meeting
relations at the airport. He kissed her coolly on the cheek,
and immediately relieved her of the bags.

" Dear Ginny, I can't say you make a very elegant traveller.
Thank God at least you're not wearing orchids."

" It was good of you to come, Eliot."

" Damn good of me. You deserved to have your wire torn
up. In fact that's what did happen, and ten minutes later
I had to fish it out of the waste-basket and put the pieces
together to get the flight number. You're late, you know.
There's only forty minutes before the London plane takes
off. They'll start boarding in ten minutes. Why the hell
can't you behave like a civilised person and spend the night
in New York? What's the sudden rush?"

She tried to tell him as they walked through the huge
spaces of the terminal. The words tumbled out disjointedly.
Abruptly he stood stock still, for a moment holding up the
flow of the crowd behind them. " I don't believe it," he
said. " You're telling me your father's dead and this aunt
is dead, and you're going off to England to God knows
what. Ginny, people don't do these things! Have you . . .
have you seen a lawyer?"

She shook her head. " I never thought of that. If I had I
probably wouldn't be making the journey . . ."

The loudspeaker cut across her words. "Pan American announces the departure of Flight 106 leaving for London. Will all passengers kindly . . ."

"That's you," Eliot said. "Quickly, get over to the desk and have them check your ticket, and tell them you have some more luggage to go aboard. I've already spoken to them about it, so they're alerted and ready to ship it as soon as you present your ticket."

"What luggage?" She was starting to run.

"I called that Barby creature, and told her to haul out all the clothes you left behind. I sent down some suitcases to have them packed, and there they are. I had to rout her out of her office to do it in the time, *and* she was spitting with fury. But then she never did like me, so it's no loss. Incidentally, she sent her love."

Ginny slipped the ticket into the waiting hands of the airlines clerk. "The clothes—*all* of them?"

"Anything I thought suitable for that unbelievable English climate. I didn't know how long you were planning to stay . . . or why . . . so I had everything packed. I'm sorry the bags have my initials on them. Couldn't do anything else in the time."

"Eliot, you're . . . I don't know what to say."

"Forget it. My kind always does these little things so well, don't you know? No—no, don't pay that. I've already fixed about paying for the excess baggage. Now quickly, Ginny . . ."

"The flight is departing on schedule, miss. The plane is loading now. Gate Nine."

He hustled her towards it. "I had them put champagne on the ice up in the restaurant—pity there isn't time for it. Though champagne's hardly the thing, is it? I didn't know about your father. I'm sorry, Ginny. This is a hell of a time and place to try to say it, too. Perhaps I just should have bought a ticket and gone with you. If I'd known about this, perhaps I would."

"I have to be alone some time, Eliot. It has to begin . . . I was frightened in San Juan when I sent that wire." Suddenly she stopped, in the way he had done a few minutes before, and in his rush he shot past her. "Come back, Eliot. I have to say something before I go. I suppose

—I really think I wouldn't be making this journey at all if it weren't for some of the things I learned when I was here . . . from you."

"From me? What could a girl like you learn from me?" His tone was suddenly angry. "Where's Jim? Why isn't he teaching you the things you should know?"

"Jim . . .? I don't know. I . . . I lost Jim a long time ago."

"All right then. Forget him. Go to England and forget him. Or if you can't, come back and hold on to him hard. Don't let yourself settle for the half measure. Your trouble, Ginny, is that you're not quite sure he's what you really want." He jerked at the bags. "Now come on. Don't dawdle. Have you got your boarding pass, and your passport? Well, don't lose them. It can be awkward."

"Eliot, you're very kind . . ."

"Shut up," he said. "For God's sake don't start getting mawkish, and don't try it on the English either. They hate that kind of sloppiness. Here, take your bags. If I were you I'd lose that old camera. It's seen better days. And here —this too."

As Ginny's boarding pass was being examined a uniformed man approached whom Ginny afterwards remembered was one of the two Russell family chauffeurs. On his arm, neatly folded and wrapped in transparent plastic, was the white silk coat. The Russian broadtail lining was discreetly out of sight. He passed it to Eliot, who in turn laid it on Ginny's arm. "I'm sorry to give you another burden. This wouldn't fit in the bags."

She couldn't speak. His good-bye kiss was light and swift, like a woman's kiss on the cheek.

"I'm sorry I tried to buy you, Ginny. It was very crude of me. This time there are no strings attached."

When she was seated on the plane she collapsed for a moment against the arm-rest, her bags jumbled on her feet and spilling into the aisle. A stewardess came quickly to try to tuck them all under the seat. "Shall I put this in the rack?" she said, reaching for the coat. "You'll be more comfortable . . ."

"No. I want to hold it. I'll put it up later."

The girl shrugged. "Well, fasten your seat-belt, please."

Ginny slipped the coat out of its plastic cover. A little

dead whiff of scent reached her from it, the Balenciaga Eliot had given her. She clutched the coat to her, feeling the incredible textures, the stiffness of the silk, the softness of the fur. Her hands trembled a little. She thought of what was behind and ahead, and for a moment her mind numbed in grief and fear. "Father . . . Jim . . . Eliot . . . between all of you where on earth am I?"

BOOK TWO

CHAPTER ONE

" I think we may begin our business, since Mark Barstow seems to have decided not to appear."

The words were spoken into the dead quiet of the room, a room in which five persons sat, and yet no one but the solicitor seemed to move or breathe naturally. There was no obvious anxiety in any of the faces of the people about her, Ginny thought, except possibly her own. There was not even any overt hostility. They had had days now—a week— since Isobel's death ; they had schooled themselves to whatever disciplines they would require.

" I think the will is quite clear—but I'll answer whatever questions any of you have when I have finished reading."

No one spoke. In a sense they all knew what was in this will, the part that mattered they all knew. Ginny's presence here answered the one important question. The will was the formal document which would dispose of the details. Ginny looked away from the group seated about her, staring into the fire that burned even on this day in May. She heard the crackle of the stiff paper as the solicitor unfolded his document. He was William Randall of the firm of Hedges, Randall, and Strong whose name had been on the cable sent to St. Nicolaas. He was the only one who was not caught and bound by this explosive silence ; no doubt, Ginny thought, he was used to it. He must often have read wills to assembled families and known that his words were another kind of death to them.

Ginny let her eyes move away, upwards past the great carved stone mantel, the carved panelling, roaming over the sculptured ceiling of the room. She remembered the only time she had seen Isobel. Isobel had sat in the high-backed Spanish chair as if its splendour did not intimidate her, nor even surprise her. Now Ginny understood why. From the moment she had first glimpsed Tilsit last night, seen only in outline in the darkness from the other side of the stream and the stone bridge, she had begun to understand a great many things about Isobel and her father.

Her gaze travelled the length of the room—a very long, high room with three square bays of windows that gave a view of the terraced garden. The wall opposite the bays —the wall that contained the two great fireplaces—was hung with tapestries that appeared to have been woven to fit above the panelling. High-backed Jacobean chairs stood at intervals down the length of the room, and pictures hung between the bays—two Van Dycks and a Canaletto, Randall had already told her. Two sofas and two easy-chairs covered in brilliant gold damask that matched the curtains were grouped about one of the fireplaces, and that was where they sat. This was Tilsit's Gold State Room, and it was never used except on such occasions as this, Randall had said. So they sat here uneasily with hardly a movement, with not a sound beyond Randall's quiet voice as he began to read. The casements were closed and no scents came from the garden; outside the rain was falling, as it had done all morning, but it was a light rain that did not penetrate Ginny's consciousness except to lay upon her a feeling of melancholy and slight chill.

Ginny had chosen the comparative isolation of one of the chairs; Randall had the other. As he read the preamble Ginny darted a look across at the man and woman who had taken their places one at each end of the sofa on her right. The man's attention was fixed on the solicitor, his expression stony and correct. Lawrence Bowen-Tilsit was a conventionally handsome man whose regular features somehow matched his correct tweeds and the way he fingered his empty pipe, not smoking it because of the occasion and the place where they sat. His thin mouth was strengthened by the thick grey moustache which he kept pulling at in a nervous gesture. The woman beside him sat with her head bent over an embroidery frame, the needle in her hand flashing in and out with the speed of long practice. It was impossible for Ginny to guess at her thoughts—the delicate, exquisite face under dark silver hair was veiled, deliberately vague and shifting. She had allowed her eyes, unusual violet-blue eyes, to rest on Ginny only for a moment as they were introduced, and then had dropped them again to the work in her hands. Ginny had the feeling that this woman rarely looked for long at anything else. She was the wife of the man on the sofa beside her. Her name was Margaret Bowen-Tilsit. On the drive down from London Airport yesterday Randall had explained the relationship of these two to Ginny.

" Lawrence is Isobel's first cousin—the nephew of the man—John Bowen—whom Isobel's mother married. It was part of the marriage contract that John Bowen should assume the name of Tilsit. When his nephew, Lawrence, became associated with Tilsit, he added the name to his own."

" The same as George Martin Tilsit?" Ginny said. " He assumed the name of Tilsit, didn't he?"

The solicitor was driving, and he seemed to be inviting a crash the way he turned to look at Ginny each time she spoke. " Your aunt told me that you knew nothing of the family history."

" The encyclopædia of pottery and porcelain," Ginny answered briefly. " It's part of the Tilsit entry that the potter George Martin assumed the name of Tilsit."

" Yes—when he married Jane Tilsit. Are you interested in pottery?"

" I don't know anything about it."

" You'll learn about it then. Everyone who's ever been connected with Tilsit in the last hundred years does learn." Ginny recalled the conversation as she looked at Lawrence Bowen-Tilsit. A first cousin of Isobel, the nephew of Isobel's father—he had, therefore, no blood relationship to the Tilsit family.

" Your aunt," Randall had said, " insisted that he take the name of Tilsit. When your father left—there were suddenly no male bearers of the Tilsit name."

" Isobel might have married," Ginny said.

" She didn't, though. Unfortunately, Lawrence had no sons. Just one child—a daughter."

Lawrence Bowen-Tilsit had been employed at the Pottery at the time John Tilsit had left England. On Isobel's invitation he and Margaret had come to live at Tilsit, and their only child had been born there. She was known as Vanessa Tilsit; the Bowen part of her name was never used. Isobel had kept to herself the information gathered over the years about her brother and the birth of a child on St. Nicolaas

—no one beyond Randall had ever known of the journey to the West Indies. In the absence of anyone else, it had always been assumed by everyone at Tilsit, that Vanessa would inherit from Isobel. And then last week Randall had told them that he must cable St. Nicolaas, and the assumption of the inheritance had collapsed. It was towards Vanessa Ginny now looked.

She sat alone on her own sofa, and she was staring, not at Randall but directly at Ginny. Her gaze did not shift or falter; she just kept staring, deliberately and coolly. She was about twenty-five, Ginny thought. She had her mother's beauty, but in a much stronger cast—the same extraordinarily white skin and the deep-set eyes, defined by dark lashes and brows, the dark hair. But her face had a stamp of maturity that the older woman's lacked; her eyes were intelligent and quick, with a bite of passion revealed in them. She was dressed casually in country clothes whose simplicity didn't conceal either their elegance or their cost. Her hair was worn in a style that was expensively artless, her finger-nails long, manicured, and painted a pale pink. Seated in the middle of her gold sofa, at home in this great room of paintings and tapestries and sculptured ceiling, she seemed to Ginny supremely suited to be the heir to this house. There was one thing wrong. Her name was no longer Tilsit.

Randall had told Ginny about this, too, on the way down from London.

"She had a debutante season when she was eighteen. Your aunt gave a small dance at Tilsit—your aunt never liked to spend money on things like that. And then she shared another small dance in London with a girl she went to school with. Your aunt wouldn't allow her to be presented at Court—there's a family tradition of keeping aloof from royalty—something connected with a story of some supposed snub from Queen Victoria. But without being presented, and without any big splash party, Vanessa became quite the rage that season in London—she's really very beautiful, you know. Even at that age she had style. She got in with a smart, rather fast crowd. Isobel didn't like it, so she kept her pretty short of money; and then she cut it off altogether and ordered Vanessa to come back to Tilsit. The Bowens didn't have money, so there was no help from her father. She came back to Tilsit but she only stayed a few months, and then she was gone again, to some job or other she said she had in London—though what kind of job it could have been I don't know, because she was never very serious about anything then. Your aunt was teaching her the whole pottery business from beginning to end, and she was furious when she left. Lawrence tried to force her to come back again—everyone, you see, expected that Miss Tilsit would leave her the whole estate, and I suppose Lawrence didn't want her to jeopardise it. But Vanessa was very independent —and she was young. She used to manage to get invited to places like Klosters and anywhere else that was fashionable. It must have seemed to Isobel that she was being thoroughly frivolous. It was then that Vanessa married her racing-driver."

" A racing-driver!"

"Precisely that. An Italian racing-driver. A famous one, I understand—though I don't know much about these things. She met him at a rally on the Continent, and then he came to England to race, and they were married. Vanessa was under age, and Isobel demanded that the marriage be annulled. But for once Lawrence dug in over that, and he said he wouldn't start the action. So nothing was done. I met the Italian once—Marcello Vitti was his name. He was as handsome as the devil, and very charming. Good manners. And I must say I think he loved Vanessa very much. In any case he told me politely to go to hell when I suggested that your aunt might be willing to meet his price for a divorce. He was insulted by that—it was a very unwise thing for your aunt to have done. And he laughed in my face when I asked if he would be willing to change his name to Tilsit. He snapped his fingers at me and laughed." There was a lingering warmth in Randall's voice as he spoke. "I must say I rather liked that man, for all the fact that he had none of the qualities we solicitors are supposed to admire. He was winning and making a lot of money then— and spending it, he and Vanessa. Vanessa had all her clothes from Paris, and she caused a sensation wherever she went. She was always being photographed all over the Continent— one of the beauties of the International Set, and always a little ahead of fashion, my wife used to say. Vitti made enough money to support that while he lived."

"He was killed?"

Randall had nodded. "In one of those terrible multiple crashes. Three racing cars were involved, I think—all the drivers killed, and a couple of spectators. That happened about eighteen months ago. Vanessa came back to Tilsit."

"And she never knew, all this time, that I existed?"

"Not until I had to tell them that I was sending for you."

"Then they know what is in the will?"

"More or less."

And so Vanessa's expression, as she stared at Ginny, held no shock. She already knew what she had lost. Her gaze was critical and appraising, but hardly hostile. As they listened to Randal reading, Vanessa took a cigarette from a gold case she carried with her, and her eyes left Ginny to glance about for matches. Finding none, she rose slowly and went to the fire. Ginny watched her lift the heavy tongs that matched the massive crested fire-dogs ; she found a red ember of the burning wood and lifted it with exquisite grace to light her cigarette. Over the red-hot ember, her eyes met Ginny's again, and she seemed to smile, not a friendly smile, but one of acknowledgment, with a hint of amusement in it. It didn't seem possible that Vanessa could be laughing, as if Isobel had played some colossal joke on her, and yet she might have been. Ginny thought that in different circumstances she would have liked Vanessa. As it was, they didn't have to like but only to tolerate each other.

They would all have to tolerate each other, Ginny thought. They were here, strangers pushed, by an improbable family history and her father's implacable mistrust of his sister, into this uneasy union. They needed one another. Lawrence Bowen-Tilsit ran the pottery, and she, Ginny owned it. That was what William Randall had explained to her on the way down from London.

"I shouldn't be divulging the terms of your aunt's will to you in this way, before the formal reading. But it doesn't seem fair to plunge you into the middle of this family with no preparation for what you'll find. They're an odd lot— it was an odd situation at Tilsit. But you'll find a good many of the English are odd. They enjoy it."

During the long drive down from London she had begun

to relax in the presence of this man, tall and kindly, in his sixties, and wearing his rumpled tweeds like a comfortable skin. She had begun to like and to trust him; he was gentle and patient with her bewilderment and her sense of having come too quickly through the happenings of this last week. At London Airport he had apologised for rushing her to the car when they had finally identified each other. " If you don't mind, we'll go straight down to Tilsit. The family is waiting to meet you—and there are reasons why it might be as well——"

One of the reasons seemed to be his reluctance to permit the press to interview Ginny. As he was stowing her baggage two men had appeared, one carrying a camera. At the sight of them Randall had thrown the remainder of the bags in the back of the car, and attempted to bundle Ginny into the front seat, while she was still clutching some small pieces and the white coat. He didn't make it in time. As he opened the door for her the camera bulb flashed.

" Miss Tilsit? I'm Peter Styles of the *Daily Post*. Could we have a few minutes . . ."

Randall had cut in. " If you don't mind, not now, please. Miss Tilsit has had a long journey and is very tired. She has no statement at this moment . . " And all the time he had been urging Ginny firmly into the car, and with the last words he closed the door. She heard him add, " All communications can be made through my office, gentlemen." He had slipped in beside her, and started the car jerkily, fumbling in his haste. " You don't mind my speaking for you, do you? It's so very awkward with the press when the will hasn't been read or filed for probate. One can say absolutely nothing." Ginny had accepted that as reasonable, thinking that this kind of behaviour was typical of her father's, and therefore to be expected. After that, wearily she gave herself up to the journey, to watching the narrow roads and little towns choked with traffic, hearing the click of the windscreen wipers as they passed through showers, listening politely to Randall's attempt to point out things of interest they passed. She felt that he was trying very hard to find a bridge in her own background, and was not able to make it because for him the world of the Caribbean islands was something from the *National Geographic* and he couldn't imagine anyone actually living there, or making a living there.

He treated her with cautious awareness, like some delicate tropical bird, fussing with the heater and constantly asking her if she felt cold.

" Most of us can't imagine what it's like to live in a place where it's never cold," he said finally. " We just can't imagine it." She noticed that from time to time he would quickly roll down his window and gulp fresh air as if he were stifling.

He kept encouraging her as the twilight faded into the darkness. " It really isn't so much farther. Just a bit past Bournemouth. It seems long the first time, but you'll be surprised how quickly you'll get used to the drive from London. There's a decent place to eat not far from here. We'll be too late for dinner at Tilsit." He sounded as if he were glad of that fact. " I've been staying at Tilsit ever since your aunt died. There has been a lot to attend to . . ."

The inn he had chosen to take her to was half-timbered Tudor. She said, " I'm surprised the real thing looks so much like the copies—except for the sagging beams."

" There are parts of Tilsit much older than this," he answered, dismissing the building with a shrug. " The Great Hall and parts of the Old House date from the fourteenth century. But the chapel is twelfth century, with a mural that was done about fifteen hundred."

She looked down at her wine. " I'm not sure that I will know how to live with a house like that, Mr. Randall."

" Those parts are not used now, except to show to the public. But even so, the house is . . ." He hesitated. " It is lived in. It has been continuously occupied in every stage of its existence—always by Tilsits."

" Not by my father," Ginny said.

Then it had been Randall's turn to look down at his wine. " Not, not your father," he said. And that was all, and she knew at once that there were going to be no easy explanations of the past, that at Tilsit they wanted to talk about her father as little as he had wanted to talk about Tilsit.

" When was Isobel's funeral?" She was not able to call her " my aunt."

" Yesterday. It was just as well you missed it. It was private—otherwise half the district would have been there.

Your aunt had no interest in demonstrations, and in any case she wasn't the kind of woman who cared whether people liked her or not."

"Yes, I know that," Ginny said.

"If you had been there a lot of people would have come to the church just to get a look at you. The word had leaked out, you see, that we had had instructions to cable to ask you to come in the event of your aunt's death. People didn't know, just from the fact that you were coming, whether or not you had a substantial interest in the inheritance. It was just the fact that you existed at all. The inquest was a big enough sensation, but they really had a field-day when the word got out that John Tilsit's daughter was coming. Thirty years isn't so long in the memory of a quiet little county like Dorset. Tilsit is important as a monument, but the Pottery is more important because it gives a living to a lot of people. There is always a great deal of interest in what happens at Tilsit. At times I wish there weren't. The crowds at the inquest. . . ."

"Why was the inquest necessary? Isobel told me she had a heart condition. Surely that . . .?"

Randall sighed. "I wish the inquest could have been avoided. I tried—but there was a doubt, and so it had to be. The doctor couldn't say whether she had fallen first and had been killed in the fall, or whether she had had a heart attack and was perhaps already dead when she fell. So there was an autopsy and an inquest."

"She fell?"

"From a cliff. Not too high, but enough to injure her seriously. No one saw her fall—there was never any way to tell exactly what happened. The death and the fall were so close together it was not possible to separate them. The coroner gave a verdict of death from natural causes, which was what everyone was hoping for."

"What other verdict could there have been?"

"Death by misadventure—meaning she had died from injuries suffered in the fall. The autopsy revealed heart failure. It could have been either. Which was why the inquest was necessary, I suppose. But it seems a pity, all the same. Those kind of things always stir up unnecessary talk. Much better if they never happen."

They left the inn and were once again, it seemed to Ginny,

playing a game in a maze of narrow country roads that
led to signposts which announced to the traveller where
he had been, and where he could choose to go, but almost
never the place at which he had arrived. Randall drove
at speeds that seemed madness on these roads that were
masked by high hedges, and he shot past other vehicles where
there seemed barely room for two.

"You get used to driving this way in England," he
remarked cheerfully, as if he knew her apprehension. "Roads
are so narrow you'd never get past anything at all if you
didn't take a chance now and again. They tell me it's quite
different in America."

"Somewhat," Ginny said faintly. "Mr. Randall, why . . ."
"Yes?"

She had been going to ask about her father. She could
sense now the close approach of Tilsit. The dinner hour
had been an interlude, a pause in the passage between the
world she had just left, and the world to which she had come.
With every mile Tilsit grew nearer and the questions more
urgent. But also the reasons that had driven John Tilsit from
here began to have more weight as she came to a small awareness of what he had left. Thirty years was a very short span
of time by comparison to centuries; but time was respected
at Tilsit, and time was needed to travel back the distance
since he had left. She had begun to comprehend that there
was more than the simple answering of simple questions.
She yet didn't know the right questions to ask. So she said,
"How much farther?"

"Some way yet, I'm afraid. You see we've had to skirt
all around Poole harbour and this long inlet. There's a car-
ferry that connects the two shores, but it closes down
at eight. St. Mary's is about fifteen miles from here—
the Pottery is at St. Mary's. Tilsit is about fifteen miles beyond
that. Tilsit's on the coast, of course."

On the coast, he had said. She could not have told it as
she sat here in this long splendid room listening to Randall
read the will and watching the fire that did not warm her. It
was possible to forget where one could not hear the sea,
nor smell it, even. Between this room and the view of the
sea lay the whole great pile of Tilsit's buildings, the passages,
the staircases, the two courtyards. Beyond that was the low
wooded hill against which Tilsit was set, and on the skyline,

the ruin of the Norman keep. The rain had stopped by the time they had reached Tilsit the night before, the thin clouds chasing swiftly across the face of the moon. Past the gate-house Randall had slowed the car for the hump of the narrow stone bridge.

"That's Tilsit there on the right," he said unnecessarily. It was above them, half-way up its hill, the outline revealed briefly by a break in the clouds. One wing only had lights, but she remembered how her hand had gripped the seat in a sudden panic at the sheer bulk of it in the half darkness; it seemed to be built on two levels of the hill, so that the walls on the near side rose as sheer as ramparts. The clouds had closed again, and the light was gone from the crowd of chimneys, the complex pattern of its roof-lines. Even now, less formidable, less fairy-tale seen by daylight, her mind boggled at the thought of it. A little at a time, she told herself; she would learn it all a little at a time. She gave her attention again to Randall's words:

"To Emily Brown and Robert Garth, if they are still in my employ at the time of my death, each one thousand pounds."

Garth. Robert Garth. That was the stoop-shouldered old man who had welcomed her to Tilsit last night, opening the double doors that gave on to a great stone-flagged hall at the instant that Randall's car passed under the archway into the first courtyard. "This is called the Hall Court," Randall said. "I've brought you to the East Front. Usually the family uses the small entrance on the South Front, but I knew Garth would be heartbroken if you didn't come in by the main door the first time."

And the old man had bowed and said, "Welcome to Tilsit, Miss Virginia." She had felt enfolded, engulfed almost, by the words, and by the long look he gave her, as if he were passing over something into her keeping. There was no more emotion in the lined face than could be permitted in a well-trained servant but she felt the weight of what he said, the charge and responsibility. And yet as she followed him past the carved oak screen that shielded the Hall from the entrance passage and he paused for a moment by the break so that she could see it, she could almost have laughed at the unreality of it, and her being here, of the place itself, the great height of the chamber barely lighted by the candles in the pewter sconces so that the gallery above was almost lost in shadow and the tapestry behind the High Table leaped to life and colour only in parts as the candles flickered in the draught from the open doors. And then there was Garth signalling to a young boy in a white jacket to take her bags, and he was leading her through a second screen that rose from ceiling to floor on the other side of the entry, and beyond this was electric lighting, and at once the medieval splendour gave way to solid Victorian comfort. They turned at right angles into a wide passage and Garth was showing them into a large, rather shabby room that Ginny later learned to refer to as the sitting-room, and whose deep sofas and chairs upholstered in worn red damask were a relief after the austere bareness of the Great Hall. A fire burned in the marble hearth and Ginny went to it gratefully.

"This whole wing was built during the late seventeenth century," Randall said, lowering himself into one of the chairs with an air of long familiarity. "It was heavily modernised about the turn of this century—which is something you'll learn to be grateful for." Then he looked at Garth, who was standing by the door.

"The family have retired, Mr. Randall. We were not sure that you would not decide to stay in London to-night. They asked to be called if Miss Virginia should arrive."

But Garth had expected her, Ginny thought, remembering the lighted candles in the Great Hall. Randall was shaking his head firmly.

"Don't call them, Garth. Miss Tilsit has been travelling continuously since she left the West Indies. I don't think she can take much more excitement and fuss. She needs to be in bed as soon as possible."

"Very good, Mr. Randall. Shall I bring you some refreshments, Miss Virginia?"

"I would like some tea, please."

Garth brought it, ten minutes later, on a huge oval silver tray; the tea-service was a rich red, heavily ornamented with gold.

"Is this Tilsit china, Garth?"

"This is our most complicated pattern, Miss Virginia. It is very difficult and expensive to make." Even into that

H

disciplined voice there crept a note of pride. " I expect you'll be learning all about it."

" No doubt she will, Garth," Randall had answered for her.

Then there was the woman who waited in the bedroom to which Garth led her—the thin tall woman in the flowered smock whose iron-grey hair was rolled into a knot at the back. It was a plain face, without make-up, the end of hair straying as if she had not looked in a mirror all day.

" Good evening, Miss Virginia." The formula was repeated. " Welcome to Tilsit. I am Brown."

" Am I to sleep here?" Ginny said, her voice faint with growing dismay. She fought it, because it was a sign of weakness, but the thought of sleeping in this room appalled her. The blue and gold damask curtains were closed tightly over the enormous windows, a single lamp burned on the carved tallboy. Massive dark shapes of furniture hardly served to fill the spaces of the room. The four-poster, turned down and ready, was topped by an embroidered blue canopy and backed by a great head-board of dark carved wood. Most of the room was lost in shadow.

" Of course, Miss Virginia, you can sleep anywhere you choose. There are many rooms. . . ." The woman's lips worked nervously. " Your aunt, though, slept here, and her grandmother, until she died. You see——" Suddenly she went and opened a door that connected with an adjoining room that seemed to Ginny almost as big as the one in which they stood. " Your great-grandmother had a bathroom made here. It used to be a powder closet in the old days."

" Well . . ." Ginny said.

" I'm sure you'll be comfortable, miss. And you see, if there's anything you want, you can just ring for me. Your aunt had me move over from the servants' wing years ago. I'm quite close. Just along the passage there."

" Yes, I see."

The whole smothering weight of the room seemed to be about to fold in on Ginny. She felt herself sway slightly as she stood. Even half lost under its heavy canopy, the bed now seemed a haven.

" I expect you're very tired, miss. You'd like to go to bed. I've unpacked most of your things. You can tell me to-morrow how you like them arranged. We'll get you settled in nicely to-morrow, miss."

"Yes. Thank you." She couldn't understand why the woman's tone should have been so persuasive, almost pleading. Between this woman and Garth, something was being thrust upon her. She was pleading, Garth had been firm, and Randall had wanted to pass it to her gently and with understanding. But all of them would pass over this charge with an air of relief that she was there to pick it up.

"Just one other thing, miss. The candle . . . you see there are only the electric sconces over the mantel, and this one lamp. I expect it was luxury in the days they put it in, miss—but it's not enough now. You have to use the candle by the bed, and if you want to do any writing . . ." She nodded towards the tall secretaire between the windows. "You will be careful with the candle, won't you, miss? The bed-hangings . . ."

Ginny nodded. "I would like the window open a little."

"Of course, miss. Your aunt liked to sleep with the windows open too. Here, let me do it for you."

It was a shock to come close to the curtains, to touch them. In the distance and the dim light she had seen only the blue sheen of their damask, the richly embroidered gold border. Close to, she realised that the silk was rotten ; it had perished along the folds, and clung in silken threads to the blue padded lining. The woman noticed Ginny's finger softly trace the threadbare folds.

"It's time they were replaced, miss. This pair has lasted over sixty years, but the pair before that hung here for nearly a hundred years. They wove better cloth then. Of course the border is transferred from one set to another. It's a big undertaking."

Even through her weariness Ginny had to ask the question. "How do you know all this? How can you know how long the set before this lasted?"

"It's all written down, miss. In the household records. This set . . ." She fingered the curtain. "This cost thirty-seven pounds five shillings more than sixty years ago. They would cost several hundred pounds to replace now. That's why Miss Isobel kept putting off having them done."

Ginny nodded, staring out into the darkness revealed by the drawn curtain. There was nothing to see, that is, nothing until her eyes, growing used to the blackness, could discern faintly the outline of the keep on the hill. "This looks to the sea?" she said.

"You can't see the sea from any of the rooms, miss. The hill there is a little higher. But you can hear it sometimes, when it's stormy. The others—Mr. and Mrs. Bowen-Tilsit and Miss Vanessa have their rooms on the other side of the passage—that's looking into the Inner Court. Miss Isobel always preferred this side. Will there be anything else, miss?"

"No . . . no, I don't think so."

"Very good, miss. Then I'll say good night. I hope you sleep well."

"Thank you." As the woman began to close the door, Ginny halted her. "Just a moment—I don't remember what you said your name is."

"I'm Brown, miss. I dust the china."

She left Ginny staring after her, fighting a wild desire to laugh aloud hysterically. "My lord——" she whispered to herself. "I'm Brown . . . I dust the china." And she did laugh, softly, a foolish child's giggle that came close to a weak sob of fatigue and disbelef.

She had slept, and had wakened in the darkness again with the feeling that she had slept only a few minutes. She lay in the bed tensely, and she heard then the sound that had wakened her, a faint and delicate scratching sound that for a moment sent a chill through her body. She drew in her breath sharply, unable to focus either her surroundings or the reason why she lay in such an unfamiliar darkness. And then she remembered that this was Isobel's room at Tilsit, and after that she was able to identify the kind of sound it was. It took a minute or more to find the candle and matches, and the single point of light in the room only made deeper its shadows. She went in her bare feet to the door and opened it slowly.

Without hesitation the dog came in, a beautiful liver and white spaniel; he seemed to pause by her only a second, one swift upward look at her that showed no evidence of either friendliness or suspicion, merely a glance from the liquid, melancholy eyes that was like a form of polite but distant greeting. This over, he started at once a slow tour of the room while she held the candle high, watching him. He examined everything, smelled the bags still waiting to be unpacked, her slippers, behind the bed and under it, disappearing for a moment beneath the hangings. And when it was all finished he gave Ginny only one more glance, but made no overture, and then he settled himself, with a heavy sigh, into the basket before the dying fire. She knew that this was Isobel's dog, and that the search had been for a trace of his mistress. The beautiful, aristocratic head was rested on his paws, and Ginny knew he wanted no comfort from her. He didn't seem to resent her presence in the room ; he simply behaved as if she were not there. Ginny went back to bed and blew out the candle, but she lay there for a long time without sleep, and at last she knew from the dog's heavy breathing that he slept before she did.

It was Brown who had come to her bedside that morning with the breakfast tray. The first thing Ginny had opened her eyes upon was the faded flowered smock cloaking the angular figure of the woman as she had drawn back the curtains fully, and the light had flooded the room.

"Good morning, miss. I see you let Trip in—I should have warned you that he might come. He misses her . . . I hope you slept well otherwise."

"Yes, thank you. What—what time is it?"

"Almost half past ten."

Ginny sat bolt upright. "I should have been downstairs long ago. Is that breakfast? I don't want to have it here. I don't like eating in bed. I should have been downstairs. There are . . . the others. I haven't met them yet."

"Mr. Garth and I thought this arrangement would suit you best for the first morning, miss. You seemed so tired . . . Mr. Randall said, if it is convenient, that you would all meet at half past eleven in the Gold State Room."

"And the others will be there?"

"Just the family, miss, I understand. And—and Mr. Barstow, if he's decided to appear. Will that be all now, miss? I'll leave you to have your breakfast. I've lighted the fire in the bathroom. Mr. Randall told me you'd be chilly, coming from that place where you've lived."

"Thank you . . . Brown?"

"Yes, miss."

Ginny poured her coffee, sipped it, and winced. "Brown, what do you do besides dust the china?"

"I used to take care of Miss Isobel. She had so much to do, running a great place like this, seeing to the pottery. I used to do whatever I could for her, besides the china. She trained me, you see. We were almost of an age—I'm a little older. I came to Tilsit when I was a girl, and she and the Old Lady trained me to do things the way they liked them."

"The Old Lady?"

"Jane Tilsit, miss. The Old Lady taught Miss Isobel how to dust and handle the Porcelain Collection. I used to help her. Then in time Miss Isobel left it all in my hands. I have the keys, miss, whenever you want to see it."

"Yes—I'll tell you when I want to see it. Brown!"

"Yes, miss?"

Ginny gave her first order at Tilsit. "I would like you to tell them that in future I would like tea with my breakfast."

Brown nodded, a quick respectful bob that indicated pleasure in the order. "I'll tell Cook, Miss Virginia."

These then were Garth and Brown to whom Isobel had left each one thousand pounds.

Garth had been waiting in the hall when Ginny had gone down an hour later. "Good morning, Miss Virginia. I'll show you the way to the Gold State Room." And he had led her back through the Great Hall, past the bottom of a winding enclosed staircase which he said led to the solar, the long Gallery and the Great Bedchamber. Then he had thrown open the door of the Gold State Room and announced her name.

They had been assembled, Lawrence, Margaret and Vanessa, and Randall had performed the introductions. A vague smile had fluttered momentarily on Margaret Bowen-Tilsit's lovely face, and had disappeared. Lawrence was the only one who stammered a pretence of welcome. Vanessa's smile had been her cool, amused one.

"One of us should have come to meet you, but Randy is much better at that kind of thing. He had a lot to tell you too—of course we all had to be prepared for each other. We were dying to know if you were black—such a lovely shock for the county if you had been. You'll have to tell me exactly where St. Nicolaas is. I couldn't begin to find it on the map."

" It's hard to find," Ginny answered. " It took Isobel a long time to find it too." As she sat down she noticed that the smile had left Vanessa's face.

Randall's voice went on:

" To Vanessa Isobel Tilsit, the farm known as Barrow's End, together with the two tenant cottages that stand on it, and the property known as Barrow Great House."

For an instant Vanessa had registered shock, and then it was gone, though her fingers gripped the welts of the sofa cushions and held them tightly.

" To Lawrence Bowen-Tilsit, the income for life on one thousand shares of stock of Tilsit Potteries. The voting rights of such stock, however, are to remain with my niece, Virginia Tilsit and the income to revert to her on the death of Lawrence Bowen-Tilsit."

Ginny didn't want to look at Lawrence, knowing that Isobel had given and withheld at the same time.

" To Mark Barstow . . ." Here Randall paused, and seemed for a second to be waiting for the door to open and the absent man to appear. He resumed. " To Mark Barstow, the income for life on one thousand shares of the stock of Tilsit Potteries. The voting rights, however, are to remain . . ." The same conditions applied as in the case of the bequest to Lawrence. After reading this clause, Randall's eyes had flickered over the group, as if watching for a reaction, a protest. The discipline held ; no one moved or spoke. Randall resumed.

" It is my wish that Mark Barstow shall continue to discharge the function of curator and custodian of the Tilsit Porcelain Collection."

Then followed the clause that Ginny had been summoned from St. Nicolaas to hear.

" The residue of my estate, all real and personal holdings, the property known as Tilsit together with the farms that adjoin it, my interests in the Tilsit Potteries, I give devise and bequeath to my niece, Virginia Tilsit. The condition of this inheritance shall be that she shall reside at Tilsit and shall assume an active interest in Tilsit Potteries, that she shall give her services in any way deemed advisable and necessary to assist in maintaining the house, and in keeping it open to the public. A further condition of this inheritance shall be that, upon her marriage, her husband shall assume the name of Tilsit, and all children of the marriage shall be known by that name only."

Ginny felt as if she had been struck. The chill was suddenly a deep cold, cold in the marrow of her bones, a cold that seemed to freeze the very spirit of her. Once before she had felt like this, that time when Eliot Russell had fastened the necklace about her throat and laid the white Russian broadtail coat about her shoulders. She was owned and possessed, the property of someone to whom the right had not been given by love. Randall's quiet, pleasant voice seemed now to roar in her ears.

He was reading on; he seemed to read on and on for pages of the long legal sheets—pages filled with conditions that were a part of the inheritance. Some were real and had meaning to which she could immediately take hold—such as the one that Lawrence and Margaret Bowen-Tilsit were to continue to reside at Tilsit without charge to themselves for as long as they saw fit; Vanessa was also to have this privilege until such time as she remarried. The firm of Hedges, Randall, and Strong of Bournemouth were to continue to administer the affairs of the estate and also the affairs of the company formed to deal with the revenue and expenses of keeping Tilsit open to the public. Virg.nia Tilsit was to head this company. "In the event that my niece, Virginia Tilsit, shall still be a minor at the time of my death, the estate shall be held in trust by Hedges, Randall, and Strong until she reach her majority."

There were other clauses that made no sense at all. "It is my wish, in accordance with the wishes of my maternal grandmother, Jane Tilsit, that my niece and all future descendants in the direct line shall refuse all title and honours which may be offered by the British Sovereign."

And then the last clause of all.

"In the event that my niece, Virginia Tilsit, shall predecease me, then I give, devise and bequeath after the several bequests shall have been fulfilled, the residue of my estate, all real and personal property, to Vanessa Isobel Tilsit, with all the foregoing conditions to apply."

William Randall removed his spectacles. "I'll be glad to answer any questions you have. But I think Miss Tilsit's will seems to make everything quite clear."

Lawrence Bowen-Tilsit swallowed and re-crossed his legs. Since no one else spoke, he was compelled to. "Quite clear, I think. It is . . . Isobel has been generous. . . ."

Something between a cry and a laugh broke from Vanessa. "Oh, Father, stop it! Stop it, now! There's no need for this any more. She's dead now—don't you understand. There's nothing more you can do one way or another, to change what's written in that document. You don't have to be nice about her any more . . . or nice *to* her. You don't have to tell her she's right when you know damn' well she's wrong."

"Vanessa!" Lawrence's pale lips worked furiously. Ginny suddenly saw that he had the face of a weak man whose good looks disguised the fault until the moment of stress. His features seemed to have lost contact with each other; his dark brows were drawn together, not in genuine anger, but in an agony of tension. "I forbid you to say any such things, Vanessa. Isobel has been generous—you can't deny that. Look, you have Barrow's End and Great Barrow . . ."

Vanessa gave a kind of snort of contempt. "And much good will they do me! What's Barrow's End but a couple of little farms that'll only bring a few hundred a year in rent? And the repairs on Great Barrow House will keep me poor— that is if I still have it when the tax men are finished." She got up suddenly from the sofa, and stood there for a moment, looking down at Lawrence Bowen-Tilsit. "Father, why be grateful for the few bones she threw us? We've been her servants, all of us, and she rewards us by flinging us the few scraps she thinks can be spared from the estate. What did you get? Nothing! What's a thousand shares worth when you have no right to dispose of it and no voting rights? You've worked in the Pottery all your life and still she turns your voting rights over to a girl who still doesn't know china from earthenware. She gives all your work and your experience to someone else. And Mark's too. And why? Because she couldn't bear to think there mightn't be one woman in this house to whom everyone had to defer. She couldn't live forever herself so she tried to create someone who would be just like herself, with all the same powers. She's stripped the lot of us to give it all to a girl she only ever laid eyes on once. So don't be grateful, Father. Continue to eat your bread in this house, and sleep in your bed, and know you've earned every bit of it."

Lawrence Bowen-Tilsit's skin seemed paste-coloured. He took his handkerchief from his breast pocket and wiped his lips. Then he looked at Ginny.

" I have to apologise for Vanessa. . . ."

" No, don't! Don't you dare apologise for me! I've only said what's in all our minds. If she's got any brains at all she must know how we feel."

" . . . Apologise," he went on, as if Vanessa had not interrupted, " because gratitude is hardly the issue. My cousin Isobel built on what she herself inherited. She inherited Tilsit and the Pottery intact, all of a piece. She made them her lifework, and she left something greater than what she found. I respect that." Having said that, he closed his lips tightly.

" But she didn't respect you," Vanessa said. " She *used* you."

" Hush, Vanessa! Hush!" Almost for the first time Margaret Bowen Tilsit spoke, her dreaming face wrinkling in reproach, the tiniest, daintiest of frowns coming between her eyes. " Can you imagine how vulgar you sound? What will Virginia think of you?"

" As if that mattered!" Again Vanessa gave that strange cry that was nearly a laugh. " Good God—can't you get it into your head? Virginia isn't here for the week-end. The visit isn't going to end. This is for keeps, and we belong to her, more or less—just the way we used to belong to Isobel. Begin to understand, Mother, will you? Virginia is the Miss Tilsit now.

As Vanessa spoke a gong boomed out, muffled somewhere along passages behind the closed doors. At once the little frown was erased from Margaret's face, as if she had not heard what Vanessa had said, or did not wish to hear it. Carefully she put the embroidery in the bag she carried with her.

" The gong is for lunch, Virginia," she said. She stood up, but they all waited, as if by custom, for Ginny to move first.

11

They went back through the Old House to the South Wing, Randall and Ginny leading, and Randall keeping up a flow of talk until they found themselves seated about the table in the dining-room. And then Vanessa broke in.

" You see it's really a very small world we inhabit within this big house—just this dining-room, the sitting-room, and Isobel's office. The rest of it "—she jerked her head towards the Inner Court, on to which the dining-room faced, towards the opposite wing—" is just for show. It's a pity, really. The last time any of those rooms were used was for my coming-out party—and Isobel was in a frenzy about cigarettes and spilled champagne. There's no electricity over there—the rooms were lighted by floodlights from the garden. It was a wonderful party. Isobel never got over what it cost, but no one who was there has ever forgotten that night."

Ginny, from the head of the table where Garth had placed her, looked with some puzzlement at Vanessa. Her expression was one of pleasurable remembrance, and seemed quite divorced from the person whose explosive bitterness had caused the scene in the Gold State Room. The resentment she harboured was against Isobel. Vanessa's attitude towards Ginny was almost one of pity mingled with amusement at finding this odd stranger in their midst. It could be, Ginny thought, that Vanessa's disappointment might be tempered a little by the belief that she would certainly make a botch of the tasks that Isobel's will had clearly laid upon her, and that, in the end, Isobel would be proven wrong. That might well be so, Ginny acknowledged, but it wasn't proven yet.

She nodded towards Vanessa. " You know the house well—the furniture and paintings. Would you take me through?" There was no humility in her request. She had to learn about Tilsit, and quickly. Common sense told her that Lawrence's inhibited personality would impart no more than the bare facts. Margaret, vague and shifting, was an unknown quantity. The hope of real knowledge and discovery lay in Vanessa.

Vanessa's delicate eyebrows shot up, and into her face came a look of recognition, almost a salute. She paused in the act of helping herself to roast beef from the platter Garth held for her, and a quick smile came and went.

" Why not," she said. " Heaven knows I've enough information to give away. Isobel's been training me ever since I could understand even faintly what she was talking about. You might do worse than follow me about when I take one of the tours. Oh, yes—I help conduct the tours. I do Tuesdays and Thursdays. And on the week-ends I handle the souvenir shop. You see, we all get pressed into service one way or another, isn't that so, Randy? We don't get our pay otherwise."

" Someone has to be paid for the job, Vanessa."

" And the money might as well stay in the family? Dear Randy, you always could see Isobel's side of it, couldn't you?" Vanessa looked back to Ginny. " Randy always tried to stand between Isobel and me. It hardly ever worked, but he always tried. But Randy always thought everyone should work because Tilsit couldn't afford hangers-on, so he didn't object when Isobel put me to work. So I do Tuesdays and Thursdays, and you're welcome to listen any time you want."

" I'll need a little more than that," Ginny said shortly.

Vanessa shrugged. " Take it gradually. There's a great deal to learn about Tilsit. I'll show you what I can—that is, everything but the Porcelain Collection. No one but Brown will show you that."

While they talked, Garth had been around the table to each person with the meat and then with the vegetables. It had taken a long time; when the service was completed, he had withdrawn. As the swing door closed behind him Vanessa said:

" I hope you'll put an end to all this fuss with Garth serving everyone individually—at least at lunch-time. It's ridiculous in this day and age. We should all be helping ourselves from the sideboard. But Isobel wanted everything kept up—and never mind that Garth's only got a little Italian boy—the son of one of the gardeners, to back him up with all this work. He's too old for it, and when there are more than three people it takes for ever to get anything to eat. I think he should . . ."

" Vanessa." Lawrence cleared his throat. " I suggest you keep your advice to yourself. Virginia will make whatever arrangements she sees fit."

Ginny looked at him carefully. What might have been an overture could also be defined as a wish to see Ginny get enough rope to hang herself. The enemy might be found more truly here than in his daughter. She said, " Perhaps it was because he's old that Isobel continued to let him do it. I imagine he would hate to have it taken away."

With a potato poised before her lips, Margaret halted. " That's true," she said with surprising emphasis. " He'd be broken-hearted if you didn't let him do it."

Now that she had everyone's attention she laid down her fork again. " What Vanessa said about the Old House not being used since her party isn't quite true. She may forget it, of course—but *I* use the Old House every day. I have a needlework room there—the very end room past the Great Bedchamber. It overlooks the chapel. I work there every day. Are you interested in needlework, Virginia?"

" I don't know anything about it—I can just about turn a hem."

" Oh—hems!" Margaret dismissed that with the faintest shrug of her slight shoulders. " I wasn't speaking about that kind of needlework. You must come and let me show you some of my things. They are of quite some historic interest." She gave a tiny sigh. " I like to keep my hands busy. I find it soothes me to have my hands occupied." And she turned her unlined, slightly blank face that denied any form of tension, fully towards Ginny. " It started as a little relaxation of mine when I was a girl, and I've never given it up."

" You mean, Mother," Vanessa said, " that Isobel made sure you never gave it up. She's had the services of an expert needlewoman all these years without a penny cost to Tilsit."

" That isn't true, Vanessa," Margaret answered, without heat. " Isobel paid for a most expensive course at the London School of Needlework. She has always shared my interest . . ."

" She sent you to the School so that you could learn how to look after and repair her tapestries and her chair-covers and her curtains. She's had thirty years of embroidery and repairing and replacing all to the greater glory of Tilsit and with nothing out of pocket."

Again the shrug appeared, and the look from the violet-blue

eyes was secretive and elusive. " I don't think of it that way, Vanessa. I have been glad to see my work on display here—there's hardly a room at Tilsit that doesn't have some of my work—either my own designs or copies of the originals that I have replaced. I have enjoyed it—Isobel understood why I enjoyed my work." Having said this she retreated once more into her silence, but later in the meal Ginny, looking at her when she thought she was not observed, caught again the secretive expression of brooding on her face, a dreaming look almost. She barely touched her food, as if she had other satisfactions and did not need this one.

" She gave you an inheritance," Randall said, " that is really a lifetime of labour. Can you accept that?"

" Can I refuse it?" It was half a jest, but Ginny knew as she uttered it that it was a genuine question.

Randall shrugged. " You can neither accept nor refuse anything until you come of age. If you do nothing about it, the inheritance will be automatic. So you have until . . ." He paused. " You have until September." He had been sitting smoking with his quiet motions, and then he suddenly squashed the half-finished cigarette into an ash-tray. " How young you are!" he said. " You're very young to be handed all this without preparation—without warning, even."

" I used to feel very young," Ginny said, " until a little while ago. Now I don't feel any age at all—not young or old. More coffee?"

" Please." He passed his cup and lighted another cigarette. They were alone now, back in the sitting-room, where they had sat last night. After lunch was finished Lawrence had refused coffee, saying that he had to get back to the Pottery. Ginny thought he was glad to go. Vanessa had said, over her shoulder as she went up the staircase to her bedroom, " Too late. It's almost two o'clock and it's time for me to start earning my living. The horde—or the trickle —starts arriving at two. Since the sun's coming out it'll probably be a horde." Margaret had simply disappeared, saying nothing.

So they were alone, and the sun was beginning to come through, as Vanessa had said. The windows were open to the precisely tended rectangular garden of the Inner Court.

The room was filled with the rich, heavy scent that Randall told Ginny was the scent of the wallflowers. " I've often wondered how an English garden smelled," she said. " One keeps reading about it . . ." A new fire burned in the grate.

" She loved it very much, didn't she?" Ginny demanded abruptly of Randall. " Oh perhaps I shouldn't say " love " —perhaps that's not the exact word."

" Isobel and Tilsit, you mean? Yes, she did love it— obsessively—fiercely. She gave it her life, and didn't mind that. Her trouble was that she wanted to hold all of it to herself until the last moment. She was so jealous over the act of its bestowal on someone else than she neglected to safe-guard the inheritance itself."

" What?"

" Death duties," he said. " Estate taxes. We haven't talked about them yet, but in England these days they're as inevitable and sometimes nearly as terrible as death itself. The Tilsit family have been more fortunate than most, though, in that respect." He flicked ashes towards the hearth. " Your great-grandmother, Jane Tilsit, was eighty-six years old when she died, and Isobel was only in her middle twenties when she inherited from her. So that's almost forty years when there have been no death duties to pay. Your aunt had time to build up—and plenty of time to prepare for this, if she had chosen to do so."

" What do you mean?"

" She could have set up trust funds for whomever she had chosen as her heir, or heirs. So long as the gifts of property had been made five years before her death, they were free and clear. She could have given away Tilsit— given away the pictures, the Porcelain Collection—even the Pottery if she had wanted to. It could all have been done, so that the inheritance was almost free of encumbrance. But she could not strip herself of these things. She could not.

" So what she leaves to you may be an inheritance that will be hardly an inheritance at all—just a long labour that has very little reward except, perhaps—though I don't know how you view these things, coming from your part of the world—the reward of trying to hold together a collection of things that your ancestors built and acquired and probably loved. It may take a long time before we know what is to be left. You can't put a value on this house, or the furnishings or the pictures in a week or two. They will be very careful in making the assessment—but unrelenting, I'm afraid. We will protest as much as possible. We will try every tactic that is open to us. But in the end you will have to pay. It may mean selling some of the things that Isobel prized most. Whatever it is, it will come hard.

" So perhaps the inheritance is not much to rejoice in— and you may need a back of iron to carry the load."

" Vanessa could have carried it."

He looked up sharply. " Why do you say that?"

" It's obvious, isn't it? She was born to do this. She was trained to do it. Listen to her talk and you know that she loves this house too, even when she's laughing about it. Mr. Randall—why, in heaven's name, didn't Isobel give her this house?—at least this house?"

" I told you. The marriage was wrong. The Italian wasn't a man whom Isobel could manage. Vanessa killed her chances with that marriage. Isobel might have set up a trust for her when she came of age—or again she might not. But the matter is academic. It was all over by then. Vanessa was married and gone. And Isobel couldn't forgive her. Even after her husband was killed and she came back to Tilsit, your aunt couldn't forgive her. You must remember —by that time she had made her journey to the West Indies and she had seen you. The decision was made then."

Ginny shook her head. " On the basis of that one meeting? It doesn't seem possible. We didn't hit it off. In fact we hardly began to talk at all. I refused to listen to what she had come to say. She couldn't have been so crazy . . ." She looked at Randall sharply. " I suppose she was a little crazy?"

He lifted a hand in small protest. " I wouldn't write off your aunt as crazy. She was a rather remarkable woman. She did great things for the Pottery—very far-sighted things that put it in the healthy position it is to-day. Eccenric, yes. Mad?—I wouldn't say so."

Ginny indicated the room with a gesture that in fact embraced the whole house. " If she wasn't mad, then why give this to me? Here she had under her hand someone trained to take an inheritance like this—someone who was born here, and loves it. Why me and not Vanessa?"

Randall sighed. He fussed with his cigarette and looked away from her.

" Mr. Randall—why?"

He shook his head. " There's more than a hundred years of the history of the Tilsit family involved in that answer, my dear. I wish I could make it simple for you. But you need time here—time—even a few weeks—will help you to understand. It could mean nothing to you now, or almost nothing. The most simple and obvious reason I can give you for your aunt's passing over Vanessa is that she is not a Tilsit."

" *Not* a Tilsit . . .?"

" Let me go over it again. Her father, Lawrence Bowen-Tilsit, was Isobel's first cousin on her father's side. He only *assumed* the name of Tilsit."

She nodded. " Yes—I hadn't thought it all through. And the name is important. But she had the name."

" The blood is important, Virginia. The direct and legitimate descent was of extreme importance to Isobel Tilsit."

Finally he packed his papers and closed his bag. " You've had enough now, my dear. And I must be on my way back to Bournemouth. Oh—you'll be seeing a good deal of me, I'm afraid. But you've enough to think about for the moment. We should let you settle down . . ."

She followed Randall to the door with reluctance. It didn't seem possible that he would go, he, her only link with the world from which she had come, the only one of whom she could ask the questions.

" Mr. Randall . . .?"

He understood what was in her voice. " Come and see me any time you wish. Or telephone me, and I'll come down here." His lips parted in the briefest smile and she knew that he had recognised her apprehension. " Things will sort themselves out in time. He nodded towards her. " They need time too—the others. Isobel had directed their lives so long. They're not used to doing without her."

He motioned Ginny to precede him along the passage, indicating the direction away from the Great Hall. " I've parked the car at the South Front. The public entrance is the East Front, where we came in last night. That," he said, gesturing briefly towards a closed door farther down the passage,

" is the room Isobel used as an office. You'll find most of her papers in there—anything relating to the household and the Pottery. I don't think they're locked. If they are, ask Garth or Brown for the keys . . ."

" You think I should read her papers?"

They had reached a kind of hall in which hung a row of coats with a matching line of gumboots underneath. Beside the big studded door a stand bristled with walking-sticks. As Randall swung open the door he looked at Ginny quickly. " They're your papers, aren't they?"

" Not yet," she protested. " Not till September."

" A formality," he said. " If I were you I'd read them." And he nodded, underscoring the point. " Yes—read them. There's a lot of time to make up for."

There were three cars parked on the gravel beside the entrance—Randall's, a small, shabby one of a faded navy colour, and a dark-green sports Jaguar.

" There's a garage round in the old stables, but mostly they're left here—too far to walk when you need a car," Randall said as he got into his own. He pointed to the Jaguar. " That one's Vanessa's. Vitti gave it to her, and she brought it back here after he was killed. The other one was your aunt's. Ask Garth for the keys. I expect you'll want to use it."

Through the open window he held out his hand to her. " Telephone if you need me. I'll be coming over from time to time. . . ." He made the parting casual, but unspoken between them was the acknowledgment that from now on she was on her own. Randall backed and turned the car as she stood and watched; she wanted to call to him to come back, that it was too soon to leave her, but a protest would only have postponed what was inevitable, so she merely answered with a half wave as he raised his hat, and the car started down the drive and made the turn to the bridge.

" Mr. Randall . . .!" She ran a few steps in a vain attempt to stop him. But the car had gone too far. She halted, shrugging. She had meant to ask him, while they were alone, about Mark Barstow. " Well," she muttered to herself. " That only makes one other thing to find out."

She stood looking down the empty drive. Behind her was Tilsit, with the burden of its people and its problems, the strangers who waited in rooms she did not yet know, who spoke of things which were her past and which she did not recognise, the world of Isobel which her father had fled. She shivered suddenly. A little wind blew at that moment so she could not say if she were chilled by that or by a new sense of doubt and mistrust.

At that moment something touched her leg. She flinched as if she had been struck.

The brown eyes of the spaniel were turned upwards to her.

" Oh,—it's you!"

She could not refuse the mute appeal. She bent and touched the soft head, hating herself because she could not feel attracted to this gentle animal.

" Well—what is it?" She remembered the name Brown had given him. " Looking for her, are you, Trip? I'm not Isobel, you know. I'm not your mistress." She squatted beside him, glad now to feel the warmth of his silken body, the little wriggle of pleasure that went through it at her touch. Encouraged, the dog diffidently placed one limp, soft paw on her knee. " You want a friend, don't you? You're lonely, Trip—well, so am I. You want Isobel back, and I want . . . I want Jim. I could do with a little of that MacAdam brand of good sense to fight off all these ghosts I'm fancying here. And you—I suppose you want the ghost back in the flesh. Well, you'll have to make do with me, Trip, and I'll have to make do with . . . with no one."

She straightened again, and began to walk back to the open door. The dog followed closely on her heels. She thought of the room that Randall had indicated as Isobel's office, with the papers waiting to be read, of the room upstairs where Isobel's presence was made by Brown to seem a real and tangible thing, of the family sitting-room which was the only place in the whole vast house where one might go, of the strangers who had paid their money to walk through all the other rooms conducted by Vanessa. None of them welcomed her.

" To hell with it, Trip. We'll get out of it for a while."

She kicked off her shoes swiftly and dug her feet into gumboots that were slightly too big for her, and took down from its peg a long cloak of soft worn tweed. It was made with an overcape in the style of fifty years ago, and its long folds reached almost to her ankles. The sudden quiver of

Trip's body arrested her as she began to fasten it. He
gave out a sound that was between whimper and whine and
he stretched up on his hind legs to paw at her with a swift
movement that expressed both angu.sh and ecstasy. She
ran her hand down the front of the cloak, understanding now
that Isobel had worn this cloak often ; that for the spaniel
it had a beloved familiarity, it symbolised a return to security.
With a ye.p of excitement the dog turned and ran through
the door, dashing out on to the gravel drive, stopping short
and wheeling back to her, plumed ta.l lifted in the classic
stance. He barked sharply and began to run again. Looking
back only once to make sure that she followed, he ran
swiftly, ears flying, down the drive where Randall's car
had disappeared.

Ginny pulled the door closed behind her, not gently, but
with a bang that resounded down the passages of the
building, her first act of sureness since she had come to
Tilsit.

III

Trip did not follow the drive across the bridge, but instead
he darted through the trees that lined it, and then started up
the slope of the hill. The wind drove a little scurry of
drops from the wet trees before it as she followed after
Trip. On the road behind her two cars went slowly by.
Visitors, she thought, and already there was in her attitude
something of detachment from them ; thinking of them
she felt that she belonged more at Tilsit than they did ; the
Tilsit family now became strangers in degree only—not
close to her, but closer than the rest of this strange world
she had come to.

She reached the crown of the mound on which the keep
stood. Ignoring the sign that warned that the ruins were
dangerous, she moved in under the shadow of the round
wall. Somewhere in among the flat slabs of fallen grey
stone she could hear Trip. He reappeared briefly, and
then seemed to vanish into the ground—to cellars, she thought,
or the dungeons of the Norman lord who had fortified and held
th.s hill. She turned and looked back towards Tilsit.

It must have been hard, she thought, for her father to

leave this behind him. It was beautiful, this manor-house, built about its two courtyards; it was even gentle, set against the hill with the stream winding about its base, and surprisingly intimate, for all its size. The crenellated decoration of the roofs and the rise of the chimneys reminded her of the Italian hill-towers set small and jewel-like in the background of Renaissance paintings. There was no classical façade for the eye to see in a glance; it had to be taken piece by piece, a mixture of periods that blended lovingly, an end result of centuries of building and adding as the wealth and influence of its owners grew. She stood there, contemplating it, wondering at what period the peace of the land had held long enough for the lord of the manor to feel secure in leaving his Norman keep to begin building this unfortified house by its gentle stream. She wrapped the cloak closely about her against the wind that was chill here on the rise, and wondered how her father could have disciplined himself never to speak of this.

It was then the voice reached her.

"Gave me quite a turn, you did—standing there in her cloak! I thought it was the old witch herself come back!"

Ginny swung round. He was there, below her on the path that wound around the base of the keep, a young man in a thick jersey, with the wind blowing his wild dark hair.

"Yes, you!" he said. "It was you I spoke to." Now he was coming up the steep slope towards her.

"You startled me." Almost instinctively she took a step backwards. Even at a distance there was an impression of strength and power about him, in his bulky body, in the rough cast of his features which still managed to have a certain fierce beauty in them.

"Startled you, did I? Well, what do you think you did to me?—standing there like a bloody ghost in her cloak, staring back at the house the way she used to. Gloating over it."

"Me?"

"Her. You might have been gloating too, for all I know. You're the niece, aren't you? John Tilsit's daughter? Yes, I thought so. Couldn't have missed it. There's a portrait of the old girl, Jane, back at the house—an awful daub done by Millais. You're the bloody spitting image of it."

He stood squarely before her now, his feet planted wide, hands thrust in the pockets of his shapeless stained flannel trousers, a figure of extraordinary force and vividness, dark and rough-complexioned, his chin with a cleft in it that looked as if it had been carved with an axe, his eyes the colour of dark grey mud. She stared at him in fascination.

"And who are you?"

"Barstow's the name. Mark Barstow."

"Yes . . . Mark Barstow. I've heard of you."

"I'll bet you have! I'll bet you've heard an earful."

"You're conceited, aren't you? I didn't hear anything, except that they decided not to wait when you didn't appear for the reading of the will."

"Well, that puts me back in my place, doesn't it?"

"What is your place?"

He shrugged, and the impression of intensity lightened a little. He almost smiled. "Who knows? All I can say is that I don't seem to have found it yet." Then he laughed suddenly, an explosive ringing laugh, laughter at himself and the whole world around them. The fierceness seemed to drop from him; he was unself-conscious and free. Ginny joined the laughter, weakly at first, tentatively, and then as her sense of release grew, she gave in to it w.th a wholeness. Relief washed through her in a surge. She felt released and liberated by this young giant of a man, with his laughter and his teasing. For the first moment since she had come to Tilsit she was participating, no longer observing. The relief was sweet and heady.

"I'm glad there's someone else who doesn't know their place. I don't know mine right now."

He thrust out his hand, a huge hand, blackened under the short, stubby nails. His grip was hard and strong, as if he had never learned to shake hands with a woman; the skin was rough.

"I suppose I should do the proper thing and say well——"

"No, don't! Don't *you* say it too!"

He nodded. "It's been a b.t much, has it—all this welcome stuff? I'll bet it has! They've got you scared a bit, haven't they? Well, listen, my girl . . ." Through the cloak he reached and found her arm and took it in his hard grip. "Don't let them get you scared. You're a gonner if you let them get you scared. I know what they're like—old strait-lace

Bowen and that idiot Randall. And Garth acting as if he had charge of the keys of the kingdom. And Brown with a bad smell under her nose all the time—that's another old witch, that one! Just you say to hell with them all, my girl, and you'll feel a lot better."

"That's what I did say—that's why I came out here."

"Good for you! I hate the place myself—it begins to close in on me after a while. I've never been able to take too much of it . . ."

Ginny was aware of a sudden and sharp disappointment. She said quickly, "Well, you'll have to spend some time there occasionally. In the will she said you were to remain as curator of the Porcelain Collection." She didn't mention the income from the thousand shares of stock in the Pottery, knowing Randall would tell him in time, and wanting at this stage to see his reaction to the lesser information.

"She said that, did she? Well, how did she know I'd agree?" But there was already a swift pleasure on his face, a kind of smile of satisfaction. "I'm glad, though," he said. "It's a lovely thing, that lot. I reckon I'm fond of it, at that. I learned a lot from it in the old days when I was a kid—just by looking at and feeling those pieces."

"Would you show me the Collection—explain it to me?"

He shook his head. "That job's not for me, my girl. That's Brown's job. She'd have my head if I took that from her. She's a touchy old hen—and I suppose, to give her her due, if looking after a thing makes it belong to you, then the Collection is more hers than it was Isobel's, in the end. There's not much for me to do there any more, to tell you the truth. All the stuff's labelled and classified. Isobel hadn't made a purchase for years. Everything's too expensive now, she used to say, and there was no money for new purchases. Is there any money?" he added.

She was startled by his frankness, and yet it compelled respect and an answer. "Mr. Randall says there isn't—or at least no money that anyone can jingle in their pocket. He says the tax men could take a big slice of it away . . ."

His thick straight brows came together in a scowl that became nearly a grimace. "You rich people make me sick! The tax men will come and have their pickings, and you'll only be left with a bloody great castle and a few Van Dycks and a Memling to keep you company—and a couple of thousand acres of farmland and a modest little Pottery that's only making the best contemporary ceramics in England. You'll be poor as dirt, won't you? Ah . . .!" It was an expression of disgust.

Ginny was aghast. "Why are you angry with me? What have I got to do with all this? It isn't of my making, is it? After all—I only got here last night."

"Yes, but you'll be just like her. I can tell," he answered briefly and illogically. "You'll ride around in that broken-down old car and wear clothes that are twenty years old because everything's so expensive these days—that's what she used to say."

"Don't you think you should stop talking about what she used to do and say. You ought to give *me* a chance."

He stared at her for a minute, and the sullen look gradually lightened; once the look of anger was gone, his features lost their heavy cast and took back their kind of blunt good looks. Ginny thought that he was the strangest man she had ever met, writhing inside at one moment with a suppressed fury, the next softening with a smile that went far back into his eyes. Now he was patting her arm, with a touch of his hand as gentle as a child's, a protective gesture, almost paternal.

"You're right, you poor little devil. It's not your fault, is it? And you're only a bit of a kid too."

"Not a kid—not exactly a kid."

His lips twitched; his gaze now was appraising. "And such an exotic bird to drop down in the midst of all us solid Dorset types—with your golden hair and your dark tanned face. A bird of paradise come to us from the sugar islands. I wonder if you'll stay, or if you'll pine away in these Northern islands, chilled by our sunless days and our ways as cold and unfriendly as our climate?"

"What nonsense you talk, Mark Barstow."

"Yes, I do talk nonsense, don't I, Ginny—that must be your name. Or do you like to be called Virginia?"

"Ginny."

"That's good. I don't think I could take to a Virginia."

"Are you going to take to me?"

"Who knows? I could try—it mightn't be hard at that." He added suddenly, "Do you want to come to my place?

I've got a fire going—and I'll make you a cup of tea. Would you like that, Ginny?"

" Yes—yes I would, very much. But weren't you on your way somewhere?"

" Nowhere important. No—that isn't true. To tell you the truth I was going over to Tilsit. I was going to cadge a cup of tea from the cook and listen to the gossip about you —as long as Garth wasn't there."

"Why from the cook?"

" Because I'm more comfortable in the kitchen than the drawing-room." He pulled at her arm roughly. " Come on. There's a path to my cottage on the other side here."

He took her hand then and led her through the fallen slabs, through a crumbling arch and through the long grass to a gap where the massive curving wall of the keep had collapsed. They emerged on the top of the knoll, the slope steeper here than on the other side. Although Ginny had been expecting the view of the sea, it came still as a shock. A grey sea, less than a quarter of a mile away. The vivid green field between them and the sea ended at a hedge and the cliff face. A herd of creamy brown cattle grazed gently.

" This is your domain too," Mark said. " And there— that's where I live." He pointed to a low white house perched precariously on the cliff face, with a high structure that looked like a barn attached to it. " There's a bit of a beach below the cliff there—nothing much. Just a strip of shingle, really. The inlet is too shallow to be any good as a shelter. And the road runs behind the cottage on the way to the next farm. It's three miles by road from Tilsit. I expect this used to be a better anchorage in the time of the Vikings and the Normans. But the cliff is crumbling away all along this stretch of coastline. There was a fall just last year—it buried some of the shingle and damn' nearly took the cottage." Over her shoulder he pointed. " That promontory over there is the Isle of Portland and Portland Bill. And this way is Swanage. Bournemouth is tucked in behind it. Farther along the channel is the Isle of Wight, You can see it when it's clear, which isn't very often. If you stay long enough you'll get used to this kind of weather. You'll start congratulating yourself any day the sun shines."

"Why do you keep saying that as if I might go away?"

"Do I keep saying that? I suppose it's because I can't imagine anyone staying who didn't have to stay."

"You mean here—at Tilsit?"

"At Tilsit. Yes."

"Do you have to stay, Mark?"

He didn't answer her, but turned away and started down the narrow path worn in the grass. He didn't look back to see if she followed, and she had the feeling that he might just have decided to leave her there. She started to run after him. "Wait, Mark. I have to find Trip . . ."

He shouted back to her, "To hell with the bloody dog. Are you coming or aren't you?"

She didn't hesitate because she did not dare. "I'm coming."

The cottage was small and low, made of old brick and wood, freshly whitewashed; the bigger building behind it, attached by a passage-way, seemed to have been built of the same brick but it was newer, its lines straight without the sag of age. There was no garden, just a worn path in the rough grass, and the cliff face not more than twenty feet away. Mark nodded to it briefly. "Forty-odd feet went with the last slide. There used to be a headland of sorts here when I was a kid." He flung open the door and waited for Ginny. "Well, come on," he said, his face wrinkling in his sudden smile, good-humoured now. "Don't stand about all day."

She turned from her contemplation of the shallow inlet, the sight of the fallen rock that stretched in a line out some distance from the little bar of shingle that was the beach. A rowboat was drawn up tight against the cliff; it looked small and far off, white against the grey shingle and the grey sea. "It's very exposed here."

A kind of pleasure lit his face as he stood to let her pass. "It's exposed all right. When there's a storm in the Channel you'd think the whole place was going to lift right off and blow out to sea."

"You like it." It was hardly a question.

"Yes." His hand rested briefly on her shoulder as she moved past him. "I like it."

There was no entrance hall; Ginny stepped straight into the living-room of the cottage, cluttered, with small windows facing the sea and the wall opposite them lined with bookshelves. The embers of a fire still glowed in the deep fireplace that filled the whole end of the room. Mark went immediately to it and thrust some kindling under the charred wood; at once a flame sprang to life.

"Well," he said, "that's better. It isn't Tilsit, but it's a damn' sight cosier. I'll get the kettle on. Make yourself comfortable. I'll show you the rest of the place when we've had a cup of tea."

She took off the cloak and followed him to the small and surprisingly modern kitchen that opened off a hall at the back of the cottage. Mark had cups out on a tray, and was slicing bread. She nodded towards the china. "Tilsit?"

"What else? These are export rejects—we all live off them." He was moving rapidly, efficiently; neat in his movements for a man of his bulky frame.

"Do you take care of yourself here—I mean the cooking and all the rest?"

"I'm a pretty good cook. Mrs. Johnston, the farmer's wife from down there "—he nodded towards the window, to the muddy lane and the distant view of the roofs of farm buildings—" comes in every week and does the place over. Makes this bread, too. Here, grab the honey, will you, and we'll go in to the fire." He preceded her with the tray. For a moment she looked around the little white kitchen, the treeless sweep of the cliff face, the bare lane down to the road. All of it had a chill about it, a barrenness that depressed her. She started at the sound of Mark's voice behind her. He stood leaning against the door jamb, watching her.

"Well—what do you think of it all?"

"It's strange," she said at once, not trying to hide her thought from him. "Lonely—and sort of withdrawn."

"It's meant to be," he answered. "Here—I'll pour you some tea, and I'll tell you." He led her back to the living-room and motioned her towards the settle that formed one side of the fireplace. "There! You'll warm up there. How do you like your tea?"

"With milk."

"Like the English, eh?"

"My father . . ."

"Yes, I keep forgetting . . . sugar?—have some bread?" He took his own cup and settled into the arm-chair with its torn slip-cover that faced her. "So you think it's too solitary here?"

"I didn't say that. I said it was—withdrawn."

"Withdrawn it is. This place"—he looked about the crowded room whose light was now concentrated between the fire and the two small squares of windows that faced the sea—"this place is my victory over Isobel. A small victory, but at least I'm not one of her row of stuffed dummies at Tilsit. I have a place to breathe in."

She put the cup down on the hearth, leaning towards him. "Mark—who are you? What *are* you to Isobel?"

"You mean you haven't been filled in? Brown didn't fill you in, or Randall? Neglectful of them—no doubt it was lack of time. They'll get round to it." He reached for a packet of cigarettes. "Fag?" When she shook her head he took one for himself and waited until it was lighted before he looked back at her.

"Officially I'm head of the design department at the Pottery—the rest of the department consists of an apprentice designer, so the title doesn't mean a thing. Unofficially I'm Isobel's captive."

"What are you talking about?" She said it with a beginning of anger, feeling that he had gone too far, and that Isobel now gained a certain sympathy because she could not speak for herself.

"A captive precisely and exactly. A captive of what she has made me and what she has given me—in a way a kind of a capture to my own bloody gutlessness in not being able to tell her what to do with it and cutting loose." He drew on the cigarette. "Sounds mad, doesn't it—a lot of bloody rot. Well, it's partly true, even if I do dramatise it. Your aunt, Ginny, picked me up out of a labourer's cottage over at St. Mary's and out of the local school when I was thirteen and gave me a kind of education—at least enough to make me presentable. Cut the corners off my Dorset accent. Then she arranged for me—no, paid for me at the Royal College of Art in London—and paid for me to work with Barry Jones, who's one of the best potters in the country and not a bad sculptor either. And then I came back here and every new shape and design that Tilsit has produced in the last six years has been mine. And damn' good ones they are too!"

"Why did she do this? How did she know when you were thirteen that you were going to be any good?" She said it doubtfully, unwilling yet to believe what he said and what it implied of Isobel.

"God knows! She had a way of feeding off people, of taking from them the things she needed."

"That doesn't explain it very well."

He threw out his hands in a sudden gesture of impatience. "How the hell should I know how she knew! I tell you she could smell anything that was to her advantage. If you really want to know the truth about that little story I'll give it to you, even if it isn't very nice. My mother worked in the Pottery—still does—as a decorator—you know, someone who paints on the designs. Well, she'd been taking home wet clay for me to model and saying nothing about it. Isobel found out and my mother would have been sacked except that she was a skilled worker and Tilsit had put a bit of money and a few years into her training. Also she happened to be nearly Isobel's equal socially—that's another story, Ginny, so don't interrupt—so it didn't do to bawl her out in front of the works people. But then, as I said, Isobel had a nose for what could be to her advantage. I suppose she wanted to know why anyone would take home clay when they worked with it all day long. So she came, and she saw what I was doing with the clay, and she wanted to grab me then and there for the Pottery. If it hadn't been for the factory act and my mother I would have been in the Pottery the next day. She was like a wolf with her teeth in. I tell you it scares me stiff even now to think about that time and the way she was."

"What happened?"

"My mother bargained—God knows with what. The assumption of talent in me from the piddling little shapes I'd thrown, I suppose. She bargained to get me into one of the decent public schools—Isobel to use her influence and to pay, of course. And then at eighteen if I wanted to go on with pottery—and only if I wanted—I was to get to the North Staffordshire Technical College and to work with a first-class studio potter. Only I did better than the North Staffordshire—I made the Royal College. She wouldn't agree to apprentice me at Tilsit at fifteen or sixteen, the way the kids in St. Mary's were. She wanted the best."

Ginny ran her tongue over her lips slowly. " She got it, then?"

" At the risk of her own job she got it. Isobel dragged me to the works one Sunday herself and watched me throw a bowl just to see that the other things weren't frauds. She wanted to make certain that her pound of flesh was there to collect. I was cross-eyed with nerves and damned resentful, I remember—and the first one I threw was a holy mess. The second one was a beauty. She decided to take the gamble."

" She won?" It hardly seemed fair now to ask the question. Mark reacted to it with a furious wave of his arm that almost knocked the cup off the arm of his chair.

" You bet your sweet life she won! She collected her pound of flesh."

" Wasn't she entitled to it?"

" God, you're like her! I worked for damn' little in wages, though, and so did my mother. Isobel was entitled to a couple of years of work, I suppose, but she wanted my soul too."

" You exaggerate."

" I do not! That woman was a greedy old bitch, and I don't care who hears me say it."

" Why didn't you leave?"

" I did. I tried that too. She pulled me back."

" How could she if you didn't want it?"

" She bribed me. It was as simple as that—and I'm no better than she for taking her bribe, so I haven't much right to talk. I pulled out of here and went to Wedgwood— they've got a big design department. Isobel knew where I'd gone, of course, and she waited until I found I just couldn't elbow out of the way all the people who were there before me even if I was the greatest genius that had come along since old Josiah himself. She waited until I was good and sick of it, and then she made her offer. I fell for it, hook, line, and sinker."

" Was it so good?"

" I would have had to be made of cast-iron to have turned it down—I was only twenty-four then, and she was offering

what every artist dreams of. She was offering me a steady
job with almost complete autonomy to design as I pleased,
and my own studio to try my hand at special pieces that
wouldn't go in the commercial line. In fact she was offering
me the money and the space and the time to try myself
as a potter and even as a sculptor. Viewed from a bed-sitting-
room at Stoke-on-Trent this was damn' near irresistible. I
didn't trust her, even then, and so I had her spell it out.
And then I came back . . ."

He rose and stretched his hand to her. "Come on—I'll
show you the rest of the place and you'll see why I came
back."

He led her through to the passage that she realised was
the connecting link between the cottage and the large
building at the back. It was built of whitewashed brick,
windowless, lighted by skylights, and its two walls lines with
shelves on which were ranged pieces of unglazed pottery and
ceramic sculpture. Ginny would have lingered here, but
Mark pulled her on.

"You can come back to them later," he said, as he flung
open the next door.

The studio was as big as a small barn, white like the
passage, and flooded with the harsh, even and deadly north
light that came from the enormous skylights and which
bounced back off the white walls and the grey cement floor.
At the far end stood two electric kilns; most of the
space was filled with the potter's tools, the benches and
lathes, the wheel, the baths for slip and glaze; the pots
of different coloured enamels and paints for decoration;
a table with a slanted drawing-board stood near the door.
Over everything, the benches, the walls and floors, was
splashed the dark greyish colour of the raw clay.

"Who wouldn't have come back for this bribe?" Mark
said. "If I'm not the best goddam potter in the world it
isn't for lack of tools."

Ginny's gaze moved upwards. From the rafters that tied
the steeply pitched roof hung pieces of metal, twisted and
welded into an incredible fantasy of shapes, in beautiful
balance and suspension so that now they turned and stirred
and did their slow rhythmic dance to the slight air currents
that the opening of the door had set up in the studio. The

mobiles were of dark bronze and copper and stainless steel, floating in a life of their own, above the earthy tools of the potter's trade.

"Wonderful!" Ginny said, spellbound and fascinated by their seemingly timeless, effortless moving upon the air.

Mark followed her gaze, and seeing her look, his own face warmed with pleasure. "I'm glad you saw them. Most people think they're pieces of junk hanging there. Isobel thought they were junk—a waste of time, she said. A waste of time in which I should have been creating new shapes, or throwing pots to send to more exhibitions to spread the name of Tilsit. But she had made her agreement, and to give the old bitch credit, she stuck to it. She had agreed that I could work on whatever I wanted in my spare time here, and she would pay for the materials. So she's been paying for bronze and copper and iron and lead, from every scrap-metal yard this side of London. I've got a lovely scrap-metal heap all of my own out the back." He motioned Ginny forward with a jerk of his head. "Look here——" He stood beside an enormous sheet of bronze, as tall as himself, about a two-inch thickness, cut roughly in a cubic pattern of a man, with strangely eloquent outstretched match-stick arms, that ended in square and enormous hands. "I call it 'Standing Figure,'" he said. "It's not finished, of course. I don't know that I have the courage to decide the finished form. It's the best thing I've ever done, though. Isobel thought it was a stupendous piece of nonsense. All she could see was the price of the bronze. She said she hadn't sent me to the Royal College and to Barry Jones to learn to be a mechanic." He jerked his thumb towards the welder's torch and mask, and the tanks filled with oxy-acetylene gas ranged against the wall.

"How could you stand it," Ginny said softly, suddenly understanding some of the sullen rage that stirred in this man.

"Where else could I have had this?" he demanded roughly. "It costs money—money to buy equipment, kilns, a place to work, a chance to make a name. I have an offer of a one-man show for the sculpture and ceramics at a good London gallery just as soon as I have enough pieces ready. Where else could I get these conditions for working? As long as I gave Isobel her share at the works, what went on here was private. And I gave her her share. I didn't cheat her. But what was mine was my own. Look here——" he said again.

He moved back into the passage-way and took from its place a rough-textured golden-red bowl, carrying an abstract line decoration in darker red. " Stoneware," he explained briefly. " Part of an exhibition of British pottery that toured Scandinavia." He presented its bottom to her. " This is what I mean. You see this—it's signed ' Barstow '—not Tilsit. She didn't like it when I did that kind of thing, but as long as I went on turning out what she needed for the pottery, there wasn't much she could do bout it." He replaced the pot, turning it carefully to the side he liked best. " Tilsit's got the name now for producing the kind of china that goes with all the modern stuff—the Danish furniture and the new kind of cooking pots and stainless steel. The market for that kind of thing used to be pretty small, but the public's growing up to it, specially in America. A lot of people are finding the traditional patterns a bit too ornate, and the shapes don't fit with their other modern things. Tilsit's never had a very great name for traditional china—there was too much competition before it was started by the names like Wedgwood and Spode and so on . . . I pushed Isobel towards the very modern designs, which really don't look very complicated—I can tell you it's a pretty devilish thing to think up a new shape for a milk-jug and at the same time make certain that it will pour milk. Well, we concentrated on that side, and now Tilsit holds second place in sales for imported contemporary china in the States. So . . ."

Ginny broke in, " So you did give her share."

" I had to. I had to earn the right to sign my name— just my name and nothing else—to these other pieces."

He came back and stood close to her, his brow furrowed, hands in pockets, his gaze on the lightly moving mobiles hanging from the rafters. " This part of my work has to be free and clear—because this is where my guts are."

He looked at her suddenly, demanding, " You understand that, do you? It's as if . . ." he fumbled for the words, " as if the work for the Pottery is the prize dogs I breed for sale to get the money to feed my cats."

Ginny looked back at the display of pottery on the shelves,

the stone and lustre-ware jugs and bowls and pots, mostly of
warm earth colours, and even her inexperienced eye could
tell that they had been fashioned with a degree of confidence
and sureness that stamped them with the mark of the master
craftsman ; of their value she was less certain ; she knew only
that the design and shapes seemed bold and fresh, strongly
masculine in execution. They seemed fitting companions to
the twisted fantasies of metal hanging from the studio rafters,
virile and tough. Looking back from these things which spoke
their own story of talent, she said to Mark, " Why do you
doubt that you gave her enough back? That debt must have
been paid off a long time ago."

" Why?" He started down the length of the studio, his
heavy shoes ringing harshly on the clay-powdered cement
floor. " Why? You wouldn't ask it if you'd known her.
You had to keep paying or you felt that you could never get
free."

He didn't wait for her comment ; he didn't look back at
her, but launched into a highly technical description of the
stages of the potter's craft. After a minute she lost the
thread of it, lost in a kind of fascination with the figure he
made, planted here, the whole length of the studio away from
her, his legs astride, his arms waving to demonstrate, his voice
thickening into what she imagined was the local accent as
he grew more forgetful of her presence. The personality
he expressed now was the blunt and forceful one of his
metal sculptured man ; here was the strength of his pottery
shapes, the free boldness of their designs. Caught up in the
rhythmic tones of his voice as he talked, she had an enormous
desire to see those clay-toughened hands at work on his
art.

" Firing's tricky. Everything shrinks in the firing—by about
an eighth You can lose your shape. Too much heat or too
little and you can lose your colour, or it colours unevenly. You
have to make moulds to hold the shapes . . ."

His powerful, attractive hands outlined what he spoke of ;
in the loving curves his hands described she saw and felt
the shape of something curved and feminine. She interrupted him.

" Some day will you throw a piece for me—so that I can
watch?"

His face darkened with sudden annoyance. " The hell

I will!" he said. " I don't make pieces just for the amusement of an audience. Some day if you're lucky and privi-
leged enough you'll be here when I'm throwing a piece. Maybe
I'll let you watch."

He strode towards her. " I suppose I've just been wasting
my breath telling you all this. In one ear and out the other.
Well, you'll have to pay more attention in future. If you're
a Tilsit you know about pottery—and for a Tilsit you're
pretty late starting . . ."

He was level with her now. " You know," she said,
" at the moment I don't care what I am. I'm just tired.
I've seen enough, and I've heard enough talk in the last
two days about things I have to understand to keep me
scrambling for the next two months." She shook her head.
" I just can't take in any more. I'm tired, Mark."

He had halted before her, and now his hand came up slowly,
to trace with exquisite gentleness the furrow between her
eyebrows, the line of fatigue under her eyes.

" Why, so you are, you poor little devil. So you are."

Ginny sat on the floor before the fire, her back leaning against
the padded arm of Mark's big chair. She closed her eyes,
and she was conscious that she thought of nothing, nothing at
all. Beyond the windows was the sound of the sea, a hollow
monotonous crash of the water against the rocks. In the
room itself was only the sound of Mark's soft movements,
and the human, real comfort of his presence. He brushed
against her as he squatted to put a mug of hot tea into her
hands, and she wanted then to seize upon the roughness of his
sweater, with its smell of salt-water and clay, to bury her
face in it. She wanted the ultimate peace of resting there;
she wanted this quietness, this absence of thought to go on
for ever.

He settled in his chair behind her to drink his own tea,
and she felt him take her by the shoulders and shift her
bodily sideways until her back rested against his legs;
the familiarity of the gesture was easy, as if it had been of
long duration. She settled against him, the bones of her
back seemed to melt with wonderful swiftness into him. She
sipped her tea, and closed her eyes again, and felt the
warmth of his body reach into hers. It was the first moment
of true peace that she had known since the hour that she

and Katrien had worked in the garden at Oranje Huis, the hour before her father had died.

Then a log slipped and crashed in the fireplace, and she started, the tension leapt into her body again.

At once his hand was on her shoulder. " Easy, love—easy." His voice was thick with the Dorsetshire accent.

She felt the alarm leave her, the tension recede. His hand remained, heavy and possessive, on her shoulder. It remained, like a barrier against her thoughts, against the misgivings and doubts that the coming to Tilsit had stirred in her, the ache of homesickness for familiar things and voices ; it was there, strong reassurance against uncertainty, the hedge against loneliness and fear, a stranger's hand no more. It was as if she had known it all her life and yet still felt it for the first time. It charged her with a sense of wonder, this combination of familiarity and uniqueness. Then it occurred to her that if she had not known this hand, this touch, all her life, perhaps she had been waiting for them.

The hold was relaxed gently, and then with slowness, but with great and unquestioning confidence, she felt Mark's hand under her chin to tilt her face upwards towards him. He said, before his lips came down to hers, " You're a lovely thing, you rare golden Bird of Paradise—you're a lovely thing !"

Mark began the walk back to Tilsit with her; he put the cloak about her shoulders himself, as if it were no longer the covering of the enemy. It had grown colder and the sunless, spring twilight was no more than a grey light on the sea ; the wind had risen and cut at them along the cliff path. And still Ginny held to her the warmth and release of that hour by the fire with Mark, the respite from the weight of Tilsit upon her, the words that had drifted between them, phrases without much meaning except that they undersood each other's talk. She faced Tilsit again with the sense that she was not alone, that it was not the only place she had to go. The cottage behind her she now thought of as a refuge.

The keep loomed up above them, higher here and more forbidding than from the Tilsit side ; Ginny could see now that it might have been once an impressive stronghold, commanding a long stretch of coastline in both directions. Watching it, wondering at what moment she would see the first lights from Tilsit, she suddenly felt Mark's hand on her arm.

"Keep in close to the hedge," he said. "You have to be careful on this path. It used to be wide enough to take a horse and cart, but it isn't safe for that any more."

He crowded her against the hedge and himself took the outside position on the path; she smelled the sweet wet smell of the leaves close to her face.

"Will you come back to the house with me—will you come in?" She hardly dared ask the question, afraid of his refusal, afraid of having his support withdrawn.

"I might," he said. "I might do that." And then he laughed, a sharp, harsh sound that surprised her. "It upsets them when I come looking as if I've just left the studio—reminds them too much of where their bread and butter lies. And old Lawrence primly offers me a sherry, and I say I'll have whisky. Then they have to send Garth with the keys to get the Scotch."

"Why do you hate them so much? What can any of them have done to you?"

"Hate them? I don't hate them. It isn't worth the effort. I despise them. They were all Isobel's servants—willing, if not content, to stay under that woman's thumb. For the same reason I despise myself—except that I don't have to sit at her table every day, even if I eat her bread."

"Vanessa too? Do you despise Vanessa?" It was suddenly important to know what he thought about Vanessa.

"Vanessa's all right," he answered carelessly. "She had a life away from Isobel—while she was married to that Italian fellow. It saved her, I suppose. Even when she came back Isobel didn't quite own her again."

They walked on in silence for a while, and now Ginny felt herself reach for Mark's arm, needing the contact with him to ward off the foreboding that the mention of Isobel had returned to her. At the base of the slope up to the keep, she said, "I suppose Trip's gone back. I shouldn't really have left him . . ." She was conscious of a kind of sympathy for the dog, the sharper because she couldn't really bring herself to like him.

"I wouldn't fuss about that animal," Mark said bluntly. "It knows how to take care of itself—a snivelling, whining thing, ready to droop or drool whenever Isobel looked at it. Just like her to have a dog that didn't have the guts of a mouse . . ."

" You're so hard on everyone, Mark—everyone at Tilsit."

In almost an automatic gesture he took her hand on the slope and pulled her after him.

" I have to be hard on them. You'll learn—after you've been in England a while. They're the natural enemy—since I came out of a labourer's cottage, and there was a time when my father used to dig the flower-beds here at Tilsit. It's part of the revolution, Ginny—no, don't smile, because that's what it is. All I have to fight them with—me and my kind—is whatever talent and gifts we have that they need. We're no longer just a pair of hands and a back, and we make them pay dear for whatever they need. And we despise them—all of us—and at the same time we envy them because they're still so sure of their world. I suppose we want their world, even when we pretend we don't give a damn about it. We tell ourselves that the Welfare State and taxes are pulling the mat out from under their feet, but even with the mat gone they're still better than we are, and all of us know it. So that's why I take care not to wear a jacket and tie when I go to Tilsit, and I ask for whisky when they offer me sherry. I make them know that they need me. And all the time they know that I need them."

" And me? Where do I come in all this?"

" In the worst place—right in the middle! You're one of them, but second-class, because you're a colonial. They don't talk about colonials any more, because there aren't any colonies, and Jack's as good as his master. But they still think that way. And so you belong smack in the bloody middle—and that's an unhappy place to be, my girl."

She answered lightly, " It also means I can move in either direction—— Look—there's Trip! He's waited all this time for me! Trip!"

The spaniel had appeared from behind the wall of the keep and leapt on to one of the fallen slabs. His excitement at the sight of her found vent in his sharp barking; he moved tentatively as if to run down to her, but at the edge of the slab he stopped, as if rooted. Ginny, hurrying towards him, suddenly felt the tug on her hand and realised that

Mark was holding back. Glancing at him she saw with shock that the look of hostility he had worn first seemed to have returned to him; his heavy brows were drawn in a frown. Impatient now with his swift and inexplicable changes of mood, she broke her hand from his grasp and hurried up the rest of the slope towards the dog. His barking ceased as soon as she laid a hand on him; he gave a kind of shiver.

"What is it, Trip? Did you think I was lost? Silly dog—you should have come with me."

Mark was coming towards them while she fondled the dog. As he approached the change in Trip was marked. His body stiffened, and the tender spaniel's mouth, not bred for battle, was stretched back unnaturally to show his teeth. A low sound, between a whine of fear and a growl, issued from his throat. Uncharacteristically he crouched down on the slab as if he would spring.

"Trip! What's the matter, Trip? Mark—what's wrong with him? Surely he knows you? He can't be frightened of you?"

To answer her, Mark made a gesture—an ugly one that looked as if he meant to aim a blow at the dog. Looking at him in wonder, Ginny had the sudden conviction that if Trip had been on the ground, it would have been a kick aimed, instead of just the gesture made.

"Damn' whining coward! Fool of a dog!"

"Mark!"

"Oh, to hell with it—you too!" And he turned and strode down the slope again, leaving her with her hand on the quivering body of the dog. Her voice reached after him with a cry that was nearly one of entreaty, and which was caught and swallowed by the wind.

At Tilsit they were waiting for her. Garth swung open the door at the South Front before she had reached it, as if he had been watching for her.

"We were beginning to grow anxious, Miss Virginia."

It seemed absurd to be compelled to explain where she had been for a few hours, but the old man's anxiety seemed to be genuine, and she felt responsible for it. "Yes—I've been to visit Mr. Barstow."

"Oh . . ." The face was too well trained to move by more

than a fraction, but the fraction was a tightening of the lips. " Well, I hope you enjoyed your walk, miss. The family is in the sitting-room."

They were waiting for her too, Lawrence, Margaret and Vanessa. A drink tray stood ready with decanter and glasses, but no one had poured a drink. Vanessa was smoking, and she squashed out her cigarette with a gesture of nervous impatience when Ginny appeared. Margaret raised her head from her embroidery frame with the faintest of smiles, but her hand did not cease its task.

Lawrence greeted her with an attempt at joviality. " Well —there you are! Had a good walk? Splendid! Well, now —can I pour you some sherry?"

Ginny looked across at the shining silver tray and the delicate stemmed glasses. It all seemed chaste and severe, and somehow grudging. It was too feminine. She looked directly at Lawrence.

" I'd like some Scotch, please—if there is some."

" Scotch? Well——" He recovered himself quickly. " Oh —well, I'll ring for Garth."

Vanessa suddenly threw up her hands in a gesture of small triumph. " There's something to be thankful for, Father! At last we're going to be able to get a drink in this house."

His face reddened dully, but he made no reply. Margaret did not raise her head again from her work. Vanessa, greeted with silence, shrugged and reached for another cigarette. Ginny stood where she was until Garth had answered Lawrence's ring.

" The Scotch, please, Garth."

" And three glasses, Garth," Vanessa said quickly. " I'm sure my father and I will join Miss Virginia."

When he reached the door Ginny called him. " And Garth . . .?"

He favoured her with more interest than he had shown the others. " Yes, miss?"

" In future I'd like the Scotch put out, please." For the benefit of them all she added, " I'm sure Mr. Randall won't decide the estate can't afford it."

" Miss Isobel . . ." Then he stopped. " Very good, miss."

When he was gone Vanessa leaned back against the worn red damask cushions of the sofa, pulling on the cigarette deeply, her head tilted towards the ceiling, eyes half closed. "You know," she said, "it's Garth and Brown I feel sorry for. They miss her. She really was the beginning and end of existence for them."

"I'm sure we all miss Isobel," Lawrence said.

"Oh, Father, you're so pious. You know that none of us will miss her except to be thankful she isn't here." She straightened a little. "And why don't you pour Mother her sherry? After all, we don't have to wait for her any more." She turned sharply to Ginny. "I don't expect you'll make us wait?"

"Of course not!" To relieve her own embarrassment Ginny moved towards the fireplace, to stand before it staring at the flames and thinking, in an instant, how much brighter the blaze had seemed in Mark's cottage. Vanessa was still talking.

"Isobel used to make us wait until she came out of the office. And that was never until a few minutes before dinner —so that there wouldn't be time for more than one drink."

"It can be changed." She heard her own voice, tense and irritated by the thought of the thousands of small things they would come to ask her to decide, things so tiny she couldn't even imagine them now. She turned and faced them, determined to get the next thing over, to face their dis- approval if it was there, and to establish once and for all that she would move in her own ways, whether they were Isobel's or not.

"I suppose you've been wondering where I've been?"

Vanessa answered for them. "We've been dying to know, but we've all been playing the English game of minding our own business."

"I met Mark Barstow. I've been to his cottage. He showed me . . ."

Lawrence, in the act of pouring sherry for his wife, put down the decanter jerkily, banging it against the glasses with a force that caused the crystal to ring.

"To his cottage?"

"Yes——"

"I wouldn't go to his cottage again if I were you."

"Why not?"

"I wouldn't go there again," he repeated.

For the first time Margaret spoke. "Lawrence—that is done with. Let us have no more scandal."

The door opened to admit Garth, and silence fell on them all.

IV

At the head of the stairs Ginny was halted by the sound of the wild and erotic music that suddenly broke the quiet. It was a raucous, strident rhythm of guitar and castanet; the loudness mocked the accustomed quiet; it was like a slap in the face to the prescribed decorum of the house. It came, unmistakably, from the open door of the room that Ginny knew was Vanessa's bedroom.

She hesitated, attracted by the sound in the way that she had been attracted by the warmth she had sensed in Mark Barstow after the cold welcome tended by this house. And yet the invitation was only tentative, and Vanessa was not her friend. What turned her finally towards the open door was the sight of Brown's patient, watchful figure standing by the door of the room Ginny now occupied, patently waiting for her to come to prepare for bed. Ginny longed to escape that engulfing presence, the sense of the past and of Isobel that seemed to be Brown's only passion. She bought herself a small reprieve by turning away, towards Vanessa.

Vanessa half sat, half lay in a huge chair before the fire, her feet propped on an embroidered stool. Her feet and legs were bare, and the long jade-green velvet robe she wore had parted to display their exquisite shape and the whiteness of the skin to which the firelight gave the same rose colours as to the marble mantel. Her hands and her expression both were empty.

"May I come in?"

Vanessa looked round, no surprise on her face, but a gesture of her hand that might have indicated welcome or indifference.

"Yes—do." With a graceful, indolent stretch she reached out and touched the volume control on the record-player. "Was this disturbing you?"

Ginny shook her head. " I enjoy it. It reminded me of Puerto Rico—they play a lot of Spanish music there."

" Puerto Rico?" Vanessa shrugged. " Yes, but have you been to Spain? Marcello and I used to go there often— between races. He was supposed to rest, but he never did. Marcello loved Spain . . . he loved to stay up all night, and to dance . . . he loved the women . . . to look at, not to talk to, he said. He never really thought women were to talk to."

" Did you love Spain?"

Vanessa looked at her fully. " I loved whatever Marcello loved."

Her expression was now one of such naked longing that Ginny was forced to look away. She waited, gazing around the room, until Vanessa pulled herself back into the present, and collected herself sufficiently to make the first gesture of invitation. " Won't you sit down?"

Ginny took the small, plush-covered chair opposite Vanessa. She sat there stiffly, her legs, too long for the height of the chair, thrust out before her. She felt awkward and somehow gauche beside Vanessa's silken beauty, her nudity under the velvet robe, the smell of her perfume that reached across the space between them.

" You have a lovely room," Ginny said, because Vanessa didn't seem inclined to say anything else.

" Yes—it is nice. Isobel let me put all these things together when I turned eighteen. They come from all over the house—nothing very good, of course, or otherwise Isobel would have had it on display. But this Victorian stuff is fun in a way. Isobel preferred to be uncomfortable, but much grander. The furniture in the room you use—her room—should be in the Victoria and Albert."

Ginny's eyes roved about openly now, approving the light-flowered hangings on the windows, the matching cover for the bed and canopy, the little gilt mirrors that hung about, silver and crystal bottles on the dressing-table, the porcelain shepherdess and her shepherd boy, the music-box, the corner what-not crowded with elaborate ornaments—all of it cluttered and somehow untidy, but with a gay charm that the other rooms she had seen at Tilsit entirely lacked. It was a light, feminine room, a triumph of determined fashioning against the austerity of the rest of the house. Ginny spoke her thoughts.

" How did you manage to do this—*here*?"

" How? It was all here—in various storage rooms all over the house. Most of it, I think, was bought for Isobel's mother when she married—she was the one who married my father's uncle, John Bowen. It was just about that time that Jane Tilsit was having this part of the South Wing modernised, having a few bathrooms made and electric light brought in. The rest of Tilsit is just as it was, of course—candles and no heat. Though Isobel always had the heat here turned off religiously on the last day of April, so I'm afraid you'll be cold now until October. Even in October you won't notice much improvement. Isobel never believed in people being warm—she thought it made them lazy. But the staff who look after the historic part of the house go around every day lighting fires in all those empty rooms to keep the damp out of the pictures and the woodwork. Strange . . . there has always been money for things at Tilsit, but not often money for the people who have lived here."

Her voice suddenly sharpened; she looked directly at Ginny. " You wonder why I stay on here now—now that you have come?"

" You're welcome to stay," Ginny said quickly. " Isobel's will . . ."

" The will . . . No one could live by that. It's not a very human document, is it?" She gave a small, wintry smile, the first sign of wistfulness that Ginny had detected in her. " You're thinking that I have Great Barrow and the farms, and that should be enough. It sounds enough on paper—in fact it's a pittance. But it would be enough if I'd never had anything else. Isobel used to say I was spoiled—and so I was."

She made a restless movement with her legs and reached for a cigarette. " Randall told you about my husband?" she said. " I was married to Marcello for more than five years, and I had everything that a girl thinks she wants from life. No children—but racing drivers seldom give such tangible hostages to fortune. And so long as I had Marcello I didn't need anyone else. He lived with the thought of dying, of course—racing-drivers do. The few times he talked about it—there weren't many because that would bring it too close—he used to laugh and say that I would marry again quickly. He said I was beautiful, and I would marry a very rich man."

"Perhaps he was right," Ginny said, shifting uncomfortably, trying to ease herself from the magnetic stare of Vanessa's eyes.

"Have you ever noticed how many beautiful young women there are in the world and how few rich men?"

"Do you need a rich man? There are the other kind."

"No one thinks about the other kind—for me. Isobel said it—she said I was spoiled and that's what everyone believes. And why shouldn't they? That was all the evidence there was. It was the way we lived. Marcello was quite famous to people who follow racing and who bet on it, and he had the looks and manners of an angel. He knew so many people—people who had yachts and villas and chalets in all the right places. We never had a permanent place to live in all those years, and it never really mattered because when he wasn't racing, there was always someone else's house to go to. Professional guests, I suppose some people called us, and in a sense it was true. But why not? Even among the rich, talent and beauty and charm are fairly rare. I think we paid for what we got."

"You're honest about it. Most people wouldn't be."

"Marcello taught me to be realistic. He knew if he had a smash-up and couldn't race any more that it would all be finished. He would be selling sports-cars to the people in whose houses we had stayed. He kept trying to prepare me for it. But I wasn't prepared when it came."

"I'm sorry." It was all there was for Ginny to say.

"Sorry? You didn't know Marcello. No one here did . . ."

"Randall did. He liked him."

"Everyone who met him liked him. Without meeting him Isobel hated him. She thought he was some kind of awful gigolo who could drive a car. She never could get it into her head that he might have been offended by the offer of money for a divorce—Randall told you all this, didn't he? And she never knew the absurdity of suggesting to an Italian that he take his wife's name—unless the wife happened to be a member of the Roman nobility. He thought the Tilsits were comparative upstarts—and I wasn't even a Tilsit." She gave her short dry laugh. " I suppose I should be like Father—at least pretend gratitude. I did pretty well for someone who wasn't a Tilsit—getting Great Barrow and the farms. You see there were only two kinds of people for Isobel—those who were Tilsits and those who weren't. It was lucky for me, I suppose, that there were so few Tilsits or I wouldn't even have Great Barrow. But Great Barrow isn't much of a dowry, and it's money I need."

" Why?" Ginny asked it directly, wondering if Vanessa said that because money was a conventional need, or if it was greed, pure and simple.

" To get married again. You don't think that's hard? Perhaps where you come from it isn't. But for me—who's there for me to marry? I'm not a debutante any more—and my picture's been splashed in newspapers all over the Continent, so I'm supposed to belong to the International Set. That's the reputation I had here in England, but it was all founded on Marcello. Without him there's nothing. Look ——" She flung out an arm. " In there—in the dressing-room—there's a row of some of the most beautiful gowns you'll ever see in your life. Balenciaga—Givenchy—Castillo. Marcello bought them, because we lived the life where women wore that kind of clothes. They haven't seen the light of day since I came back to Tilsit There are no young men here to take me to balls in London—none of the right young men who will waste themselves on the widow of an Italian racing-driver. So don't tell me about being beautiful. I know I'm beautiful, and it doesn't count. All that counts is what I've got, and that's an uneconomical manor-house, and two small farms. Yes—I have been spoiled. I've been spoiled because I like life to have some gaiety, some charm. And I'm spoiled because I'll never be resigned to the fact that it can have none for me. I used up everything in five years. All the beauty, all the fun. And I'm not a penitent prodigal. I'm not grateful like Father for what I have here—it pays for perfume and cigarettes and petrol for my car."

Then she added thoughtfully, " But if that's all I had, and Tilsit were mine, it would be enough. It was enough while I thought Tilsit could belong to me. But then she died, and

Randall produced you—like a rabbit out of a conjuror's hat."

"It was a shock for me too," Ginny offered defensively.

"You? I don't blame *you*. If she had only told me I would have had no hopes and no expectations. I think I would have made a better effort to find something for myself away from Tilsit after Marcello was killed if I had known about you. But she told no one except Randall. To keep me on a string, of course—on the unlikely chance that you would refuse to come here, refuse to have anything to do with all this."

"Unlikely? Was it unlikely? Yes, I suppose it was."

"Of course it was. It would have seemed unlikely to me if I had known about you. I would have bet that you would have come. And you see—here you are."

"Yes—here I am."

The words fell between them, and each sat and thought her own thoughts about what the words contained. They were no more enemies than before, and no more friends, but somewhat less of strangers to each other. There was no struggle between them because it was already over and done with before they had seen each other; Isobel had decided the struggle that day back in the convent of Santa Maria. It had been won and lost then, and both of them now recognised the futility of expending emotion upon it. Their eyes met each other in a kind of a recognition.

Suddenly Vanessa stood up with a swiftness that belied the seeming indolence of her posture; Ginny was beginning to understand that there was more energy and will in Vanessa than she wanted the casual observer to detect. It was as if there was an earnestness there over which she laid a veneer of levity. She went and closed the door and then turned back to Ginny at once.

"Why did you go to see Mark Barstow?"

Ginny understood now the reason for the music and the open door, the scene before the fire that might attract her when she would have to walk along the passage outside. Vanessa had meant her to come in order to ask just this question.

"I didn't go to see him—I met him. He invited me to the cottage for some tea."

A slight flush had risen in Vanessa's face as she seated herself again. " You *met* him? Are you sure it wasn't a contrived meeting. Mark's more devious than he seems."

" I wonder why you say that? He told me himself he was on his way to Tilsit. Not to meet me, he said, but to gossip to the servants about me."

She nodded. " He might say that too—it sounds like Mark. It's one of his gambits to play the simple, country-boy, but he's as clever as three foxes. I suppose he filled your ears with his tale of Isobel and her pound of flesh?"

" Yes . . ." she said reluctantly.

" Well, don't take too much notice of what Mark says about Isobel—yes, I know, it makes a good story of exploitation, but you always have to remember it's only half the story. There's her side of it too."

" There always is, isn't there?"

" Isobel was good to Mark Barstow," Vanessa said firmly, as if Ginny had not spoken. " Or if not good to him, then decidedly good *for* him. She forced him to be better than he ever dreamed he could be. It's probably true what she used to say of him—that she fashioned a craftsman and so forced on him the basic skills to be the artist he is now. If Mark has great work to do in the future it's because Isobel made him prepare himself to do it."

" I somehow thought . . ." Ginny said slowly, " I always thought that an artist found the ways and the means if he had it in him to do at all."

" Nonsense! You're still thinking of all that artist-in-a-garret nonsense. These days it takes money to train to be anything. The garret was only possible and habitable at a time when most people lived the same way. These days you can be mediocre and be paid much more money for mediocrity than greatness. Greatness needs time. No, don't be mistaken about Mark. If Isobel had not come along and lifted him out of his cottage he would have been a mechanic or a TV repair man, or maybe, with his big strong shoulders, he would have been pushing round a trolley at the Pottery. There really isn't much chance for the Mark Barstows of this world if there isn't an Isobel behind them."

" You've switched sides."

" There isn't any ' side.' I know Mark, and I know what he came out of. It was one of those hopeless, stupid marriages

that should never have been. His father was a labourer
—he worked on the roads for the county. And his mother was
a vicar's daughter. She's had most of the false gentility rubbed
off her now. There isn't much in Millie Barstow except
the bitterness of the kind of woman determined she was going
to get her own back on the world through her son."

" Mark said she worked in the Pottery still."

" Yes—she took the job when Mark's father deserted them.
From what you hear of him, the father must have been
a pretty brutal type. He was fined once for ill-treating a
dog, and then he had a couple of spells in jail for getting
into fights. He drank, and there was some talk that he
used to beat up Millie Barstow. Of course you'd never
get *her* talking about it. I don't know how much of this
is the truth. Mark was only about seven when his father
deserted them and the people in St. Mary's are inclined to
embroider the facts because Mark's story seems a kind of
fairy-tale to them. Most of them don't have an inkling about
talent, even the ones who work in the Pottery. They've been
used to seeing the shapes thrown and moulds made all
their lives, and they just think of the designer and model-
maker as someone who's rather handy with his hands. They
don't know anything about the prices Mark can command
for any of his signed pieces, or have any idea of the commercial value of the designs for the contemporary china he
does. He's still the man who's handy with his hands to them
—and damn' lucky, they think, that old maid Isobel Tilsit
took a fancy to him. They think that it was because he was
nice to look at when he was a boy that she sent him to school
and had him here to live during the holidays——"

" He lived here—at Tilsit!"

" Why, yes—from the time he was about fourteen. I
was about ten then. I remember him in the holidays—a sulky
boy with terrible manners who did everything he could to
frustrate Isobel."

" It must have been quite a jump from a labourer's cottage
to Tilsit," Ginny objected, knowing that she betrayed herself
in this hot and swift defence of him.

" I told you he was clever as three foxes. Artists always
are quick imitators. He learned his manners quickly for the
occasion that it suited him to use them, and he dropped
them for the times that it would most embarrass and annoy

Isobel. I'm not denying that she was hard on him. Isobel always exacted the most from everyone. But his dislike of her—fear, it might have been too, when he was younger—was the stick she used to make him jump. He was ungrateful and sullen, and she put up with everything he did for the sake of his talent."

" But she had need of his talent."

" How could she know then how he would turn out? And as he got older she knew that the bigger part of his talent might never be of use to Tilsit. Mark could be a great sculptor some day if he sticks with it—perhaps so great that he won't bother any more with mere cups and saucers. He has a wonderful feeling for the material he works with —clay, wood, metal, stone . . . And Isobel pushed him to try every medium."

" I don't believe that. He told me Isobel begrudged everything that wasn't for the Pottery."

" Mark was quite a good liar when he was a boy. He hasn't lost the knack of it. She knew that he worked best against opposition so she kept it up. But even if she hadn't he would have imagined it for himself. Mark needs to build up his monster of oppression and injustice. He has to have his scapegoat for whatever is wrong in his life. So do I."

Suddenly she threw her cigarette butt into the fire with a kind of repressed violence.

" Isobel served as a scapegoat for both of us—in different ways. We both needed our monster. But the Isobel Mark thinks of and the Isobel I knew must be two different women."

Then she leaned forward and took an ember from the fire with the tongs. Ginny sat, fascinated by the subtle grace of this complicated act of lighting a cigarette which seemed to be her habit. She wondered how often in the past Vanessa had used this gesture to command attention. She seemed to wait until she was certain that Ginny's eyes were fixed on her before she looked up.

" And yet he's wildly attractive—Mark is, isn't he? Even with his sullenness and arrogance. I mean—he's the kind of man one could go mad for . . ."

" *One* could go mad for—or *you* could, Vanessa?"

She nodded faintly, and her knowing smile was affirmation. " Any woman. I—if you like."

And then she stretched over and turned on the record-player again; the strident noise seemed to leap at them, ending conversation. Ginny got to her feet. But at the door she turned back and took a few steps nearer Vanessa.

"I want to ask you one thing."

"Yes?"

"Why did your father tell me I shouldn't go to Mark's cottage again? Was it because of you?"

"Because of me? Heavens, no! Mark hasn't shown any signs of wanting me . . . yet."

"Then why?"

Vanessa shrugged. "Perhaps he was trying to protect you."

"Why should he try to protect me?"

"Randall didn't tell you then about how Isobel died? No, he wouldn't—like my mother he doesn't believe in unnecessary gossip. But it caused quite a sensation at the inquest and it will be a long time before people stop talking about it, and putting their own interpretation on it." She drew at length on the cigarette and Ginny felt her body freeze suddenly in a wave of apprehension.

"Isobel was killed in a fall from that cliff, and it happened only a few feet from Mark's door. She had been to see him, and Mark swears she was all right when she left him. And he swears that he heard nothing. Not a cry from her or the dog. Trip was with her, you see—he always went with her to the cottage—and instead of trying to rouse Mark, Trip came running all the way back here. People couldn't understand why, and nothing was explained at the inquest."

"What are you saying, Vanessa?"

"Nothing—I'm saying nothing, because no one knows, except Mark. No one knows. What they do know is that Mark and Isobel had quarrelled violently at the Pottery that day—they were always quarrelling, of course—it was part of their relationship. But this one was fierce. It had to do with Mark's sculpture. He was giving too much to it —not enough to the Pottery. She implied that she was at the point of ending their arrangements about the cottage and he accused her of breaking her word, said he should have known what her promises were worth. Isobel didn't like that. She shouted back—some pretty shocking things. She said she would make it her business to see that he never got employment anywhere else. I don't suppose she could have done it, but it was a dirty threat. They all heard it—all the office staff at the Pottery. Mark stormed out and didn't come back that day. It was that same night she went to the cottage——"

Ginny felt her lips quiver as she broke in. " All this proves nothing."

" You're right. It proves nothing. No one is actually saying that he caused her death. The question was did he fail to go to the aid of someone in danger of death? Did he just close the door and pretend that she was not out there in the darkness? He might have wished her dead sometimes, but the question is could he have let her die and do nothing to help her?"

" I don't believe it!"

" You and many others don't believe it. Some do."

As Ginny fled along the passage to her room, she uttered again aloud the words that had already been said. " I don't believe it—I don't believe it!" Behind her the wild flamenco music pursued her, the volume turned up again, haunting, restless, mocking.

V

Brown waited for Ginny in her room, sitting straight as a rod on a high-backed Jacobean chair against the wall—a long way from the fire. Ginny pulled up short when she saw the other woman, the words of rebellion and dismissal rising on her lips because all her senses at that moment craved the grace of solitude, the space in which to think over what had been revealed to her this day, and what had been learned. But the long day was not ended yet. Brown, too, it seemed, must have her time.

Brown rose at once. " Good evening, miss. I hope you don't mind my waiting here." She added, a little hesitantly, " It is cosy here with the fire."

" Good evening, Brown," Ginny wondered by what stretch of reasoning this great chamber could ever be termed cosy, and what degree of comfort and relaxation anyone could have drawn from a fire so far distant. " You needn't . . . it wasn't necessary for you to wait up for me."

" I always waited until Miss Isobel was ready to retire.
miss. Just in case there was something she wanted. I've
laid your nightgown out, miss. It seems too thin, I must
say. But I've put a hot-water bottle in the bed." She
looked hopefully at Ginny, pleading for a request, an order,
any kind of recognition of her presence and of her function.

" Thank you, Brown. You're very kind." To meet the
woman's need she threw another sop. " I'm sure I shall be
most comfortable. If . . . if there's anything I need I'll
remember to ring."

A faint glow came to Brown's face, as if she had suddenly moved close to the fire, and Ginny was appalled to sense
the emptiness that could be filled by such a small thing.
" Very good, miss. Anything at all. At any time. Miss
Isobel . . ." She halted, and for a moment Ginny thought
those bloodless lips trembled. " Miss Isobel trusted me with
everything."

" I'm sure she did. I expect I shall need your help in many
things, Brown. There's a great deal I have to learn yet . . ."

" So there is, miss. And you mustn't try to do it all at
once. You mustn't let them take too much out of you.
They took too much out of Miss Isobel—always demanding,
always asking. All their problems . . . she let them all climb
on her back and she carried them all. You mustn't let them
do that to you."

" I'll try not to." Ginny walked across the room to the
beautiful inlaid eighteenth-century dressing-table where Brown
had set her cheap nylon and plastic hairbrush down beside a
worn, silver-backed one that must have been Isobel's. She
tilted the little gilt-framed standing mirror to catch the light,
staring at her own face, shadowed and hollowed by weariness.
She hardly recognised her features, the skin stretched tightly
on them as if she were suddenly grown older, or had been
ill. She turned away from her own image. " Good night,
Brown."

" Good night, miss. Oh—just one other thing, miss."

" What is it, Brown?"

" The key of Miss Isobel's desk." Ginny followed her gaze
to the tall secretaire with its front closed that stood between
the windows. " I knew where she kept the key—she told me
herself. I didn't give it to Mr. Randall," she added defensively. " I thought I would wait until you came."

"It should have been given to Mr. Randall. He is dealing with all the estate matters."

"What's in that desk has nothing to do with the estate, miss. All of that's down in the office. What's in the desk is private—Miss Isobel's private papers."

"Her private papers are not mine, Brown. If they're private they're not mine. Perhaps I should tell Mr. Randall and then have them destroyed."

"Destroyed?" A look of shock and outrage came into the woman's face. "You surely couldn't do that, miss! Miss Isobel wrote at that desk nearly every day of her life. I can't believe anyone would want to destroy what she wrote down over all those years. What's in those books, miss, belongs to you, like everything else at Tilsit. And I'll just leave the key . . ."

She took the key from the pocket of her smock and laid it on the dressing-table near Ginny. Her eyes were appealing. "You couldn't have them destroyed," she said again.

Ginny laid one finger tentatively on the key. "This isn't mine, Brown. Nothing at Tilsit belongs to me."

"Who else's then?" the woman demanded in a passionate whisper.

Ginny shook her head. "Not mine—not a stranger's. It should have been Vanessa's—you know that!"

"Vanessa? That one!" The words were spat out with a kind of contempt. "She with her cheap husband and her fancy clothes! What right had she to come back to Tilsit? She left it, didn't she? Left Miss Isobel? After she'd been born here and lived here all her life."

"Sometimes people have to go away from what they've known all their lives—and then they know how much they love it. Vanessa loves Tilsit," Ginny finished, knowing that this was the truth. "She's been trained to it—she knows it and this life, the Pottery, everything."

"How can you say that, miss, when she lays her nasty tongue to everything here to criticise it? Don't think we don't hear her—we do hear her, Garth and I. She's discontented and greedy. She's not willing to work for what she's had from this place and from Miss Isobel."

"But she loves Tilsit," Ginny insisted. "She knows it and I think she would take better care of it than I could. She has a long start on me, Brown . . . Tilsit is a charge, and it needs a long preparation."

" Nothing that you won't be able to manage, miss—and manage very well. I'm here, aren't I, to help you, to tell you what you need to know? And Mr. Randall? And Garth? Mr. Bowen-Tilsit runs the Pottery. You can do it if you want to, miss. You're a worker—like your aunt. She picked that too, miss. That's what she said to me. ' Brown,' she said, ' she's young for her age now, but she'll come on quickly. She's got spirit—and she's a worker.' That was when she decided you should have Tilsit, miss, and she's never been wrong."

" How do you know all this? Randall said no one knew about me except him."

" It was different between your aunt and me, miss. She told me everything. The week she went to the West Indies that time, everyone but me thought she was in London. When she came back she told me all about it. All about you ' She's right for here, Brown,' she said. And *I* knew it the minute I laid eyes on you. Your aunt's very walk—the way she moved, the expression sometimes. ' She's the image of my grandmother, Brown,' she said—that's Jane Tilsit, miss— the Old Lady. But I see more of Miss Isobel in you than she could see for herself. She wasn't vain, miss—I suppose she'd forgotten what she looked like when she was young. Before she was disfigured. But I remember her—a lovely young lady. If she had ever had a daughter she might have been very like you. But your aunt didn't have any children, of course. She wanted a lot of children. ' I need a lot of children for Tilsit, Brown,' she once said to me. That was when she thought she would marry. But she didn't marry."

Ginny sank down on the tapestry-covered stool before the dressing-table. She could wring no more endurance from the long day. " Brown . . ."

" Yes, miss—you're tired. I can see that. I've talked too much. But you remember what I said, miss—remember what your aunt said about you. She knew you would come here—even after you didn't reply when she sent the cheese knife. You remember that she knew you could manage anything you wanted to. And don't let them all jump on your back, or put you off what you want to do. And remember, miss, that you've only to ask me—ask me anything at all."

"Yes, Brown," Ginny answered faintly. "I'll remember."

Sleep would not come and so the long day had still some further endurance to be wrung from it. Ginny lay in Isobel's canopied bed and watched the embers of the fire sink lower, the light only dim on the high ceiling. The wind came in gusts against the house, and between the gusts, far-off and distant, the sound of the sea. She thought of Mark in the cottage at the cliff's edge, and with the thought the restlessness grew. "I don't believe it," she said again aloud, so that the whisper seemed to echo in the room. She felt again the gentleness of his hands, and the strength of his lips upon her, and her mind rejected the thought that he could bring violence upon another person. Mark was talk and passion and energy—but not violence. The creative instinct in him would stop short at the act of destruction. Mark, she told herself, who could create, would never destroy, or would not mutely stand by to witness the end of life. His gift was the life force, and any diminishing of life by his own act, must necessarily wither and chip away at his gift. "He could not have done it," she said. And then questioned herself why she cared so passionately that what she said should be the truth. He had taken her hand in their first meeting and she had been drawn by the magnetism of his power and energy. And then he had kissed her, and she had seemed to feel the breath sucked out of her by that kiss. The arousing of full passion still trembled in her body, and would not let it be still or at rest. Mark could do this to her—with a touch of his hand he could summon her to follow him. And with a mere kiss he had seemed to take possession of her.

There was nothing in her whole life that had prepared her for this hour and for this feeling. Nothing in the slow dawning of her love for Jim had prepared her for the swiftness and brilliance of this new awakening. Her body had stirred with desire before, but never in her soul had she known this instant's moment of intuition, the rare flash of lightning in which the whole terrain is revealed, the highs and the deeps, the second of illumination which contains both the beginning and the end. She was not prepared to call it love, because the beloved was still unknown except by the touch of his hand and by his kiss. And yet she knew no other name to call it. It bore a resemblance to nothing else she knew by name, no way to evaluate by past experience this new emotion, less of joy than an anguish of longing. She did not know herself; she did not recognise the new creature of Mark's creation. He had seemed to put out his hand and in that act to have called forth a different woman. The response and the knowledge of it was both agony and delight.

She stretched out her arm in the vastness of that bed and met only the wasteland of its emptiness; she turned her face against the pillows to stifle the cry of his name in the darkness.

As it had been the night before, she heard the plaintive scratch of Trip's paw against the door and the snuffling sound of his breath as he thrust his nose against its edge and the floorboard. With no fear to-night, but a certain resignation, she lighted the candle and went and opened up for him. He gave her only a moment's scrutiny in passing, and then once again he began his circle of the room, seeking the traces of Isobel. Defeated and disappointed once more, with no further look at Ginny, he arrived at the basket before the fire and settled there. Ginny stood with the candle held high, watching him. She was aware that she, like the dog, in this unfamiliar world where the mainstay had been removed suddenly, had lost her point of contact. She could go down in the rush of the unfamiliar, or she could struggle to re-establish the link.

Abruptly then her hand fell on the key that Brown had left on the table; a minute later she had thrown on her robe and Isobel's secretaire was unlocked and the flap down. Without giving more than a glance to the two rows of leather-bound books on the shelves which were now revealed, she searched the drawers for paper and pen. In a fury of need and bewilderment she wrote the first words on Isobel's thick white paper—the paper that she remembered from the letter that had arrived that Christmas Day—engraved in heavy black with the name of Tilsit.

Dear Jim—the pen, strange to her hand, stuck and spluttered, and the ink blots lay all at once across his name.

*To-day I met a man who touched my hand and kissed me,
and I think I fell in love with him. I don't say I love him—
how could I love him when I love you? But I fell in love
without understanding and without much reason or without
reason that I can put on paper. Is this some kind of madness
or is it only because I seem to have stepped into a world
where madness is normal? Shall I ever again be sane and
shall I look back on this afternoon as a rush of folly,
the passion of inexperience? Are there any answers to these
questions, Jim?—do you know any answer? I have asked
you because you loved your wife well and deeply, and
because my knowing about that love—and my loving you
—has given me what small recognition I have of what has
happened to me. But why, I wonder, don't I ask my
questions of myself, and get the answers I want to hear.
Why do I tell you this—that I love someone else when I
thought I loved you? Why do I risk losing even what little
I ever had of you . . .*

The words would not come any more and the pen halted.
She read back, with a sense of unbelief, what she had written.
And then she laid the pen down. She would not send it, of
course. To send it would be to cut off her way back to that
other world where Jim lived and where her heart had had
its being. But the feeling persisted that Jim was friend and
this new love was stranger, and might even, by the very
nature of his being, become enemy. No, not enemy, she cried
inside herself—not enemy, but lover. That was what she
had so suddenly wanted that afternoon, still wanted now,
and the thought of Mark had halted the words to Jim.
She knew that she would write no more of this letter—not
now or ever. She folded it but her fingers fell away from it
as she made the first motion to tear it.

She had pushed back the chair from the desk and half
risen before she was struck again by the sight of the two
rows of books, of uniform size—the first half-dozen of the
set bound in faded soiled blue velvet, the rest in prim blue
leather, with ornamentation of dull gold. There was nothing
to identify them, either by title or name. She reached down
the end one, the one whose gold stamp was newest and opened
it in order to bury Jim's letter there. She flicked the thick

gold-edged pages, and saw, with a slight sense of shock, that all of them were blank.

Quickly then, at random, she took down another. It was filled to the last page with Isobel's writing, that blunt masculine hand, but distorted here, small in size and difficult to read. The pages were crowded, some dated, others not; the dates and the faded ink were of a long time ago. She paused a few times to try to make out some of the phrases. "*A new kiln ordered for the Pottery to-day, a fearful expense but we must stay abreast of the others—the only way to pull ahead,*" and then, "*Margaret thinks it would be a good idea to have a special birthday tea for Vanessa, and Vanessa is insisting on a new velvet dress. The child already has too much her own way.*" An earlier book came down then, the white pages marred by the brown spots of age and mildew. "*Granny and I discussed with Richards, the architect she got down from London, the business of having the Inner Court wall of the Long Gallery reinforced. A big job because he must go right down to the foundations. Half the Inner Court lawn will be torn up and must be replaced. A great nuisance and expense, but Granny says it must be afforded somehow.*" And then a break in the writing, as if Isobel had paused. "*John had promised to be here to meet Richards. It is important to understand what the work will entail, but he said they needed him to make up a double match at Long Kedston. I suspect someone else was there.*" A few pages forward in the book she read, "*The Van Dyck of Lady Rowena Blake came back from London where it was being cleaned. Granny and I went to watch it being hung. Granny joked about the fortune she had been offered for it by the dealer. She thought he probably wanted it for Lord Duveen. I had a horrible fear she might be tempted, but of course she was only joking. The picture is marvellous. It must never be let go from Tilsit. When John came back from the Marstons he went to see it and he only said they had made the gown too yellow. Granny was annoyed.*" The small domestic matters were recorded alongside the important ones. "*Brown is having trouble with her teeth and is being stubborn about having them seen to.*" And on the next line, "*The Bishop came to lunch to-day—a new man. Everything was very formal and grand, and Granny wore*

*her pearls. She even took him through the whole house,
though it is such a long walk at her age. He loved the
chapel, but she didn't let him stay very long."* The domestic
matters sometimes bore into the personal. *"Twelve dozen
linen sheets ordered to-day. Granny upset because the last
sheets were bought when she was first married."* *"A small
fire at the pottery to-day. No one hurt. Granny says parts
of it are unsafe and it should be rebuilt. John was away
in London so Granny came with me to see the damage.
A couple of the older workers cheered her."* And then,
*"To-morrow John goes up to Cambridge. He spent the
last day at the Marstons."* And then alone on a page the
words penned so swiftly and with such force that they were
nearly illegible. Ginny studied them a long time. *"Edward
Ashley came again to-day. Third time in two weeks. We
walked in the garden."*

Ginny paused here, filled with guilt that she had intruded
so far into the private affairs of the young Isobel. She
remembered the woman who had stood before her at Santa
Maria, with passion and self-pity all schooled out of that
horribly marked face, the body so disciplined that it appeared
impervious to discomfort; those things she remembered,
and the strangely beautiful hands. The woman had been
young once, and perhaps in love, and she had written down
that she had walked in the garden with a man called Edward
Ashley.

Ginny closed the book, feeling that enough of Isobel
had been exposed and laid bare in this one brief look. But
she would be back, she knew. Too much of Isobel was
here to leave unknown. Too much of the world of Tilsit and
her father.

Ginny's hand went now, without much hesitation this
time, to the row of velvet-bound books on the shelf above.
The writing here was different—copperplate, immaculate,
precise; the ink had turned brown on the yellowed paper.
The first entry was dated 1865.

"To-day," it ran, *" I have met a man who touched my hand
and kissed me, and I think I fell in love with him."*

The breath exploded from Ginny in an audible gasp of
shock; she felt the goose pimples break on her flesh to see
the words that she had written to Jim that night set down

in this Victorian lady's hand of a hundred years ago. She understood now that this was the book of Jane Tilsit.

The entry continued, " *His name is George Martin and he is a potter, and I have determined that I will marry him. He does not know it yet, but it shall be so. He is a common man—of the people—almost a rough man if anyone rough could be so gentle. We met and he did not know who I was or where I had come from, and before we parted he had kissed me. If this is folly then I shall commit folly, for I have had my inheritance these five years past and no man has sought my hand and there will be, I know, no marriage that is not of my contrivance. I will marry this rough potter, and raise him up, and people will say that I have made a mésalliance. Let them say—I will close out the world. I must have this marriage because I must have many children for Tilsit.*"

Ginny read no further. Her eyes blurred with fatigue and by too many emotions, she sat and held the book between her hands, her mind going back to the picture in the Tilsit New York showroom, the picture of the bewhiskered man with the solemn, kindly eyes, the master-potter, George Martin Tilsit. The entry in the Encyclopædia of Pottery and Porcelain was explained: " *assuming the name of Tilsit in 1865 . . .*" Jane had married her rough potter and had indeed raised him up. But there had not been " many children for Tilsit." There had been only one, Elizabeth, the mother of Isobel and John. She had left no mark at Tilsit, nothing save the few gay and charming things that Vanessa had gathered in her room. And of her children only Isobel had endured. Jane—the " Granny " of Isobel's diaries, the " Old Lady " of Brown's remembrance—had passed the inheritance to Isobel. And now the inheritance waited—something not yet understood, something not earned by love or work, for her, Ginny, to pick up.

Once again her hand went back to the second row of diaries, to the last book with the blank pages. As she finally inserted the letter to Jim and closed it, she recognised that with the words written down that night she might, unknowingly, have made the first entry of her own journal.

CHAPTER TWO

"I am not an educated woman, you understand, miss," Brown said, "but your aunt tried to teach me what she knew."

She said this as she and Ginny were walking across the Hall Court, bathed in a bright wash of morning sun that softened and lightened the grey stone walls so that they took warmth and some colour from it. A sudden whirr of seagulls above their heads caught Ginny's gaze, the blurred grey and white against the gentle blue of the morning sky. The arch of the gatehouse framed the pastoral of wooded park and stream below them. Ginny was suddenly deeply conscious of the peace of the scene, of the remembrance that this had been a family's home for a very long time before it was a showplace, that the pursuits of family and love and commerce had taken place under the walls of this court. She pictured this court peopled with those who came to do business at Tilsit, and those whose life was Tilsit, master, family, servants and serfs; she sensed the whole cycle of innocence and maturity, war, famine, pestilence and death, and the joy of the new birth.

She said to Brown, "Why is the family called by the name of the house? It isn't usual, is it?"

"As long as the records go back, miss, the family has been called Tilsit. No one knows whether the first lord of the manor gave his name to the place he settled, or if he took the name of the place because he had no name of his own. If there had been a title—an important title—I suppose the family name would have changed. Your aunt used to say the Tilsits had been wise in being without ambition. For the few miles around here they were kings, but they kept to their own little corner and to the rest of the world they were never anything but local squires. When other men lost their heads and lands, the Tilsits kept theirs because they were careful never to attract attention. That's how Miss Isobel explained it to me, miss."

As she spoke Brown was unlocking the outside door to the old South Wing, which balanced on the same side the one

where the family lived. " I'm taking you through the visitors'
entrance, miss, because you'll get a better idea of what the
people see when they come in. This," she said, indicating
the flag-stoned ante-room, " is where we sell the coloured
catalogues of the Collection. And this room through here
is the souvenir shop, where Miss Vanessa sometimes works.
You see, we have a whole line of little china pieces relating
to the house that the Pottery makes for us—some of it has
the coat-of-arms, but your aunt never cared for that much.
Most of it is the regular Tilsit line—you see, miss, these
little coffee cups and ash-trays and the cheese knife, all
in their special boxes. It's surprising how much people will
pay for these tiny things once they feel they have some
connection with the house. Surprising the kind of people
you find paying a guinea for a cup and saucer."

" And the money goes—where?"

" The money goes to the separate company that keeps the
house open to the public—for repair and maintenance—all
that kind of thing, miss. All the cleaning is done by special
people—not the regular staff we have for the family wing.
You'll see a lot of people cleaning and dusting around in
the public rooms that have nothing to do with Garth—or
myself. But here in the Porcelain Gallery I'm the only
one who has the keys of the exhibit cases. I dust and wash
the china. Your aunt trained me to it long ago."

She abruptly halted and stretched out her hands to Ginny,
holding the fingers wide. " You see I have to take care to
keep the skin soft and the hands exercised. Otherwise I might
grow clumsy."

She remained standing in the middle of the souvenir shop,
a figure of supreme dowdiness in the thick cotton stockings,
the long baggy skirt and flowered smock, the wisps of straight
grey hair for ever escaping the bun, but the thin face now
wore a look of dedicated fervour that transformed it, and lit
it with a sort of beauty.

" You love the Collection, don't you, Brown?"

The woman nodded. " I do, miss. In the beginning I didn't
understand it. I thought the pieces were pretty, of course, but
it was a long time before your aunt was able to teach me
what went into making them. She had me over to the Pottery
several times to try to make me understand why it was
so hard to get certain colours, and why it all took so much

time. As I understood it, miss, I began to love it. Of course
the Collection isn't anything to do with Tilsit—there are
pieces from every country, and almost every period. There
are the kind of pieces that people will never be able to make
again. So it was important for me to understand the process
of making ceramics so I would understand why it would never
be possible to make them again. Though here," she added,
her gesture sweeping the souvenir room, "there's only
Tilsit china. It wouldn't do to stock other kinds, would it,
miss?"

"I shouldn't think so," Ginny said, laughing. "Why
give them the space and the publicity?" She picked up a plate
of the same pattern as the family normally used. Then her
hand went to a cup of the pattern that Garth had used to
serve her first cup of tea at Tilsit. "That is Rose Imperial,
miss. That was created by George Martin Tilsit himself—the
husband of the Old Lady. It was one of her favourites. That's
the Bluebell pattern, miss," as Ginny's hand lingered over
a plate of the pattern that her father had smashed in the
sitting-room at Oranje Huis. "I like that one the best. So
simple and pretty. It was created just about the time John
——" She broke off. " —And over here are all the new
patterns—all new shapes, too, as you'll see. Not in my
taste—too plain, and some of them downright ugly, I think.
But then, I'm not modern, am I, miss?"

"Did Mark—did Mr. Barstow create these?"

"He did," she acknowledged unwillingly. "Some of them
won awards—though I can't see it myself. Ugly, twisted
things, they are!"

"My aunt didn't think that, Brown. She put a great deal
of trust in what he did."

"Yes—and perhaps the poor creature lived through minutes
long enough to rue that she trusted him, that she could
never see the ugly and twisted thing he was inside. But if
God was merciful, miss, she died quickly."

Ginny laid down a plain white coffee-pot whose shape she
had been examining in silhouette. "Are you saying, Brown—
are *you* one of the people who think that Mark knew that
she fell or had an attack—and refused to help her?"

Brown returned Ginny's gaze without wavering. "How
can I say what happened? I wasn't there. No one knows
but him. All I know is that he is capable of it."

" Are you sure of that?"

" As sure as anything I've ever known. He's always been that way. A wild and violent boy he was when she first brought him to Tilsit—shocking manners and nasty ways about him. None of us liked him, but she kept insisting that he would turn out all right."

" Brown—that's not fair! He'd had no training then . . . no reason to be well-mannered or polite. He'd never known any different."

" It's not that I'm talking about. He learned his manners well enough when he chose to use them. Don't forget his mother was a gentlewoman. It was the other things that I didn't like. He was always clever with his hands, of course —could make anything and fix anything. It was people he was so bad with—and animals and plants, and things like that. Anything that was living he didn't seem to know how to handle. Three dogs, I think Miss Isobel gave him, inside of two years, and all of them run-over or died. And Miss Isobel's horse that fell dead under him because he rode it past its limit. She gave him his own plot in the kitchen garden. Do you think he could make anything grow? I tell you, miss, everything died as soon as he touched it. A bad and twisted nature—that's what he had and still has. Just like these ugly things he makes and those old twisted-up pieces of scrap that he calls statues or sculpture —or whatever they're supposed to be. You'd only got to look at them to know what he is. Evil . . ."

" Brown, no!" The words tore from Ginny. She wanted to cry out that this was ignorance and prejudice, the suspicions of a closed mind that knew only one loyalty. The woman's eyes glinted in her emotion, the hands clenching convulsively.

" A destroyer—that's what he is," she insisted. " Destroys everything he touches—except what he makes for himself. Himself, that's all that matters to him."

" You can't condemn him for that. A lot of people are like that."

" Not the way he is. He's had so much from her that he's come to take it as his right. I feel sure that when she went to him that night she might have been going to take some of it away. And he couldn't endure the thought of it. So . . . he let her die."

K

"Have you said this to anyone else? Is this the truth, or is this just what you *think*?"

"Why should I say it to anyone else?" Brown demanded, her tone growing stronger. She had lost her respectful demeanour in the grip of her agitation. "Do you think I would bring scandal on Tilsit if I could help it? I knew you were coming here and I would not have brought you more trouble in your days than what you had to bear. So I said nothing—there was nothing to prove, in any case. They had had a row in the works that day and he had walked out on her, as he was always doing. She went to the cottage that night to finish whatever it was she had to say. He'd been neglectful of his duties at the Pottery— attending only to his own concerns, making his own weird and sinful things. She was going to refuse to let him go on with it. She could have taken it all away from him, you know—the cottage, the studio, even his job——"

"The job wouldn't have mattered. Mark could have a job with any pottery in England. You know that!"

"That much might be the truth—but what kind of a job? You don't think, do you, miss, that he could walk in any- where and get anything like he has at Tilsit? Someone of his type and class? Even with all the talent in the world he couldn't have had again what he has at Tilsit. There's no one here to say him nay. She made him his own master. Where else could he have that—and him hardly thirty and with no money or family or connections? I think he thought he might do better if Miss Vanessa were running things—as everyone supposed would happen. He could have let Miss Isobel die—he *could* have," she repeated.

"There is no proof, Brown."

"No proof, miss—that's true. Only the word of a woman who's watched him since ever she brought him here and who knows him through and through."

"You're entitled to believe what you want, Brown, but not to speak it." Behind her back, away from Brown's sight, Ginny gripped the edge of the display counter, holding it tightly, willing herself to stay and to hear calmly what Brown had still to say, willing herself to confront the sus- picion and stare it down.

"Why do you tell me these things, Brown? You know it's wrong to say what can't be proven."

"Why—because you have to be protected! That's why! This house, the Pottery—everything is on your shoulders now. You have to deal with Mark Barstow and whatever evil he creates. You have to be warned."

"Very well, Brown." To her own ears Ginny's voice sounded eerily like Isobel's had been on that day at Santa Maria. "Let us say I have been warned." She stood straight and let go of the table behind her. She could argue no more about Mark, say nothing more to defend him because if she did her control would snap. He was already, less than a day after she had first laid eyes on him, too precious and too much beloved to be given over to the slaughter of this woman's accusations. The new love was yet too fragile to endure it.

With a gesture of authority which she deliberately made as close to Isobel's as she could remember it, she said to Brown, "Now—could I see the Collection?"

"The Collection was begun by Jane Tilsit about 1870," Brown began as she unlocked the farther doors of the souvenir shop. Her voice had gone back to its usual tone, submissive, dull. She almost chanted the words, as if this were a guide's recitation. "It is representative of almost all important and interesting aspects of the potter's art, ranging through archæological finds from fifth-century Attica, the great Ming Dynasty of China, the European hard and soft pastes, and examples of the best work of the English potters of the eighteenth and nineteenth centuries. It is held to be one of the finest private collections in Europe. . . ."

Ginny broke into the recital. "Was it actually Jane who made the collections, Brown? Or was it in fact George Martin?"

"You forget, miss—it was the Old Lady who had the money. I don't say she wasn't *advised* by George Martin Tilsit, but whatever was bought was paid for by her. Of course, it was possible then to make such a collection for much less money than it would cost to-day. This, miss," she added, opening both of the double doors wide, "was once the old kitchen wing of Tilsit—the kitchens are underneath here—dungeons, almost. It was not in use at all when Jane Tilsit's collection grew to a size where it needed special housing."

The long room before them was the full width of the

wing, windows on both sides; a highly polished floor of random-width boards, wooden pegged, reflected the glass display cases that lined each wall, and formed a double row down the centre of the room. The sunlight streamed in through the south windows, playing on the shining glass, giving to the thousand colours and hues of the ceramics an astonishing brilliance. The colours sang like an exuberant painting, like an epic poem that ranged the whole story of civilisation.

"It isn't, as you see, miss, a very large collection. Over the years the Old Lady discarded and sold anything that was not of the very first quality. What you see here is the cream skimmed from the top. Miss Isobel had these modern display cases made when it was decided to open the Collection to the public—you see they light from top and sides so that the porcelain can be seen to best advantage even on very grey days."

Standing there in the doorway, Ginny's eyes flicked along the cabinets, lingering now and then on an individual piece whose like she remembered from the museums of New York— the red and black Greek vases, the famous blue of the K'ang Hsi hawthorne jars, an exquisite four-sided vase of *famille noire*, the Chelsea birds and flowers, the unmistakable Wedgwood Black Basalte. So much her glance quickly told her. She looked back to Brown for guidance.

"Any one of these pieces would be prized by almost any museum in the world. It's become an increasing expense to insure and protect it. We try to advertise the Collection wherever Tilsit china is sold because we depend on the admissions and the catalogue sales to keep the Collection intact and here at Tilsit."

"Are there any pieces of Tilsit china?"

"Over there—the last case. For sentimental reasons, really. George Martin Tilsit was a good potter and his manufacturing process was an excellent one. But he doesn't rank among the great English potters. Certainly not good enough—even for sentimental reasons—to belong with the others in this room. But he inspired the Collection, you might say, so for that reason some examples of his own potting are here."

"I like it. It makes it less like a museum and more like the family china cabinet to have him here."

" Exactly, miss. That's what Miss Isobel used to say. But make no mistake—it is a great collection. Miss Isobel had bids from all over the world for individual pieces, and several new museums starting up in America have wanted the whole collection. But it is part of Tilsit and it should stay here. Miss Isobel used to call it a burden and a treasure.

" And to think," she added, the keys rattling savagely in her hand and her voice betraying an anger she was unable to hold back, " to think that in her will she gave it into Mark Barstow's charge. She made *him* custodian of the Collection—that savage! "

II

The sound Ginny had been waiting for all morning, and through lunch, finally came in the middle of the afternoon. Joyfully she lifted her head from the papers spread before her on Isobel's desk. At first only his tones were audible, talking to Garth—the assured cockiness, the suggestion of rough vigour and freshness. Then she heard some of the words. " . . . Keep them away. They can do none of us any good." Garth's low-toned answer was not audible.

The door of the office burst open, and Mark stood there. He was tidier than yesterday, wearing a tie and tweed jacket, but his shoes were caked with mud and he seemed to have forgotten to comb his hair. Without preliminary, with no excuse for leaving her yesterday on the mound of the keep, he simply smiled and said briskly, " Come on, my girl—on with your coat. I'm taking you to the Pottery."

She sat still and said nothing; she could feel the warm flush rise in her face. For almost a minute they watched each other, and then she could see the change in his face; he shook his head slowly and his expression crumpled into the contriteness of a child.

" All right—I can't get away with it, can I? I should have said I was sorry at once." He stepped into the room and swung the door closed behind him. " Yesterday was bad— bad of me, I mean. And I was sorry the moment it was done. These things happen quickly for me, and I don't know how to explain them. There I was thinking all the time at the cottage that finally I'd got a friend at Tilsit.

I was believing that you were understanding what I was saying—in *my* terms, Ginny, not dimly comprehending as if we were communicating through a glass wall. It was a big thing for me—a kind of discovery, and I was nearly off my head with excitement over it. And then suddenly there you were fussing over the damn' dog as if it were the most important thing in the world. And I was firmly put back in my place. You seemed just like all the others here, and I'd lost contact again. I felt sick. . . ."

" We lost each other," Ginny answered. " And I didn't know why." She got to her feet. " And if you'd only known—I would have let you get away with it. I would have let you get away with anything just as long as you walked through that door and rescued me from this . . ." She indicated the papers spread on the desk, the cupboards lining the opposite wall whose open doors revealed the shelves crammed with manila envelopes and dusty yellowing papers tied with tape.

" Is that all I'm good for—to get you away from Isobel's junk?" he demanded.

" That isn't all—and you know it!"

" That's better!" he said, and his face brightened. He jerked his head towards the bulging cupboards. " And as for that lot—my advice is to put a match to it. What good is it?"

" There are all kinds of financial statements from the Pottery—the trouble is that you have to come across them by accident. Isobel and Jane Tilsit must have had their own private filing system. I can't make head nor tail of it. I'm looking for financial statements and I haul out laundry bills and estimates for top-soil."

He clicked his tongue in disgust. " The Pottery has an accounting department. It's run like every other business, except that it's so tightly controlled. But Isobel had to hug every bit of information to herself and she had copies made of every single financial transaction at the Pottery and brought every one of them back here. God knows what for."

" They might be useful—if I could read financial statements," Ginny said, moving round the desk towards him.

" Randall can handle all that for you. For God's sake, Ginny, don't get caught up in her trouble. She could never let anything go—burying herself here with her old papers." She drew level with him and he suddenly caught her chin and tilted her head so that he was staring into her face. " You could turn into dust here among all these senseless records. We can't let that happen—you're worth too much to let that happen."

He didn't release his hold, but kept looking down at her, his gaze seeming to go beyond the flesh to the bones themselves. " You know, you've got a good face for a sculptor —the old-fashioned kind of sculptor whose work you could look at and know what he meant. I couldn't do that kind of work any more. If I were to try to do your face it would come out as some expression of the way I see you inside— the way you are now—bewildered, searching, not really knowing what you're supposed to look for—or why. The rest of it would be me—rough as bags, and probably angry about something. You'd look at it, and you'd think, ' That's what he thinks of me—ugly, distorted mass of junk!' And that wouldn't be true at all. All the time I'd be trying to say, 'I'm glad you've come, Ginny.' "

Without any self-consciousness his fingers traced the structure of her face slowly, examining, exploring—a movement of great tenderness and growing knowledge. " Oh, yes," he said softly, " I'm glad you've come."

Mark's car was a new and expensive one, and for its age astonishingly battered and unkempt. The back seat was littered with books and papers, a few tools whose use Ginny couldn't discern, two apples, and a two-foot square of bronze.

" Can't waste time fussing with how a car looks," he said, when he caught her staring at the disorder, at the mud dried on the carpet. " They're purely machines for what they'll do for me—but I'm damned if I'd do anything for them beyond feeding them what they need to make them run." The car went hurling down the drive and lurched over the bridge with a sickening bump.

" I see your point," Ginny murmured. " But can the bridge stand it?"

" Don't be sarcastic, my girl," Mark answered, with a kind of shout of laughter. His high spirits, the overwhelming good humour were as pervasive as yesterday's mood of dark passion. She found herself swayed by it just as she had been then, carried along, willing, grateful, humble. Now that she was again touched by the magnetism of his presence she was able to thrust aside the doubts that had been summoned by Vanessa's cryptic warning, by Brown's conviction that he had indeed let Isobel die. The gift of life Mark possessed made the idea that he could kill impossible to Ginny; his ability to evoke a response in her destroyed the doubt. On this day there was no evil in Mark—nor on any other day, she told herself. There was only joy. She found herself laughing with him, at nothing in particular. The car roared through the arch of the gatehouse and out on to the road without slowing, swerving at the last moment to avoid another car parked in closely to the hedge. Mark put his hand down hard on the horn, turning back to look.

"Silly bastard—leaving it there! God—it's that awful journalist type I told to get off the place half an hour ago. He didn't go far."

"What journalist?"

"I don't know which one in particular. From some London paper. He seemed to think I should have known his name."

"What did he want?"

"What do any of them want? They want an interview with you—that's what they want. You know—lost heiress. All that kind of bloody rubbish." He glanced at her sideways. "You don't mean to say you'd have given an interview? You ought to know that the gutter press in this country is about the nastiest in the world. They'd blackguard their own mother if it would make a story . . "

"I thought Tilsit needed publicity," she said, to tease him.

He leapt to the bait with a jealous protectiveness that pleased her. "Not that kind it doesn't! You stay clear of them, you hear. Bloody bunch of liars!"

"Have there been others then?"

"Garth's been keeping them away."

She straightened, the half-smile vanishing. "He should have told me—he shouldn't just assume I wouldn't see them."

"For once Garth's instincts were right, so you needn't get your back up. That last one back there in the car was a particularly nasty lot—damned pimp snooping around the place. I told him to get the hell out, and reminded him that this wasn't one of the days the house is open to the public. So then he asked who the hell I was. So I used that fancy title Isobel gave me—I said I was curator of the Tilsit Collection. He didn't seem very convinced—or very impressed. But he went."

"Are you always like this, Mark?"

"Like what?"

"Laughing and shouting. Hating and . . . loving?"

He shrugged and didn't take the question seriously. " I don't think much about what I am. There isn't time. All I know . . ." He looked again at her, taking his attention dangerously from the road for a long time. "All I know is that to-day the sun is shining and I am—what did you say?—laughing and loving?—well, yes. I am laughing, and loving too, perhaps. And that's how it will be to-day. And I don't intend to let anything change that."

She nodded, said nothing, and was well content.

They drove then in silence through the green and sunlit country, the country of narrow lanes that were called roads, of swelling little hills, high-hedged fields, of villages with the houses crowded together, the red telephone boxes and the pub signs painted bright, babies in high carriages in the front gardens, and the flash of the red letter-boxes. The flowers were everywhere, orderly, trim, and tiny greenhouses tacked to the backs of the houses. The stretches of open road were few, the villages strung together on a seemingly endless chain. To Ginny it had the look of something deliberately reduced to less than human scale, as if she looked at it through the wrong end of a telescope. Orderly these villages were, and clean, not showing to the casual eye too much of the centuries that had gone into their fashioning ; only knowledge would tell that at a glance. She was reminded of the miniature work of the artist's hand on the *famille noire* vase, the beauty seeming to disguise the infinite patience and the time behind it.

She said, "Brown took me through the Collection this morning."

"What did you think of it?"

She shook her head. "I don't know enough to say. It's beautiful—of course it's beautiful. Anyone could say that. But I have the feeling that so much of it escapes me. Brown did her best—and I think she was very good. But I don't even begin to see the fine points."

"Yes, Brown's good in her way. She would make you see the things that she thought were beautiful. Don't despise what she has to teach you. But it will be limited—the way all of our loves are limited. Walk through with Vanessa some time. She'll show you something different—she has a more sophisticated eye. Go through it by yourself and after a few times you'll begin to feel something for some particular pieces. After that it's the time to get out the books and learn why you feel that way. Isobel has a good library on ceramics—most of it though has ended up at the cottage. By that time you're going to want to go about and see other china—the Victoria and Albert and all the rest of the places."

"Yes."

"You're starting on a long road, Ginny. It could take a lifetime to become an expert—and you should be something more than an expert. There are enough people who can walk through that gallery and put a pretty accurate price on what any piece would bring at Sotheby's. But that isn't enough. You will grow to love it, or it will be an impossible burden to you. Without love you'll only think of the price it would all bring at Sotheby's. This is St. Mary's. . . ."

Bigger than the villages they had passed through, it was a small town. The red-brick houses faced the streets in terraces; a lot of the green was missing here.

"This is where George Martin was born—or at least at Torrington, which used to be a couple of farms on the edge of St. Mary's. It's been incorporated since. He drew all of his early workers from St. Mary's, and a good many of the people living here are Tilsit people—those that aren't working in the shoe factory that started after the war."

"I always thought," Ginny said, "that all the potteries of England were in the Arnold Bennett country."

"They are there because the coal is there. The china clay comes from Cornwall and Devon and Dorset. There's always been a small pottery industry in Dorset because of the local clays. The coal was brought by sea to Poole. George Martin learned his craft here. Then he served an apprenticeship with Wedgwood. Later he came back here and experimented for a few years with the local clays. There is a quarry on the land his father farmed. It's worked out now but it's still here. He finally arrived at a formula that produced a china that was very strong and yet had quite a look of delicacy. This was just at the time when there was beginning to be lots of money in the middle classes in England for fancy things. He turned them out by the million—big ornate dishes and jugs and pot-plant holders —most of them ugly as sin by the way we look at them, and decorated up to the eyes. But the Victorians loved them, and Tilsit made a mint. You'll see Tilsit's own collection at the works—it's so horrible it'll fair blind you. But old Lawrence won't hear of tucking it decently out of sight. I think he's actually quite fond of it, if you can believe that."

" Why did George Martin "—she found herself dropping the Tilsit because Mark had done so—" make that kind of thing if he had enough taste to start the Collection?"

" You don't understand. The Tilsit Pottery was for money —the Collection was for love. George Martin's genius was in turning out all the over-decorated soup tureens the Victorians wanted at reasonable prices. The Pottery made money—but that doesn't mean his heart was there. I have to assume that he knew it was awful, even when he made the models himself—otherwise there would have been no Collection to offset it. But I don't know how he felt. Nor does anyone else. George Martin seems to have been a very quiet man. And a very prudent one. He left nothing written down."

" How do you know he didn't? How does anyone know that it isn't all hidden away somewhere among all those papers back there?"

" Then it'll stay hidden," Mark answered cheerfully, " because no one's ever going to have the energy to go through that lot. It's the best hiding-place I can think of."

" But Jane . . ." Ginny had almost begun to speak of the diaries. Then, in a visitation of caution that she didn't quite understand, she closed up again. She suddenly knew that the diaries were not to be spoken of; no one had said they were a trust; there were no directions from Isobel that they should be treated as such, and yet the trust implied by their possession was binding. Whoever had inherited the room, the desk, the key, had also inherited the thoughts and feelings of the two women whose lives were there written out. If she had seemed to write to Jim last night with the pen and the words that Jane Tilsit had used a hundred years ago, this also laid a charge upon her to protect them as she would have protected her own words. So even to Mark, beloved and desired, the words would not be entrusted. She began the first deceit, the first omission, of love.

"God!" Mark groaned as he parked the car before the long, one-storey brick building that bore the legend of TILSIT POTTERIES on a sign across its face. "I thought we might be able to sneak in without Lawrence seeing us. But it never works. He has his desk beside that window and he doesn't miss a thing." He nodded towards a window near the main entrance where Lawrence was signalling to them frantically. Almost before Ginny was out of the car Lawrence had appeared, bearing down on them with his long stride.

"Ah—Virginia! I'm glad you've come. I telephoned the house but Garth didn't know where you'd gone. I was about to propose that you might like to make arrangements to visit the works to-morrow."

"Well—she's here this afternoon," Mark answered for her. "That much the better, isn't it?"

"Quite—only perhaps it would have been nicer to have informed some of the department heads so that they could have had some interesting pieces in process to show. Just a thought . . ."

"Who the bloody hell do you think she is—Princess Margaret? This is Ginny's pottery! She's going to be here every other day for the rest of her life! Do you have to turn it into a state visit?" He slammed the car door shut angrily. "If that's the case, Ginny, you'd better go home and get all dressed up. White gloves and the lot."

"Now look here, Barstow! There's no need at all to take that tone! I made a perfectly simple suggestion. . . ."

Mark wheeled round to face him. "You make me sick! Who do you think these people are—peasants or something? They're craftsmen—all of them. Day in, day out, they're craftsmen! There's nothing special that they do that Ginny won't learn to appreciate in time—and no way to teach it all to her in one easy lesson. She's coming here as a student—no state visit, no white gloves. And if she's wise she'll stay a student for a long time, or Tilsit is going to start to mean a lot less than it has up to now. If you think the people here are going to stand and wave flags because the new owner has arrived you're bloody well mistaken. Those days are over—whether you recognise it or not. I know what the people here think—how they think! Don't you forget that I'm one of them, Bowen!"

"I never," Lawrence answered, "forget *that*. You are——"

"Enough! Now that's enough!"

Both men turned in shocked surprise as the words came coldly from Ginny. She was aware that at that moment she did not think of Mark nor of Lawrence as separate individuals, nor of her feelings towards either of them, nor even of the right and wrong of what they were saying. All she knew was that this scene, played out before the fascinated gaze of a dozen or so watchers from various windows that overlooked the parking space, was an intolerable thing to be happening. The Tilsits, she was sure, had never aired their family quarrels before an audience. It must not begin now —not especially while Isobel's death was fresh in their minds, and while the talk about Mark's part in it was still so strong. A show of solidarity had to be maintained. And she, Ginny, had the power to demand it, and enforce it.

"I will see the Pottery to-day," she said, her tone kept low and deliberately calm. "Since Mark has offered to show it to me, I would like to accept that offer. I would like you, Lawrence, to come with us, if you can spare the time."

They stared at her for a moment in silence, and she saw from their faces that they were not deceived by the polite reasonableness of her tone. They knew what she meant. They too, by now, could see the faces at the windows.

She gestured towards the entrance, starting to walk, and knowing they would follow. "Do we go through here? I think I should meet the office staff first . . ."

She didn't look back to see if they followed. Their footsteps sounded after her.

What remained of the afternoon was interminably long.

Ginny felt that she dragged the weight of the hostility that existed between Mark and Lawrence with her on the tour of the Pottery, and that having assumed responsibility for the appearance of all of them before the workers, they let her bear it as a matter of course.

Ginny's face ached with the smile that was fixed there. It had begun with the tea she had shared with the three members of the office staff who had been at Tilsit longest— two men from accounting and Miss Phillotson, who ran the showroom. The conversation, Ginny found, had to be initiated by herself while their eyes devoured every detail of her appearance, and when their awkwardness dropped away from them in brief moments of forgetfulness, the conversation was almost wholly based on Isobel . . . " Miss Isobel said . . ." and " I do recall Miss Isobel telling us . . ." She felt the burden of their gaze upon her—hopefully, wonderingly, the fear underlying, but vis.ble, that changes would be made. She tried to give them reassurance and realised that they found little of that in her youthfulness, the terrifying, indisputable fact that this was the first time she had stepped through the doors of the Tilsit Pottery. And the uneasy presence of Mark and Lawrence made it harder.

Mark was the first to break the tension generated by his outburst. He began to relax as they toured the showroom, tea mugs in hand, Lawrence trailing them at the distance of a few feet. Mark warmed to his subject, drawing Miss Phillotson into the discussion of the merits and sales value of several patterns, joking with her in a natural, easy way that proved what he had said to Lawrence that he belonged with the people at Tilsit. It was not a pose, but real, and Ginny knew he talked with Miss Phillotson this way because it was the way he had always talked, and because it was on this spirit that Tilsit had always been based and on which it would continue to function. As they finished the circle of the display counters and came back towards the door again, which Lawrence already held open, Mark parted from Miss Phillotson with an affectionate slap on her broad, tweed-clad bottom.

" We'll teach her yet, won't we, Phillotson? Between all of us we'll teach her what it's all about."

Miss Phillotson blinked at him through her glasses; her

lips registered a slight wobble of emotion. " As long as she's in your hands, Mr. Mark, there'll be no need to worry."

Lawrence trailed them through the Pottery in much the way he had done in the showroom, hands clasped behind his back, saying nothing, and gradually Ginny grew less aware of him, and Mark seemed to forget his presence entirely as he grew absorbed in what he was trying to impart to Ginny. Ginny never entirely left behind the feeling that she dragged them both with her, but it grew easier as she discovered that in the works itself Mark was supreme, and that Lawrence had long ago established the front offices as his only domain and he seldom ventured beyond it. He was there only as the token of solidarity she had demanded, and they all accepted that. " The whole place was rebuilt in two stages —during the twenties, and then just after the war," Mark said as he led Ginny into the first of the long shed-like buildings, well lighted, the steel girders painted green, and all of it wrapped in a kind of antiseptic air of cleanliness. " It took just about all the fortune that George Martin had piled up, but I have to hand it to Isobel that she knew where to spend her money. After Wedgwood this is about the most modern plant in England—only a quarter of Wedgwood's size, though. Isobel copied everything they did— the electric kilns, the overhead conveyors—everything as automated as is possible in an industry that still relies on a man's or a woman's hand in every stage of its being. She copied them in manufacturing process, and she even tried to hire away some of their key people." He laughed suddenly, ignoring Lawrence's disapproving frown. " They know all about Isobel Tilsit up at Wedgwood. But they don't worry—it would take four Tilsits to make a Wedgwood.

" This," he went on, " is the sliphouse where the blunging and grinding is done—these machines here mix up the ingredients—the ball clay, china clay and china stone and flint are all ground into a powder and mixed with water, and then whatever quantity of either we need goes into this tank— arks we call them—for blending. What goes into them depends on whether we're making china or earthenware." He bent and picked up a handful of small bleached bones from a pile of burlap sacks filled with them. " Here—look at this! Most people never realise that bone actually goes into bone china—very expensive it is, too. It was the discovery of English potters in the eighteenth century, and it's the ingredient that makes bone china so strong. . . ."

Ginny followed him obediently while he explained rapidly the filter-presses and the pug mill, striving to remember what he said, and the names of the people to whom she was introduced. As with Miss Phillotson, Mark's relationship here with the workers was an easy and effortless thing; his Dorsetshire accent thickened as he talked. The plate-makers and the cup-makers acknowledged him with a nod and sometimes bandying words passed between them in an accent so thick Ginny couldn't understand them. He seemed to forget her presence for a few moments in the absorption of watching the operation—as keenly, Ginny thought, as if it were the first time for him also—then he turned to her.

" These two machines—the jigger for making plates and the jolly for making cups—are as close to mechanics as you get in pottery—except for pouring slip into moulds—and you can see that it still needs the human hand to throw the clay on to the machines and it needs handwork to combine with the machines, and the good sense and judgment of the operator. If you never let yourself forget, Ginny, that all this is still a craft, and not mechanical manufacturing process, you'll understand pottery that much quicker, and you'll live with it more happily."

He took her through all the stages of the work with a pride and understanding of each part of it as great as if he himself handled each separate item, calling each worker by name, touching the pieces, even the most routine product of the moulds as if it were a small work of art. He spent a long time with the mould-makers, but by-passed the special room where the throwers worked on the potter's wheels. " You'll have to come back and spend a couple of days in here—this is the heart and guts of pottery, even though it's the most expensive way to make anything. All of these men are artists and they deserve more than ten minutes."

The two electric kilns were his greatest pride, long brick tunnels through which trucks stacked with the hardened pieces of clay in the biscuit state, moved on rails. " The firing takes about seventy hours—the trucks are moving slowly all the time. It's much easier to control the temperatures of these electric kilns than the old coal-fired type. When it comes out the other end it's cool enough to unpack." He gave a rueful grin. " By that time it's too late to do anything about any mistakes you might have made. Once it's been through the fire it can never be raw clay again." He shrugged and added in almost a mutter as he turned away, " It almost has a human quality that way."

He took her through the rooms of long benches where the decorating was done. "This is where we need women's hands—for the hand-painting and enamelling, transferring the paper prints on to the ware, the aerographing, the lining. You see here, Ginny—the engraver cuts the design into copper plates and then they're printed on tissue. The transferrer rubs them with this hard brush on to the ware, then washes the tissue away. The design stays. The art of the hand-decorator is a good deal more skilled. After whatever kind of decoration goes on the ware it's sent to be dipped in glaze—the decoration is then what we call ' underglaze ' —and then back in the kiln again for the glost firing. When we make very complex patterns of a lot of different colours we have to keep putting the stuff back in the kilns for almost every colour, blocking out the other colours every time so they won't change. That's why the very rich designs and colours cost so much—they could have been through five or six firings. Like the Rose Imperial pattern we do."

They stood for some time watching a woman working a hand-operated turntable, her brush, dipped in gold, deftly outlining the handle of a coffee-pot, the rim of its lid, the rim of its base. " The gold has to be put back into the kiln to be fired—it's real gold specially prepared. You see how dull it is? When it comes out of the kiln it has to be hand-burnished with fine sand."

Suddenly Lawrence, whom they had both forgotten, reached over and took up a plate. He cleared his throat awkwardly. " You see this, Virginia? This is a piece of fine porcelain, fashioned and decorated by methods that are costly and demand skill and time and love." Now he looked at her directly, and she was astonished to see that a faint flush had crept into his cheeks ; he was embarrassed but his gaze didn't waver. " Love," he continued, " is the element which fine china needs most. With love it will endure almost for ever—one of the toughest substances we know. With love it will endure my lifetime and yours, and seven more life-

times. Without love it can be destroyed in a second. All
I have to do is smash it."

Mark looked round at Lawrence and Ginny saw him nod
slightly, the first sign of mutual respect she had seen pass
between the two men. After that gesture Mark turned
abruptly and began to stride down the length of the room,
joining the stream of workers.

"Come on, Ginny—it's knocking-off time."

"I shouldn't have let fly at Lawrence like that," Mark said.
He put down his beer mug, reached out with the toe of
his shoe and poked at a log on the fire that threatened to
fall. Besides the two men wearing workmen's cloth caps who
stood at the bar, they were alone in the single room that
comprised The Golden Cap. The sixteenth-century inn on
the road to Poole was, Mark said, his favourite in the
district. He had been greeted by name by the landlord, who
had brought their drinks at once, but Ginny was forced to
conclude that these Dorsetmen were a reserved lot, because
although the two men at the bar had nodded with familiarity
to Mark, not a word had passed between them. They all
looked oddly comfortable with the silence, Ginny thought,
as if it were something made just for their pleasure. The
landlord polished glasses and said nothing about the weather.

"I let myself get too damn' involved," Mark continued,
looking at her. "Lawrence isn't such a bad stick—it's just
that I've only thought of him as being Isobel's dog's-body
and I forget that he's human. And he's able enough, too,
in his way—which is administrative. Perhaps I'm even jealous
of him, and annoyed because I think the designer shouldn't
have to listen to lectures on costs. This is what I think
about him when I'm not with him—I turn into my ideal
self very quickly in my imagination, Ginny. Then as soon
as he comes into sight all I can see is the old school tie
and the twitching nose, and no matter how nice he tries to
be to me I think he's patronising me. I somehow turn
into a clumsy oaf who can't hold a knife and fork—not
because I am one, but because my father was one. Lawrence
and all his kind get the back of my hand because of it."
Ginny saw at once that he regretted having said what he
did. He rose and picked up her glass.

"I'll get you another. Double Scotch, please, Mr. Williams."
The landlord reached for the bottle and filled the order at
once, still wordlessly. The door opened and another customer
entered, favoured the company with the briefest of nods,
and without question the landlord drew a pint of mild and
bitter. "Fine evening," he murmured as he took his first
swallow.

"Looks like rain to-morrow," the landlord volunteered.
They all nodded together in comfortable agreement.

Mark handed her the glass, seated himself again, this time
beside her instead of opposite, his back to the bar.

Ginny leaned in close to him and whispered, "Am I
inhibiting them?"

Mark grinned. "Probably. They've got you picked as
Miss Tilsit because you're with me and because your clothes
are American and you've got a tan the like of which they've
never imagined. What's probably got them stupefied is that
you're here, sitting in a pub instead of dining with the Lord-
Lieutenant of the county or toiling away at the books at
the Pottery. Isobel created such a formidable myth of all
work and no play—the few times in her life when she did
dine with people like the Lord-Lieutenant she made it seem
like hard work—that it's a bit of a shock to see you here with
a Scotch in your hand and your toes stretched out to the
fire. But they're enjoying themselves immensely. There's been
nothing so exciting for them since the Cup Final."

His smile broadened. He slid down in his chair and his
outstretched legs reached closer to the fire than hers.

"Nor for me, either, Ginny."

"To hell with it," Mark said as they drove away from The
Golden Cap. "I'm not taking you back to Tilsit—or to
any other place to be stared at. You ought to see another
side of England that's just as real as Tilsit or any sixteenth-
century pub. You ought to come and visit my mother. She
lives in a council house in Torrington."

"Your mother . . ." Suddenly Ginny remembered. "Mark
—you told me she still worked at the Pottery! Was she there
when I . . .?"

"She was—but she wouldn't have wanted to be introduced then. She'd rather no one noticed her there. She's
an odd fish, my mother. Very touchy."

" Then won't she be upset if we just come in on her like this?"

" That's the only way I ever see her. I don't make appointments—she doesn't expect them. She let the strings drop long ago, Ginny—the time when she handed me over to Isobel."

" Mark—you say so many exaggerated things. No mother hands over her child . . ."

" You don't think so? You've been lucky. And very sheltered, my girl. My mother handed me over to Isobel Tilsit and all of us knew it was for my own good. And I suppose none of us really liked it. It wasn't such a strange thing for my mother to do, after all. She came from the class of people who regularly send their sons away to school at seven or eight. Her father was the vicar at Tenton—that's inland from here. They had no money, but her father was a Balliol man with all the right traditions. I never knew him. He refused to see my mother again after she ran away and got married. Of course he must have thought she'd gone out of her mind, marrying Joe Barstow. Perhaps she had. When you see her you'll wonder how she had it in her. My father deserted us when I was a little kid—but I remember him. Attractive devil, and a hell of a way with women. You'd wonder what he could see in the sort of prim, strait-laced kind of girl she must have been. But still, I suppose she had her great moments with him—who knows? She never has talked about him . . ."

The face and the eyes and the manner of Mildred Barstow were not those of a woman who talked much about anything. To Ginny she had the look of a person who has lived much alone and has grown to prefer it that way. If she was surprised by their arrival she did not show it. She welcomed Ginny with perfect gravity to the neat, bright, modern semi-detached cottage on the council housing estate at Torrington, and she did not exclaim or fuss over Mark, accepting his perfunctory kiss on the forehead, but not returning it. The house was tiny, everything touched with the flimsy look of post-war building, everything painted and waxed and shining like a doll's-house. It was sparsely furnished in contemporary furniture that seemed to Ginny oddly out of keeping with this quiet, neat woman in the navy dress. She led them through to the sitting-room that was at the back, with french windows that gave on to the long, narrow garden.

"This house is not much my style," she said suddenly, as if she guessed Ginny's thoughts, or as if she herself was not used to it and still had need to explain. "But Mark bullied the council into letting me have it, and then he insisted on furnishing it *his* way—the better for us to see and understand his talents, I think."

"Well, it has a bathroom, hasn't it?" Mark demanded.

Mildred Barstow looked at Ginny. "Mark can't accept the idea that a basin in the kitchen is not necessarily a degradation. Will you have some sherry, Miss Tilsit?"

"Her name's Ginny, Mother—and she prefers Scotch. What have you done with that bottle I brought last time?"

The woman shrugged. "If you brought it, it must still be here." And then back to Ginny. "I'm old-fashioned, Miss Tilsit. Sherry was all we ever served when I was a girl. I haven't changed."

"You'd better not," Mark said with rough affection. "You're too old to start kicking over the traces now." Then he left them to go to the kitchen for the drinks.

At once Mildred Barstow closed the door. She stood in the middle of the room looking at Ginny, her arms straight by her sides, thin, tall, her fine white skin marked in a network of lines.

"What do you think of my son, Miss Tilsit?" It was said with no attempt to lighten the tone. The question was meant to be answered.

"I . . . I think he's a most unusual person . . ." It was weak and untruthful, or only a particle of the truth. Both of them seemed to know it, for Mildred Barstow shook her head impatiently.

"What do you really think of him?"

Ginny took a long breath and again evaded the question. "I hardly know him." Suddenly she thought of how shocking it would be to say simply, "I love him," and what a relief it would be. And yet the truth might not have shocked this woman. At one time her own young love must have come as swiftly and as terribly, and recalling that unsuitable, irrational love she would not be shocked. But the words would not come for Ginny, and the time and the chance passed by.

" It makes no difference with Mark how long you've known him. All that he is is right there, plainly. He has never hidden anything, has never been capable of hiding anything. It all comes out, whatever he feels or thinks. Which all makes nonsense of what they've been saying about him . . . you've heard what they've been saying about him and Isobel Tilsit—that he caused her death?"

" Yes," Ginny said reluctantly.

" It could never be. Mark is capable neither of the act nor of hiding it."

" I know that."

" You know it? Then you know him better than you admit. I'm glad you know it quite surely. It is important."

She gestured suddenly towards the shelves that lined one wall of the room. On them, stark and sparsely, were displayed pots and vases and jugs like the ones at Mark's cottage. " That's all his work. He brings his best work here. As a potter he's a genius. As he matures he will grow better and stronger—but already he's outstripped most of his generation. But he has greater things to do, I think. Look!"

With a sudden motion she went and pulled aside the net curtain that screened the window opening to the long garden. Her motion and words were charged with the kind of nervous excitement that belongs to the person who does not often speak or act, and is all at once compelled to do both.

" You see that! He did it when he was only twenty-five. His first bronze full-size figure."

The sculpture stood slightly off-centre in the garden, the figure of a young girl in abstract, arms upstretched, strangely appealing in its immaturity and a certain crudity of execution.

" My neighbours petitioned the Council to have it removed. They all think it's a monstrosity. I wasn't sure at first. So I spent my holidays travelling to see what the great ones had done—Mark told me where to go. I saw Epstein's work, and Moore and Hepworth. Then I knew it was all right for Mark to be doing what he did."

She let the curtain drop again. " But my son is his father's son as well, Miss Tilsit. He needs to be pushed—he needs a goad. He has had all I can supply."

She stiffened and grew wary as the sounds from the hall

announced Mark's return, the tinkle of glasses, his amiable mutter as he half tripped on a rug.

Before the door opened she turned and looked at Ginny. "Perhaps," she said, "he needs another Isobel Tilsit." And at once Ginny felt herself swamped with a kind of fear and dismay that had no right, no part, in love.

III

It was late when Ginny returned to Tilsit. Trip was in his basket in her room, and Brown was waiting, as Ginny knew she would be, as she also knew it was useless to protest the fact.

"Ah—there you are, miss. I was getting worried . . . well, you *have* got a colour, haven't you? You must have been in the wind." Brown's eyes were on her searchingly, and Ginny was suddenly aware of how she must have looked, with burning cheeks and tumbled hair, and her lips still warm and crushed, from the last kiss that Mark had given her. Not tender kisses this time, not kisses to comfort her fatigue or ease her bewilderment as had been yesterday's, but the hard and passionate kisses of a man who is aware only of a woman, with no special reason to kiss her except that he wanted to. This far they had gone since yesterday, and it seemed an extraordinarily long way to have travelled. It seemed they had entered a whole new era of time together, and Ginny felt that she moved in new elements, a strange and unimagined world, different from the one she had known up to this, transformed by this man she had not seen until yesterday.

So to-night no pallid face looked back at her from the mirror. She smiled as she picked up her brush. "Yes, Brown—I have. I've been out in the wind."

When the woman was gone she went at once to the desk and unlocked it. More important than Brown, the diaries were waiting also. And the letter to Jim that had never been finished and would never be sent. And yet her hand wavered and hesitated before she took down the first little velvet-bound book in which Jane Tilsit had written the story of her love for a potter. Some last surviving sense of caution urged her to resist the diaries, lest she become lost to them, given over to what their pages contained. Two women, stronger than she, had written out their lives here; she risked falling under their dominance and yet she seemed hardly able to help herself as the little book came down finally, and she opened it to the entry following the one she had read the night before. Here were the words, she knew, to flesh out the bare bones of the story of Tilsit in the last hundred years, and, perhaps, if she searched long enough and had the heart to discover it, much of the truth of her father and Isobel.

Yet, as her eyes struggled with the microscopic script in the ink faded to brown, her mind sent a lingering thought to Jim. He was St. Nicolaas, he represented all the serene and calm world of Katrien, the sunlit world of beauty to which all of his life, her father had never completely succumbed. Her father was Tilsit, a world half in shadow, a place where there was more of passion than of love, more of ambition than of kindness. And yet a place whose hold and fascination were so strong that they had lasted through her father's lifetime and had laid their claims heavily on her.

" Jim . . .?" she said suddenly, aloud, her voice thin and hollow in the quiet emptiness of the room. At the fire Trip raised his head, searching, inquiring of this name that was spoken and was strange to him. He found no answer, nor did Ginny. The world of St. Nicolaas and of Katrien and Jim faded and receded back in time and distance, and the words written in the copper plate script before her took on the reality of the spoken word. She almost believed, if she strained hard enough, that she might have heard them.

There was no maidenly Victorian reticence to screen the thoughts of the writer, no coyness to cloak her intentions. "Mr. Martin was surprised to learn that we would be married." This entry came a bare two weeks after the first mention of his name. "But I am convinced that he will see, as I do, that it is the right thing." And then underlined, as if the writer had to convince herself anew, "It is the right thing for Tilsit." The entries continued, filled with the practical details of the wedding plans, and not again did Ginny discover the flush of passion and love that had illuminated the first entry. The wedding gown was ordered, of serviceable blue alpaca. "In my situation," Jane wrote, " white would be frivolous and out of keeping, for there will be no one

to see it." It was a winter wedding; she permitted herself
"*a little fur trimming.*" There was no self-pity, but an
unconscious note of sadness in the words she added: "*No
further trousseau is necessary, for no one will come to Tilsit
to be entertained. There will be no one to see how I look
. . . George Martin accepts me as I am. He will never know
how thankful I am that I sense no shrinking from me in him.
For I lack the words to tell him this.*"

The entries ran on, prosaic domestic matters, with no
indication of a bride's pleasure or nervousness at her coming
wedding. The matter, however, was accorded a page to
itself.

"*It is over and done with. George Martin and I were
married this morning—no one present other than the witnesses.
Afterwards we drank champagne and then went about our
business. George Martin confessed himself disappointed that
I would not agree to a wedding journey, but there is the
new pottery works to be built and much here at Tilsit
to be attended to. Neither the time nor the money can be
spared for such things.*" A trace of wistfulness appeared then,
and the first evidence of a bride anxious to please her
husband. "*I think my husband missed the dancing and
laughter of the village weddings he is used to, and of course
there was no one of my own level to wish us well. The*
bride who is disfigured does not expect the usual flatteries,
but for his sake I regretted their absence. At dinner I tried
to be gay to make him forget . . . but he was not deceived.
He knows I am not accustomed to laughter or to pleasantries.*"

The next words came on another line, as if they had
been added later. "*My husband is most kind to my infirmities.*"

Ginny turned the page, wondering over the words " disfigured " and " infirmities," remembered, too, the phrase
from the first entry, "*no man has sought my hand.*" What
disfigurement had George Martin not shrunk from, what
infirmities had he been kind to? The entry on the next page,
dated a few days after the wedding, was written in a larger
hand, with less care, as if in the heat of emotion or anger.
"*The vicar has called at Tilsit to-day protesting that the
marriage, which he was informed of just yesterday, was
performed by a non-conformist minister. He reports that
his Lordship, the Bishop, is seriously annoyed. To which*

*I replied by reminding him that his Lordship and all the
churchmen around drew back in holy horror from giving me
my name at baptism, shrinking in alarm and disgust from
the thought and sight of me. I told him he might go and
remind his Lordship of the circumstances of my baptism,
and of the kind of minister who had given me my name. If
I were so displeasing at birth was it the fact of my inheritance
that made me now fairer and more deserving of the kind of
looks of the church?* He went away angry—and I hope
humiliated, as I have been." She added to this, " *The scar
does not diminish, as I had hoped it might. When the wound
is probed, I bleed again.*"

Ginny knew that she would have to have the answer
to the riddle of these entries—of the bride of a few days, the
heiress to an ancient house and its lands who would invite
no one to her wedd.ng, who wrote, not of love, but of anger
and humiliation, who could look no higher than a humble
potter, and who must be grateful for his kindnesses. She
wondered if the disfigurement were an obvious thing or was
it hidden by the blue alpaca gown with the little fur trimming
that was the only adornment of Jane Tilsit's wedding day?
Or was it more mental than physical that the words and
presence of the vicar could open the wound that she had hoped
was diminished? It was the cry of anguish from the young
woman, so self-possessed until this moment, that touched
Ginny. She knew that she must have the answer to this
before she could read further. It was an unholy intrusion
to read of suffering whose cause she did not know. She
got up and went and opened the door, standing staring down
the length of the empty corridor where now only a single
light burned. She looked at all of the closed doors that
faced her, and wondered where she might go to ask her questions. Brown? She rejected the thought because the woman
was too close already, and too possessive. Vanessa? Too
young, too much of her own age . . . perhaps Vanessa did not
even know, perhaps had never questioned why Jane Tilsit
should have married a local potter of low birth. It was
possible that Vanessa might laugh at such pretensions, and
suddenly Ginny knew that now it would hurt unbearably to
have Jane Tilsit laughed at. The woman of the diary was
not a woman to be laughed at, not her pain, nor her fortitude.
Obsessed she might be, but never absurd. Ginny rejected

Vanessa, and that left only Lawrence and Margaret; at once they were rejected also. You did not wake a man like Lawrence in the middle of the night to tell him that you had been reading Jane Tilsit's diary. Brown or Vanessa, who each in their own fashion were creatures of the night, might have understood the sudden urgency to know, but Lawrence would not.

Ginny returned to the secretaire and carefully put away the diary and locked it. Then she picked up the lighted candle and went back to the door. This time Trip seemed to understand that she meant to go farther. He rose at once and he was at her heels as she moved quietly down the passage, down the stairs, through the entrance hall of the South Front until her way was barred by the great oak screen that divided this part of Tilsit from the Old House. The oiled bolts hardly made a sound as she slid them back and passed through.

She wondered if she should have felt afraid in the immense blackness of the Great Hall, the single candle wavering in a draught that came from an open window somewhere high up in the gallery. Yet she was not afraid, not even uneasy. She paused for a moment in the centre of the hall; the light from the candle barely reached the edge of the dais where the High Table stood, did not illuminate the colours of the tapestry behind it. The gallery was lost in the shadows above her head. She should have passed on quickly to the winding stairs that led to the solar, and from there to the Long Gallery. But she lingered, waiting— perhaps for a sound, for something to happen. Then finally she herself stepped up to the dais and stretched up and lighted from her own candle the two thick tapers in a pewter sconce on the wall to the right of the High Table. Trip had followed her; she felt his warm body press against her leg, but he stood firmly, without trembling. She wondered if perhaps Isobel had made this journey sometimes at night, walking alone through the empty house. Now in the light from the sconce the high roof beams were visible, and visible too were the faded, tattered silk of the pennants that Brown had named for her that morning, the names of the battles in which Tilsits had borne arms— Agincourt, Flodden Field, Blenheim and Ramillies, Yorktown,

Vittoria and Salamanca, Waterloo. "They were humble country squires and after they had done their duty, they came home and stayed home," Brown had said. Brave or cowardly, changing religions, sides and kings when they must, they had survived, the Tilsits, until the last of them stood here, she thought, their history embodied in her presence.

There were no tales of high drama to tell of Tilsit—and no Tilsit had lost his head for honour or for greed. If there were ghosts they were friendly domestic ghosts, more concerned with getting in the crop than winning glory, living the humdrum life of the manor with only the great wooden salt-cellar here in the middle of the table to mark the master from the serf. So she felt no fear of them, the ghosts of these country squires and their ladies bent over the tapestry looms; they were ordinary people, probably not better or worse than they should have been. They had built a great house, and kept it intact, but one of their descendants, a woman who thought herself deformed in some fashion, had had the energy and will to move them beyond this house and this narrow frame, to take their place in a modern world of industry and manufacture. Ginny reminded herself that her business was with Jane Tilsit. She picked up her candle and moved towards the stairs.

Vanessa had pointed out the windows of the Long Gallery directly above the Gold State Room. She found it without difficulty—only one door opened off the circular stairway to the left. But the candlelight would illuminate only its width; the length of it—over one hundred and twenty feet, Vanessa had said—stretched away ahead of her in blackness. She could see the dark mass of space broken by the faint outlines of the windows on each side of the gallery, but the moon was cloud-covered so the candle was all she had to light her way. The flame was gently thrown back in reflection from the silver-grey panelling, the silver sconces on the walls, the broad boards of the softly waved oak floor. She moved down the gallery, diagonally back and forth from one portrait to another; the artists' names engraved on the plaques beneath each portrait of a Tilsit formed a rough history of the fortunes of the family—there had been prosperity in the middle of the eighteenth century and two portraits by Gainsborough and a Reynolds, one Kneller from a century before. Other than that the artists were unknown to her until she came to the one near the end of the room bearing the name of Millais. There she stopped and raised the candle high to look at the portrait of Jane Tilsit.

It had been painted when Jane Tilsit was young and it was dated the year after her marriage to George Martin. Somehow he had prevailed upon her to spend the money for the portrait but she still permitted herself no indulgence in dress. She was clothed as a young governess might have been, the blue gown long-sleeved and high-necked, trimmed with a narrow edging of fur down the bodice—the wedding gown, Ginny wondered? The pale gold hair was drawn severely back to a knot. She wore no jewels, no adornment of any kind, and she stood tall and unrelaxed. The painted draperies behind her, richer than the gown, had been the artist's attempt to soften his subject, but in that slender, high-breasted figure there was no softness. Jane Tilsit had been beautiful then, and in her youthful sternness, slightly forbidding.

Ginny moved in closer. Millais had painted his subject in the most uncompromising of poses, full-face and standing alone. No wrap or shawl, no lace or ornament relieved the composition. There had been nothing to hide in the rather cold perfection of her figure or face, there had been no disfigurement or deformity for him to attempt to disguise or conceal. Whatever had disfigured Jane Tilsit had not been apparent to the beholder.

Ginny acknowledged that Isobel and Mark had been right —or partly right. It was an idealised, stylised version of her own face that looked back at her, a face so tightly controlled that no emotion was permitted to record itself there. A bride, the mistress of a great house, the wife of a potter— none of these things had registered here. It was the portrait of a young woman in a blue gown, offering her challenge of pride and arrogance to the viewer. Jane Tilsit asked for nothing—not flattery nor love.

"I don't understand," Ginny said softly, and at the sound of her voice Trip raised his head to her inquiringly, the sad spaniel's eyes seeming to melt in the candlelight. "We'd better go back, Trip—this doesn't tell me anything—except that I don't like it when they say I look like Jane . . ."

Her voice trailed off as, suddenly, the dog's head turned and he stared in the direction of the door through which they had come, his body at once alert and listening. A low warning sound came in his throat.

"Trip? What do you hear, Trip?" She moved closer to him, to the comfort of his presence. She now also heard the sound. It was distant, muffled, the echo of a door closing, perhaps—faint, but still of shattering loudness in the silence of the house. No voice came with it. She waited for a minute longer, seeming unable to move, and then distinctly she heard the creak of the stair-treads. In an instant's panic she looked about her, seeking escape, but behind her was only the darkness of the remainder of the gallery and, for all she knew, perhaps no door. And then as quickly she rejected the idea of flight, as if she felt Jane Tilsit's eyes upon her, scornful of this descendant who could not stand her ground in the place where she should be most at home. As the footsteps approached the door by which she had entered, Ginny moved slightly forward to meet the intruder, holding the candle high to cast the light as far as possible.

It fell far short of the door that opened then, and its pale radiance was no match for the powerful beam of the electric torch that cut the darkness. Its ray was played directly upon her, blinding her.

"Who is it? Who's there?"

There was no reply, only the hollow footsteps on the boards. The figure that moved beyond the dazzling brilliance of the torch was vaguely seen, but unrecognisable. Ginny dropped her eyes and waited until the figure should come nearer. The long walk down the gallery seemed to take an age—it seemed a small age of time before the hem of the jade velvet robe came within the circle of light cast by Ginny's candle.

"Vanessa?"

"Yes—it is I."

"Have the goodness to take your light out of my eyes. I'm not a thief." It was a shock to hear her own voice; she could be back in the sitting-room at Santa Maria and Isobel, with Reverend Mother's porcelain in her hand, was saying the words.

The flashlamp was lowered. "I'm sorry." The phrase came reluctantly. As the flashlamp went down, Vanessa's face became visible, sharp and white in the surrounding darkness, the velvet robe wrapped round her as gracefully as the painted draperies of the Gainsborough. Even here, even at this hour, Ginny thought with a stab of jealousy, Vanessa belonged.

"Why have you come?" Ginny said coldly. "There was no need to come."

Vanessa shrugged. "I thought there was. My windows look directly across the court to this side of the house. I saw your candle and I had to come at once. We never bring candles into this part of the house. It's too dangerous. There's always the chance of fire." She gestured suddenly, the flashlamp cutting an arc of light across the paintings, the silver-grey panelling, the carved ceiling. "This wood is like tinder—and there's too much to be lost here."

At once Ginny was filled with a hostile anger and a sense of shame that she had to be taught the value of her inheritance and how to care for it. She felt herself a clumsy interloper here among these things that Vanessa understood so well. "Thank you. I won't need to be told again."

"I'm sure you won't." She made to turn away. "The torches are all kept in that big cupboard near the Hall Screen. It's convenient there, and we all know where to find them."

"I'll remember."

"Yes. Well—I'll leave you." No question as to why Ginny should be there at all at that hour, and no offer to stay with her. If she had been surprised, she gave no sign of it. "Shall I take your candle for you and leave you the torch? It's safer, I think."

"Why should it be safer with you?"

"I know my way about—the floors are very uneven here, and there's always the chance of stumbling. The place is full of mice. I don't know if you're nervous of mice. . . ."

"I'm not, thank you. I assure you I'll be careful. I don't jump at shadows. You may leave me the candle."

Again Vanessa shrugged, and the movement tried to be casual, as if she didn't care very much whether a careless or frightened action from Ginny put an end to all that was Tilsit. But she did care. There was a kind of agony of reluctance and dread in the slowness of her turning away. "If you want it that way—there's no more to be said."

"Yes, I want it that way."

The velvet robe billowed in the swiftness of her walk back down the gallery, as if she would be done with it quickly now that she must go. Ginny made a gesture to recall her, but the gesture was never completed. Her hand fell back, and she said nothing. There was humiliation in having to admit the fierce jealousy and possessiveness that stirred in her, but it was there, undeniable, a canker that had suddenly made itself manifest. At that moment, watching Vanessa's retreat, she knew that Isobel had counted on this very thing happening when she had summoned her to Tilsit. Tilsit had its own way of working on the senses, and Isobel had known it. So Ginny stood, as if she were helpless, and watched Vanessa go. She made no further movement to detain her—nor would she. Not ever.

Vanessa opened the door and the flame danced wildly in the draught. Then from below, from the direction of the Great Hall, the shout reached them.

" Is that you up there, Vanessa?" It was Lawrence's voice. " Vanessa . . .?"

" I'm here, Father."

" Someone's lighted a sconce down here and left it burning." His footsteps sounded on the stairs, running almost. " Is Virginia up there?"

" She's here . . ."

He had reached the gallery now. Vanessa stood aside to let him past.

" What the devil are the two of you doing up here at this hour? Are you both out of your minds?" He was bewildered and somewhat shaken, the flashlamp in his own hand swinging between the two of them. " And leaving the candle burning in the Hall. Do you want to burn the place down?"

" It was I who left it burning." Standing still half-way down the gallery, Ginny made no effort to advance towards the two. It was a kind of compulsion of power to draw Lawrence to her side as irresistible as the compulsion to show to Vanessa her will to act with her own property as she chose.

He began to move towards her, as she had known he would. His tone was lower. " We never do that," he said apologetically.

Ginny nodded. " And quite right. It was very stupid of me."

He kept advancing. " I woke up . . . perhaps it was the sound of the door in the Hall Screen opening. It was

a shock to see the light over here. It made me think for
a moment that she . . . Isobel used to come over here
sometimes at night. But she never carried a candle. It was
her strictest rule. For a moment I thought that it was she
. . ." He shook his head, as if to deny what he had just
said. " And then there's always the chance of someone
breaking in. The exterior windows are wired from the
outside with an alarm system, but I've never felt it was
adequate. Vanessa always said that we should . . ." The
flashlamp swung abruptly back to the doorway. Vanessa
had gone.

" She will put out the candles down there," he said quietly.
" Vanessa is very careful. She has always taken great care
of the things here."

" Yes—I see that."

He was close to her now. The handsome face looked odd
without the protective enclosure of striped shirt and correct
tie ; the rumpled pyjamas under the robe and the hair
fallen across his forehead and over his ears gave him a slightly
rakish air she would never have suspected in him. His
concern had shaken him out of his aloofness. " You must
try not to mind us, Ginny," he said, using that name for
the first time. " If we seem to fuss too much it is because
Tilsit means a great deal. It has been our lives, you
know."

It was said very simply, a statement of fact that she could
at once accept.

" Even for Vanessa," he added, " it is so. Even though she
pretends to laugh at it."

Again Ginny nodded, accepting this also, knowing that
it was the truth. " And I am the intruder here?" She thought
that perhaps never again would she and Lawrence talk
like this, never again break through the barrier of inhibition
and reserve.

He shrugged very slightly. " What is best for Tilsit must
be."

" How do you know that I am best for Tilsit?"

" Isobel thought so. She was seldom wrong." Suddenly
the flashlamp swung upwards, to the portrait of Jane Tilsit
behind Ginny. " You came to look at that, did you?"

" Yes."

" Then you know how Isobel must have felt. A *real* Tilsit,

you see. No assumed name. No need to pretend you are something you are not."

Ginny followed the beam of the flashlamp towards the unrevealing face of the portrait. "If it means so much to be a Tilsit, why did she feel as she did about the world outside of Tilsit? She didn't seem to feel as if it was an honour —it was a burden to her, almost. Lawrence"—the name broke from her without thought—"why did Jane feel the way she did? Why did she feel—disfigured?"

She looked back at him quickly enough to catch the expression of shock. "Disfigured? Is that how she thought of herself? I never knew it went so deeply . . . Disfigured? Yes, perhaps she might have thought that. In her time that might have been true." He turned to her sharply. "How do you know what Jane Tilsit thought?"

"The diaries . . . her diaries are in Isobel's desk."

"Ah, yes—the diaries."

"You've read them?"

"No one has read them except Isobel. We knew they existed."

"You knew they existed—but you never read them?"

His lips twisted slightly in a smile that could have carried a suggestion of scorn. "They were private. They belonged to Isobel and now—to you. Isobel," he added more slowly, "never told us much of what was there. She was very close to her grandmother while the old lady lived . . . I think she probably didn't feel like discussing her."

"You knew Jane Tilsit, didn't you?"

"Yes—I knew her. You forget—my uncle was her son-in-law. She encouraged me to visit at Tilsit even after my uncle died. It was she who first made the suggestion that I should work at the Pottery."

"Then you must have known why she felt that way . . . in the diaries she talks about her infirmities. What did she mean?" Suddenly Ginny held the candle towards the portrait and Lawrence gave a nervous start. "I can see nothing wrong with her . . . she's not sitting or leaning against anything . . . What was wrong with her?"

Lawrence gave a faint sigh, as if he did not relish what he was embarking on. "Your great-grandmother," he said "never leaned against anything in her whole life. At the

time of her death, when she was eighty-six, she was a strik-
ingly handsome woman still, straight as a ramrod, and still
with all the spirit and fight of a terrier. There can't have
been many women as well favoured—as well endowed—as
Jane Tilsit. If she had been born a little earlier—a generation or two earlier, perhaps, she would probably have been
a very happy woman as well. As it was she lived a life of
bitterness and hate for the rest of the world, and I can
see now—now that you've said she actually wrote it—that
she might have regarded herself as disfigured."

"What are you saying? What exactly are you saying?"
Ginny pressed.

"Your great-grandmother was illegitimate."

"Illegitimate . . .?"

Thoughtfully, Ginny looked again at the face in the
portrait, the stern young face of Jane Tilsit, and her mind
was crowded with memories of the phrases written down
in that Victorian hand, the phrases of hurt and anger and
mistrust. "I never knew that," she said. She turned back
to Lawrence, her tone regretful, puzzled. "Did it matter
so much?"

"That's what we might say now—that was what they would
have said around the turn of the century before Jane Tilsit
was born. But by the time Jane had come to marriageable
age, Queen Victoria had established a kind of rule of
universal respectability. But Jane was the child of a notorious
illicit relationship that flaunted the rule, and she was
marked by it."

"Everyone knew then?"

"The churchmen called it a public scandal—and it involved three of the most important families in the county.
Jane's father was Sir Henry Tilsit, who was a widower,
without children. Her mother was Katherine Parley—married to one of the Parleys—and Lord Broderick's daughter.
They went off to Italy together, and Katherine Parley died
giving birth to Jane. Henry made no attempt to cover up
the birth. He brought his daughter back to Tilsit, and
after that he closed his door to the world. The county couldn't
afford to sympathise with the guilty ones, so Jane grew up
here at Tilsit quite isolated from her own kind and class.
It must have been a very lonely and strange childhood.

Henry Tilsit became a recluse—refusing even to see his own child for months at a time. It might have been different if she'd been a boy, I suppose . . ."

" Then her name wasn't Tilsit at all. How strange—after all the fuss there's been about the name . . ."

" She was legally called Tilsit. She changed her name by deed poll when she came of age. That didn't make any difference to what people thought, though. Henry Tilsit hadn't shown any signs of being contrite, so they weren't going to forgive the child. Still . . . I've often thought that the whole thing might have been forgotten if Sir Henry had done the right thing by the system—if he'd searched out some obscure cousin to whom the inheritance could have been passed, and the title—anyone, just so long as he was male and, preferably, respectable. But he named Jane his heir, and let the title lapse—no male relation ever turned up to claim the baronetcy. I suppose Henry was trying to make some compensation to Jane—I suppose he thought that providing her with money would automatically provide her with a suitable husband. But it didn't work—and Jane herself must have made things more difficult by being an exceptionally able and independent woman in an age when the status of a woman counted for almost nothing."

" Yes . . . Yes, I see. I see why she wrote those things."

Lawrence continued. He was staring straight at the portrait, speaking his thoughts slowly, as if they were coming to his lips for the first time. " If she had been a woman of no ability and no stature her history might have proved Sir Henry's critics right. But she *was* an exceptional woman—and she made an exceptional and impossible marriage. It has been the great good fortune of the Tilsits that Jane was born illegitimately and had to look outside her own class for a husband. It's true that she provided the capital to build George Martin's pottery, but George Martin was himself a man of industry and patient genius. George Martin's pottery returned a flow of money to Tilsit just at the time when land had ceased to be the prime source of wealth—at the time when Tilsit needed it most. It held the inheritance intact. It might have seemed an impossible marriage at the outset, but Jane knew what she was about. It was a lucky marriage—at least for Jane. One hears very little about George Martin. Just the way one hears very little about any of the men of the family since Jane's time. Funny——it has become almost a local legend of these strong women who dominated the men about them. There have actually been only Jane and Isobel, but their influence has been felt over a long time. There has never been, in that time, a man in the family strong enough to challenge them."

" My father . . .?" Ginny said.

He gave a short and bitter laugh. " He was no better able than I to challenge that domination," he said. " And I am not even a Tilsit."

He swung back to her, his voice sharp with emotion. " Do you wonder we're afraid of you? The inheritance is in the female line. You are Jane and you are Isobel, and there's nothing any of us can do about it."

CHAPTER THREE

The garden at Tilsit sloped away in broad terraces from the North Front until it met the flat meadow where the stream wound among the trees. Ginny stopped several times as she walked slowly along the near bank, turning back to look at it, and it came to her mind that there was a superficial resemblance here to the terraces of Oranje Huis, though these were perfect and orderly, with wide bands of green turf where the overspill of green vines had been, and in place of the ripe lushness of the trop.cal blossoms there were the disciplined beds of gentle English flowers whose names she did not know. She wondered how often her father also had made this comparison during the years on St. Nicolaas, and she thought that at times he must have ached to speak of it, and yet he never had. She wondered if he too, looking back quickly from this point as she did, had sometimes fancied that a movement among the massed shrubs swaying to the breeze was the figure of a woman, distant and small, in a prim Victorian gown of blue, pacing the walks between the flower-beds. Or had Jane Tilsit never spared the time to walk merely for pleasure in her lovely garden, as she had never spared the time for a wedding

journey? Was it she to be seen there, in the soft sun
of the herb garden on the lowest terrace, bending diligently
with garden shears among the sharp-scented fronds, the blue
gown fading to the colour of the lavender? Ginny shook
her head and blinked quickly, looked back again, and
there was no figure to be seen now. She would not have
sworn, though, that she had not, just for a second, seen
it. And why, if there had been no one there, did Trip stand
poised, listening, one paw raised and pointed, as if he
too had seen something that his senses knew? Or was
the figure of Trip's vision that of another woman, strong
and spare in outline, dressed in old-fashioned tweeds, the
cropped grey hair indifferently dressed, the scarred face
mercifully hidden at this distance? If there were ghosts that
walked the garden at Tilsit, then the beholder might see,
Ginny acknowledged, that which was foremost in the mind.

To break the spell, to distract herself and the dog, Ginny
bent and picked up a stick and threw it for him. He
ran joyfully, ears flying, and there were no more ghosts on
the terraces of Tilsit.

She wished she might have had a particle of his swift
joy in this English morning when the air was as soft as the
brush of a petal. It had been a morning of rebuffs—the
empty dining-room when she had come down to breakfast,
only her own cup unused on the sideboard, Lawrence,
Vanessa and Margaret all finished their meal and gone. She
had wanted to see Lawrence again, to reassure herself by
the sight of him returned to his normal order and precision,
that last night's conversation had been no fantasy, that
someone so eminently sensible as Lawrence could not have
invented his tale, nor could he have, under the push of his
emotion, been driven beyond the border of truth. Even that,
though, would have carried the sting of apprehension in it, for
he had, without time or space to judge, linked her irrevoc-
ably with Isobel and Jane. "The inheritance is in the
female line," he had said, and she knew that he had not
meant the inheritance of this house or the Pottery. They were
dismal and lonely thoughts in the big and empty dining-room,
drinking her tea and eating the last boiled egg from the
silver bowl on the hotplate.

After breakfast she had gone again to look at the portrait
of Jane Tilsit in the Long Gallery. Built more than two

hundred years later than the Great Hall, it was a less utilitarian place than the other, a place for the ladies and children of the household to take their leisure when the weather forbade the garden, a place to show the treasures of a family. In the morning light it was a place of beauty, the silver-grey panelling and the silver sconces reflecting, not her single candle of the night before, but the sunlight that streamed from the south windows and sparkled on the diamond-paned casements. Seen this way it was a friendly, luminous place, but it belonged far less to her now that it had done in the hours of the darkness.

She had forgotten that this was one of the days when the house was open to the public. A long strip of drugget had been laid on the waxed boards, and crimson velvet ropes protected the pictures. Two women in aprons, heads tied in flowered handkerchiefs, were dusting. They both stopped and stared at her as she entered. They were strangers to her, but she saw the recognition dawn in their faces.

" Good morning, Miss Tilsit," they both said, almost in unison.

" Good morning—I'm afraid I've disturbed you . . ."

The older woman spoke. " Don't you worry, dear. Just finishing up . . . you can have the place to yourself in a minute." As she began to collect her dusting cloths she added, prodding Ginny to conversation, " Gave me quite a turn, you did, miss—I thought for a moment it was your aunt, come to check up on us, like she always did."

" I . . . I'll come some other time . . ." Nervously, Ginny closed the gallery door with a clumsy, inelegant bang that echoed down the stairs.

She had gone next to Mark, counting on him being there at the cottage as he had said he often was in the mornings. The walk had brought a lessening of her tension, the certainty that he would talk them away, or laugh them away. The cottage had seemed peaceful in the sunshine, and the sea was calm and blue, the freshness of the hedges, the bright green of the pastures with the dairy herd was a scene of tranquillity. And the keep was no more than a picturesque heap of stones, without history, without menace. She sang to herself a little as she stood for a moment on the crest of the hill, sang as Trip hunted among the slabs for the rabbit warrens.

The mood was broken though when Trip again refused to come on the cliff path with her, cowering at the edge of the keep, barking, imploring her to stay, she thought, and refusing to come to her command. She had to turn and leave him at last, but the brightness of the day was suddenly overcast with foreboding, and the memory of what was said about Mark. She kept her eyes away from the fallen cliff face as she walked.

It was no better when she reached the cottage. Mark's car stood in the muddy lane that led down to the farmhouse, so when he did not answer her knock, she went through the cottage to the studio. He was there, at the end of the building, the two big doors open to the sunlight. A sheet of bronze was held between clamps, and he was working on it with a welder's torch, the mask pulled down over his eyes, his whole attention concentrated on his work. When at last he became aware of her he did no more than lift his arm in vague salute. He kept the mask on his face, and he said nothing. She watched his powerful body as it squatted before the bronze; the intense glare of the acetylene flame seemed to throw him into silhouette. He was cutting the bronze along a line that only he could determine, and his attention did not falter. She knew she was at worst a nuisance, at best a hindrance to complete concentration. She left him quietly, without speaking, and she thought it would be some time before he knew that she was gone.

Trip waited for her at the keep and together they had gone back down the hill, following the course of the stream along under the bridge until they had come to the edge of the gardens. She wondered if she had imagined the figure on the terraces above out of a sense of need, a need to establish contact. Her two worlds seemed out of reach this morning—the world of Tilsit lonely and peopled with strangers, the world of St. Nicolaas farther away with every hour that passed. The letter she had begun to write to Katrien that morning before breakfast had been stiff and self-conscious; not being able to explain the extraordinary world of Tilsit to Katrien she was not able either to render it in ordinary terms. She felt a little afraid by her own powerlessness to fight the current that swept her on, and yet to ride with it held its own dangerous excitement. Her senses quickened with a spark of fear that was also pleasure.

"Miss Tilsit? Miss Virginia Tilsit?"

She swung around with a guilty start, feeling as if her thoughts and pain and pleasure had been open for the world to read. Trip was a long way down the stream, and the man who had spoken was on the other bank, just a few feet away.

"I'm sorry if I startled you," he said. "I was certain you must have seen me."

"No . . . who are you?"

"May I come across? I find it difficult to babble across this babbling brook." He indicated the causeway of stones that offered precarious footholds above the water.

"If you can," Ginny said dubiously, noting his shining shoes that were never intended for tracking across wet fields, the bright yellow waistcoat, the country tweeds that had never been farther than the race-track. He was middle-aged and fat, but he crossed the slippery stones with surprising agility, arriving on her side of the stream with a little smile of pleasure at his own cleverness.

"There now!" he said. He teeth were nicotine stained, and he was even now reaching for a cigarette case. He proffered it to Ginny, and when she shook her head he lighted it before he spoke again, never taking his eyes away from her face at all.

"I'm not exactly a trespasser, you know," he said. "I've paid my half-crown—look, I've got my ticket to prove it."

"I somehow don't think the admission price includes as much as you seem to have taken," Ginny said sharply. She was unhappy under his scrutiny. "What do you want?"

"I want to see you, Miss Tilsit. I've tried every other civilised means I can think of—I've telephoned, I've called. It seems you are never at home." He held out to her a slip of pasteboard. "Raymond Nettle of the *Daily Post* . . . London," he added.

She held it gingerly. "What do you want to see me for?"

He uttered a sound that was meant to be a laugh. "You're a very unusual young woman, Miss Tilsit. These days most people don't ask a newspaperman that question—they just begin talking at once. Publicity is the food of this century. . . ."

"Perhaps I'm not hungry."

He laughed, more genuinely this time. " I think I might like you, Miss Tilsit. But I wish you wouldn't keep closing your doors to newspaper people. It makes life very hard."

Ginny came close to smiling at him ; he was so reassuringly ordinary a person after the figures of her imagination on the terrace, so obviously hoping to win her confidence a little, contrasting to Mark's indifference that morning. " You don't look as if life were hard for you." It gave her a feeling of independence to be standing here in conversation with this man when she knew both Mark and Garth had turned him away. She felt a little more in possession of her own self.

He sensed her thawing at once. " It really isn't hard, Miss Tilsit—not usually. You see, I do a daily column for the *Post,* and columnists are not in the habit of hiking across several muddy fields to get their stories—there are legmen employed to do that for them. But I am staying near here with friends for a few days. The paper asked me . . . oh, well, let's say I was curious myself. Or rather, my friends made me curious—you've been the subject of some conversation these past few days, as I suppose you must know. Yesterday I tried the front door, and was turned away—I had hopes this morning if I stayed in the garden long enough I might see you . . ."

Ginny called to Trip, and then turned and began to walk towards the lower terrace. Nettle followed, as she had thought he would. " I wonder what makes you think I'd be any more ready to talk to you to-day than yesterday."

He was half running to keep up with her. " Let us just say that I had the faintest suspicion that you hadn't any notion that I or anyone else was asking to see you. By the way —you don't mind my coming along, do you?" It was said teasingly, hardly a question at all.

" I thought you said you'd paid your half-crown—that gives you admission to the grounds as well as the house."

" Very gracious of you, Miss Tilsit."

By the time they reached the small door in the wall that led to the herb garden, Nettle was panting. Ginny felt a little sorry for him, but she had kept up her pace because she meant him not to think her too easy. Even in this small thing she was conscious of a kind of betrayal to Tilsit, but her curiosity was stronger. Nettle halted suddenly by a bench at the edge of the flagged path.

"Do you mind if I catch my breath for a minute?" He shook his head towards the steps that led to the terrace above. "I'm not much of a climber—too much wine and good living in London, I'm afraid. I just can't see myself pursuing you all the way up to your door. In fact, Miss Tilsit, I'm asking you if you'd mind staying here with me—just for a minute or two?"

Ginny looked at him, red-faced, panting a little still; his hand trembled slightly as he lighted a fresh cigarette. She shook her head. "I can't say you haven't earned it. But I'm afraid it's no good. I really don't have anything to say to you."

"Well then . . ." He shrugged, and sank down on the bench. "Well, it's been charming meeting you, Miss Tilsit. Oh —by the way—did you see this picture our paper printed of you. A good likeness, isn't it? I knew you at once . . ."

"What picture?" Without meaning to, Ginny found herself back at his side, her hand outstretched.

"Arriving at London Airport, I believe. You seem to have been well guarded, even then. It's a pity, if I may say so, Miss Tilsit, to pick up our English habits of reserve too quickly. Spoils such a lot of fun for a young person, I think. I remember when your cousin's husband—Vitti— was alive they were always good for a picture and a paragraph. Wonderful people—what a stunning girl she was! I wonder how she finds it back here . . ."

Ginny wasn't listening. She was staring at the picture of herself, looking as she had when she got off the plane, her arms loaded with small pieces of baggage and the white silk coat, looking untidy from the long plane journey, her hair straggling a little, looking apprehensively, questioningly into the camera. The caption was quick and crude. HEIRESS ARRIVES. *Miss Virginia Tilsit arrived in England to-day stirring speculation that she has been named as sole beneficiary under her aunt's will to the historic mansion, Tilsit, in Dorset, and to the Tilsit china works. Her arrival also revives memories of the law case fought in the twenties between her aunt and father for control of the famous pottery.*

Ginny dropped down beside Nettle on the bench. " Is this true about a law case?"

He blinked, and his reply was deliberately understated. " True? Why, I imagine so. Papers keep files on those kind of things, you know. And we don't exaggerate more than we have to. Don't *you* know whether it's true, Miss Tilsit? How interesting! My friends knew, of course—they remember it very well. Now, Miss Tilsit, I wonder if you'd mind telling me why you never knew? Was your island very remote? . . . Did you never hear about Tilsit or the law case from your father? How dramatic! Really, Miss Tilsit, you must let me work this up into a Sunday feature. You'd have people swarming down to see your house . . . think of all the half-crowns . . ."

" Can I keep this?" Ginny demanded, rising, waving the folded paper at him.

" Of course you may keep it—but must you go? It would be very good publicity, you know. . . ."

Ginny had turned and was running along the path towards the steps. Her urgency had communicated itself to Trip, who ran with her, barking sharply.

" Miss Tilsit—just one more thing, Miss Tilsit!" She looked back and was surprised to see that Nettle was running also. There was no choice but to stop and wait for him.

He was breathing heavily again as he came up to her. " I have a ' true or false ' question for you now, Miss Tilsit, if you don't mind."

" What is it?"

" About Eliot Russell. Is it true that you are going to marry Eliot Russell?"

Ginny took a step backwards, shocked and troubled by the insidious ability this man possessed to creep in under the fences of privacy. His pleasant fat face seemed all at once filled with menace, potent with the unspoken threat of what he would invent for his public if he did not have the truth to write. " How . . . how do you know about Eliot?"

He shrugged, his eyes wide with hapless innocence. " My dear Miss Tilsit—I told you we have our files. And an old newspaperman like myself develops a memory for faces. I saw a picture of you with him some months ago in

Time. As I said, you photograph very distinctively. After I saw the picture in the *Post*, I telephoned the office and had my people pull the file. The clipping came this morning. Now, I wondered . . . our readers would be very interested to learn that you were going to marry Eliot Russell. The joining of two inheritances . . . you know that kind of thing. He *is* very rich, isn't he?"

Ginny's fear of him went down before her outrage. " You . . . you're even worse than Mark said you would be! I should have listened to him. How do you dare come poking around here, asking your questions . . ."

He smiled mildly. " I'm sorry you take it this way. May I remind you, Miss Tilsit, that you sell tickets to view your lovely house. I am quite within my rights."

"And I'm sure that somewhere in the fine print there's something about the owner's right to refuse entrance. Now I'm refusing you entrance, Mr. Nettle. And I'm telling you to leave the grounds. By the front gatehouse. At once!"

He spread his hands as if to indicate astonishment at her reaction. " Please don't get excited, Miss Tilsit. I never push my way in where I'm not wanted." He paused, smiling at her coldly. " It's interesting, though—very interesting. My friends were wondering what kind of girl you were. I shall be able to tell them that you display all the characteristics of your eccentric aunt. Good day, Miss Tilsit."

11

Ginny took the keys of Isobel's car from Garth without telling him where she was going. She thought it was a small price for her independence that she got lost several times driving to William Randall's office in Bournemouth. There was the moment, driving off the car-ferry on the short-cut Randall had told her about, when the ancient car stalled; a line of honking vehicles stretched behind her and she thought that in the matter of cars, at least, Isobel had been no better off than her father. But mostly she thought not at all—just concentrated on the road and let the questions she would ask Randall go unformed.

When she got to Randall's office he was out to lunch. When

he returned an hour later she made no answer to his surprised greeting but just laid the folded copy of the *Daily Post* on the desk before him.

"Mr. Randall—why?" She paused and took a deep breath. "Why didn't someone have the sense to tell me about this? Why have I got to get all my information by roundabout ways? *Was* there a law case, Mr. Randall?"

He merely glanced at the picture, as if he had seen it before, and sighed. "There was." Then he stopped, and she thought he didn't mean to go on.

"Well . . . ?"

He rose from the desk and went to stand by the window, staring down at the street. His hands were clasped behind his back. She suddenly noticed how much better his rumpled pepper-and-salt tweeds became him than the suit Raymond Nettle had worn. She was surprised at herself for thinking this, because she was angry with him at the same time.

"Why, Mr. Randall?"

He turned back. "I'm sorry, Ginny. There's no reason why you shouldn't have been told—except that for so many years no one has talked about this, and it's not easy to begin again."

"You mean the family have not talked about it? Other people have! I know that!"

"Yes—other people. It died down, of course, after your father left, but your aunt's death and your coming have naturally stirred up speculation again." He nodded towards the newspaper on the desk. "And in more distant places than you would expect."

He came back and sat opposite her again. Now he tried to smile faintly and she was aware once more of the concern for her that had attempted to ease her entrance into this family and this house. Her anger faded a little.

"There was another reason, Ginny—something that I think was in your aunt's mind, though she never spoke of it directly. When she went out to see you in the West Indies she refused to speak of the reason for the quarrel—is that right?" When Ginny nodded he went on. "I think she had a hope that you might come to Tilsit and judge what you saw for yourself, without prejudice, without feeling the tug of loyalty to your father's cause. Perhaps we all hoped that—unrealistic, of course. But it seemed that Tilsit needed you . . . and if you could have some time there first . . ."

" It *was* unrealistic, Mr. Randall. My father died when he got that cable from you. Did any of you expect me to forget that?"

He gestured with a kind of helplessness. "No." And then he appealed to her. "You mustn't be too hard on us, Ginny. We all see our own side of it."

She reached over now and tapped the newspaper lying between them. "But there *were* two sides to it! It got into a law court, didn't it? That says there were two sides."

Randall sighed again, and gave in to her. "Yes—two sides. But being your aunt's solicitors we never believed that your father had any case at all. As it turned out, he didn't. He brought the action because Jane Tilsit left the whole estate and the Pottery to Isobel. In other words, she was the sole beneficiary. That left John with nothing. He decided to contest the will. It's as simple as that!"

" I don't regard that as very simple, Mr. Randall. My father was not the kind of man who made law-suits for the fun of it."

" I wouldn't doubt it. It must have been hell for him. And he borrowed heavily from Lord Chardley, who was at Cambridge with him, to pay the costs. Since Chardley is one of the old Dorsetshire families, that didn't make for very good feeling, either."

" He lost, though . . ."

" He lost. He contested on grounds of undue influence on a woman who was senile. The case wouldn't stand up."

" Why not? Jane was eighty-six when she died. And it does seem unfair that Father got nothing . . ."

Randall shook his head. " Isobel was able to produce a score of witnesses who could testify that Jane Tilsit had never had a moment of uncertainty or confusion in her life. At eighty-six she was still visiting the Pottery regularly, giving orders that made more than good sense, still running most of the household matters at Tilsit . . . overseeing the gardeners and even showing a profit on the sale of the surplus vegetables and fruit. There was no senility in Jane Tilsit when she died."

" What was my father's case?"

" Very little. He pointed to her eccentricities—she was very tight with money, and wore the same clothes till they fell apart, and refused to have a motor car at Tilsit. She said she didn't trust them. Many people agreed with her on that. She had refused for many years to entertain at all at Tilsit—she would have nothing at all to do with the other county families. John even dragged up the fact that she had made her husband refuse a knighthood. All of this was irrelevant, of course. This was not the result of senility, because she had always been like that. Unfortunately for your father's case, these are the very qualities which the English admire and applaud. They cherish their eccentrics. Jane Tilsit might not have been popular, but she was respected. Everyone knew that she was no more senile than Isobel was. And Isobel had been her grandmother's shadow. People's sympathies might have been with John for a while because it seemed wrong that the only male descendant should have to beg his bread from his sister. But there was never any doubt in law. Jane Tilsit knew what she was doing when she made her will. Your father didn't have a chance."

Ginny slumped back in her seat. " Well—that's that! I wish I'd known long ago. He would never talk of it . . . I had the feeling of something worse. He seemed so bitter about Isobel."

" It *is* a bitter thing to lose an inheritance, and lose a fight for it," Randall said quietly. " Before the case came to court John had a good deal of local sympathy—which is probably why he went ahead with it. But during the hearing it all seemed to drain away from him. People changed their minds. You could feel it."

" Why?"

" I suppose part of the trouble was that the case was pleaded in this county. It was too close to home. John made the mistake of going back into Jane Tilsit's past. All the old stories were raked over—Jane's illegitimacy, her strange marriage. The gossip that had almost been forgotten was raked up again. It involved the whole Parley family— who were very prominent in politics—Jane's mother had been a Parley. There was the feeling that what John did was a lot of bad form, and the county wasn't likely to forgive him that—that was from the county point of view. On the other side John lost sympathy from the working people because Jane Tilsit had created a very going concern in the Tilsit Potteries, and during the hearing Isobel made it very

clear that up till then John had hardly put his head inside
the door. She, in fact, was the one prepared to step into
her grandmother's place. The working people began to feel
that John would mismanage the Pottery. There were a lot
of jobs tied up there, people wanted to keep the *status quo*.
John lost on all counts."

" How old was he then?"

" I don't remember exactly. Young—early twenties. He
seemed even younger, though. He had a gullible look about
him—and he appeared a rather foolish and greedy young
man because he'd let himself be talked into a law-suit that
just had no foundation. People thought he was arrogant. . . ."

" Not my father!"

" Perhaps not the man you knew, Ginny. He seemed so
then. He was inexperienced, and he lost his head a few times.
By contrast Isobel seemed supremely suited to carry on the
inheritance. To do your father justice—although she was
our firm's client—I have to admit that Isobel was ruthless in
exploiting her advantage. She stripped John of everything—
his pride and self-esteem, the confidence that is still so shaky
in a young man. What really amazed me was that after the
judgment was handed down, she seemed to assume that
John would be just as he was before. She saw him immediately afterwards, and she obviously expected him to come
home with her to Tilsit and settle down as if nothing had
happened. She would be in charge, of course . . . and he
. . . well, it was clearly implied that he would do exactly
as he was told. It never seemed to occur to her that he
might refuse."

" But he did refuse." Ginny's voice grew warmer, feeling
the rightness of that decision to have taken the sting from
the defeat. " He refused to be Isobel's servant—like the
others." She was echoing Vanessa's words. " So you see she
didn't take everything from him."

" No . . ." Randall's answer carried a note of doubt.
" Though I remember wondering at the time what he would
do. He had been trained for nothing—he was barely down
from Cambridge. And he was in debt. He paid that off,
though. I heard from Lord Chardley himself years later that
it had been fully repaid. I think Chardley meant me to pass
the information on to your aunt."

" But she already knew, didn't she? She kept track of him

all those years . . . and never once a letter, an offer of
help . . ." Her anger was rising again to remember Isobel
having taunted her with her father's near bankruptcy for
twenty years. It hurt now to think how close they had lived
to the edge of poverty at Oranje Huis—the poverty itself
not the hurtful thing, but the fact that her father had suffered it in bitterness and hatred for his sister. "There was
nothing from her—no word of reconciliation, no message—
nothing until she wanted me." Ginny looked hard at Randall.
"She didn't change, did she? When I saw her that one
time she just expected I would come exactly the way she
expected Father would do as she ordered him." Her eyes
glinted at the memory of it. "I didn't know what any of it
was about. But I think I answered her the way he would
have done. I said . . ."

Randall gestured to cut her short. "Perhaps he gave her
no chance at reconciliation. She had her own bitterness
to bear, and she stayed and took the blame for something that
was partly John's fault."

He spread his hand before him on the desk. "John's
action against her had automatically tied up the estate—the
whole business dragged out to nearly a year. During that time
the court appointed a board of trustees to run the Pottery
—and John got a court order to bar Isobel from entering
the works itself. He claimed that she might influence
decisions that would be detrimental to the future of the plant.
The Pottery continued to function, of course, but John's
action had stopped some rebuilding at a crucial stage. The
money for rebuilding was tied up, and the board of trustees,
who knew nothing much about the pottery business, held
maintenance down to the minimum. There was an accident
at the works the day after the decision was handed down.
A man was killed in that accident, and another had his arm
crushed."

"Oh, God . . ." Ginny said softly. She put the back of her
hand against her mouth, pressing her lips. "But he was not
to blame . . ."

"There was bad feeling at the Pottery. The people said
that the procedures were unsafe—the temporary conditions
because of the rebuilding had gone on too long. It was
a very haphazard operation for that year when Isobel wasn't
allowed inside the place. John had been responsible for that

—but it was Isobel who stayed behind to take the blame."

"He wasn't to blame," Ginny repeated, her tone rising in an attempt to convince Randall. "You didn't know him . . . he must have suffered more than she did. He wouldn't have hurt anyone. You . . ." she said accusingly, as if Randall had committed a betrayal, "see only her side of it."

"She was our client," he answered simply. "And then, your father didn't give anyone the chance to know how he felt about the accident. He left the day after it happened. No one ever saw him in England again. I didn't think much about John after that. Most of my sympathies were given to your aunt."

"She didn't need them," Ginny said cruelly. "A woman of that kind needs no one's sympathy . . . or help."

He shook his head. "It seemed to me at that time that she did. The day your father left was also the day Isobel had her accident—the time that she cut her face so badly. It was a very difficult period for her. There wasn't much in the way of plastic surgery in those days, and she was stubborn about seeking help. Eventually she did go to a man in Vienna, but she wouldn't stay for all the operations he said were necessary. She came back to Tilsit, but by that time her own chance of personal happiness seemed to have slipped away from her." He paused. "Isobel Tilsit was a very proud woman. She couldn't accept love if she thought there was pity in it. She was to have married Edward Ashley, but she never did."

For the first time Randall looked away from her. His fingers played absently with a paper clip from the bowl on his desk.

"She had her own tragedy to live with. Perhaps she didn't give thought then to your father's. I think, Ginny, your aunt suffered very much in the knowledge that she would never have children. Already, even at that age, when she was still in her twenties, she was concerned about passing on the inheritance."

III

Mark was waiting in the sitting-room when Ginny returned to Tilsit from the visit to Randall. He rose at once when she entered, his smile tentative, almost humble. It seemed out of place on him.

"Am I welcome?" he said.

She stopped for a second, and then moved towards him again quickly, thrusting out both hands to him, and finding them caught in his own. The roughness of his skin was like a caress.

"I think," he said, "that we should go back and start from the beginning again. We should pretend that you've just arrived—the new Miss Tilsit from some remote tropical island. And I've come to pay my respects in a decent fashion as I should have done the first evening. And you ask me to stay to dinner."

"And do you accept?"

"Of course I accept! Foolish girl! Why else do you think I got all dressed up?"

She stepped back from him, laughing, looking him up and down. "I was wondering why you looked like a stranger. Of course—I see it now. A dark suit—and a tie and white shirt, no less. And you've even remembered to comb your hair. What has happened? This morning you wouldn't look at me."

He gestured with a kind of helpless innocence. "I was working."

"That's it, is it? You were working."

"That's always it. When I'm working there is nothing else. Afterwards, when I realised you'd gone, I began to think you might have been upset." He shrugged. "There was nothing I could do about it—and nothing I can do to change it in the future. It's better if you try to understand it now than later. No, wait——" He motioned her to silence as she was about to speak. "I thought I'd try to soften the hard facts just this first time—just to let you know that you have your hour in my life too. So I brought you this—and it's a piece of myself."

He turned and took from a table near him a small stoneware bowl, darkish grey at first glance, but as it was moved, revealing the greens and blues that seemed to live there as a part of the texture itself.

"The marks of a man's hands and heart are in this, Ginny. It was the first piece I ever had accepted for exhibition. I threw it at a particularly dark period of my life—the time when I left Isobel and went to work for Wedgwood. I was pretty unhappy then, and all my thoughts and hopes about the future were somehow centred in this little bowl. I can think of nothing I own that I want less to part with."

She fondled the rough beautiful surface with fingers that had swiftly grown in appreciation of such things. " Why are you giving it to me?" she said softly.

" A man usually brings gifts to his beloved. I think I've come to court you, Miss Tilsit."

" Are you serious?"

Mark answered her with a question. " Are you?"

She couldn't reply to him directly. She looked down at the bowl in her hands. " Thank you for this. It's very beautiful. I'll cherish it always."

He nodded. " See that you do."

Mark's bulky frame seemed ill-at-ease in the dark flannel suit, but he bore it with the same kind of obvious restraint with which he bore the interlude for drinks before dinner with the family, and the meal itself. He sat quietly, almost sedately, and sometimes Ginny, catching his eye, would nod in recognition of the effort, and he would smile at her, demanding her approval. He behaved with Lawrence as if yesterday's scene at the Pottery had not taken place, and Lawrence fell in with this. They talked, with no real cordiality but also without hostility, about the weather, the repairs that must soon be carried out at the Tilsit gatehouse where the tickets were sold, and about the coming by-election in St. Mary's. Having exhausted these subjects, Mark moved over to sit on the sofa beside Margaret, asking her about the origin of the pattern on the seat-cover she was working.

" It's an original pattern," she said. " I'm very fond of the flowers and birds motif. I use it wherever it seems appropriate through the house. This, of course, is styled to resemble the seventeenth-century design—it's one of twelve seat-covers I'm making for the chairs in the Long Gallery. This will be the first time they've been replaced since the time the gallery was built."

" Yes—it will suit them very well," Mark said, nodding. For a moment he rubbed the silk texture of the *petit point*, and then went on to talk to Margaret about the difficulties of adapting needlework patterns from large subjects to a smaller scale. Margaret entered the discussion with unusual animation, and in the middle of it Mark shot Ginny a look that seemed to say " See how good I can be when I try." And she had to acknowledge silently that it was so, and that the charm was there for every woman to respond to, and that Mark himself knew it.

Vanessa came to dinner in a dress of soft white wool, loosely tied, as simple as a nun's habit, and devastating in its effect ; her dark hair was held back by a band of crimson. Ginny instantly felt, by contrast, shabby and dull, wondering with quick jealousy why she herself hadn't put on one of the dresses that she still thought of as " the Eliot clothes," one of the sophisticated wools bought for the New York winter. She wondered if Mark would have reacted to her dressing up in the way he did to Vanessa's, with the lighting of appreciation in his eyes, the quick nod of approval. From his scrutiny of Vanessa he turned too quickly back to Ginny, and she thought he seemed apologetic, as if he wanted to say to her, " I can't help it. I respond to beauty —and she is beautiful."

It was hard, too, for Ginny to listen to the talk between them at dinner. They seemed to play at scoring off each other, and yet it was done in the fashion that suggested that they understood each other very well—the places, people and happenings of their childhood were a common background which Ginny could not share and from which she felt excluded. She listened as Vanessa began to draw Mark out to talk about the piece of sculpture he was then working on, and he, forgetting that he had come to show Ginny that he knew how to behave as everyone else did, was caught up in her questioning, and reacted with the inevitable egotism of an artist, so that the food grew cold on his plate while he tried to explain the symbolism of his metal pieces, his hands gesticulating and reaching in the air as he grasped for words to convey his purpose. He forgot to eat, the service of the meal was held up, and still he talked on, his eyes ranging round the table so that no one could escape them. He was oblivious to everything but the struggle to express what he felt, not caring that the time and place was inappropriate and unsympathetic. Ginny saw Lawrence's shoulders hunch together in a faint shrug, indicating that this was what must be expected from Mark Barstow. Finally, she herself had to nod to Garth to remove Mark's plate with the food almost untouched on it. And while he talked Ginny saw that Vanessa's gaze never moved from him, and her questions, intelligent, shrewd, followed what he was saying, and complimented it. She interposed herself between Mark and his other audience with effortless skill, leaving Ginny a listener, but not a participator. Mark was still talking, exclusively to Vanessa now, as they filed out of the dining-room.

At the doorway Margaret came up beside Ginny. " Some day when you have time you must come and visit the needle-work room. I think there are some things there that would interest you . . ."

" What?" Ginny said, straining to listen to what Mark was saying, not hearing Margaret.

" Garth will show you how to get there—it's through the solar in the Old House. Any time—I am there every day."

" Yes," Ginny said automatically, not knowing what she replied to. For a second Margaret frowned, the tiny faint lines appearing on her smooth forehead, and then almost at once her face switched back to its habitual expression of serene blankness.

Ginny walked on in a daze of uncertainty and unhappiness; at the entrance to the sitting-room, Mark's hand suddenly cupped her elbow. He leaned in close to her.

" Are you running away from me?"

She felt herself tremble and his grip tightened. " Don't run away from me because . . ." She heard his breath drawn in. " Because I need you, Ginny."

Ginny took her place behind the coffee tray that Garth had left ready, and while she poured Mark carried the cups to the other three. Once again his face wore the look of self-conscious virtue; he seemed pleased with himself and utterly unaware of having monopolised the talk through dinner, and Ginny knew that if it were pointed out to him that it had been so, he would be unrepentant—and he would also be right. In a house like this one, she thought, no one should be made apologetic for an extreme of enthusiasm or of love —and his talk had been both. So she answered his eyebrows questioningly raised with a smile and a nod, and he moved on, even more pleased with himself than before, and happy. He went to stand before a display case of small china pieces, whistling tunelessly beneath his breath. Without a glance at any of them he suddenly set down his cup, and opening the cabinet he took down one of the pieces and began to examine it closely. Lawrence stiffened at this attitude of freedom, and an amused expression came to Vanessa's face.

But it was Ginny who spoke. "Put it back, Mark!"

He spun round his face darkening with fury. "Who the hell do you think you're talking to? You sounded like her —just like her!"

Ginny's hand gripped the edge of the tray to steady herself; she felt a kind of dismay at what she had let herself say. "I'm sorry . . . I didn't mean that. I meant . . . well, I meant I'd like you to listen to me. I have something to say." She looked around the room. "I have something to say to all of you."

Grudgingly Mark returned the piece to its place, and closed the door. He walked slowly to stand before the fire. During this time no one spoke. The silence was complete enough for them to hear the dull sound of the silk being pulled through the fine canvas as Margaret worked on steadily.

"Well?" Mark said. He seemed the only one willing to speak.

"I want you all to know . . ." Ginny began nervously. She looked around their watchful, searching faces and she once again felt the mood of the morning—that she was alone here. And with this her anger returned. She put her cup down sharply on the tray, causing the spoon to rattle loudly.

"I have been to see William Randall to-day," she continued. "I'm sorry that you have forced me to learn from a stranger—a journalist—and from a newspaper cutting, the extent of the disagreement between my father and Isobel. I just want to say to you all that I don't appreciate—and I won't stand for—any of you making up my mind for me about what I ought to read and whom I ought to see. If I want to see a newspaperman, I will! At the same time I think it was pretty foolish of any of you to think I'd be left in ignorance about the law-suit for very long. For how long," she demanded, "did you think I would be the only person in the county who didn't know?"

Lawrence cleared his throat. "It was Randall's idea—and I must say I thought it pretty unrealistic. He knew from Isobel that you had never been told about anything that happened here in England. He thought that these first days would be trying enough as it was . . ."

"Randall," Vanessa interrupted, "is a sentimentalist. At times I think he's a very bad lawyer."

"That's hardly the point, is it?—not any longer," Ginny said. "I know now—I know about the law-suit and the way my father left here. And I just want you all to know that you can stop pretending that it was any other way. I knew that my father hated—yes, I think he *hated*—his sister. There had to be reason—and this seems enough reason to me."

"Reason enough—but not good reason. John was right to spare you the details. For all he knew it would never be necessary to know."

"But now it *is* necessary—half-truths generally appear worse than the whole could be."

Lawrence shrugged. "Whatever you wish, of course. But sometimes one's innocence is a happier state."

"No doubt," Ginny said. "But I didn't ask to be taken out of my state of innocence, Isobel decided that."

Lawrence nodded. "You're right. Of course you have questions to ask. But I can't see that it concerns anyone else here but myself. After all—I am the only one left of those who were at Tilsit at the time when the suit was going on."

"But all of you seem to have been involved in Randall's conspiracy of silence," Ginny said. "I just wanted you all to know that I am now aware of the circumstances in which my father left Tilsit, and so it won't be necessary to keep telephone calls and newspapers and callers away from me any longer."

Lawrence shifted his position in his chair. "It is an unhappy time to recall—can you blame me that I fell in with Randall's suggestion? Sufficient unto the day . . . Everything seemed to happen at once then. The judgment was handed down on the inheritance, and then there was a serious accident at the Pottery which should have been avoided. And That was the time, also, when Isobel had her own accident.

I was away from Tilsit . . . your father was gone. They sent for me . . . Isobel sent for me."

"That was when she hurt her face?"

"Not only her face—she was badly injured about the head, too, but of course when her hair grew again the scars didn't show. . . ."

Mark turned and kicked a fallen ember back into the grate with his toe. It seemed a movement of desperation. "For God's sake!" he cried suddenly. "Do we have to go all through this again? The woman was disfigured—hideously disfigured. Does it matter how?"

Lawrence wheeled from Ginny to look directly at Mark. Their eyes met as Mark turned back to face the room.

"Perhaps it does matter. Isobel's life was tragic. I believe it adds to her tragedy that she should have come to grief twice in the same fashion."

Ginny leaned forward, but Lawrence did not take his gaze off Mark. "What do you mean?" she said urgently.

"You didn't know that? She injured herself in a fall on the cliff—Isobel fell twice on that cliff. The second time, ten days ago, she met her death."

CHAPTER FOUR

After the first days, the self-perpetuating routine of Tilsit absorbed Ginny effortlessly. Isobel's death and her coming was a small ruffling on the surface of its ways, but its history and its rhythm were too old to be disturbed to their depths by happenings of such short duration. At least this was what Ginny began to feel as she sensed the flow of its routine close over her. She rose in the mornings and went to bed at night at almost exactly prescribed hours because the household was long accustomed to Isobel's habit of doing so, and Isobel had taken her habits from Jane. Ginny guessed that Jane had done so because her father, Sir Henry Tilsit, had ordained it. The continuity seemed unbroken. So strongly did Ginny feel this that she grew certain that if she searched long enough among the papers in Isobel's office that somewhere she would

find it all written down. Each day she told herself that
to-morrow she would make the first change—she would do
something, however slight—to mark the fact that time had
passed. But each day she did nothing, and the current of
the ways of Tilsit carried her with it.

The habits of Tilsit being immutable, they could absorb
the shocks that would have destroyed more fragile institu-
tions. Not only was Tilsit unchanged by Isobel's death,
but by the manner of her death. Scandal and rumour and
accusation came and were heard, and died down again.
Lawrence would continue to live and work alongside of Mark
because Tilsit needed him, as would Brown, although she
hated and mistrusted him. And while all of them might
deplore Ginny's growing closeness to Mark, in a fashion
they also welcomed it because she was the instrument of
drawing that strange alliance together again. Mark was
as much a part of Tilsit, whether or not he would acknowledge it, as if he had been born within its walls and still
inhabited them. Isobel had laid down the custom of the
acceptance of Mark long ago, and custom prevailed. In
the moments when loneliness was uppermost in her being,
and the remembrance of St. Nicolaas and Jim and Katrien
brought into sharp focus the strangeness of the world in
which she now dwelt, Ginny would question if perhaps
custom had not taken the place of decision at Tilsit.

The letters from Jim and Katrien were voices from an
experience that even this short span of time at Tilsit had
made seem incredibly remote. Katrien's letters were as
she was, sane, calm, tinged with her own earthy wisdom,
writing of the island affairs as if they had great moment; she
asked no questions of Ginny, barely referred to the fact
that her daughter was living a life that her husband had
kept locked up inside himself for all of the years he had
known Katrien. Katrien's patience was no small thing;
she had waited for John to speak, and he had never spoken.
She could afford to wait a little longer. "*Nothing happens
here*," she wrote, "*and yet things happen every day. We miss
you.*" She did not ask Ginny when, or if, she was coming
back.

Jim's letters were different. "*What in God's name is happening to you?*" His exasperation and anxiety boiled over
into words that tried to be funny but never succeeded. "*Are*

there suits of armour on your stairs at Tilsit?" he demanded.
*" Better get one of them to write—it would probably be more
informative."* The letters were long chronicles of the progress
of the building, the little events of Willemstad, the arrival of
a new real estate man, the debate over the new school—
all of them things Ginny had known before she left. Jim
sensed, as truly as she knew, how much change had already
been wrought in her, and so he had to paint the colours
of the island as brightly, as boldly as if she had been a stranger
to them; he had to reiterate its own particular way of life
to try to counteract whatever influence it was that had laid
its own claim on Ginny at Tilsit. He was a man fighting
something of which he had no knowledge and in desperation
he would seek to evoke the image he possessed that seemed
truest to Ginny. *" I look along the beach in the mornings
and I don't see you—and I wonder where you are, and if
you will ever come back. Bo wonders too—he's getting older
and he's less optimistic than he used to be when you were
gone before. Sometimes he doesn't even bother to look for
you. I say to him, ' Not to-day, Bo. She isn't coming
to-day,' and he grunts and lies down again."*

Ginny laid these letters aside, wondering how to answer
them, pondering the impossibility of answering in any vein
that made sense of their questions. The replies to Jim
and Katrien were stiff and awkward. She wanted to ask
them to suspend judgment for a while. But that in itself
would have been to ask the question, " Judgment of what?"
So she wrote as a child, as if nothing had happened to her.
And they all knew that the replies were false.

The diaries became a counterpoint to the letters—they spoke
with their own voice to pull her back towards Tilsit. They
waited, as surely as Brown waited each night, a presence
as real as hers, but secret, a communication between herself
and the two women who were in their graves. The thread was
invisible but it was strong, pulling and compelling her back
into the past of Tilsit, making her a sharer in the minds and
wills of these two women who had outlived and outlasted their
men, whose strength had been the life of Tilsit in the last
hundred years, whose impress seemed worn into its very
stones. Ginny looked into the mirror these written lines held

up and saw, half fearfully, a blurred and indistinct image that could be herself.

The two women had written of the minute of life at Tilsit in exhaustive detail. In one of Jane's velvet-bound books. "*The wall of the lower terrace is crumbling and must be replaced. We are replanting the border . . .*" Then followed a whole list of perennials. She enumerated her purchases of damask tablecloths and kitchen knives, and recorded the dismissal of the second footman for smashing a Chelsea figurine. They entertained very seldom at Tilsit, despite its splendour. Jane's defensiveness was on guard against the whole of life that lay beyond the house and Pottery. "*We have received cards for the Eccleston garden party—no doubt because they need George Martin's support to turn out the vote of the Pottery workers. We shall not go, of course. This overture should have come years ago.*" There had been a reconciliation of a sort with the vicar. "*The vicar came to tea. He wanted a donation for the new roof. I refused him, since we never go to church. The new recipe for plum cake is excellent. George Martin ate half of it in a sitting. He had to be dosed with bicarbonate of soda.*"

The trivia were there, set down like a journal of housekeeping. The things that were blows to the heart of Jane Tilsit were recorded with great sparseness, as if the pain were too great to permit more.

"*The child was born, and is dead. We named him Henry John.*"

The record of joy was brief also. Two years later, the entry, "*A daughter, Elizabeth. A healthy child.*" The next years contained many references to Elizabeth, to her growth and progress. Then, among the housekeeping details, the cry of anguish broke through. "*Are there to be no more children for Tilsit?*"

After that, the bitterness that hope had kept at bay seemed to close in. Ginny could sense the handwriting and the woman grow tighter and more withdrawn. Her pride grew with her age, and her feeling of exclusion from the affairs of the county. She marked the great social events of the county, and always that they either were not invited, or did not attend. And then the overtures from the families living about them stopped, and Tilsit was left in its isolation.

Although this isolation was of her own making, Jane resented it. "*Am I to bear this all my life, and my children too?*" She did not see her own bitterness as part of the reason for this—and she persisted in her belief that there would be more children. "*This cannot be all!*" she wrote. But she could not call them to life the way she could order George Martin's existence.

The Pottery was prosperous and becoming well known, selling by the million its heavily decorated mugs and tureens and vegetable dishes. George Martin would have stirred himself out of the limits of Tilsit if Jane would have permitted him. "*They have been here to ask George Martin to stand for Parliament. I have told him he must certainly refuse. Do they think they can make us suddenly respectable when they find we can be of use?*"

Six months later came the entry on a page by itself. "*The Queen is giving a great garden party at Osborne, on the Isle of Wight. The whole county has been invited, all except the Tilsits.*"

The oversight—or the snub—rankled. Six years later Ginny found the entry, "*George Martin has been offered a knighthood by the Queen. I have told him to refuse.*"

In 1887 came the words, "*George Martin Tilsit died peacefully to-day.*"

Jane's only child, Elizabeth, was a disappointment to her. The events of Elizabeth's life, her marriage to John Bowen, who assumed the name of Tilsit, were recorded dutifully, rather than with great interest. "*I have waited for maturity to add to Elizabeth's character, but at this age I am forced to conclude that Elizabeth is frivolous, and her husband is a weakling. My hope lies in the children.*" Elizabeth and John Bowen-Tilsit died within a week of each other during an epidemic in Paris, Jane dryly wrote that she had given orders for the bodies to be sent back to Tilsit for burial.

From then on the diaries concentrated on Isobel and John, but from the beginning, the emphasis was strongly on Isobel. "*John betrays his father's characteristics of weakness and indecision. He must be watched and shaped.*" By the time John was barely turned eighteen and not yet enrolled at Cambridge, the decision had already been taken. "*John could never stand alone. He must be guided always by Isobel. I have settled my will accordingly.*"

Like Jane, Isobel had filled her diaries with a great mass of domestic detail, and Ginny had to search among it for the points of drama that had high-lighted her life. Like Jane, Isobel also had not recognised the high moments, or had been too overwhelmed by them at the time of their happening to do more than merely mark their event ; in retrospect they may have proved too painful to elaborate. There was hardly a record at all of the law-suit her brother had brought to contest the will. After searching a long time, Ginny found the entry. It was remarkable only in that it followed the record of Jane Tilsit's death. " *Granny is dead.*" No word of mourning, but the sense of desolation was in the brief words. A week later was the entry, " *John has been foolish enough to bring suit to contest the will. Of course it will be upheld.*" There followed the words, " *Poor John—he has learned nothing and must be taught.*"

In the next six months there was very little mention of the progress of the case—Isobel apparently was certain that no case at all existed. Instead there was the anguish of being barred from the Pottery; she recorded secret meetings away from the Pottery with the chief designer, the plans she was making for when she would take complete control. There were many mentions of Edward Ashley. But Ginny never found the record of love. There came the final bald statement. " *Edward Ashley and I are engaged to be married.*" Either she did not love him, or she was cursed with Jane Tilsit's inability to write down her deepest emotion.

The end of the law-suit was noted. " *The judgment has been handed down. It was inevitable that it would be in my favour.*" And then, set down in an agitated scrawl, as if Isobel had at last been touched in some spot that hurt deeply. " *A terrible accident at the Pottery—John is to blame for halting the rebuilding at this stage, but of course it is I who must bear it before them all. To the rest of them I am Tilsit Potteries.*"

On the next page, undated, written in the usual clear, sober hand, Ginny found the entry, " *John has left Tilsit and England and I—I am destroyed.*"

The remainder of the book was blank.

Wonderingly, Ginny took down the next volume of Isobel's diary, and on the first page the entry date was more than a year after the last one had abruptly ended. The script was careful, studied, as if the writer were unaccustomed to the act, as if she were very conscious of the new volume and the unwritten pages ahead.

"*I am back from Vienna, no better—worse, I believe, than when I left. They can do nothing—and I must make myself forget what I look like. It is an act of will to look in the mirror and not see myself.*" Without a break the script went on, as if the next sentences were inevitably linked to the foregoing. "*Of course there is now no question of marriage. I have broken the engagement to Edward Ashley.*"

And thus, with such sparseness, did Isobel Tilsit record the most momentous happenings of her life. After that the record went back to the daily life of Tilsit, the rebuilding of the Pottery continued, and whatever heart Isobel had was slowly buried under the mass of small events that was her life. Ginny would come to the end of her night sessions of reading with the candle beginning to splutter as it reached its end, the feeling of frustration acute in her that she was only permitted the barest suggestion of what had loomed large in the lives of these two women, and an avalanche of facts about what she did not need to know. The questions persisted—something untold that had happened at the time when her father had left Tilsit, something untold also in Isobel's stark words "*I am destroyed.*"

From the nightly reading of the diaries, which were the tale of pride and death, Ginny sought the reassurance of life and love. When the candle had been snuffed out she went to stand by the darkened window, seeking the pattern of the dark fuzz of trees on the hill which were outlined by the glow that came from the skylights in Mark's studio. She could not see the studio itself but the light in the sky proclaimed his nearness and gave back to her a sense of hope. For her he became the affirmation of life.

The habit had grown upon her now of going in the mornings on the familiar walk up over the hill of the keep and along the cliff path to his cottage. It no longer disturbed her that Trip refused to come farther than the keep, that his sharp barking seemed to implore her not to venture there herself. She understood his fear now, tied as it was to Isobel's death, and she had ceased to question that it had anything to do with Mark. She found it was even possible to put out of mind the fact that Trip still cowered at the sight of him, and that Mark seemed barely able to restrain his hostility. In the midst of all the strangeness of Tilsit these became minor things; she practised a small dishonesty with herself by not allowing either of them too much importance.

What was important was the lift of her heart when she entered the studio each time. It no longer seemed an austere place to her, and the steady north light was not harsh but dispassionate, dealing with everything in even quantities. And it was no longer troubling her that Mark did not stop work when she arrived—how stupid, she thought now, that she had ever expected it. If he was working at the potter's wheel the motion never hesitated even when he gave her his brief glance; but a shade of warmth came into his expression. For more than a week he was polishing the stainless steel of a new abstract sculpture, and he would pause to give his aching arms a rest.

"Come to disturb me again?" he would say, but pleased just the same that she had come. And she would nod and go into the kitchen and make coffee for them both. He made a mock grimace as he drank it. "I don't know why I expected you to be able to make good coffee—because you've been in New York, I suppose. But what a hope—you've got all the English knack of ruining it."

She never minded him saying the mocking, half insulting things that he did habitually. It occurred to her that it was a strange kind of love-talk in which they indulged, teasing and provocative. Often as Mark spoke like that he would be reaching over to pull her closely to him, a little rough, a little possessive. "God—you're a lovely thing in the morning. Did you know that, my girl? All pale and golden, and not quite awake. Give me a kiss now, and let me get on with this—all this mucking about isn't going to make anyone rich or famous, you know." And he would kiss her, and then push her from him playfully, and he was back at work again, and she nearly forgotten.

It was disturbing that in these moments of absorption in his work he reminded her most strongly of Jim.

And he did work. Denying what Lawrence implied, making nonsense of what Brown said of him having an easy position, he worked like a man possessed. Ginny would often find work on the drawing-board, rough sketches that were developed through all their phases to come close to what

M

the design might look like seen on the roundness of a plate,
tried again on the cup and a teapot. These appeared endlessly as he strove to find the most worth-while for the
purpose—different developments day after day and she
knew what kept the light burning into the morning hours.
The designs for the sculptures were laid there on the table
beside them, and Ginny could never have said which had
preference. Working on his beloved bronze and stainless-
steel abstracts or sketching the most domestic coffee-pot, she
knew that his commitment was complete and total. It did
not take her many days to know with certainty that Isobel
had never been cheated.

Once, as she entered the studio on a misty morning, with
droplets of moisture clinging to her hair and coat, he laid
down his tools and got to his feet, stretching his powerful
frame with a kind of crude grace whose very vitality made
her recognise again the reason why she came here. The
whites of his eyes were bloodshot, but he still seemed to
radiate that compelling energy and magnetism that had first
drawn her. Even his fatigue did not dull the inner sheen
of that energy.

"God—what time is it?" he said. "I haven't been to
bed." He put his arm loosely about her shoulders, and
walking her through the passage to the kitchen. "Boil me
a couple of eggs will you, love? I'm starving." He began
hacking huge pieces of bread from a loaf and cramming them
into his mouth. With the second one he paused long enough
to spread solidified fat from a bowl he pulled from the
tiny refrigerator. "Dripping," he said, his voice muffled
by the mouthful of bread. "Always tastes best when you're
hungry. Used to live on bread and dripping when I was
a kid. When you're hungry—and you're poor—it has the
taste of last week's meat in it."

Then he smiled, and once again yawned, his mouth stretching wide open, revealing the half chewed bread. The coarse-
ness of the gesture was redeemed by its very naturalness and
warmth. He saw her eyes on him, and he grinned. "I'm
an oaf, aren't I, Ginny?"

"You work hard," she said, lighting the gas under the
saucepan.

Abruptly he was serious. "Work!—my God, I haven't
begun! Just give me ten years like this last one!" His hand

gripped the edge of the table, fiercely tense. His voice seemed to shout and boom through the tiny space of the kitchen. "There just aren't hours enough—or days enough. My head teems with ideas I want to try. Sometimes I think I'm going mad because there's too much to hold. I have to keep pushing on because something might get away from me. . . ."

And yet there was discipline in him. By noon he had put away the stained sweater and trousers and was on his way to the Pottery. "The tie and clean shirt are my gesture to being an executive and the head of the Tilsit design department . . . even now it seems to be vaguely sinful to wear a clean shirt every day. Wasteful, you know . . ."

He would never take Ginny with him to the Pottery. "You must come by yourself," he said. "It wouldn't help morale if people saw you arriving with me every day. It wouldn't seem fair . . ."

But the way to the Pottery grew very familiar to Ginny just the same. She went there very often, and it was not to see Mark. After a time it became a habit of her days, just like reading the diaries, and coming to breakfast and walking with Trip and always ending at Mark's cottage. It grew to a point of familiarity where the Pottery workers didn't take much notice of her any longer, and Lawrence would nod briefly from his desk near the window and go on with his work. She would wander slowly through the place, stopping where she felt like it, watching the motion of the workers' hands, feeling a small gràtification when one of them, looking up, simply nodded in recognition, and the work went on. She still didn't know what much of the process was about, but it was simpler to ask her question of the person nearest at hand, and to stand and watch and listen until the answer began to make sense.

"Why is the raw clay coloured with all these different colours—this pink and blue and green?"

"That's to distinguish the various kinds—china and earthenware—so there won't be any mistakes. It's only a vegetable dye. It burns out in the kiln."

She grew more familiar with the terms, began to use them with a sense of pleasure—biscuit and glost, frit and slip, over-glaze and under-glaze, ground-layering and aerographing. She was shy to use them at first, expecting to make

blunders. But she came to understand that there was a
certain pride among the workers in what she attempted and
succeeded in, and they helped her forward, as if she had
been a baby taking its first steps.

But the best of it, as Mark had promised, was watching
the throwers. She stood for so long before the spinning
wheels, watching the shapes grow with astonishing speed from
the ball of raw pounded clay, that the men began to take
her presence for granted. It seemed at times to Ginny that
the shapes of the bowls and vases and pots seemed almost
to spring out of their hands; it was like a small miracle
at last to begin to comprehend the centrifugal action of the
turning wheel and the impress of the hands on the wet clay.
From the hundreds of pots that she saw come off those
wheels it was gradually impressed upon her that even in this
commercial manufacturing process, where the object was
to copy a set pattern and shape, no pot was absolutely
identical with the next. She remembered what Mark had said
once, talking of studio potters: " All their work has the
feeling of a man's hand on it. You know without question that
it was a human that fashioned it, not a machine. That's
why, Ginny, a Greek vase, or a Roman pot—perhaps from
quite an ordinary potter of that day—has the power to
move and touch us across all this great distance of time.
The potter's art speaks the oldest language we know."

A humility and reverence grew in her as she stood and
watched the shapes come to life. One of the throwers, having
forgotten her presence, looked up suddenly and blinked in
a kind of shocked recognition. " Your aunt used to stand
just there. Always watching, she was—always able to tell
what wasn't going well. But standing just as quiet as you
when things were all right. I reckon you'll be getting ready
to take her place . . ."

And Ginny had turned and left him in sudden panic.

The life beyond Tilsit began to claim her also, in a small
way. Gradually, in a somewhat diffident fashion, the neighbouring families began to call at Tilsit. Ginny left a comb
and lipstick in the downstairs cloakroom so that she would
be ready for the sudden summons to the sitting-room.
The vicar came first, and he talked in conventional terms

about Isobel, talking about the funeral service as if any of it had meaning for Ginny, who had seen Isobel only once. The callers were mostly of a type—well-bred faces, the men usually better-looking than the women, dressed suitably in faintly dowdy country clothes. Their diffidence puzzled Ginny, because she guessed it was not their usual manner; it was explained to her by one woman, whose ugly, engaging face peered at her from under a hat that could have been identical with Isobel's own. "You must forgive me— all of us, my dear—for behaving around here as if we might be put out at any moment. It's gone on for so long, you know—this attitude of Tilsit not being able to forgive the county, and the county not being able to forgive Tilsit. It was all quite absurd—but Isobel took it from that ridiculous old lady, her grandmother. At times I didn't think she was quite right in the head, you know—either of them— I'm old enough to remember the Old Lady. But I'm glad it will be different now. It's high time Tilsit took its own place in our affairs here. We can't afford hermits any more. The times are against it, my dear."

They were not all like that. A little, tired-looking woman in faded brown clothes presented herself one day. "I've come about my boy, Rick, Miss Tilsit. Your aunt was interested in him—she saw his work at the local school exhibition. She had said she might be willing to help get him into some art school when the time was right. He's breaking his heart since she died, Miss Tilsit. I was wondering if there was anything you could do . . ."

And the woman looked at her in plain disbelief when she tried to explain that she had, as yet, no legal position at Tilsit, that she had no money or influence to help anyone. "But you're Miss Tilsit, aren't you?" the woman said.

Of all those who came the memorable one was Lord Chardley. Even Garth's announcing his arrival was something to impress itself on Ginny's memory—his whitish, pinched, old-man's cheeks high-lighted by an unfamiliar spot of colour.

"Lord Chardley to see you, Miss Virginia."

She rose at once, the look in Garth's face compelling her. "What's the matter, Garth?"

"Nothing, miss—it's just that his Lordship . . ."

Then she remembered that Chardley had been the one who had loaned money to her father at the time of the lawsuit. She guessed from Garth's demeanour that he had not been at Tilsit since. It was a shock to see the withered face of the man who struggled to his feet with the help of a cane as she entered the sitting-room. By this time she had also remembered that Randall had said that Chardley and her father had been friends at Cambridge. Surely, she thought, her father had never been as old as this man?

"I'm glad to see you, my dear," he said, taking her hand in such a way that his frail weight seemed to rest on her. "It's been a very long time since I was in this house. Not since Johnnie left . . ."

Someone, then, had once called her father Johnnie. She could get no picture at all of a man called Johnnie—a man who had been young when this withered man was young.

"I loved Johnnie," he said. "Many of us loved Johnnie—he was my best friend. I missed him very much when he left. . . . I had to come and see what his daughter was like." He smiled and the wrinkles etched deeply into his face. "You're thinking that I'm an old man—older than your father. We were much of an age—but you see what arthritis in a climate like this does to one. I hear that Johnnie died quickly. He was fortunate."

He leaned in close to her on the sofa, peering at her face. "I had to come and satisfy myself. I had to see you. They've been saying around here that you're very much like Isobel. That isn't true, of course." His hand, twisted and swollen in the joints, was laid briefly on her arm. "You are yourself—I could see it in the second you walked in here. You're neither Johnnie nor Isobel. Perhaps I was disappointed you weren't more like Johnnie. But all the same I'm glad to have seen you while you're here."

"I expect to be here . . ."

He cut her short, shaking his head. "I can't see you here. You belong to yourself, not to Tilsit. To me you seem a bird of passage . . ." He rose again, painfully. "I must go now—I was on my way to a meeting when I had the sudden impulse to come and see you. I would like you to come over to visit me at Long Knedston if there's time while you're here. But I don't expect you'll be staying that long."

She rang for Garth and wondered why she didn't have tongue or wit to protest the old man's prophecy.

It was only Mark who spoke out against this committing of herself so completely to an existence and a routine that another woman had lived before her.

"For God's sake, Ginny, break away from what she was! Get away from here for a few days. Where's your curiosity? You haven't been farther than Bournemouth! Take a week off and go up to London. No, I'll *take* you to London—that's what I'll do!"

But they didn't go. They talked about it, but it was something that might happen in the indefinite future, and in the meantime there were things for them both that seemed more pressing. How was Mark to leave when the moulds were being prepared for a new style of china? And how could he leave the sketches for a new sculpture of the Resurrection that were beginning to form on paper? How leave it and risk that the mood and the excitement of it would never come back? And how would Ginny leave when day after day more of the history of the house, more understanding of the pottery was opening up to her.

These were the reasons they gave to each other. But the truth was that they were afraid to trust themselves or each other beyond the confines of the world of Tilsit. Here they were close and the routine sustained them. Too often there were reminders of the other world. Katrien's letters continued to restate its values in her direct, uncomplicated terms, the values that for Ginny seemed to be suspended at every fresh encounter with Mark. Katrien, had she known of Mark, and the questions that surrounded him, would have stated the matter simply. "Thou shalt not kill." But what, Ginny wondered, would Katrien have done confronted by Mark himself? Would she not have thrust it aside?—or condoned?—have found an excuse in the insupportable domination of Isobel? It was no use, though, to ask what Katrien would have done when it was she, Ginny, who must bear the burden of the choice. She seemed to burn with a kind of fever of love, and the price she paid was the guilt and torment of eternally wavering between one emotion and the other. And yet it needed only Mark's presence, his touch, to wipe out the guilt.

They stretched and reached for each other, and they were all but lovers.

The cottage on the cliff became their haven and Ginny's refuge. She began to go there in the evenings after dinner, and she knew that it was too often, and that with each meeting the impulses that attracted and bound them to each other grew stronger. They were alone in the cottage, before the fire with the sound of the waves on the rocks below closing out the rest of the world. It was their world, this small enclave of space and time, with their lips and bodies close, and demanding more insistently, with their hands caressing and growing more accustomed. They were ripe for love and they held back.

" This can't last," Mark said. " I want you and soon I will have to go to bed with you—or I will have to be done with you."

She lay where she was on the sofa before the fire, where he had left her in the fierce rejection of frustration. She put her hands on her bare breasts where his hands had been, feeling the coldness of loss.

" Not yet," she whispered.

He had lighted a cigarette and was staring at the fire. " I know that well enough," he said. " And I'm afraid of you because of it."

" Afraid?"

" You will have all of me before I have any part of you. I will be bound and clamped and tied to you before you give me that marvellous body. I don't know that I can accept those terms."

" Did I make terms? . . ." Her voice was muffled by the sofa pillows as she half turned her head away from him, feeling the agony of loneliness, and again the knowledge of rejection.

" You don't make terms consciously. But between you and me the terms were made long ago—before we ever saw each other. You are Tilsit, and I am the one Tilsit lifted up. From me to you there could only be complete and utter capitulation. I'm not prepared to give it. I love you . . .!" He suddenly jerked around and faced her. " Yes, I do love you—but do I love you enough to wrap myself up and hand myself over—body, soul, the lot? I have to ask myself if Tilsit hasn't had enough of me. What would be left over for myself, I wonder . . .?"

She felt a sudden shame and reached for her sweater. And then his hand was there once more, and she felt its warmth and was reassured.

"No—let me look at you . . . if that's all I can do. Do you love me, Ginny?"

"Yes," she said. But she didn't know what was the complete truth. Did she mean to say " Here and now, I love you—in this time and place "? Or if she had been apart from him would she still have felt as she had felt for Jim, would she have striven in her mind as she had striven for Jim? The thought left her confused and tormented. She lay back against the cushions again, but her hand still pulled at Mark's, and she kept it pressed against her breasts, fearful of experiencing the loneliness and coldness again.

"Have you been in love before?" she said.

"Of course—what man hasn't? A dozen times, or so I've thought. But before this it's always been light-hearted, and I've always known it would come to an end in its own good time. Once I almost got married . . ."

She made an agitated stirring among the cushions. "Why didn't you?"

"Isobel stopped it. It was when I was a student at the Royal College in London."

"How did she stop it?"

He shrugged. "Very simple. She just went to see the girl and told her that any backing from Tilsit would cease if I got married. That put an end to it. I was twenty . . . and I hadn't a penny."

Ginny thought that Isobel, without knowing it, had saved Mark for her. She wondered if she should be grateful. "And you accepted that?"

He nodded, and his hand stroked her softly, almost absently, "Isobel was right. The girl would have been a drag on me—I was lucky I hadn't got her pregnant. I was moving up, and she would have held me where I was. Isobel knew it. The devil of it was that Isobel always seemed to know these things. For whatever cold-blooded reasons she made her decisions, they nearly always turned out to be the right ones. So I didn't marry her, and since that time Isobel has seen me imagine myself in love a good many times and she's never interfered. Or not that I'd noticed. I suppose she's known that it didn't matter, and until now she would have been right."

Ginny stilled the motion of his hand on her breasts by clamping down on it tightly. She rolled on the cushions so that she faced him directly.

"Would you marry me?"

He moved in close to her, his hand grasping now. "I would marry you. I want to marry you. But I don't want to marry what's up there." His head made a jerking motion. "I don't want to marry that house. I don't want to be called Tilsit. I don't want to marry everything that Isobel has left behind her. If you were simply—Ginny No-name—I'm marry you to-morrow. But I've been used enough, and I have to be free. If you were not a Tilsit . . ." His voice grew muffled and died away as he buried his face against her breasts. She held his head there, almost as if she would comfort him, and the bleak and bitter thought occurred to her that perhaps the very fact of being a Tilsit made the attraction inevitable. It seemed to be Mark's fate to be haunted by Tilsit, possessed by it, bound to it. He struggled against it, but without conviction.

She suddenly brought her face down to his, and her lips pressed on his were angry and wounding. "Love me," she demanded. "Love me for myself."

But when she felt the instant response of his body she drew back, ashamed of having demanded and taken his will at this moment when his desires made him powerless to resist her. "No . . ." she whispered. "I can't do that. I can't do that to you this way. When you come freely, then we will love one another."

II

Garth brought the news of Eliot's arrival to the second terrace where, under the supervision of Crawley, the head gardener, Ginny was being permitted to weed a bed of stock. Garth loomed above her on the gravel path, looking perturbed. "An American gentleman to see you, Miss Virginia. A Mister Eliot Russell. I came to tell you myself, miss—because . . ."

Ginny scrambled to her feet. "Eliot? Eliot here! Where s he, Garth?"

"He came to the public entrance, miss. He's in the Great Hall at the moment. I wasn't quite sure where to put him. He's come with his baggage. Was he expected, miss?" Garth's tone expressed outrage that such arrangements might have been made without consulting him.

Ginny thrust the trowel and her gardening gloves towards Crawley. "Not expected . . . no, not exactly expected. But welcome." She started to run along the path towards the steps. Then she recalled Garth's age, and she stopped and waited.

"Shall I bring in his bags, then, miss?"

Excitement and exhilaration rose in Ginny so that she beamed at the old man. "Yes, Garth—by all means bring in his bags."

"Which room shall I put him in, miss?"

"Well . . ." Ginny could remember in particular none of the empty rooms she had looked into in the South Wing. "What do we have that's dry and aired?"

Garth looked hurt. "All in South Wing are dry and aired, Miss Virginia. It's part of the routine."

"Yes—I'm sure," Ginny said hastily, starting to mount the stairs at the pace he could manage. "But is there—is there a special room, Garth? One that's grander than the rest?"

He seemed to hesitate, and she had to wait for him to catch up. "Do you mean the Rose Room, miss?" His expression was stricken with doubt. "It has been very seldom used. The furniture is in dust-sheets. There are some extremely valuable pieces in there, Miss Virginia. Are you sure the young man . . ."

"The young man," Ginny said firmly, "will understand fully the value of every one of those pieces, Garth. You may trust the Rose Room to him. And Garth . . ."

"Yes, miss?"

"Ask Crawley to cut flowers . . . and Brown will help you to get things ready." She was hurrying on, conscious for the first time of having possessions to display and to order. "For dinner we will use the best service, Garth . . ."

He was falling into the mood of her excitement, his

distrust of those who came without arrangement dispersed
by her pleasure. " And the gold flatware, miss?"

" Gold . . .?" Ginny stopped short. " Do you mean to
say, Garth, that we have a service of gold?"

" Only for a dozen, miss," he said deprecatingly. " It
came as part of the dowry of Miss Arabell Lacy when she
was the bride of Sir John—that was Sir Henry's father, miss."

Ginny clutched the balustrade for a moment, weak with
the kind of helpless confusion that had gripped her on the
first night at Tilsit. Garth peered at her in concern.

" Is there something wrong, miss?"

She shook her head, controlling herself. " No, nothing
wrong, Garth. Nothing at all wrong except that I've just
discovered something else to pay inheritance taxes on." Then
she turned and sped up the steps, leaving him there.

Eliot stood, thumbs lightly resting on the slits of his coat
pockets in his usual stance, in the middle of the Great Hall,
staring upwards at the banners that hung from the gallery. It
was not the tourist's unseeing stare, but an appraisal of
warmth and appreciation. He was immaculate as always,
showing no sign of having travelled that morning. And
as always, whenever she saw him afresh, Ginny was struck
again by the crisp, beautifully modelled lines of his face and
again she was touched a little by sadness at the sight of
him.

" Eliot!"

" Ah, Ginny!" Characteristically he made no move towards
her but waited for her to come to him. As she advanced he
spread his hands sparingly to indicate his surroundings, the
Great Hall and the pile of the buildings grouped about it.
" Magnificent—and wasted on you, Ginny."

She took no notice of his words. " I'm glad you've
come."

He bent to kiss her cheek briefly, a gesture to the occasion.
" Are you glad? My arrival seemed to disturb your butler.
He wasn't quite sure he could trust me here alone."

" Can you stay? You have to stay, Eliot."

" I'll stay—yes," he answered, as if it were long ago
arranged. Suddenly he put his hands out, holding her at
arm's length, looking her carefully up and down.

" My God, Ginny. How did you do it?"

"Do what?"

"Here you are—you've been in the country just a few weeks, and already you're a pretty good copy of every well-brought-up young Englishwoman. Tell me—did you inherit that skirt from your aunt too? And the sweater has definitely seen better days—about five years ago, I'd say. If I'd only known I'd have brought you a string of pearls of indeterminate length to complete the costume. I wonder what happened to that entrancing girl who used to accompany me about New York? Look at your nails . . ."

She pulled her hands away from him defensively. "Is that all you've got to say to me? I wouldn't have thought it was worth the journey. I don't always look like this . . . I've been gardening."

"You would have had to be doing *something* to produce that result. I suppose you *have* been doing something . . ." He peered at her face closely. "No, don't turn away from me. Those absurd letters you've been writing . . . You must think I'm some kind of a fool to be taken in by all that schoolgirl nonsense. You've inherited one of the loveliest houses in all England and a not-bad pottery, and all you can write is that the gardens are nice. Nice! What kind of innocent do you take me for . . ."

Ginny choked. "Eliot, don't. If that's the only reason you've come, I wish you'd stayed away."

He shrugged, and permitted himself the faintest smile. "I'm sorry. I didn't mean to lecture you. Not immediately, that is. But it was partly the reason I came."

"Partly?"

He took her arm in a motion of rare warmth in Eliot, bending confidentially towards her, walking her across the Hall as if he already knew the house and were long established here.

"Partly," he repeated. "There was an interesting report in one of the New York columns that you and I were going to be married. I thought I'd come over and find out if it were true."

She stopped short, pulling her arm from his grasp, and at once regretting the action when she saw its reflection in his face. "That man!" she said. "That horrible man—he went ahead and printed it. I should never have talked to him at all. What a fool I am—what an inexperienced, gullible fool! I should have known that if I didn't deny it, he would print it."

His face had resumed its expression of smooth imperturbability, a wintry expression. " My dear Ginny—don't fuss. It's of no consequence." Then he added, reluctantly, as if it were a question asked against his will, but one which must be asked for whatever power the answer still had to hurt him. " You didn't deny it—but it isn't true, all the same? Is it?"

" No, Eliot. It isn't true." She wanted to look away, but she made herself face him. " You wouldn't want it to be true, would you?"

For only a second he hesitated. " You're quite right. I wouldn't want it to be true."

And then he took her arm again. His manner was brisk, whatever he felt—relief or disappointment—well concealed. " Well, now that we have that matter disposed of, we can start being comfortable with each other again. Show me the house, Ginny. I've been reading about it since we last saw each other. What a gem! And you don't understand the half of what you've got, do you? There must be someone around who knows every inch of it. I warn you I'll want to see it all. And the Porcelain Collection . . . When my mother read that paragraph about us she telephoned me to ask if it were true—hopefully, I suppose—though she should long ago have given up hope. After I'd disillusioned her about that, she then said she'd once come to see the house and the Porcelain Collection. You know, I think she might have *wanted* that paragraph to be true . . ."

He went on. As they walked from the Great Hall through the screen and down the passage to the South Wing, he didn't stop talking. He commented on everything he passed, facetiously often, praising what was good, but with a merciless eye for the errors of the Victorian modernisation. By the time they reached the sitting-room, Ginny knew that it was talk for the sake of talk, a cover for what was more deeply felt than his face would allow him to betray. Incredible as it seemed, Ginny suddenly knew that Eliot had been prepared for either answer to his question. In his heart he did not want to marry her, but if she had agreed, he would have made no objection. Eliot was tired of himself and of his face before the world. He would have been glad to shift the weight of his ambiguity to her, who would demand so little of him. He saw her as his pupil, almost his creation, manageable, pliable, never troubling him with passion. He had felt her dependence on him and for that reason she was welcome in his life. She was made fully aware now, for the first time, of the desperate emptiness of his existence, the loneliness of his ways, that had brought him to this willingness to settle for so little. And she also knew, with gladness, that in some things she had outgrown him.

When they entered the sitting-room Vanessa was there, smooth, beautiful, cool, at that instant engaged in that act of consummate grace, lighting her cigarette with a live ember from the fire.

" Here," Ginny said, " is the person who will show you the house. She knows it very well." Unregretfully she led Eliot forward.

III

Tilsit was itself diverse and varied enough to be able to absorb Eliot, so that his exotic, slightly perfumed quality seemed not out of place, nor scarcely even remarkable. After two days he seemed to have been there always—in the Long Gallery with Vanessa, making pointed remarks about the portraits by provincial artists hung beside the Gainsboroughs and the Reynolds ; staying for hours alone in the Porcelain Gallery, long enough to worry Brown, who couldn't believe he was there merely to look ; somehow convincing Garth that he could be trusted with the keys of the store-rooms so that he could hunt among the furniture under the dust-sheets for good pieces that had been overlooked. As she moved about Tilsit Ginny heard his voice constantly—discussing in knowledgeable detail with Margaret the possible origin of an undated tapestry in the Great Hall, pointing out to Lawrence that a grouping of poplars in the lower terrace would better define the course of the stream, endlessly pointing out to Ginny what he thought she was missing.

On the third day he came in to her in the office. " Did you know there's a whole library of books in fine bindings

—probably some rare editions among them—in the room right next to this one. And it's been *locked up* for twenty years!"

Ginny laid down the financial report from the Pottery she had been trying to understand. She sighed. "I don't think Isobel read books, somehow. They might have contained dangerous ideas . . ."

"Don't be funny!" he said sharply. "How could anyone live with a room like that one, and not use it. She must have been out of her mind."

"It must have been locked up during the war—it probably would have needed one extra in staff to keep it open. She couldn't afford it. *We* can't afford it." She tapped the papers on the desk before her. "Isobel wasn't out of her mind. No one who could understand all this was ever anything but eminently sane."

"Here," Eliot said, gesturing. "I'll explain it to you if you really want to understand it. I'm very good with balance sheets. I'm forced to be. I don't intend ever to be robbed. I'll give money away—but I don't intend ever to have it stolen from me."

"How extraordinary you are, Eliot," Ginny said quietly, half amused. She got to her feet. "Let's leave the figures. Let's go for a walk. You haven't been to the keep yet . . ."

"I was there this morning," he said, "before anyone else was up. If you don't mind I'd rather go back to the Long Gallery again and have another look at the Gainsboroughs. Oh, yes—and have another look at that extraordinary young woman that Millais painted—the one that you're so much like."

"Jane Tilsit," Ginny supplied.

"Yes—Jane," he said, as if he had been intimate with her for a long time.

Indeed it did seem a long time that Eliot had been at Tilsit. He was accepted by the household; they were used to his questions and his polite but firm probing, and they didn't even resent them. It was impossible to resent what was asked from such deep interest, not merely for the sake of gossip. In three days Eliot had informed himself of the whole history of the Tilsits in the last two hundred years. More gently, but no less pressingly, he had questioned Ginny about the immediate history of Isobel and her father, and she found herself answering with the full truth. She talked to him with the same freedom with which she had talked that first night when they had sat on the palisades of New Jersey looking across to the lighted towers of Manhattan and the outline of the bridge growing darker as the sky paled. But this time, instead of her tale of love for Jim MacAdam, she had talked to him of Jane Tilsit and her marriage, of Isobel, her disfigurement and the manner of her death, of the fight over the inheritance and her father's long self-exile from England. And finally, unable to help herself, she had talked to him about Mark.

Gossip about the guest at Tilsit had already reached Mark by the time he came, by invitation, to meet Eliot. He came, his bullish good looks heightened by antagonism and jealousy, expecting to demolish this elegant fop. Instead he encountered Eliot's steely coldness with which it was impossible to fight.

" Damned pansy! " he muttered to Ginny.

Ginny thought it was not so much Eliot himself that so disturbed Mark, but the effect he had had on the household. He saw in one jealous appraisal, what Eliot's presence had done to the three women. Ginny had brought out the New York dresses to wear, and Vanessa came to dinner in a black dinner dress which Eliot had looked at and correctly named as a Balenciaga model. Vanessa had smiled her pleasure.

" This is the first time it's been out of its dust-covers for over a year. There seemed no occasion to wear it . . . how clever of you to know Balenciaga's work."

Eliot said, " Great dressmakers have a signature as distinctive as—potters." He made a faint bow in Mark's direction, a small and delicate gesture of propitiation.

Mark uttered a sound that was a small explosion of contempt, that tried to hide his wounded puzzlement over the hold that Eliot had come to have on the household in so short a time. He noted the gold flatware, which had already become a small joke between Ginny and Eliot, and he recognised that Eliot had somehow come to command Garth's respect, and that Lawrence tried to spark the conversation with old stories from *Punch*, and he was at great pains to issue the invitation for Eliot to visit the Pottery in such a way that there could be no mistake about who had the right to do it. But the greatest change

Mark saw was in Margaret, quite startlingly beautiful because some animation had come into her face, wearing dark-blue velvet and a string of aquamarines he had never seen on her before. She said little, as usual, but she listened with her eyes, and after dinner she didn't return to her embroidery frame. He was shaken by what he saw.

"What's happened here?" he said to Ginny, as they stood together, apart from the others. He leaned in to her closely as if he had to make his claim upon her. "This fellow has turned the whole place upside down."

"Do you mind?"

"Yes—I mind. I mind because he can do it. I mind because I'm jealous." He nodded back towards the group at the fireplace. "I would like to be able to do it, but I only succeed in upsetting everyone. If it was only money he had, I wouldn't care. I could challenge money—but he has more than that. I'm damned envious of the way he has everyone eating out of his hand without having to force anything or pretend. And I don't like him because he makes me feel it's not worth-while to be a man when something only half-way between will send women fluttering to dress up and to preen as if his admiration were worth something . . ." His voice was very low and strained, and Ginny saw that his face was contorted in a grimace of frustration. For once he was not forceful. His tone had dropped to a whisper, as if it were an inner voice with which he questioned himself. He suddenly looked down at his hands, which were clenched.

"God, Ginny," he said, "I never thought I could be jealous in this way. I never thought I could care what anyone like that was able to do or say or be. His kind never mattered to me—money or background or the way he looks or wears his clothes. Truly—they've never mattered because I've always been able to tell myself that I had a talent that made me equal—no, not equal—I'm superior to most other men. But now, here I am, furious with him, and burning up with jealousy just because you're wearing a different dress to-night and your hair looks different and I begin to see the Tilsits in you more than ever . . . and I feel like a clumsy ox who's blundered in here by accident." He suddenly slapped one clenched fist into his big palm.

" I don't want to feel this way. I never have before. I don't know what to do about it . . ."

In sight of all of the others she stretched her hand towards him, holding the lapel of his jacket. " Nothing . . ." she said. " Do nothing about it. It is Eliot who envies you."

He caught her hand fiercely. The conversation by the fireside had not been able to ignore them; it had faltered and stopped. All of them now seemed to turn and look at Ginny and Mark. He knew it, and he still ignored them. He said then to her in a low voice:

" And I'm afraid, too. You don't know what this place is all about . . . and I'm afraid he'll tell you. I want you to stay as you are—without knowing. I don't want you to be Isobel again . . ."

She drew her hand away very slowly. " If I'm not afraid, you shouldn't be."

IV

A new atmosphere, almost gala, came to Tilsit with Eliot's presence.

" He stirs things up," Vanessa said gratefully. " And he has such a superb sense of an occasion. You find yourself living up to Eliot." She was rejoicing in the huge *flacon* of perfume which he had ordered by telephone from Fortnum and Mason and had had delivered by special messenger. " It destroys a woman a little when she has to buy her own perfume. That's what I've been doing since I came back here . . ."

For Ginny there were half a dozen cases of champagne which nicely filled out the empty wine racks of Isobel's cellar, and there was a box of caviare and cheeses. " We should have a party," Ginny said, " but I don't know anyone to ask. And I suppose it would look odd to have a party when Isobel's just dead a few weeks . . ."

Eliot looked up from his study of *A Scholehouse for the Needle*, dated 1624, which a London rare-book dealer had found for him to present to Margaret. " Don't you know yet," he said, " that it will be a long time before this house begins to feel as if Isobel is really dead and buried. Have your party any time—you'll still have a disapproving ghost at it."

Eliot also moved them a little beyond the radius of Tilsit's influence. " Good God, Ginny—this is England! Do you never intend to see any of it? There are other Stately Homes to look at besides yours."

In the Austin Healey he had rented, he and Vanessa and Ginny made trips into the neighbouring counties, to Salisbury and Bristol and down along the Devon coast. Sometimes he let Vanessa drive, admiring her skill and coolness. " She has style," he said, and Ginny knew he was not talking only of the way she handled the car. Looking at Vanessa, in her Emilio Pucci pants and shirt, with the cardigan hung on her shoulders with just the right degree of nonchalance, Ginny had to agree that he was right.

Eliot's presence also took her away from Mark, and Mark was resentful about it. He would not say, though, that he missed her morning visits to the studio or the times when she had left Tilsit after dinner to visit the cottage. He made his complaint about Eliot instead. " If I want to see you these days I've got to go up to the house and sit there and watch you all make fools of yourselves over this stuffed dummy. How long is he going to stay? Doesn't he have any work to do?"

" Eliot works," Ginny said icily.

" Yes—I suppose it's considered quite hard work looking after money. He must be exhausted."

Eliot had been almost two weeks at Tilsit before he went to Mark's studio. There had been a certain reluctance in both him and Ginny to make the visit, Eliot because of the natural irritation roused by Mark's hostility towards him, and Ginny because she had delayed as long as possible the moment when Eliot would see Mark's work and make his judgment.

They went in the afternoon when Ginny knew Mark would be at the Pottery. The day was warm ; there had been no rain for ten days, and the path through the woods and up the slope to the keep smelled of dry leaves and earth. Trip went on ahead of them, side-tracking through the undergrowth in search of rabbits, emerging before them at the top of the hill, and at once diving again out of sight among the fallen slabs. They paused before the descent on the other side of the mound, and for once the sea was calm and warm-looking, the unexpected blue of English summer.

Ginny's spirit rose at the sight of it. Mark's cottage on the headland looked secure and anchored, not the threatened structure she often thought of it as being; the scene was tranquil. All that troubled her was the guilty feel of the key in her hand, the key that Isobel had kept to Mark's cottage and which she had taken this afternoon from Garth. She had asked Mark's permission to bring Eliot, and the consent had been given grudgingly.

"Do what you like. It's no concern of mine. I don't give a damn what he thinks of my work."

They had started down the slope towards the cliff path when Trip's frantic barking arrested Eliot. He turned back towards the spaniel who had taken his usual rooted stance on one of the slabs at the base of the crumbling wall.

"What's the matter with him?" Eliot said to Ginny. "Why doesn't he come?"

"Oh, he never comes down here," she answered tersely. "Leave him be, Eliot."

As usual, Eliot persisted. "But why not? He goes everywhere else with you."

"Because . . ." Ginny faltered on the edge of lying to Eliot, and then decided that it would do no good. "Because he's afraid of Mark. He's afraid of the cliff path and the cottage—ever since Isobel died here. Now, come on," she added shortly, "if you really want to see these things . . ." For a while after, as they made their way silently along the cliff path, the golden warmth of the afternoon seemed chilled, and there was no more beauty in the riot of wild June roses that hung over the fence at the back of the cottage and their dusty scent in the afternoon sun had the reminder of death in it.

Inside the studio though the feeling was different. As always whenever there was something of Mark's, it was dominant. The sculptured shapes, the hanging mobiles swinging eerily through their endless patterns of flight seemed to Ginny to be shouts of affirmation, an understanding of life and a vigour to live it. They were cries of aspiration towards the future. Eliot walked among them saying nothing, the only sound the grating of his heels on the cement floor. He stood before the largest, the man in bronze with the outstretched arms which seemed to dwarf him, for a long time. He looked through the drawings for the Resurrection piece, laying them one by one on the drawing-board and studying them carefully. He mused too, for a long time in the passage where the pots were displayed, turning them about, feeling their texture, while Ginny felt her palms grow wet with the sweat of apprehension. When the silence had become almost damning, Eliot spoke.

"He's good. He's wrong-headed about some things, but he's marvellously, wonderfully confident, and he's brought off some remarkable things. Let's concede his technique is a bit ahead of his humanity—but then he's still young and perhaps that chip will fall off his shoulder and he'll learn he's much like the rest of us. A little compassion in his work, a little more subtlety, and he might be great." Eliot paced back towards Ginny, the tense lines that his face always assumed whenever he became immersed in the study of something harshly played up by the brilliance from the skylights and making him look older and slightly worn. Then he shrugged. "But let's say he never does achieve compassion—let's say that crudity of his is never touched or softened, then the technique would still make him extremely convincing to all but the very few who really care what's at the soul of an artist." He jerked his head to indicate the whole array of the studio. "He could become very fashionable, your boy—and if something should happen to move and shake him sufficiently, he has even a chance to become great."

Then Eliot turned and stood with his back to Ginny, hands in pockets, the light striking his blond head.

"I'll say something else, though. I wouldn't own one of his pieces—except some of those pots out there that he threw when he still had his innocence. But these things—marvellously clever as they are, they give me no warmth. There's no comfort in them. Perhaps they're meant to strike you in the face, so that you know you're still alive because you hurt. Why, I wonder, does he take a devilish delight in telling you all over again that life is awful?"

They walked back along the cliff path without speaking. Trip waited for them at the keep; as Ginny bent to run her hand along his back, she felt the moisture of the unshed tears prick her lashes, an overwhelming sense of desolation at what Eliot had said, a sense, even, of fear.

Back at Tilsit she did not leave Eliot at once, as she had

thought she wanted to do. On impulse, as they entered at the South Front, she said to him, " Come and walk through the house with me. I like it best at this time when the visitors have gone, and the late sun is in the rooms . . . it feels almost then as if it might belong to me."

He nodded, and moved on with her to the Great Hall. The only sound was the gentle scraping of Trip's claws against the stone floor. The western sun still touched the top windows, but the shadows under the gallery were beginning to deepen. A faint draught from somewhere stirred the banners above them as they walked. Eliot stopped before the High Table and turned back to look once again at the carved screen, his gaze seeming to see its hundreds of years all in one instant. " If this belonged to me," he said, picking up her train of thought as if there had been no break, " there'd be no one here except those I wanted. No one would pay their half-crown to come and stare. I would have all of this for myself."

Ginny shook her head. " That wouldn't be right. I've come to feel that it wouldn't be right at all. Even if it were possible to do without the half-crowns, it still wouldn't be right to shut out those who wanted to come. This place can only live by people . . . people within its walls. No one person could pump enough life into it to keep it going . . . It isn't meant to be only a museum." She gestured suddenly to include the whole house. " In any case, even if you could afford to have it all to yourself, it's just not possible. There have been too many people here before you. You must always make room for them—you must always remember that they're here. You always must save space for them, like laying an extra place at table . . ."

Eliot spun round. " Ginny, I think perhaps you're in danger of becoming as crazy as your aunt."

" Perhaps," she acknowledged. " Let's go into the Gold State Room."

She led the way, hardly remembering how strange it had all seemed when Garth had brought her through these passages on that first morning when the will had been read. The Gold Room was splendid, but familiar now, admired, but no longer awesome. The late sun had almost gone from here too, so that the pictures were shadowed. The carved ceiling cast shadows upon itself. The velvet ropes were down, as she liked them to be, giving her the sense that this wonderful, brilliant room was actually to be lived in. She moved to one of the bays and stood looking down over the garden. The gardeners, like the visitors, had departed. The shadows of the balustrades were long on the gravel paths. She breathed in the warm, dry scent of the garden. Some of her mood of fear and apprehension had lifted. " I come here every day," she said.

Eliot stood beside her. " I can imagine your aunt might have done it too," he answered. " And perhaps that stern young woman up in the Long Gallery that you look so much like. Be careful, Ginny. You're treading dangerous ground. This house—this family—is ingrown. There haven't been," he said, with pointed emphasis, " enough men in it in the last hundred years to give it the checks and balances a family and a house needs. It's out of balance."

" There have been men when they were needed," Ginny replied, not defensively, but as a fact.

" But what kind of men?" Eliot persisted. " Your own father was driven out by the express will of Jane Tilsit. He could only have stayed by making himself subordinate to Isobel. Jane Tilsit must have been out of her mind to have excluded him completely—as if she were bent on destroying all her own work here and at the Pottery. How did she suppose it was to carry on? After all, not everyone could expect to have her luck. You don't find a George Martin very often—not right on your own doorstep . . ."

" Isobel did. She found Mark."

" And you think Mark is for you?" Eliot moved in close to her, his eyes seemed to glitter in sudden, uncharacteristic intensity. " You think you will be Jane Tilsit all over again with her humble potter? If that's what you think, then I'm telling you to watch out. This is no humble potter you've taken hold of—this is a man with a creative drive so strong he could destroy you and this house and everything it stands for. The way he destroyed Isobel."

" He did not! He did not do that!" Ginny turned on him in a kind of desperate fury. " How could Mark destroy anything? You said it yourself—he's a creator, Eliot!—a maker, a builder!"

Eliot shook his head. " He's also a man so obsessed with his own vision of what he has to achieve that he's capable of striking down whatever seems to threaten that end. He's jealous, this man—he won't share credit for what he's done with anyone else. Isobel forced him to be what he is. She even gave him the resentment and the anger that made an artist out of a craftsman. He won't acknowledge that debt. And he is capable of letting her die so that she would cease to make her claims on him."

She drew in a breath of horror. "This is only what you *think*. You don't know—no one knows."

"Mark knows. Have you asked him, Ginny? Have you dared to ask that question?"

He took her arm, a gesture in Eliot so rare that it was startling. "I know this man," he said. "I know men in ways you never could. I know strengths and weaknesses because I search for signs in a man that a woman doesn't look for —and signs a normal man doesn't look for, either. There's nothing that pleases me in Mark Barstow. But I have to respect his talent, and because of it I'm afraid for you. As much as he's capable of twisting his metal and shaping his stone into images of power, so he's capable of destroying whatever interferes with his own image of himself. You could tear each other to pieces. You'd not be able to handle him, Ginny. You're neither as skilful as Vanessa, nor as strong as Isobel. And you're not that poor tormented creature in the portrait upstairs either. You're not poverty-stricken in the way she was—you were far richer than she when you stood on the steps that night in New York when I first saw you. You don't have to settle for her kind of life. Don't be fooled, Ginny." He repeated the warning, more urgently, his fingers digging into the flesh of her arm. "Don't let yourself be fooled by all this."

The words seemed to echo through the length of the room, a soft whisper, an intimation of danger: " . . . don't be fooled . . . be fooled . . ." His hand dropped away from her, and she was left with the warning and the renewal of the fear.

V

Eliot left Tilsit the next day, announcing his departure with a suddenness that shook Ginny. She had a feeling as she watched Garth fuss over stowing Eliot's bags with great

nicety into the Austin Healey, that she was not the only one
at Tilsit affected by his going. Vanessa came to say good-
bye, and lingered, as if she regretted his leaving, and even
Margaret came down from the needlework room. There was
a kind of false animation in them all as they stood there—
but not in Eliot. It would be lonely at Tilsit when he had
gone, Ginny thought, and the problems that his presence had
seemed to hold in abeyance would mount again ; they would
go back to meals for which no one bothered to dress
and at which the conversation died a slow death. There
would be no Eliot to shield them from each other.

The dull throb of the Austin Healey's engine almost drowned
Eliot's words as he gave her his brief cool kiss on the
cheek. "Save yourself—while you still can."

Then he was gone down the drive and over the bridge.
The sense of let-down was already sharp. Ginny waved,
but there was no answering wave from Eliot. From behind
her in the doorway came Vanessa's voice. "Well—it was
fun while it lasted." And then the sharp little laugh. "Now
we can creep back into our cells again."

Ginny made a move to call Trip, thinking that she would
walk to Mark's cottage. But something held her back, the
memory of Eliot's inescapable question yesterday in the
Long Gallery. "Mark knows. Have you asked him, Ginny?
Have you dared to ask that question?" She had never dared
—she did not dare now. But she could not trust herself to
face Mark with the anguish and fear freshly reawakened.
So she turned and went inside with the others. Garth
closed the door with his usual deft, quiet movement, but
it seemed to Ginny that it slammed shut on her, and all the
light was blocked out. The house took her back and engulfed
her, and upstairs in her room, Brown was hovering, eyeing
her with a strange eagerness, as if she had just returned
from a journey.

CHAPTER FIVE

The weather broke after Eliot left ; they had days of inter-
mittent showers, with gusty winds that blew in from the
Channel. The petals of the June roses lay wetly on the

gravel walks. At Tilsit they settled back into routine, and the festive air was gone. The hours now had a leaden feeling about them, and the days appeared to pass so slowly that to Ginny they seemed to be double their length; it seemed much longer than only three days after Eliot's departure when the routine was broken abruptly by Trip's disappearance.

The spaniel was not waiting for Ginny when she went to her room after dinner; she listened for the gentle scratching at the door but nothing happened to disturb her as she reached, by habit, to take down the diaries. She had made the pretence, up to this point, of tolerating Trip because his grieving and searching for Isobel had made it impossible to deny him cursory comfort. But without the silken body curled in the basket before the fire the room seemed emptier than ever before, and bigger; she knew she actively missed the spaniel, the occasional raising of his head, the ceaseless inquiry of his brown eyes, the sigh and the stretching before he settled down again. These things had given her comfort also, but she had not known that until they were missing.

Before she got into bed she went downstairs again, checking all the rooms, even unbarring and opening the door of the South Front to peer unseeingly into the rainy darkness, and to call the dog's name uselessly to the wind. As she closed the door Brown was there on the staircase, a scarecrow figure in a long, faded robe and a grey plait of hair hanging on her shoulder.

" Is something wrong, Miss Virginia?"

" It's Trip—he hasn't come in. I can't find him."

" I fed him myself, miss—and then he went outside. I felt sure someone in the kitchen had let him in again. It's not like him to stay out. He's never given any trouble like this before. . . . He was always with Miss Isobel, so no one ever had to go and look for him . . . Shall I call Garth, miss?"

" No, don't do that. He'll be here in the morning, I'm sure. He's probably in the stables, or somewhere like that. I don't think he would have gone looking . . . well, he'll be all right, I'm sure."

And yet she didn't quite believe the words, even as she spoke them. A vague uneasiness troubled her, and she slept badly, waking several times to go and open the bedroom door on the chance that Trip might be there. And each time she went back, passing the window, she saw the reflected glow from the great lighted skylights of Mark's studio; she was able to take a small comfort from the sight.

In the morning she was up before sunrise and out searching the garden, working her way down the terraces and along the course of the stream, away from the sea, making detours to several farm-houses to make inquiries about the dog. After an hour's walking she turned back again and cut across the fields to join the stream again where it ran under the stone bridge near Tilsit. When she drew level with the keep she hesitated, wondering whether to follow the stream in the wide bend it took away from the house, or to climb the slope of the keep and begin the search among the half-buried cellars and the rabbit holes. At that moment she turned and looked back at Tilsit, and the sight stopped her short. With the rain and the wind spent, the calm of early morning had a kind of radiance that dazzled her, and in this radiance Tilsit was like something remembered from a fairy-tale, the chimneys and crenellated roofs like a shining city, the pale washed blue of the sky a silken back-drop to its pale stone pile. Every leaf and every blade of grass trembled with its weight of moisture brilliant in the early sun, the damp earth was dark and sweet-smelling. The whole scene seemed to Ginny to be as it might have been when Tilsit was new, when the first roof was laid on the first walls that rose, the age of its innocence, fresh and untouched.

Into this world of purity and peace burst the anguished sounds of Brown's outrage. The woman had appeared sud-denly on the skyline at the edge of the keep, her gaunt figure racing through the fallen stones like a driven fury. She cradled something in her arms like a child. Ginny began to run up the slope.

Trip's body in Brown's arms was convulsed with pain, and had stiffened in that attitude, the long curling hair was matted with blood.

"That man did it!" Brown cried, her voice rising to a shriek. "He had to do it to this innocent creature as well as to her!"

Ginny fought her sense of horror as she laid her hand on the cold wet body. "Where did you find him?"

"Down the cliff—where that man threw him. I had to

climb down the cliff!" Now a sob of rage tore at Brown. "He couldn't let this poor dumb animal live because it knew what kind he was! He couldn't be easy while the dog was alive—so he had to kill it!"

Ginny experienced a swift and sickening growth of doubt. "Take him back to the house," she said to Brown. "I'll be along in a while."

Brown's rage faded into concern. "You're surely not going near that man, miss . . .? Miss—come back! Miss Virginia . . .!"

Ginny didn't wait to answer her as she started to run through the long grass and the fallen slabs towards the cliff path.

VI

Mark sat in the living-room of the cottage, an overflowing ash-tray on the floor beside his feet. He was not smoking when she opened the door; he was collapsed limply in the chair, his arms hanging over the sides as if he could not support the weight of them. His face was pale and drained-looking, the black stubble of his beard lay like a thick shadow on it. He barely turned his head as Ginny entered, and that was the only acknowledgment he offered of her presence. Ginny closed the door and stood with her back against it.

"Brown found Trip," she said.

There was no response from Mark, only the smallest movement of his lips.

"I said," she repeated, "that Brown has found Trip."

"What?" He turned and looked at her, his eyes dull and red-rimmed. "What did you say?"

"Didn't you hear what I said?"

He shook his head, as if trying to clear it. "I'm tired, I've worked all the night. What time is it?"

"Didn't you hear what I said?" she asked again.

"What did you say, then?"

"Brown has found Trip."

"So . . .? Was he lost?"

"Trip is dead. Brown found him on the cliff." She

stumbled over the ugliness of it. "Did you kill Trip, Mark? Did you hit him—or something—and then throw him down the cliff?"

His body exploded into life; he jerked upright in the chair, the toe of his shoe catching the brimming ash-tray and overturning it.

"What in God's name are you talking about?"

"Trip! I said Trip, didn't I?" Her voice was rising, slicing shrilly into the air. "Did you hurt him? Did you kill him?"

"Do you think I killed him?"

"Did you?"

"Why would I do that?" His face had flushed in a dark rage. The sinews of his neck stood out like cords; he clenched his fingers back into his palms. Now she felt the menace of his strength.

"Because . . . because . . ." She shook her head, suddenly covering her mouth with her hand. When she spoke again her voice came out as a shaky whisper. "Forgive me . . . I don't know what I'm saying."

He was not appeased. "I know what you're saying, all right! You think I killed that miserable creature just because he happened to have been her dog? You think I'm mad enough to do that!"

"Brown said . . ."

He cut her off. "Brown! What the hell has Brown to do with it? We're listening to Brown now, are we? What she says is suddenly more important than what I say. And why am I supposed to have killed the bloody dog? Go on —say it! Why—why?"

"Because Trip *knew.*"

"Knew—knew what?"

"Trip knew what happened the night that Isobel died. He knew what happened. He's the only one—besides yourself."

Now he got to his feet, his fatigue obvious in the clumsiness of the movement. He thrust his hands into his pants' pockets, taking the familiar stance with his legs wide apart. His voice was a low rumble of anger. He seemed to be striving for control.

"At the inquest I told them that I knew nothing about what happened to Isobel after she left this place."

"That's what you told them."

" And you don't think it's the truth?"

" I want to hear what's the truth. Now I want to hear it. *Now*, Mark!"

His movement was slow and deliberate, heavy. His foot kicked the ash-tray again as he turned; he walked across the room towards the passage that led to the back. She knew at once that if she didn't stop him this was probably the only answer she would get.

" Where are you going?"

" Where? Where doesn't matter." At the doorway he wheeled to face her once more. " Anywhere that's not here."

" You mean you're leaving—leaving Tilsit?"

" Leaving Tilsit? Does that shock you? Are you really so much like her that the thought of leaving Tilsit seems impossible? Well, I *am* leaving—and the time for it was long ago. I should have left before Isobel had her chance to bind me so close I couldn't breathe, and long before—yes, long before I was daft enough to imagine that loving you would change any of this—or that you could be different because I loved you. You can't be different. You are Tilsit—no, don't shake your head at me because you're not able to stand outside this and see what you are. You were Tilsit the first moment I laid eyes on you, and I said it truly then and didn't have the sense to know how right I was. You were Tilsit long before that time—without you even knowing it. The Tilsits never could love and be damned to the consequences. They have to say first, ' What's good for Tilsit?'—and the rest of it always follows that."

" I said none of that! I came because of Trip . . ."

" Because you think I might have killed the bloody animal? And because that would mean I have been responsible—directly or indirectly—for Isobel's death."

Suddenly he raised his hand and pointed at her. " Then let me tell you. You still came here as a Tilsit. You came to hold me to account. If you believed I had nothing to do with what happened to Isobel you wouldn't even need to ask about Trip. If there is any doubt, then it exists to the very heart of this thing—all the way through. And I've been a blasted fool to think of loving where doubt existed. The two don't live together. And I've been more than a fool to think of loving a Tilsit."

His hand dropped down to his side again limply and he

suddenly let out a wild and bitter laugh. "Love a Tilsit? Expect a Tilsit to love me? I must have been out of my mind. The Tilsits don't love men—they use them!"

Ginny slumped back against the door, the strength of anger and suspicion that had brought her here suddenly seeming to desert her body. She heard the cry of her father's bitterness here. She had no answer.

"And let me tell you another thing," Mark went on. "You didn't inherit me along with all the rest. I belong to myself. Remember that!"

As he walked along the passage back towards the studio his booming voice reached back to her. "You can get someone else to fill in at the Pottery—and you can find another tenant for this place. I'm finished here!" The pounding, exultant triumph of his voice hit her like a blow. "Right now—I'm finished with the Tilsits!"

CHAPTER SIX

"So Mark has gone . . ." Vanessa said. "Well, he'll be back. Mark always comes back."

Ginny raised her head to look at Vanessa, who stood before her on one of the terrace walks. Ginny had been sitting huddled on a garden seat since she had come back from the cottage, and because the sun was shining and it was near noon, she knew that the coldness was in herself. "How do you know he's gone?"

"He telephoned the Pottery. Father telephoned here. It will be a nine-day wonder. Some people will hope he doesn't come back, but he will come."

"No," Ginny said. "I don't think he will come back this time."

"Nonsense." Vanessa gave her strange laugh. "Tilsit's as much in Mark's blood as in yours and mine. What you don't realise is that you don't have to be born a Tilsit . . . it's a disease, an addiction. Mark has it. He'll be back."

Ginny did not believe that, and the days of regret were long and slow after Mark went. They were bitter days, days of self-questioning and doubt. The routine was broken with

a vengeance and nothing came to take its place. Ginny
did not go to the Pottery, nor did she try any more to work
through the bundles of papers in Isobel's office. There was
no longer the necessity to walk with Trip, and no reason
at all to go near the cottage. Letters came from Randall about
matters that concerned the estate; she laid them aside without
reading them. Stripped of the morning's visit to Mark, the
daily observance of his work, the silent and tender hours
before the fire, the day now had no heart or core. She
found herself wandering the passages and galleries of Tilsit
opening doors of rooms she had never seen before, opening
cupboards, flinging back the dust-sheets from furniture in
the storage-rooms; but she did none of this as Eliot had
done it, sparked by curiosity. It was done only to attempt
to assuage the restlessness that gnawed at her, to tire herself a
little so that there might be a few hours of sleep at night to
give her respite.

" Did I love him?" She said the question at last aloud
as she came face to face with her own image imperfectly
reflected in one of the showcases of the Porcelain Gallery. The
strained and pinched face of a stranger looked back at her.
" If I loved him could I have doubted him? He knew that
I doubted him . . . and so he went and I lost him. And what
if he did kill Trip? . . and what if he did let Isobel die?
Do I care so much—or do I love him so much that I can
say none of it mattered? Do I love him that much—not to
care?"

The image gave her back no true answer, and then suddenly
she was aware that two visitors had entered the gallery and
were standing staring at her, listening to this dialogue of
fantasy and despair. She had forgotten that it was one of
the public days at Tilsit, days when she would encounter at
every turn strangers who had paid their half-crown and had
a perfect right to stand and stare at her as these two did.
In their expressions of shock she caught a glimpse of the
kind of madness they had ascribed to her.

She turned and raced out of the gallery, through to the
new wing, and upstairs to her bedroom, and there waited, not
Trip, and for once not Brown either, but only the diaries.

Isobel's diaries were the only thing that held her through
these days because by careful searching she found the many
references to Mark that Isobel had made during the years

N

of his growing up and his working at the Pottery and the cottage. She even found the first entry of all that related to Mark. "*I have found a young boy, hardly more than a child, who shows remarkable skill and subtlety with his hands. Whether this is a mere childish facility or whether he has the capability for growth and development we will only tell in time.*" Then a year later Ginny found: "*Mark Barstow visited the house to-day. What a boor that boy is, and how unfortunate. But what vitality—and his talent grows.*" The year that Mark had been seventeen Isobel had written, "*Mark has spent the summer living at Tilsit and working at the Pottery. A disaster in many ways—things have been damaged, a horse dead through carelessness and bad judgment, a dog dead, a kitchen maid in hysterics—and yet all of us have been aware of a dynamic presence here whose upsets must be endured for the things he brings to the place. His confidence must not be shaken. He responds, though, to firmness.*" Later was the entry: "*When he is fully in control of himself and his material, his talent is formidable. Tilsit has much need of him. There must be a way to keep him for Tilsit.*"

As Ginny read through the following years in the diary her interest was only for Mark—the triumphs, the setbacks, and Isobel's growing concern with how she would keep him there. But if nothing else interested Ginny, she still could not miss that the greatest passion of the diary at this stage was poured out over Vanessa's marriage, the efforts to have it dissolved, the attempt to bring her back to Tilsit. When everything had failed there was a sullen silence from Isobel on the subject of Vanessa. It was as if Vanessa did not exist any more.

A little before the date at which Isobel had appeared in the convent of Santa Maria Ginny found the words: "*Mark is showing signs of far too much interest in a girl from Bournemouth—Sara Conyingham. It has to be stopped. She would never do at Tilsit.*" Then two weeks later: "*I have talked with Sara Conyingham. I think she will not be any further trouble.*" In that way, with or without his knowledge or consent, Mark's life was disposed and ordered.

On the last page of that diary Ginny found the first reference to herself:

" *John's daughter is now old enough to judge where her best interests lie. I mean to bring her to Tilsit.*"

After that there were no more entries. The remainder of the pages had been neatly clipped from the book. With a sense of frustration Ginny searched among all the other notebooks bound in the dark-blue leather that was Isobel's mark, but all of them pre-dated the one in which the entries stopped. Isobel had never recorded the visit to Santa Maria, nor the sending of the cheese knife to St. Nicolaas. Isobel's story ended at this point, as abruptly as if it had been then, not two years later, that she had died.

II

Margaret raised her head and looked at Ginny without question as she entered the room. For a moment she said nothing, then faintly she nodded.

" You've come then. I have wondered when you would come." It was said without reproach, only as a statement of fact. Ginny had the feeling that Margaret might have spent many years waiting in this room for those who had never come, and that if no one at all came it was of no particular concern to Margaret.

Ginny offered no excuse or apology. To reach this room one had to go through the solar and the Great Bedchamber where hung the Memling and the Holbein drawing that Eliot had loved, through the velvet ropes, through an ante-chamber with a gilded ceiling, to this room at the very end of the wing, whose windows looked north, south and east, and whose brightness thus served to offset the darkness of the ancient panelling. It was a smaller, more intimate room, and a very beautiful one, with the smell of wool and canvas, and the smell of the bowl of flowers set on a small table, and the oblique shafts of the late afternoon sun showing up the dust motes in the air, and silvering Margaret's hair as she sat bent over the standing embroidery frame. The room was sparsely furnished, just two chairs and a large oak side-table, and two oak presses placed between the windows. A loom was set up in one corner.

Ginny closed the door and began to walk slowly around

the length of the room, regretting now that she had so far avoided coming here, and had been driven here now only because her restlessness had brought her finally to this door and for the first time she had opened it. The impression she received was at once stronger and more forceful than anything Margaret herself projected away from this place. The deep quiet, the tranquillity suggested not so much a retreat as a fortress manned against the intrusions of the outside world. Ginny saw now that Margaret did not escape to this place, but that she withdrew.

"This is a lovely room," she said.

Margaret had resumed her work. "Yes," she said. "Isobel gave it to me at the time when I started the work of repairing the big tapestries. We had to have special frames—and I need a place that has the natural light for as many hours as is possible. In this wing, of course, there is no artificial light so my working hours are much longer in summer than winter. It makes me very conscious of the seasons."

"You have a good view."

"Yes—I rest my eyes every half-hour by getting up and going to look out. The view over the garden is my favourite. From the east windows you can see over the whole valley— only the Porcelain China Gallery would have the same view, but the east windows there were blocked up and the second floor was taken out to give it its height." Her voice went on gently, imperturbably, while the needle flashed with speed and accuracy through the canvas. Ginny came closer to the frame at which Margaret sat.

"What are you working on?"

"This is the centre panel for a new bed-cover for the Great Bedchamber. It will be appliquéd to a blue velvet background."

"It seems different from the one there now."

Margaret nodded. "As far as I've been able to research, the one there now was made in Jane Tilsit's time with the coat-of-arms decoration. That was an innovation, and out of character for Tilsit. So I've reverted to the flower and bird motif that's in the wall-hanging in the solar. It's almost a copy—a few additions of my own. It's true seventeenth-century style—which was when all the rooms on this side were repanelled—the same time the Long Gallery was built. . . ."

Ginny leaned back against the casement. "You know the history of this house as well as Vanessa."

With Margaret's head bent over the frame it was impossible to read her expression. "I've had a long time to learn it."

"Did you . . . did you know this house before you were married?"

"Yes. I grew up near here. In those days, when Isobel and her brother were growing up, there was a good deal more visiting around, though Tilsit never was a place for much social activity. It was only gayer by contrast to what it had been when Jane Tilsit was young, and her daughter Elizabeth. When Jane was an old lady—I met Jane Tilsit several times —she tried to open up the place here to encourage the young men to come round courting Isobel. But one always felt that it was only temporary, and as soon as Isobel and her brother were married, Tilsit would close up again. That's how I knew it when I was young."

"You knew my father then? You must have known him quite well."

There was the briefest break in the rhythm of the flashing needle. It spoke more strongly than the slight change of tone. "Yes, I knew him quite well."

In the next half minute the pace of the hand speeded up as if to catch up for those lost seconds. Finally, when Margaret spoke again her voice had the finest edge of eagerness to it, a shade of difference that matched the increased speed of her hands.

"I've often wondered," she said, "what your father's life was like after he left Tilsit. It was so hard to imagine him away from Tilsit. All I knew—we knew—was that he was somewhere in the West Indies. I have never travelled, you see . . . it was difficult to picture him . . ."

"On St. Nicolaas . . .?" Ginny paused and caught her breath, and then, for the first time since she had come to Tilsit she was able to talk without restraint of St. Nicolaas, about the life there, without watching words or wondering if she bored her listener. The needle continued to flash in the sunlight in steady rhythm as she began to talk about Oranje

Huis, about the gardens that were a small rendering of Tilsit's terraces, of the days under the hot sun and the nights of unclouded skies and swift rain squalls, of the gentle monotony of life, the quick exhausting months of the sugar harvest, the slow months of cultivation. Somehow into her words came the picture of a life lived richly on the verge of poverty, of acceptance and loyalty. Somehow, also, she must have suggested love, because once Margaret interrupted her.

"And your mother—what kind of woman is she? I wondered . . . it was hard to think what kind of woman your father had married . . ." It was said so gently that there was no possibility of taking offence, and for Margaret to have asked this question at all precluded any refusal of an answer.

"My mother . . . I think she is beautiful . . ." Ginny visualised her mother and was at once conscious of the contrast between these two women, and wondered if it were possible to describe Katrien's earthy solid qualities of strength to this wispish vague creature who only here in this room had taken on some real substance. "She is very different from my father," Ginny said. "But I think she suited him very well. She was . . . good for him."

Margaret nodded over the frame. "One didn't know what his life was like. He loved Tilsit—it was hard to picture him away from here . . ." The words, spoken softly, seemed to suggest that what Ginny had said was not quite the truth. Suddenly Ginny knew that Margaret hoped it was not quite the truth. "It doesn't sound like him—working so hard for all those years, missing all the things he used to enjoy so much—tennis and sailing and seeing his friends. But—I'm glad he was happy."

"Happy?" She had never asked the question herself fully, because it seemed too much to commit her father either way, and too childlike to expect a life to be summed up in such an easy word. Content, perhaps? No, John Tilsit had never been a contented man, never could be. She had to risk the stronger judgment. "Happy?—yes, he was happy. I believe he was. Finally I think he knew it. At least that's what I think he tried to tell me. It was a shock to find out that he might only just have realised it for himself. It was late but it was enough, I think."

"I'm glad," Margaret said again. This time it was more

than a polite formula; the tone carried more conviction and even a hint of acceptance. " I'm glad Johnnie was happy."

" Johnnie . . ." The name was breathed like a gentle sigh, handled carefully like something prized and seldom used. Only Lord Chardley, her father's friend, had ever called him that.

" You called him Johnnie," she said.

The needle stopped completely; the hands came to rest on the tapestry frame.

" Anyone he loved always called him Johnnie. He loved me."

Ginny's audible gasp caused Margaret to raise her head. She looked directly at Ginny and the vague voice was suddenly crisp and almost decisive. " You don't believe that? I tell you that he loved me. And I loved him. We would have been married if Isobel hadn't stopped it."

" Isobel stopped it? I didn't think my father would have allowed . . ." There was a doubt in Ginny that grew as she saw that Margaret's brilliant blue eyes had a strange fixity in them, nearly a hypnotised stare; and Ginny remembered how very seldom it was that one was able to see directly into Margaret's eyes—they were veiled or turned away, their direction wandering if they did not focus on her embroidery. Now they compelled Ginny with their riveted gaze.

" She stopped it! Yes, she stopped it!" The words burst out as if they had waited for a long time to be said. " It was not that Johnnie allowed it. He loved me—I know he loved me. But Isobel didn't want us to marry. I was all right for Lawrence, you see, but not for Johnnie. Johnnie was a Tilsit and he had to have someone of more importance, someone with some money. That's what Isobel thought. She didn't understand what it was to love someone, or how it could hurt . . . Oh yes, it hurt. It hurt so much that I let myself be tricked. If I had trusted Johnnie's love enough I wouldn't have let myself be tricked. But I was young, you see, and Isobel was a strong woman. Everyone always did what Isobel said without question—I always did it. I didn't think that she would trick me. I didn't understand that she would lie to make things come out as she wanted them. One never thought of Isobel as having to lie about anything. Whatever she wanted always seemed to come about without her having to do anything more than to say it would be so. She didn't seem the kind who lied, you see . . ."

Now the slim white hands were clenched; two patches of colour showed crudely on Margaret's cheeks, oddly at variance with her delicate looks. With a kind of pity Ginny said softly: " How did Isobel trick you?"

The words came in a rush; it hadn't been necessary to question her; there was no stopping the flood now. " It was just after the law-suit had gone against Johnnie—the time of the accident at the Pottery. I hadn't seen Isobel all the time the suit was on—she knew whose side I was on, of course, and Johnnie wasn't living at Tilsit himself then. He had a court order permitting him to stay at Tilsit, but he was actually living at the cottage that Mark has now—it used to be a sort of a playhouse for Isobel and Johnnie when they were young. So I always went there to see him, and I never came near the house. When I heard about the accident I knew how upset Johnnie would be. I had to come and see him. But he wasn't at the cottage. I was really desperate to see him, you understand. I hadn't seen him since the judgment—that was the day before. It affected us very much, you know. He hadn't actually asked me to marry him—I was only eighteen that year—but it was understood between us that we would make things definite when the decision came about the inheritance. We didn't expect it—Johnnie and I—to go against him. So there I was. I was uncertain what he would do . . . whether he would stay on here, or go. But he wasn't at the cottage, so I came to Tilsit in the hope that he would be here. But he wasn't. I was shown in to see Isobel instead."

A faint shudder racked her now. " I can remember it all so well. She was young then, you know—in her twenties. Very good-looking, with her fair hair. She hadn't had her accident then. But very strong features for a woman. I was afraid of her. I always had been. That day I was shown into the office. It looked just as it does now. I expected her to be upset about what had happened at the Pottery, but when I tried to say something about it she cut me short. I had the feeling that she thought it was none of my business, that I had no right to interfere. That hurt me, because I knew that she knew how it was between Johnnie and myself. She wouldn't talk about the Pottery or about Johnnie. She was

opening up a box of new china that had just come from
the Pottery, and she went on with it with me standing there
watching. She said it was a new design, and I asked her
how she had managed that when she hadn't been allowed
to have anything to do with the Pottery. She just laughed
at me and said, ' You don't think I've paid any attention
to all that nonsense? I've gone on just as before, but I've
been a little discreet about it. After all, one of us had to
carry on—there had to be new lines prepared for the time
when I could go back officially to running the Pottery. I
couldn't hold things up completely while John played his
ridiculous games. I knew he would thank me when he
realised how foolish he had been. He'll come to his senses, of
course, and start acting as he should have done from the
beginning.'

" I remember very well what she said because all that time
she was lifting the packing from around the china. And
then she brought out the first cup. 'How do you like it?'
she said to me, and she put the cup into my hand. It was
cruel—so cruel. I remember that my hands couldn't hold it.
It fell to the ground between the two of us, and broke."

Now the hands were wrung together in remembered anguish.
" It was the Bluebell pattern, and the idea for it had come
on a day, just before the Old Lady died, when Johnnie and
I and Isobel had been together in the woods on the other
side of the stream, and Johnnie had picked bluebells for me.
I had said how pretty they would look on china, and Johnnie
had said he'd have a pattern created to see how it would
look, and perhaps it should go into the line . . . Well, she
had had it done behind his back, and now it was here in my
hand. I turned it over, and there, beside the Tilsit mark,
was stamped the name Edgeley. I knew at once what it meant.
It wasn't very usual to put the name of a pattern on the
china itself. I said to her, 'It's called Edgeley.' 'Yes,'
she said. ' I thought it would be a nice gesture to D ana
Edgeley when the engagement is announced.' ' Engagement?'
I said. And Isobel just shrugged and looked surprised, as
if I should have known all about it. ' You are out of
touch, aren't you,' she said. ' There's been an understanding
about an engagement between Diana and John since they
were children. But of course nothing could be announced
while all this nonsense of the will was going on. But John

knows what he has to do now. He's going to marry Diana as we always planned, and the Edgeley money will come into the Pottery. It won't be like letting in an outsider then —after all the money will be in the family, and we do need the money. So it's very satisfactory all around, isn't it?' And she gave me that queer smile of hers. 'What about me?' I said. She smiled at me again, as if I were a child. 'You? —my dear, I imagine you'll marry Lawrence as he's been wanting you to. He's been very patient, you know—he's really been wanting to marry you since you were fourteen. That's what you should do. You should marry Lawrence.'"

Margaret focused glassy, brilliant eyes once more on Ginny, dragging herself out of a scene of more than thirty years ago. "I believed her," she said. "I believed that Johnnie would have chosen to stay on at Tilsit no matter what happened. And there wasn't any place for me. I believed her, and she knew I would. She knew I could never go and ask Johnnie if it were true. I wasn't sure enough of myself to do that. I wasn't sure enough of Johnnie. I wasn't really sure then that he loved me."

"How were you sure—afterwards?"

A flash of triumph and pleasure came into Margaret's eyes, the beginning of a return to her normal posture which, for the first time, Ginny recognised as having always contained a degree of smugness.

"I knew. I was very sure—afterwards. You see, I did as Isobel told me." The hands fluttered helplessly. "After all what else was there to do if I couldn't have Johnnie? I went to Lawrence and said I would marry him."

Fascinated at this assurance, Ginny said, "But did you know before Isobel told you that Lawrence wanted to marry you?"

"Of course," Margaret said with a touch of impatience. "He'd wanted to for a long time—but Johnnie was the better match, of course. I told him I would marry him at once—I didn't want to wait around then. We just got into Lawrence's car and drove to Scotland. Lawrence didn't want to do it that way, but he gave in. We were married in the morning in Scotland, and Lawrence sent a telegram to my parents and to Isobel. And then we came back. Isobel had had the accident that ruined her face, and Johnnie was gone. *That* was how I finally knew he loved me. You see, he'd gone. There never was an engagement. And when the new china pattern did get to be manufactured it was never called anything but the Bluebell pattern. So you see! I got that back."

Margaret's tone had gone back to its familiar dead calm again. The hands no longer moved agitatedly. She stroked them together as if to restore their normal momentum, and then she took up the needle again and threaded a fresh piece of silk. The needle began to flash in and out of the canvas once more.

" So you see," she continued, " I've often wondered about Johnnie—what *his* life was like. He always stayed the way he looked to me then, always young and handsome. There has never been a change in Johnnie. And as for myself— I've had my work here, and Tilsit."

" And that has been enough?"

A brief, secret smile came to Margaret's face, and was quickly wiped away. " Yes. I've had my satisfactions. It was something to know that Isobel had many years to regret stopping Johnnie and myself marrying. Johnnie would have stayed if we had married. And every time I looked at Isobel, at her dreadful face, I had the greatest proof that Johnnie had loved me."

The morbid pleasure in Margaret's tone laid a chill on Ginny. " What do you mean by that?"

The flood of words had run dry. Ginny could almost see this woman's personality shrinking and fading, closing up like the night-blooming flower before the heat of day. The speeded-up action of her hands indicated that there had been one question too many. She had withdrawn again.

" Just what I said, my dear. No more than that. There was no need to know more than that. What I knew was enough." With a deft movement the little embroidery scissors snipped off a thread.

It was then that Ginny leaned in closely to look at the work on the frame, suddenly now seeing with enlightened eyes Margaret's long obsession that lay revealed. Around the central motif was a stylised border of a chain of bluebells, the innocent, unsophisticated blossom worked in incredible detail so that it was possible to see that the edges of the petals were darkened and curling, as if they had been stung with some blight. And Ginny at once remembered how many dozens of times, in all the lavish needlework at Tilsit, on bed-covers and curtains and chair-covers, the same theme was repeated, so that wherever she went within these walls, Isobel's eyes could not have avoided it. And Ginny shrunk back a little in horror and awe at the thought of this woman who had had a lifetime of silent revenge, and of Isobel who had had silently to endure it.

III

When she left Margaret, Ginny wandered through the passages and rooms of Tilsit with a deepening conviction that in all its vastness there was nowhere to go. Whatever she encountered—pictures, books, ornaments, tapestries—all of it was marked and somehow soiled by the thought of the price that had been paid to keep it, and the thought that each person within its walls had paid their own price to stay here. The knowledge that possession was costly grew in her; the price had always to be paid in whatever coin. The struggle to deny this knowledge, or to evade it, drove her out of the house and along the familiar path to the cliff and Mark's cottage.

The emptiness of the cottage greeted her with a savage reproach, and the sense of loss was sharp. "Why did I let him go?" she said aloud to the empty sitting-room and the dead ashes of the fire. She moved slowly through the cottage touching things that were Mark's, fondling the small pieces of pottery that stood about, the contrast to Tilsit, where she had wanted to touch nothing, fresh in her mind. He had taken very little from the place—most of his clothes still hung in the cupboard, a book was open where he had left it, the overturned ash-tray from that last morning still lay on the floor. The place spoke strongly of his presence, intimately and closely, so that she kept glancing towards the door to the studio half expecting him to come in. But he didn't come, and she knew that he had telephoned Randall to say that he was making arrangements to have his personal belongings and the pottery and sculpture removed. But the place still breathed of the life he had given it, and she remained grateful.

The dusk advanced, and she had no inclination to go back

to Tilsit. In the still air, with the arrival of the darkness, a mist came down on the surface of the sea, hanging along the cliff face and growing thicker until it pressed wetly against the windows. More to dispel the sense of forlornness than against the chill, she got a fire going in the grate and brought a supper of sardines and biscuits and tea to the hearth. Then she brought Mark's Scotch from the cupboard in the kitchen and added it to the tea. As the warmth of it met her lips it only seemed to heighten the sense of the coldness inside her, the wretched groping for him, the desolation and self-blame because the knowledge grew that when she had confronted him in this room a week ago she had placed Tilsit before him, and had lost him. He had spoken the truth when he had said, " You *are* Tilsit . . ." In those minutes she had been Tilsit, and as much a mouthpiece for Isobel as if the dead woman had spoken herself. And Mark had chosen freedom rather than submission.

She wondered if her father had ever understood himself the freedom that he had won by the circumstances that had driven him from Tilsit, the freedom from bondage to two women, Margaret as well as Isobel, both of them half mad with their obsession. She wondered if he had gone in the realisation that he sought his own salvation in leaving, or had he gone sick with defeat at Isobel's hands and the sudden knowledge that Margaret was married to another man. She hoped that somehow her father had come to realise, even if it had been late, what a g.ft was the freedom to be his own man. She thought of Katrien and hoped desperately that John had known what a rare prize had been her sanity and her strength, her lack of possessiveness, the marvellous restraint, the ability to keep her hands off those she loved. She had a sudden conviction as she sat staring into the fire, that Katrien would have understood Mark's going, would have believed it necessary and right.

She stayed until the supply of wood by the hearth was used up, and the flames had died to red embers. Then she put the fireguard carefully about the grate, thinking that the only good she could now do for Mark was to safeguard the things he treasured. And then she took his flashlamp and started along the cliff path, the beam from the lamp deflected and dulled by the curtain of mist.

IV

" The family were beginning to grow anxious, Miss Virginia." Garth regarded Ginny reproachfully as she entered the
hall at Tilsit, staring at her mist-soaked hair, the flashlamp
in her hand. " It might be as well, miss, if in the future . . ."
His voice trailed into silence because it was plain that Ginny
had paid him no attention, was not hearing his words.

" Of course, Garth," she said automatically as she began
to mount the stairs. " Of course." He stood below her in
the hall, and a sense of foreboding touched him as he noted
the rigidity of the slender figure, the way she did not touch the
stair-rail, the air of withdrawal that moved with her. He
was about to call to her, unthinkable as it was that he should
raise his voice, " Miss . . ." but the words died there as
he recognised that he had no power at the moment to break
into that trance-like state. He let her go, the rich blonde hair
like a warm light in the dimness of the panelled stair.
She was lost to sight then, her footsteps muffled on the
carpet of the passage. Then came the sound of her bedroom
door opening and closing. Garth sighed, and began the
lengthy process of locking up for the night.

The fire gave the only light to the room when Ginny
entered. She did not flick the switch that would have lighted
the electric sconces, the sudden glare being no part of her
mood then. She moved softly across the room towards the
candle on the secretaire unable, in spite of herself, to avoid
a glance towards Trip's empty basket by the fire. Brown
should have taken that away, she thought: no—she should
have told Brown to take it away, because Brown would never
willingly remove anything at Tilsit that served the purpose
of continuity. The empty basket would remain as a reminder
of accusation and violence, and in time the next of the long
succession of dogs at Tilsit would occupy it, Ginny sighed
and turned away from the sight of the basket, gripped now
by a feeling of hopelessness and confusion, filled with
a need for Mark, for the human comfort of his presence,
for the sheer reassurance that his crude vitality and strength
gave her, the knowledge that he was living while half in this
place were dead. She moved to the window and stood with
her fingers gripping the sill, wishing with desperate urgency

that the dark curve of the hill where the keep stood would
be softly illuminated by the lights from the studio. But there
was only the unrelieved blackness.

" We are well rid of him."

Ginny spun round, staring into the deeper darkness of the
room behind her, from which Brown's dull and sombre voice
had come. A shape moved on one of the high-backed chairs,
and then Brown's figure crossed the path of the firelight
towards her.

" We are well rid of him," she repeated.

The gaunt figure loomed. " Mark . . .?" Ginny said. She
pressed back against the sill, trying to escape Brown's
closeness. " You mean Mark?"

" I mean him—murderer that he is! It does no good
for you to be watching for the lights from that place.
You've never stopped watching for them since he went.
Well, there's nothing good for you down there. He was
evil—a bad influence for Tilsit, and on you. We are well
rid of him—as we were of the other one."

" The other one?" The question came as a whisper in
the darkness. All Ginny's unexpressed dread of this woman
suddenly came to the surface. She was afraid of the physical
presence and of the repressed hysteria in Brown's voice.

" John."

Now Ginny stiffened in defence. " There was nothing wrong
with what my father did. Isobel never gave him anything but
good reason to loathe the sound of her name. He hated
her—and no wonder. She shut him out from Tilsit except
on sufferance, and she stopped him marrying the woman that
he . . ."

Suddenly she felt the cold iron grasp of Brown's hand on
her arm, and under it her flesh seemed to creep.

" So she told you! I knew once she got you finally into
that room that she wouldn't be able to resist telling you.
She held it over Miss Isobel all these years, and she's waited
for so long to say these things. She *did* tell you, didn't she?"
The last words were accompanied by a violent shake of
Ginny's arm. " Didn't she . . .?"

" Yes, Margaret told me."

" Ah—but did she tell you the rest of it? Did she tell
you what John did to Miss Isobel in return?"

" She said nothing about my father and Isobel."

"No, of course she wouldn't. She wouldn't like to admit that it happened. All those months afterwards she stayed away from Miss Isobel, pretending that nothing had happened. Weak and foolish, she is—as Miss Isobel knew long ago. Not the right kind for a Tilsit to marry——the blood line needed strengthening, not what she would bring it. Miss Isobel was never more right than when she put a stop to that marriage, but John didn't see reason. All he could see was her face—oh, yes, she was beautiful, I'll grant you that—but he couldn't see that there was nothing behind it, nothing but softness and that foolish ambition to be a Tilsit. She wasn't the right stuff, and only John couldn't see it. When the telegram came from Scotland that morning it was no thanks he gave to Miss Isobel for saving him from that—only ruin, and near death. Do you know *that*? She would have been dead if he had had his way."

Ginny twisted and tried to break the grasp; the hand remained as if it were clamped.

"You don't know what you're talking about," Ginny said. "I don't believe you—you're mad!"

"Mad, am I? Didn't I see it with my own eyes? It was a sight I'll never forget to my dying day—nor did John Tilsit, either. I'd guarantee that."

Ginny's lips quivered as she struggled for control. "What did you see?"

"She'd gone to the cottage with the telegram. And she'd taken him a piece of the new china, thinking it would please him. She was gone for a long time—she didn't come back to lunch—so I went over after her. From all the way along the cliff path I could see that the cottage door was open, but it was very quiet, as if everyone had gone away."

"She had fallen," Ginny said. "That was the time she fell on the cliff."

"Ah!" In the darkness the sound carried Brown's contempt. "That was no fall, and she wasn't on the cliff. I found her in the cottage lying there in front of the hearth. It was a sight to frighten the heart out of a person. The whole place was torn apart as if someone had gone mad. Things smashed and overturned, and she was battered about the face and head, and only God knows what saved her from the madman."

"He couldn't have done that—he *couldn't!*"

"He did it—John did it. And he left her there in her own blood. If I hadn't come she might have died. But she was strong, and she had endurance—she had more than a man's endurance and courage. So she stayed alive and I came and found her that way."

"And he was gone." It was no longer a question.

"He was gone. Running, like the weakling he was. And I had to do what I could for her—I myself, because she wouldn't let me bring a doctor to the cottage. She said that we had to get back to Tilsit, and that we were to tell no one what had happened."

"She went back to Tilsit—the way she was?"

"I told you she had endurance and courage beyond a man's! The bleeding had stopped and she made me bandage her up with torn sheets. She had concussion—even I could tell that, and I knew it was dangerous for her to move. The cuts across the cheek and nose were horrible, but I knew the head wounds were the dangerous ones. But she made me wait until it was almost dark before she would let us start back. It was a terrible journey. The bleeding started again, and it soaked through the head bandages and ran down into her eyes. But we got back, and she even had the courage to have me leave her and go in and open up the big main door so that we could go in that way where no one would see us. Only when she was back on her own bed would she let me send for the doctor. She told me to tell them all that she had fallen on the cliff, and no one was to be allowed in the bedroom except myself."

The grip on Ginny's arm would not relax, nor would the voice cease. "The doctor knew, of course, that it was no fall that gave those injuries. He said it was his duty to report it to the police, and to get Miss Isobel into hospital. But she would have none of it. He had been the Old Lady's doctor, too, and he understood how things were at Tilsit. She managed to convince him that no good would come of bringing the police into it, and that I could nurse her here in her room at Tilsit. And we managed it. Between us we managed it. The doctor came every day, and we changed the dressings, and for four long months she lay in that bed —first getting over the concussion, and then waiting until the bandages could come off, until the hair grew back where the doctor had shaved it off her head. She had been a lovely young woman, and what came out of the bandages was a ruin——her face destroyed, and her hair turned grey in streaks. She had the courage to face the world like that and say it had been an accident. And she had the courage to do all the other things. Think of it! That same night she remembered to send me back to the cottage to clean it up and lock it, so that no one would see it. I put the place to rights as best I could, and got rid of what was broken. It was horrible to touch those things—I never did know for sure which one of them he had used to strike her —or if it was all of them. There was a lot of blood, and I burned the hearthrug the next day. I remember it all very well, and I even remember seeing the pieces of the china—the Bluebell pattern, it was—ground into the floor."

"Then—then she felt guilty over what she had done to him that she went to these lengths to protect him."

"Guilty? She had no reason to feel guilty—why should she? You're no Tilsit if you don't know the reason why she kept it all quiet. There'd been too much talk and gossip about Tilsit in the past year, with your father going to the courts to try to steal away what was hers. She had the courage to go through with it all because the very least that would have come of it if the authorities knew was a warrant for your father's arrest. It was no simple matter he had involved us all in. He meant to kill her——I know that. He meant her to die!"

She said it because she had to, even against a sickening growth of certainty. "No!" Ginny said. "He could never have meant her to die! He was not that kind of man!"

"Wasn't he? Are you sure? Then I ask you why he was afraid of her. And why he never came near Tilsit again as long as he lived, or allowed her to come near you. Doesn't this say what he was—and what he knew he meant to do that day in the cottage? I never saw John Tilsit again but I would swear that he never passed a day without thinking of it, and that if there was any guilt between the two of them then it lay with him. I would swear that he was ridden by it as long as he lived."

And then at last the hand fell away from Ginny, and she was free.

She turned, leaning her hands against the sill, her head bent and forehead pressed against the cold glass pane. There was no way to deny what Brown had said, and it was a fantasy too great for her to have invented. She had only to do what Brown had said, to remember her father, his closed and silent nature, his refusal to permit any part of the past to touch their lives on St. Nicolaas, a morbid dread that something would reveal it. Her own sense told her now that his containment and self-exile had been too complete and absolute to permit of any such explanation as a simple quarrel over an inheritance. An act of violence had been committed by a man who was essentially a man of peace and restraint. That it had nearly become an act of murder was the horror that had stamped and marked him for the rest of his life. Ginny knew that the last of innocence died with the death of this, the last of her illusions.

And then she raised her head and saw that the lights from Mark's studio had cast a glow along the edge of the sky. "It's him! He's come back!" A cry of joy broke from Ginny, almost a cry of liberation.

She turned from the window and at once Brown's arm shot out to hold her. "You mustn't go! You must never . . ." The words were choked off; the hand dropped again and Ginny was free.

It felt like a flight to freedom to speed down the stairs, rejoicing in the clatter of her shoes on the wood, to snatch up the flashlamp from the table where Garth had placed it. As she threw back the locks on the door of the South Front, she was aware that someone—Vanessa, Lawrence or Margaret—had opened the door of the sitting-room to investigate the commotion. The vigorous and defiant slam Ginny gave to the front door was like a declaration to the whole of Tilsit.

The mist greeted her, thicker now, with the density of fog, the way along the road was easy, but up the path to the keep the shrubs and trees, their shapes distorted, seemed to be in unfamiliar places, so that twigs reached out to catch her skirt, and once, a low bough brushed wetly across her face, and she choked back a cry of terror. The fallen slabs of the keep rose up bigger than she had ever seen them before, the walls above her were lost in the mist. It took her some time to find the path down on the other side, twice she took the wrong way through the slabs that ended in a fallen wall and a heap of rubble. But the path was there at last, and the way seemed certain, although the curtain of fog obscured each step ahead of her.

She heard him coming, but the flashlamp could not penetrate the white swirling mass. "Mark?" she called.

He loomed before her suddenly, breaking the curtain. For an instant of doubt she felt the menace again of his physical power, of the animosity he bore towards Tilsit. The flashlamp illuminated his face, black and craggy, the expression of a man agonised and desperate. She checked, afraid.

His arms were about her. "Ginny! It's you! I was coming—I was coming over to get you." His strength wrapped about her, he cradled her close to him, her face thrust into his sweater ; he rocked her in his arms like a baby, joyfully, humbly. "Ginny—I had to come back. I love you. Do you hear? I love you, my bird of paradise."

She sank herself into his arms.

V

"I had to come back because I love you," Mark said once more—the fourth time he had said it.

Their loving was swift and needful, the reaching of one body to another in a wild and final expression of the hurt and pain and desire of separation, and the joy of their coming together, the mutual seeking for comfort, the salving of their individual wounds. They fitted as if born together, their understanding of each other's body instant and complete, as if, in all the weeks of holding back, their senses had already explored each other intimately, so that now there was no gaucheness and strangeness. And in this, after the exquisite pleasure, there was for Ginny the taste of sadness.

" It's as if," she said, "we have had our loving all at once. When something is perfect, how can it be better? And how can it continue? Any change would take something away. But things must change . . ."

He stopped her words with his mouth pressed hard against hers, and when he released her she had no breath for any more. "You'll have to learn to stop talking," he said. " I can't stand a woman who talks in bed. No—no, talk if you want to. Do anything you like—just so long as it's my bed, and I'm the one who listens. Oh, God, girl! I love you!

Do you hear me? I love you! I shall say it to you every day of my life. When we're married you will be the most loved woman that ever lived. I'll love you in such a way that you'll think every other man in the world has disappeared. Do you understand? It will be an exclusive love, and none of the rest of the world will exist."

" Do you want to be married?"

" Why else do you think I came back? Why else? We can't go on as we have been. And I can't do without you."

" Can you do with me? Can you take what has to go with me?" Almost imperceptibly her head jerked in the direction of Tilsit.

" All of that?" For a second, searching, she saw the trapped and frustrated expression back on his face, but it was quickly gone, so that she had to ask herself if it had been imagined. " I'll have to, won't I? Look—I came back, didn't I? I'm here, telling you that I love you—and I've never said that truthfully to a woman before. I've capitulated, you see. The citadel has fallen. I'm back, and I've thrown away all that cherished freedom and independence. I'm bound and tied, and somehow I don't care."

" Will you always not care? Will it always be this way?"

" What a child you are! Of course it won't always be this way. Sometimes it will be better—many times it will be worse. But I'll tell you something, girl. We're lucky— damned lucky. We know what we've got—and we've had."

It was there again, the feeling, involuntarily expressed now by Mark, that they had already had the best of it.

" I'll tell you something, though." He turned on his back and stared up at the ceiling. " We don't have to accept the way it's always been up there. We don't have to play out the Tilsit legend. We're ourselves, Ginny—and never you forget it. We don't have to repeat the pattern. You don't have to be an Isobel or a Jane Tilsit. And I don't have to be a George Martin. And goddamn it, we're not! You just have to break the pattern—we have to break the pattern."

Suddenly he pulled an arm from under her and reached out and took the cup from the tray where she had left it when she had eaten her solitary meal by this fire. It crashed and splintered against the fire-brick at the back of the hearth.

" You see—like that! It can be broken. All you have to do is to do it."

Then he turned back to her, rolling on his side and staring at her, his expression brooding and tender, the belief in what he had just said and done plainly there. He pulled her closer, his hands seeking, but a little less sure than before.

"Now come here to me, girl, and we'll begin again. Because I love you, and I'll have you, and if I lose myself and the whole world for you, then I'll have to count it well lost. Because—God help me—I can't help myself."

And the first premonition had been right, because for Ginny this time it was a little less the exercise of love, and a little more the exercise of power, the power she had just discovered was coupled in Mark's mind with the image of Tilsit. What, she thought, if they could not break the pattern? What if they were doomed to repeat what had happened before? What if the pattern and the legend were stronger than they, and with love grown to familiarity, would the habit of power grow also? And would she see in the years ahead the gradual erosion of this man's strength and will because he was already half convinced that the tradition must be served? That he thought of it seriously at all at this moment was the beginning of emasculation.

Then she put these thought away from her in the pleasure of the next minutes, telling herself that it was surely only a little less than before, hardly more than the spirit or the body could notice, if, in the first time, she had not had all of it, the beginning and the end.

VI

Brown's face was grey and drawn in the early-morning light. Her movements were stiff as she rose from the chair, their ponderous, measured slowness suggested a resignation that had somehow been reached through the night. Ginny knew that Brown had sat there the whole night.

"So—we are to have him here."

Ginny didn't reply. She stood before the fireplace, before Trip's empty basket, and her gaze at Brown was defiant.

"We are to have him here, then," Brown insisted. "It has come out exactly as she said it would."

"Who said—Isobel?" Against her will Ginny was drawn into talk—talk about Mark. She had meant not to talk, just to announce that they would marry, and that would be the end of it. Walking back to Tilsit from the cottage she had decided that it all must happen very soon, and there must be no time or place for argument. But Brown had sat there all night, knowing what was happening in the cottage, and now she would have her say. So she waited for the rest of it.

" She knew it all along. After that one time she saw you she knew it would be. That's what she wanted, of course—what she'd planned. She wanted Mark Barstow for Tilsit and she wanted you."

Ginny stiffened, and Brown read the look of incredulous rejection on her face. The old woman's voice croaked harshly. Two livid spots of colour had come into the grey cheeks.

" You think she hadn't thought it all out as long ago as that? You were the only real Tilsit left. And he had the talent. She was looking to see him do again for Tilsit what George Martin had done, and she was thinking of what the fresh blood-line—his kind of blood-line—would do for the future generations. I tell you she had it planned, and you see it has come out."

" That isn't true," Ginny said flatly. " How could she be sure I would ever come here? How did she know Mark wouldn't marry someone else?"

" She had her own way of arranging things. Twice she stopped Mark Barstow from marrying, and she would have done it again. She had decided to go to see you again when you came of age. John Tilsit couldn't have refused for you, then. It was to be left up to you, and no one in their senses would have refused. Her worry was that in time you would marry someone else. She died before she could be sure it would all come about. But it happened in any case. It has happened exactly the way she had it planned when she wrote it all down."

" She *wrote* it . . ." Ginny's gaze shot at once to the locked secretaire. She felt herself at ease suddenly because now she knew that Brown was lying. " No," she said. " No— she didn't write it. There's nothing written there. There was nothing ever written about me."

The colour had died again in Brown's face. Now she had assumed the look of a person who knows that they will be proven right; she shrugged with a kind of weary patience. " Do you suppose there's anything in this house that is a secret from me? Tilsit is my life—as much as it was hers. Whatever was written in those books I had a right to, you understand—*a right.*"

" You read them?"

" I read them. They were my life, too, don't forget. I read them all, and I took away the parts I believed you should never see. I knew what would be planted in your head about Mark Barstow if you read those parts. So I took them away. I thought she was wrong about Mark Barstow. I thought he was no fit person for a Tilsit—he carried death in his hands—and Tilsit would have no peace from him with his waywardness and his eyes for women. But what I thought didn't matter. It has come out that way. And I suppose if it is to be, it must be. The line has to endure, she used to say. And she decided that this was the way it would be."

Now Brown drew out from the pocket of her smock the familiar stiff white pages, saw-toothed at one edge where they had been clipped from the diary. " I have the last book locked away," she said. " You can have it when you want it. There's no reason to keep it from you now."

For a moment Ginny could not bring herself to touch the pages. But Brown held them there before her steadily, and her gaze compelled her; the woman's tired grey eyes seemed to challenge her to read this and still hold the ecstasy of Mark and think that it had been of her own volition. Unwillingly then she took the pages, and saw that her own hand trembled. The top one was dated a few days after the time Isobel had come to the convent of Santa Maria. The writing was large and rapid and strangely exultant, as if the writer had come to this the instant of her return to Tilsit:

" *I have seen her—with no success this time, but I am certain that she will come. She is a true Tilsit. She has spirit and courage, and her face is the face of the portrait. She is young for her age, but the strength is there, and she will develop quickly. It is fortunate that she is beautiful, because Mark is captivated by beauty—and, whether he accepts it or not—captivated by the traditions of Tilsit, which she surely embodies. With them the line will be secure. It is a matter of waiting, of being patient until all of this can be brought about. She must be worked on, and the ferment of curiosity will grow until that island becomes too confining—until John can no longer stand her questioning. Then she must be brought here, and once confronting each other they will fall together as I believe they are meant to do—as it will be best for Tilsit that they do. I see them as the instruments of Tilsit's continuance . . .*"

Ginny read no further. She crumpled the pages in her hand and tossed them on the dead ashes in the grate. A horrified sound of protest broke from Brown, but Ginny had already taken a match from the holder and struck it against the brick.

"You must not . . . you must not destroy what has been written!"

The little flame leaped up at once. Ginny spoke, not for Brown, but for herself. "Eliot said I must save myself while I still could. Perhaps—even now—it's not too late to save Mark."

In the seconds while the paper burned, she had imagined she would not feel the pain of leaving until the act was done —that the momentum of the wrench would carry her past the first things almost without noticing them. But it began at once; the loss of Mark and the knowledge of losing him was pain from the second that Isobel's pages were firmly consumed, leaving their own ash whiter than the wood ash.

She packed one suitcase under Brown's unbelieving gaze. Brown spoke only once.

"You can't go. You can't leave us. There must be someone to carry on . . ." But the words faded as Brown stared fully into Ginny's face in the growing light.

"It will all carry on," Ginny answered. "Isobel provided for that too."

The early morning quiet was still on the house when Ginny went down the stairs. It was not even time for the first alarm clock to ring. The sun was up now, but it was still very early so that the sound of starting up the worn engine of Isobel's car was like an explosion upon the gentle hush of the summer's morning. But nothing stirred and no one seemed to wake. She thought of Mark lying asleep and realised that she had never known the actual sight of him asleep. She thought of the countless other things she had missed—days and years and decades that had been lived, unknowingly, in one span. It might be possible that Mark would understand why she had gone, but she doubted that he would. He had believed that they could break the pattern. He didn't know that they were already part of the pattern.

So she left quickly because the resolution was strong enough to carry her only as long as she did not feel his touch or hear his voice. She had the sense that she was running and must keep runn.ng, because if she stopped she would be caught once more; and now she was nearly out of breath.

The gates to the main entrance to Tilsit were locked, so she had to blow the horn for someone in the gatehouse to come and open them. She hadn't known until this moment that the gates were locked every night; there was so much at Tilsit she was leaving without knowing. The wife of the gate-keeper, who was also a gardener, appeared; she was in her dressing-gown with curlers in her hair; her face, still crumpled with sleep, wore an expression of surprise.

"Good morning, Miss Virginia. Out early this morning?"

"Good morning, Mrs. Taylor. Yes—out early."

There was an agonising wait while the gates were unlocked and swung back. Ginny could not stop herself then from turning and looking back at Tilsit. And she knew at once that she had been foolish to do so. As with everything she had ever loved, the leaving became harder with every look.

"There you are, Miss Virginia. Pleasant journey, miss."

Ginny wrenched her gaze away, and the pain hit deeper now. She felt the tightening in her throat so that it was difficult to answer the question that came.

"Will you be back late, Miss Virginia? It's just so that I can tell Taylor to leave the gates . . ."

"No," Ginny said, and she lied, "I won't be late."

VII

The towns and villages and the narrow winding roads were much as she remembered them from the journey down from London Airport with Randall, and they were no more familiar than before; they were still a strange country. She felt that she had not been in England at all, but only at Tilsit, and that it was a country unto itself, that it had existed for her only as a country of the heart. She supposed that some day she would come back to England when the hurt had nearly ceased to hurt, but she knew she could never go back to Tilsit.

When Bournemouth had been passed and the practical details of the return had begun to present themselves, she planned that she would cable Eliot from the next post office to cable back her flight money to the Pan Am desk at London Airport. But when she glanced over the flight ticket while she was drinking a mug of coffee at a petrol station, she noticed for the first time that when Katrien had bought the ticket on St. Nicolaas she had paid for a round trip. And she wondered, and was grateful, that Katrien, knowing nothing of Tilsit, had also known that she would be back.

At London Airport she parked the car, and put the keys into an envelope with a note to Randall apologising for putting him to the trouble of sending someone to collect it. At the Pan Am desk they put her on stand-by for a cancellation, and then she sorted out the change in her purse and went to a telephone booth to call Randall

When she got through he said at once, " I've been expecting you. Lawrence has telephoned me and told me you'd left."

When she tried to answer him, the words would not come clearly. She just made an incoherent sound.

" Ginny—are you still there? Do you know what you're doing? Do you understand what this means?"

She found the words, or some of them, that had to be said. " I can't fulfil the conditions of the will, Mr. Randall. So I can't accept the inheritance."

" Are the conditions so hard—for what goes with them?" He spoke gently, persuasively, as if the decision was not already taken and there was still space and time to reason.

" It costs too much," Ginny said slowly, feeling her way. " I found out that the inheritance isn't really Tilsit or the Pottery—it's a way of life. It's those two women—it means being what I don't want to be." She stopped now, defeated, because there was no way to explain that power had already begun to taste sweet, and she feared that the future would make it sweeter. So she said, to finish it, " It costs too much, Mr. Randall."

He tried again. " And the money? There is money involved, even if I have talked strongly about the taxes."

" Money?" She thought of Eliot, who had understood money, and who had taught her in some measure what it was worth. " Money like that isn't something you can own, Mr. Randall. It's there only to be looked after. It came out of what is past, and it belongs to the future. They charge a high interest rate on that kind of money."

After a long pause he said, " You know you can't turn it down until you come of age. It will still be held by the trust for you until your next birthday."

" I understand," she said wearily. " It doesn't make any difference. Nothing will have changed. Oh—you can send me the proper papers to sign at the proper time, just to make it legal. But nothing will have changed. As far as Tilsit is concerned—and everything there—I've already come of age."

" Ginny—don't hang up, Ginny. What of Mark?"

" Mark . . ." So Randall knew—she supposed everyone at Tilsit had known. She leaned against the glass of the booth, her hand gripping the receiver tightly, her eyes closed, fighting the wave of pain and longing that threatened to submerge her. " I can't be the instrument of tying him to Tilsit, or wearing him down so that he has to become less than he is now. It would happen. Isobel knew it would be that way. The only way I can break the pattern for him and myself is by leaving. There is no other way. If he's caught just the same—if Vanessa takes him, it won't have been my doing. No—don't!" she suddenly cried, as Randall's voice attempted to break in. " Don't say anything. Tilsit is a hard spell to break out of. But it's cost too much already, and it will go on costing. I can't pay that price, Mr. Randall." The image of Tilsit and Mark became mixed and confused in her tired brain. " Because—I do love him."

His voice came, but she didn't hear the words. The public address system was sounding and she opened the door of the booth. Her name was repeated twice, being called to the Pan Am desk, and she knew she would be on the next plane when it left. Very gently she replaced the receiver.

Out over the Atlantic, when the cabin lights had been dimmed to let the passengers sleep, Ginny lay wakeful, her mind crowded with the thoughts that would need a lot of time before they would submit to being put aside. And then, incongruously beside all of the things that she had left behind her at Tilsit, she thought of the Eliot clothes, the lovely gowns unworn, the white silk coat. She wondered if Brown would send them on. Then it occurred to her that it didn't matter what Brown did with them. She wouldn't be needing them at home.

CHAPTER SEVEN

Katrien leaned against the door-frame of Ginny's bedroom, watching her unpack. It was hardly more than an hour since the telephone had rung at Oranje Huis and Ginny's voice had been on the line announcing that she had come in on the last plane of the day from San Juan. Katrien had driven with Bo to the airport to pick her up; the surprise and joy of the arrival still shook Katrien a little, but they had drunk their rum punch on the gallery, fanned by the warm wind from the sea and the night scents of the garden, and Katrien had held back her questions, making herself wait until Ginny would begin to talk. By this means Katrien knew that she had held John Tilsit to her through the years of their marriage, and she also knew that nothing less would work with his daughter. So she held her tongue, and simply watched.

The single suitcase Ginny had brought back lay open on the bed, looking as if it had been hurriedly packed and containing barely more than toilet articles and underwear. The paucity of those possessions struck deeply at Katrien; it seemed to her that Ginny had stripped herself to the bare bones, that on this return journey there had been no room for anything that was not essential to her existence. What did not matter had all been left behind.

It was revealing then to see her lift from her flight-bag, carefully wrapped and padded by a sweater, a small grey pottery bowl, in whose rough texture, as it moved, lived flashes of colour, greens and blues. Ginny placed it carefully on the broad ledge of the window within hand's reach of her bed, the ledge that had, all her life, held the treasure of the moment—the most beloved doll, the book of poetry, the first bottle of perfume. There was a kind of brooding tenderness in Ginny then as she turned the bowl to the angle she liked best, a certain finality in the way she placed it that gave Katrien the thought that this would be the last of Ginny's possessions to occupy this place, that nothing would ever supersede this small grey bowl.

Ginny turned and caught Katrien's fixed gaze on her. She looked quickly between the solitary suitcase on the bed, the bowl on the ledge, then back to Katrien.

As if to explain its emptiness she said, " I left behind me at Tilsit a good deal more than they'll ever be able to pack up and send on. And I came back with a lot more than was in this suitcase."

Katrien wakened at the first light of dawn. She had fallen asleep only about an hour ago, but last night it had not been the emptiness of the house that had troubled her, as had been the case since John Tilsit had died, but the very fullness and magnitude of what her daughter had brought back with her. She had heard it all last night in the darkness of the gallery, no light between herself and Ginny to show the shifts of emotion on the younger woman's face, only her voice as she had told Katrien of Mark Barstow and Tilsit had revealed the joy and the pain. In the end though it had had surprising strength and conviction. " So you see—I'm back where I belong. I know who I am here."

Katrien had lain awake and thought of all this, and worried over it. The slight sounds that had awakened her had come from the kitchen. Katrien went out on to the gallery and saw that the lights were on there, and Ginny's figure moved back and forth before the screens. When Katrien entered, her eyes burning a little from lack of sleep, Ginny looked up from the picnic basket she was packing and smiled faintly.

" You're up early—have some tea? I've just made it."

Katrien accepted a cup and sat at the table drinking it slowly. She watched the preparation of the food without comment, but it was easy to see that it was far more than Ginny would have packed for herself alone.

Finally Katrien stood on the gallery and watched Ginny start down the path to the beach, Bo trailing her. She understood, as Ginny meant her to, that the small grey bowl would keep its place on the window-ledge but that Ginny had returned to St. Nicolaas not to live with the past, but to break with it, to reach out and take up the future.

Katrien nodded with satisfaction, went back to bed and fell asleep at once.

II

It was the slack season in the islands—the time during the summer when the residents drew breath, and the cottages at Oranje Cove, now finished and with the sea grapes and the creepers already obscuring their outlines, were quiet. It was too early for anyone to be on the beach, too early for anyone even to be awake, except Jim, who still woke when the first light hit the beach, and who lay in bed until the scratch of Bo's paw against the screen door summoned him.

But this morning Bo did not come, and the light grew stronger. Finally he got up and went and showered, and put on the coffee, standing over the stove while he smoked the first cigarette of the day. He carried the cup to the window, and lighted another cigarette. It was going to be one of those days, hot and restless, when the yeast of frustrated waiting worked in him. Later, when he drove to the post office, he would look first of all to see if there was a letter from England, and if there was not, it would be like all the other days when letters had not come, a long wait until the next day and the next mail. The first ray of the sun struck the ridge of the hills behind, and touched the high roof of Oranje Huis.

And then he saw her as he had seen her for the first time, the long-legged girl in the faded shorts, with the blonde hair brushing her shoulders, and the dog by her side as they both waded at the tide's edge. For a moment he could not move;

he stood there, his breath drawn in, as she seemed to hesitate at the place where her father's outboard was drawn high on the sands where it had been since the last time she had used it, the morning she had gone out alone and left him behind. But then she moved, and his breath was released in a long jerking sigh of relief and wild happiness. She was coming to his end of the beach.

THE END